ACHARYA CHATURSEN

Acharya Chatursen (1891–1960) was one of Hindi's most prolific writers. He studied at Jaipur Sanskrit College, where he obtained Shastri and Acharya degrees in Literature and Medicine. He started his professional career as a physician before devoting himself to writing. Over a writing career spanning four decades, he published more than eighty works spanning the genres of fiction, drama, politics, literary criticism, poetry and medicine. *Vaishali Ki Nagarvadhu* (literally, *The Bride of the City of Vaishali*, of which this book is a translation), *Somnath*, *Goli* and *Vayam Rakshamah* are among his famous novels. His novel *Dharamputra* was adapted into a Bollywood film and won the National Film Award for the Best Feature Film in Hindi in 1961.

PRATIBHA VINOD KUMAR

Pratibha Vinod Kumar (1941–2020) obtained a BA in English Literature, Philosophy and Sanskrit from Maharani College (Jaipur), MA in English Literature from Rajasthan University and BEd from Annamalai University. She won gold medals at the intermediate (senior school) and BA levels. She taught English at Banasthali Vidyapeeth (Rajasthan, 1961–1963), St. Michael's School (Durgapur, 1963–1985) and Rotary Public School (Gurgaon, 1985–1991). Her previous published work includes translations of two classics of Hindi literature – Jaishankar Prasad's *Kamayani* and Bhagwati Charan Verma's *Chitralekha* – and an anthology of new writing, *Hindi Tales of Mystery and Imagination* Vol. I into English. A.K. Kulshreshth is her son's pen name.

BRIDE OF THE CITY

VOLUME 1

First published in Hindi in two volumes in 1948–1949

This translation © 2021 Ashish Kumar

Published by Cernunnos Books Pte. Ltd., Singapore, 2021
www.cernunnosbooks.com

Literary editors: Balwant Kaur (Hindi) and N. Henaff (English)
Hindi advisors: Archana Verma and Balwant Kaur

Interior design and composition: 52 Novels
Cover illustration and design by Zoya Chaudhury

ISBN: 978-981-14-9550-2

BRIDE OF THE CITY

VOLUME 1

'VAISHALI KI NAGARVADHU'
वैशाली की नगरवधू

ACHARYA CHATURSEN

Translated by
Pratibha Vinod Kumar and
A.K. Kulshreshth

Cernunnos
BOOKS

*Dedicated to the memory of
Archana Verma*

INTRODUCTORY NOTE

The original text uses ancient Indian units of time, such as mahurt. For the sake of simplicity, these have been converted in this translation into their modern equivalent. A 'watch' equals three hours.

The traditional units of distance used in the original text such as dhanush and kos have been converted into miles and feet. Ten feet are equal to one metre and one mile is equal to 1.6 kilometres.

Some names and descriptions of places have been shortened in this translation for readability. The cities of Vaishali, Rajgrih and Champa, are in the present-day Indian State of Bihar, while the Kingdom of Kosala is in eastern Uttar Pradesh, to the west of Bihar.

Names are spelt in a simplified way. Generally, an 'a' at the end of a name should be pronounced as 'aa', as in the end of Africa.

The book contains several references to the distant University of Takshila, the world's first university established 2,700 years ago in the Kingdom of Gandhar. Takshila is in the Punjab province of Pakistan.

Northern India
c. 500 BCE
KAMBOJ
Takshila
GANDHAR
KURU
PANCHALA
Hastinapur
Sravasti
VATSA
KOSALA
KASHI
VAJJI
Vaishali
Kaushambhi
Kashi
ANGA
Champa
Pataligram
Rajgrih
MAGADHA
AVANTI
Vidisha
Ujjain
© Cernunnos Books Ltd
Not to scale

CAST OF PRINCIPAL CHARACTERS

VAJJI REPUBLIC

Ambapali, Bride of the City.
Mahanaman, her father.
Madlekha, her maidservant.
Lallbhatt, her guard.
Harshdev, her first lover.
Sunand, the chief minister.
Singh, a leader in war.
Kapyak, his principal aide.
Jayaraj, a soldier.
Balbhadra, a bandit.
Bhadranandini, a courtesan.
Prabhanjan, a barber.
Kritpunya, a merchant.
Gautam, the Buddha – the Shakya Sage, sometimes referred to as
  Tathagat.
Mahavir, the founder of Jainism, born in Vaishali.

KINGDOM OF MAGADHA

Bimbisar, the emperor.
Acharya Varshkar, the chief minister.
Chandrabhadrik, a senior general.
Somprabh, a soldier and a scholar.
Kundani, his sister.
Shambh, his follower and assistant.

KINGDOM OF ANGA

Chandrabhadra, the princess.
Dadhivahana, the king.

KINGDOM OF KOSALA

Prasenjit, the king.
Vidudhab, his son.
Kalingasena, a princess.
Bandhul Malla, a general.
Karayan, a general.
Ajit Keskambali, a priest.

PREFACE

I had dreams of making bags of money when I started out on the writer's life. I was young. This was in 1909. In the four decades since then, I have written eighty-four books of various lengths and on diverse subjects. My articles in magazines would run into, perhaps, ten thousand pages. I did not gain anything in material terms from my writing journey. I did lose a lot. I could even say that I lost everything – wealth, peace of mind and rest. My youth and my reputation wilted away.

Today, I gladly declare that my previous literary output over the last forty years of my life – this body of work that cost me all that I had – is worthless. I humbly gift this book to my readers as my first work.

It is true that this is a novel. But it is even more true that this is a serious enquiry seeking to peer through the haze of two millennia that has shrouded the ebb and tide of religion, literature, politics and culture and that historians have chosen to ignore.

That I have declared my past work to be worthless and this to be my first work is an outcome of my belief. However, I have no right to take pride in my work. I request you, dear reader, to see if you can discern a latent meaning that is separate from the narrative. You may find the fundamental truth that drove me to research the Aryan, Buddhist, Jain and Hindu literature for ten years as I wrote this book.

Chatursen

1 January 1949
Gyaandhaam
Shahadara
Delhi

PROLOGUE

1

A paved road heads west from Muzaffarpur. Eighteen miles down this road is the hamlet of Vaishod. About thirty families still live there. Most of them are of Bhoomihar Brahman caste; some are Kshatriyas. For miles around, ruins and remnants of statues dot the hilly landscape, suggesting that there was a splendid city here in the past.

In fact, there was. About two-and-a-half millennia ago, a metropolis bustled on the banks of Gandak river, then called Singhi. Today, it flows miles to the north of Vaishod. Back in those days, its course ran to the south of the magnificent city. After kissing the city's feet, it met the mighty Ganga river near Didhivara. The city was called Vaishali and it was one of those cities of which it is said that their streets were paved with gold. It had seven thousand, seven hundred and seventy-seven each of mansions, treasuries, gardens and ponds. It had no equal.

Vaishali was the capital of the Vajji Republic established by the eight clans. The eight clans were the Videha, Licchavi, Khatrik, Vajji, Ugra, Bhoj, Ikshavaku and Kaurav. The first four of these clans dominated the others. The Videhas had their capital at Mithila, Licchavis at Vaishali, Khatriks at Kundpur and Vajjis at Kallog. This eastern Indian Republic, with Vaishali as its power centre and main capital, was a mighty amalgam that formed the one and only political and military threat to the Magadha Empire.

Vaishali was fortified with three wooden walls, each of them with many spiralling watchtowers from where sentries could view the surroundings for miles. The sentries' brass horns would instantly put citizens on the guard and call soldiers to action. Within minutes, the walls would swarm with soldiers armed to the teeth, their quivers and swords glinting, and outer walls would vibrate with the thuds of the cavalry.

An assembly governed the Vajji Union. Its members were elected by the eight clans for a seven-year term. The assembly was charged with running the affairs of State. The city had three other unions – those of the sculptors, artisans and merchants. Each of these unions had subdivisions that were headed by elders. Trade was controlled through formalised channels – markets were established for import and export, while internal produce could be freely traded. The union of merchants was headed by a chief called the Nagarsetthi – Merchant of the city – and he carried much political and commercial influence.

Surrounded as it was by the kingdoms of Vatsa, Kosala, Kashi and Magadha, and sitting astride the highway from Sravasti to Rajgrih, Vaishali was a centre of the struggle for commercial and political supremacy. It became a magnet for merchants, jewellers, sculptors and tourists. The central market of Shreshticath-var was adorned with the mansions of jewellers whose networks spanned India from the north to the south. From the distant Pathitthan, through Mahishmati, Ujjain, Gonard, Vidisha, Kaushambhi and Saket, across the foothills of the Tarai region, from Setavya, Kapilvastu, Kushinagar and Pawa the prominent merchants of the times had established business relations with Vaishali.

The east-west direction was traversed on rivers. Boats plied the Ganga up to Sehjai and the Yamuna up to Kaushambhi. Through a network of intervening cities and ports, merchandise flowed to and from Babylon, China and Gandhar. Through the Champa region, the tentacles of trade extended to the islands of Tamraparni, Suvarnadeep and Yavadweep.

At Shreshticathvar, well-fed and well-to-do merchants reclined in spotless outfits on their soft couches, chewing betel leaves, as they did business with smiling clients. Jewellers would assess and trade in emeralds, rubies, pearls, sapphires, diamonds and other precious stones. Their skilled craftsmen would mount the unhewn stones on their cutting machines, while others were setting inlaid gems into gold ornaments. Perfume makers shook bags full of saffron and mixed them into sandalwood oil to make products that the citizens consumed in copious volumes. Long-cloaked merchants from Persia and Babylon flocked to the cloth shops that were festooned with yards of silk and fine, expensive muslin. The narrow lanes of that part of the city were lined by towering mansions, and their dark basements held mounds of shiny bullion and jewels.

In the evenings, the affluent would flock to Royal Avenue in their well-decked chariots and palanquins, or on horses and elephants. The elephants moved in their stately way, and their masters reclined on them adorned in their finery, with their retinues of slaves and bodyguards surrounding them.

2

Morning had not yet broken. Vaishali's imposing mansions and towers basked in the dim light that seeped through the eastern horizon. The roads were still dark, but the first light played on the palace's main gate. The guards lay asleep at the security post. A formidably built man stood right in the centre of the entrance, napping with his head nestled against a gleaming spear.

Daylight covered more ground. The movements of men and women fell into their daily rhythms. From somewhere inside the city, the mixed melodies of stringed instruments and vocal rehearsals wafted out to the gate. A group of soldiers reached the gate for the change of guard. Their chief called out to the man who dozed against his spear: 'Sir Mahanaman! Watch out – be careful. And please go home.' Mahanaman stretched his already expansive limbs, exhaled deeply and said, 'Bless you, Sir.' He marched to the third gate, his heavy spear thudding as it landed on the ground with every step he took.

The Saptbhumi Palace – or the Palace of Seven Worlds – had a royal garden attached to it on its west side. Mahanaman was in charge of its upkeep. He had lived there for thirty-eight years with his wife, serving the city and facing storms and rain, cold and heat with equanimity.

His feet were still unsteady, and the light faint. His bleary eyes narrowed as he sensed something out of place. A few steps ahead, in the mango orchard, there was a white shroud laid at the foot of a tree. His footsteps quickened, and he saw that it was a newborn baby, wrapped in a clean cloth, peacefully sucking its thumb. Wide-eyed and with trembling hands, he threw the spear aside and picked up the baby. It was a girl. He clutched her close to his heart and ran to his wife, calling out her name. Before his nonplussed wife knew it, she held the calm baby in her hands. 'See – this is how the Almighty works', Mahanaman said, 'We have got what we have wanted all our lives.'

The baby grew up in the same mango grove, under the watchful eyes of the couple. She brought light into their lives. They named her Ambapali, in remembrance of the way they had found her.

3

Eleven years passed.

In a tiny village about four miles north-west of Vaishali, an old man stood outside his house, cleaning his teeth with a twig from a Neem tree. The patter of dainty footfalls made him turn back. A little girl, pretty as a frangipani flower, with her curly hair streaming in the wind, lunged forward to hug him. She slipped, fell and burst into tears. The man threw his brush aside, picked her up and clutched her tight. The girl sobbed as she said, 'Father, did you see Rohan's jacket? He says I do not have anything like that. It seems the girls in Vaishali all dress very well. I want one like that!'

The old man's eyes went moist. He smiled and said, 'All right, all right now. I shall get you one from Vaishali.' He stroked her upper arm.

'But father, do you have dammas? A jacket like that costs six dammas, do you know?' Her teary eyes were wide, but she had stopped sobbing.

'Yes, yes, I do know.'

The old man's forehead was lined with worry. His wife had died eight years before. Finding it hard to balance his work as a courtier with his duties as a father, Mahanaman had resigned his service of the city. He settled down in the village to give his attention to the girl, on whom he had doted all these years. His savings had dwindled despite his frugality. He had had to resort to selling off the few ornaments and souvenirs that his wife had left behind, to stave off hunger.

Now, he sensed that Ambapali was entering a new phase of her life. This cynosure of his life would have new aspirations. Each day would bring new desires. He felt a heaviness in his heart at the thought. He shook her and smother her with kisses. 'I shall get you one, don't worry.' He looked into her eyes and smiled. Her face lit up and she jumped out of his lap and ran back into the house.

The old man walked over to a platform and sat down. He realised that his cheeks were streaked with tears. He must head back to the city he had left behind, he thought. He must seek the job he had resigned from. His shoulders had lost their steely strength, but what else could he do? His daughter was his biggest concern, but for years now he had had another worry nagging him. However old he might be, he knew he was strong enough. Ambapali's extraordinary beauty worried him – a thousand girls together could not match her divine looks. Vajji tradition did not allow the city's most beautiful girl to be the wife of one man. She must be the Bride of the City – a courtesan on whom all citizens had a right within a prescribed code of conduct. That was one of the reasons that had driven him to leave Vaishali. But now he must go back. Their borderline existence in the village was not sustainable.

4

Spring was beating a retreat. Evening had descended, but the lights of thousands of lamps lit the city of Vaishali. Throngs of people were on their way home after the day's work, on horseback, in chariots and on foot. Some people, dressed in bright colours, were clearly out to socialise. Slowly, the bustle subsided, and the lights became fewer and farther between. Then darkness descended on Royal Avenue.

There was a wine shop on the southern fringe of the city. A single oil lamp bathed it with a flickering light in which the large pots of wine seemed to perform a drunken dance. The old shopkeeper sat slumped on his bench. The roads outside were mostly deserted by then. The remaining trickle of pedestrians consisted of the poor – fishermen, butchers, boatmen, barbers, potters. These were the trades that dominated this part of the city.

Old Mahanaman stood outside the shop, holding his child's finger. His knees and feet were hurting, and he could imagine the little one's state. 'We are there, girl. It took time, but we got there.' His mouth was dry, and his words came out hoarse.

'Is this the city? Where do they have those jackets?' she asked.

'Hmm…it is the start of the city. The city itself is still ahead. But we can't walk anymore, can we? Let's see if we can rest here. Sit here, and I will be back.' He patted her head, and she sat down on the cool earth.

Mahanaman stepped into the shop, bending to cross the doorway. The shopkeeper had already started awake at Mahanaman's first words.

'Yes, Sir!' he said with a practised smile. 'I have everything you could want. Which wine will you have? Dakha, Laja, Gaudiya, Madhvik, Maireya?' As he spoke, he scanned Mahanaman from head to toe. The scrutiny led him to add quickly, 'But friends, I do not offer credit. Show me your dammas, and we can talk.'

Mahanaman stepped closer. 'Bless you, citizen. But I don't need wine. I need shelter. I am here with my little daughter, and we have walked from far away. Is there a place for us to sleep? I shall pay, of course.'

The old shopkeeper's eyes narrowed. 'Hmm…you can pay, but, Brother, if you don't mind my asking, who are you? This city has become a magnet for thieves and bandits who present themselves as honest citizens. It is the nature of the city – it reeks money. These old eyes of mine have seen it all by now.'

He would have continued, but two young men sauntered up to the shop, talking animatedly. The shopkeeper sized them up. Their glittering clothes and arms made it clear that they were courtiers. His hands came together by reflex in a polite salute.

'What will the Gentlemen prefer? Gaudiya, Madhvik–'

'Hey, tell me about the bandit first!' One of the men said. His sword made a metallic sound as he unsheathed it.

The shopkeeper gulped twice before he could speak. 'Oh no, no, there is no bandit. This old man looks like he is from a village…He wants a place to rest. I am not afraid, Sir, oh no, never, never. But I just thought, you know, who this man is. You, Gentlemen, know how our riches draw the biggest brigands around…'

'Stop your nonsense, old man!' the young one shouted. He brandished his sword. 'I shall capture all of those bandits. Today! Get us some Madhvik.' He lurched as he spoke. The other man steadied him, and they collapsed into the two nearest seats.

As the shopkeeper scurried to serve them, they studied Mahanaman, who stood by in the dark. Ambapali's head had sunk between her knees, and her breath was steady. The pale lamplight lit her face and her black locks.

The man who had not yet spoken studied Mahanaman from head to toe and then stared at Ambapali. He asked Mahanaman, 'Old man, where are you from?'

'For far away', Mahanaman replied.

'And who is this, with you?'

'My daughter.'

'Is she? Or have you picked her up? Here in Vaishali, a girl like that would fetch a high price. Will you sell her?'

'No!' Mahanaman's nostrils flared, and his lips pressed tightly. He stood still, ramrod straight.

The young man did not notice all this. A smile played on his lips. His companion drained his cup, and said, 'Why – will you marry her?'

The other one said, 'Oh no. I need a slave. A small, pretty, slave.' He turned to Mahanaman, and his jaw dropped. Mahanaman had slowly pulled out a sword from below his tunic.

Mahanaman spoke softly. 'Sir, I bow to your royal uniform. I do not recognise you. Perhaps you are my friend's son, his son's son, or his daughter's son. Eleven years ago, I was a commander within these walls. I wore the same uniform as you for forty-two years. I respected it. So should you. That's what I think, and that's what made me draw my sword. This sword is old, and so am I. My hands are weaker and less practised than they used to be. But that's all right. Young man, unsheathe your sword and step over to the open field outside. Let's not wake the poor child with the clanging of weapons.'

The young man had his cup in hand. He flung it down, and as it thudded against the soft ground, he drew his sword and leapt up in a fluent move.

The other man, who looked a bit older, authoritatively signalled with his hand, and the man with the sword stopped as if he had been pulled back.

'If you were a commander', the seated man said, 'you must remember Commander Chandramani.'

'Of course, he was my best friend. My constant companion. Is he alive? Well?' Mahanaman advanced two paces with his sword lowered.

'Indeed, he is alive. This is his son. What is your name, Sir?'

Mahanaman hid his sword. 'My name is Mahanaman. And since this man is his son, his name will be Rishidev.'

The man who had his sword out hung his head and laid his sword at Mahanaman's feet. He spoke with some difficulty. 'I am Rishidev, Sir. Forgive me.'

Mahanaman stood still for some time, then threw an arm around Rishidev's shoulder and drew him closer. 'Son, you have played on my knees. I am lucky to see you today. May I see Chandramani soon?'

'Of course!' Rishidev now spoke with more ease, but still seemed troubled. 'We must go to him, he is immobile – paralysed.' He hesitated. 'Sir, I was not…please forgive me.'

'Do not worry about it now, young man. But do think about it later. Well, I shall come over tomorrow to see Chandramani.'

'Tomorrow? Oh no, Sir, now! I know very well that you are tired. And your girl…how shameful, I have sinned so terribly…'

Mahanaman squeezed his shoulder and gave him a hug. He felt Rishidev's agony abate. 'Her name is Ambapali', he said.

'I understand, Sir. Father has talked about you often. Let us go home. You cannot spend the night on Royal Avenue.'

Mahanaman did not argue. He woke Ambapali up gently, and they entered the city with the two youths, walking at a slow pace.

CHAPTER 1

THE CURSED LAW

The city seethed. At the crack of dawn, men had started thronging towards the assembly. Royal Avenue was choked with men on foot, in palanquins, on horseback, and in chariots. The big merchants, tradesmen, courtiers – they were all in the crowd. The outer corridors of the assembly were jammed with men jostling each other. The imposing marble steps were occupied by men sitting on them. A little further away, in the open field, some men stayed in their chariots as they surveyed the large building. Some of them raised their glinting spears and shouted out, creating a cacophony.

The members of the assembly were dismounting where they could and gravely making their way through the unruly mob. A platoon of guards cleared the way for them, and gatekeepers announced their entry into the hall.

The assembly was built mostly of gleaming white marble from the Matsya Kingdom. Inside, its main conference hall had a black stone floor and a hundred and eight black stone pillars that supported the ceiling. Nine hundred and ninety-nine ivory floor pods were neatly arrayed all around the hall. On these, the members of the assembly – representatives of the clans – sat quietly in their demarcated areas. In the centre of the chamber was a raised jade-coloured and intricately carved altar housing two silver pods and covered with a silver canopy. The canopy was ornate with paintings and festooned with flags. Its pillars and the two floor pods had gold inlay work. The pods belonged to the chief minister, Sunand and to the supreme commander, Suman. These two luminaries had not yet reached the assembly.

The altar had steps on three sides, and these steps seated the aged clerks who recorded the minutes of the assembly meetings. Their assistants stood ready with rolls of black and red notebooks in open baskets. Some middle-aged officials directed the preparations in their usual efficient and unobtrusive ways. The rest of the staff scurried to follow their commands.

The chief minister and the supreme commander took their seats without fanfare. The rising tumult of the assembly was drowned out by a blast of the trumpet signalling that the proceedings had started.

The crowd outside became more restive. As they chanted and paced, their faces turned red, and their eyes glowed with anger. The courtyard was packed with the sons of courtiers and merchants. The former brandished their swords and spears, shouting phrases that were lost to all but those next to them. The latter, trained to smile and create bonhomie, looked ready to pick fights. With these crowds thronging the assembly building, it was clear that all the markets and guilds in the city and up-country were closed. Inside, the two chiefs and the members of the parliamentary council were in a pensive mood. They fidgeted as if an unwanted event was about to be thrust on them. The guards were deployed in full strength, their faces taut and foreheads furrowed.

A sudden hush descended on the vast gathering, broken only by the deep, loud creaking of a chariot's wheels, accompanied by the tinkling of what seemed to be a thousand of its bells. The men in the restless crowd stopped pacing, as if bound by an inviolable command. All eyes were trained on a chariot that advanced at a stately pace towards the courtyard. The chariot was covered with a white cloth, and a white flag fluttered on its golden top. It traversed the courtyard and stopped in front of the steps that led up to the assembly. The quiet throng looked on as an imposing man stepped out of the chariot. His clothes were a spotless white, and so was his flowing beard. A long sword nestled in a sheath at his waist. The sheath and the handle of the sword glittered with inlaid gems. The old man wore a white turban that was topped by a solitaire. A young man joined him, and the old man climbed the steps slowly, but without faltering, leaning on the young one's shoulder. The men made way for him. The silence remained unbroken as he took the first few steps.

Then a murmur started that grew into a clamour. A young man, his nostrils bristling, walked down to confront the old man and stood in front of him, planting his spear on the step with a loud thud. His chest was heaving. 'So, Sir Mahanaman, you have come alone? Lady Ambapali has not come?'

Around them, first dozens, then hundreds of men – the sons of courtiers, merchants, artisans, all of the city – shouted hoarse words. Some phrases rang out clearly above the tumult: 'Insult to all of us!' 'Rule of law!' 'Intolerable!'

And then the shouting spread outward from that epicentre. 'There will be rivers of blood! We cannot allow this! The law cannot be treated this way! No, we shall protect the law at any cost!' The excited protestors included the most urbane men of the city.

'Yes, at any cost!'

Mahanaman's face grew stony. Without seeming to make an effort, he drew himself up so that he became even more towering. With his physical presence, fluttering white clothes and beard, and the diamond on his turban, he exuded a charisma that would make the most reckless of young men flinch. In a smooth move, his hand gripped the handle of his sword.

The man in front of him shrank back. It was as if an invisible hand had nudged him aside. Mahanaman continued up the steps.

Now it was the conference hall that fell silent. One could have heard a needle drop.

Chief Minister Sunand said, 'Gentlemen, may I have your ears? You all know the pressing reason for this august gathering of the eight clans. I request you, Sirs, to observe decorum, to maintain peace. Do not let excitement get the better of you. The city looks up to you, Gentlemen. If etiquette is violated, I will be compelled to break this assembly.

'First of all, I will ask the record clerk how many members of the council are present here.'

'A total of nine hundred and two', was the answer.

'Gentlemen, each member of the Vajji Union was informed of today's meet, and all who could be present are here. Is each member of this assembly in possession of his senses? If you think your neighbour is not, speak now!'

Complete silence greeted the announcement.

'If you know of someone here who is unfit, hysterical or drunk, speak up!'

The silence continued.

'Very well', the chief minister continued. 'Now listen, Gentlemen of the city. Sir Mahanaman,' he nodded towards Mahanaman, 'today, your daughter attains eighteen years of age. The Republic of Vaishali has chosen her as its foremost beauty. In keeping with the law, this assembly seeks to appoint Ambapali Bride of the City of Vaishali. She will receive the title of Benefactress of the Republic, bestower of blessings to all. It has ordered her to present herself here and take an oath to serve her duties. You are her guardian. You must present her here. Now, do you present her, and accept that she is lawfully appointed Bride of the City?'

Overwhelmed by the thousand pairs of eyes, Mahanaman slumped and lowered his eyes. His lips quivered – for a fleeting moment. He recovered his poise almost immediately. He stood erect as he proclaimed in a composed tone: 'Sir, I am a Licchavi. For forty-two years, I have served the Vajji Republic with this sword.' He patted its hilt. 'I have upheld the honour of the Republic many times. With the strength of these arms, I quelled the toughest enemies. I have respected, followed and protected the constitution, law and honour of the Republic. I shall continue to do so.'

Mahanaman fell silent. It was as if his lips, so eloquent until now, struggled to form the words that were to follow. His eyes took in the burning, seething gazes of all around him. He took a deep breath and continued in a calm, steady manner. 'Knowing what this assembly had decided regarding my daughter Ambapali, I had postponed her marriage till she became eighteen. Now–'

'Postponed!' A courtier's son shouted. 'What does that mean? This sounds suspicious!'

The floodgates opened, and many voices joined in. 'This is suspicious!' 'Be clear!' 'Lady Ambapali cannot be one man's wife. She belongs to all of us!' 'And we will use our weapons if we have to!'

Chief Minister Sunand raised his hand, and the commotion died down. 'Young men, be quiet. Do not disturb the functioning of the assembly. Sir Mahanaman has not completed his statement. Let him say what he has to.'

Once again, there was pin-drop silence in the hall. All eyes were on Mahanaman. He looked at the members of the assembly and at the raging crowd outside. He cast his eyes downwards.

This time he spoke without raising his eyes. 'Gentlemen, Ambapali is eighteen years of age today. According to the laws of the Vajji Republic, she is independent and responsible for her decisions. So, from this day onwards, I am not her guardian. She herself will speak her mind to this assembly.'

It was as if a wave of indignation had fanned out from where Mahanaman stood. Many of the young men drew their swords, and others raised their spears. There were screams of fury. 'Treason! Treason!' 'Sir Mahanaman has tricked the Republic!' 'Punish him!' 'She is for us, all of us!' 'If the Republic can't get rules followed, we shall do it!' 'Yes, with our swords and spears!'

The shouts subsided as men followed their neighbours' examples to gaze, stunned, at the door to the hall. It was as if a spell had been cast on the whole tumultuous crowd. A veiled woman stood in the doorway. Her presence seemed to light up the hall and to scent it. It was as if the pent-up anger had dissolved in an instant. The young men gave way to her without a murmur of dissent. The men inside the assembly and those outside gazed at her as they would at a goddess.

She removed her veil when she reached the altar. The gathering viewed for the first time the beauty that had been the talk of the city for more than three years. That beauty had brought the assembled multitude to their state of desperation. As the hundreds of eyes fell on her, the limbs of the viewers became still, their hearts pounded, and their breath became ragged. Like a silvery autumnal moon, her presence soothed every corner of the hall. The ferocity of a few moments before had dissipated.

Ambapali wore a spotless, golden-hued silken dress around her waist. Her hair was tied perfectly in a bun, adorned with tiny flowers. Her breasts were covered only by a necklace of large, flawless pearls. A girdle studded with precious stones divided her slender waist from her exquisitely curved buttocks. She wore glittering anklets that seemed to enhance her brilliance. Even her slender feet, encased in slippers with inlay work, were chiselled to perfection. It was as if a divinely gifted sculptor had carved out her body from a single diamond in an inspired frenzy, in homage to all that was beautiful in this world. She exuded a radiance, a subtle and tender energy that held the assembly captive. She had reduced the assembly, and the belligerent crowd outside, to a powerless, stunned mass.

This was the Ambapali for whom the citizens of Vaishali were ready to create rivers of blood. To see her, the rich and powerful often displayed ingenuity. Many had gone to ludicrous lengths to express their desires. They had commissioned images, painted based on hearsay by the most skilled painters, barring no expenses. They had hoarded the paintings away from the gazes of their friends. Today, Ambapali stood before their eyes, in the flesh, embodying all that was glorious about beauty and youth. It was as if the men in the gaping crowd had lost themselves in a state of meditative contemplation, far removed from their frenzy of a few moments ago.

Ambapali went and stood by Mahanaman, with her gaze lowered. Sunand said, 'Gentlemen, Ambapali has appeared in person to express herself before this assembly. All, please listen to her statement.'

The young woman stood still for a moment. The assembly vibrated with loud cheers and slogans from the hall and from outside. 'Long live Lady Ambapali!' 'Victory to the Bride of the City!' 'Victory to the Benefactress!'

Her lips quivered like rose petals caressed by a morning breeze. When she took a deep breath and spoke, her voice flowed like music. 'Gentlemen,' she said in a firm but dewy tone that sent ripples of pleasure around her, 'I have considered your order. I will accept the abominable, cursed law of the Vajji union if this august assembly will be so kind as to accept my terms. Gentlemen, the chief minister will convey these terms.'

A shocked silence greeted her words, and then a murmur picked up in volume. A middle-aged councilman, who had his moustache between his teeth, let go of it and protested in a reedy voice, 'What did you say? Abominable, cursed law? Take back what you said, Ambapali. It is an insult to this assembly!'

'Yes, yes!' more voices joined in. 'Take back those words. You cannot use such words!'

Ambapali spoke with ease, without seeming to raise her voice, but in words that rang out loud and clear in the hall. 'Not only will I not take back those words, but I state that I shall repeat them a thousand times. This cursed law of the Vajji union is a blot on the great name of the Republic of Vaishali. Gentlemen, what is my crime? It is that God gave me the beauty that seems unfathomable in your eyes. For this, my life from this day onwards becomes different from other women born on the same day as me. For this, I am to be deprived of the rights that every bride of a family has. I cannot give my body and heart to one man that I love. I must sell this affectionate heart and this body oozing with all that men desire to those men that bid for them. You force me to do this by law. Cursed is the law that these courtiers' woman-loving sons burn to protect with their sharp swords and the points of their spears. Cursed is the law that these merchants' sons are keen to protect with the influence their money buys.' Her voice was louder now. 'This law is fit to be cursed a million times.' She stopped, her flushed face and trembling fingers betraying her agitation.

There was a deafening silence in the assembly hall.

'Gentlemen,' Ambapali continued in a sober tone, 'I have said what I had to say. If this assembly accepts my conditions, I offer my purity, womanhood, honour, beauty, youth, body – all that I have – to the Republic in the name of this cursed law. If you do not accept them, I shall await my executioner in the Blue Lotus Palace.'

She veiled her body, took Mahanaman's hand and said, 'Let us go.' He first clasped her hand and then, put his hand on her shoulder. Together, they walked towards the chariot, followed by the young man who had accompanied Mahanaman earlier.

The people of the Republic of Vaishali looked on as if they had been struck dumb.

CHAPTER 2

THE ASSEMBLY DELIBERATES

All eyes followed the chariot until the tinkling of its bells had faded out, and its flag dwindled into the horizon. Ambapali had cast a spell on the citizens of Vaishali. That she was no ordinary beauty was only expected. What they had not imagined were the energy that she radiated, her charisma, her courage, her firmness. Her few, carefully chosen words in the assembly had left her audience stunned. Some men became instant opponents of the law. One of them spoke with eloquence. 'Who will force Lady Ambapali into serving the city? We will colour the earth with their blood. She is right, this is a cursed law, a blot on the Republic of Vaishali and the Vajji union. It is an institution of slavery in a civic society that claims to have independence in its soul. Which of our neighbours has this law? Anga, Banga, Kalinga, Champa, Kashi, Kosala, Tamraparni, Rajgrih – none of them have this assault on womanhood. What use our democratic ethos is we allow this abduction of beauty? It is an insult to our women.'

'We will not accept this!' another man joined in. 'We will revolt!' a third said. 'Against the eight clans, against society, against this republic and this assembly!'

One courtier drew his sword. His chest heaved as he spoke. 'Ambapali's words pierced me like arrows!' he said. 'She waits in the Blue Lotus Palace for her executioners! Who will send the executioners? I shall cut that person to pieces.' Many others drew their swords to support him. One of them cried, 'We will raze the assembly to the ground!'

Some of the merchants' sons were walking around as if in a daze.

'To hell with this Vajji union!'

'We will leave for Rajgrih!'

'We shall give up all we have here for her!'

Soon, a large group of men was shouting, 'Long live Lady Ambapali! Victory to the Benefactress of the Republic!'

A group of horsemen was pacing up and down, brandishing their swords and throwing their spears up in the air to catch them neatly.

'The executioners will not kill her!'

'We must enjoy her divinity!'

'Yes, she was like an autumnal moon – I need that feeling again!'

'Oh, her exquisite form, her youth!' 'She will be Vaishali's life-giver, the focal point of our lives!'

'She must become the Bride of the City!'

'Yes, we shall accept her terms. We shall accept anything to get her and give up our lives if we don't.'

The guards and officials looked on helplessly at the chaos. For the first time in his life, Sunand's gestures were impotent. He sat slumped, head in his hands for some time. Then he stood up with his arms stretched high and wide. The turmoil slowly subsided as men nudged their neighbours to quieten down.

'Young men!' Sunand spoke with fervour. 'Be quiet! Listen now to the conditions laid down by Lady Ambapali. The approval of this house is needed for the conditions to be accepted and passed into statute. She herself has said that she will become the Bride of the City on these terms!'

There was utter silence for a few moments. Then many voices joined in a single cry: 'The terms! Sir, read out the terms!'

Sunand resumed in a calmer voice. 'Yes, the terms and conditions. Her first condition is to be handed the Palace of Seven Worlds, with all its facilities and staff. She will live there and be given ninety million dammas in gold.'

The assembly and the citizens were stunned. Some senior officials gaped at each other, with raised eyebrows. A senior minister stiffened and spoke angrily: 'Gentlemen, this is impossible. The Palace of Seven Worlds is an important monument and a treasure. It has no parallel in all of India. It is a stately building that should be at the centre of statecraft and governance. It surpasses the royal palaces of Tamralipti, Rajgrih, Sravasti and Champa. And ninety million gold dammas? That is ruled out. Our treasury will be wiped out!' He stopped to gather his breath.

From outside, one of the merchant's sons chimed in. 'Why is it ruled out? If the treasury is depleted, we will refill it!' 'Yes', said another, 'and the eight clans can build another palace. Even a hundred million dammas of gold can be raised.' Many others joined in the chorus of support.

The courtiers' sons shouted out their views: 'We can meet her terms!' 'That palace is ours, it belongs to the Republic and the people. Our sweat went into building it and our blood into protecting it.' 'Just as Ambapali's beauty is a public good, so is the palace. Why not make it a centre of entertainment?'

Sensing that the discussion could get out of hand, Sunand stood once more and raised a hand to calm down the gathering. 'Gentlemen,' he said. 'I now ask you, the assembly, do you agree to meet Lady Ambapali's first condition? Those who oppose it, speak now, or hold your peace.' He was greeted by silence from the assembly. 'I hear no objections', Sunand said. 'I ask a second time. Does any assemblyman object to the first condition? No.' He paused and looked around. 'Gentlemen, I ask a third and last time – does any of you object to the stated first condition? No? Then I declare that this assembly has accepted Lady Ambapali's first condition.'

The mood became festive, inside the assembly and outside it. The hall vibrated with slogans for Ambapali.

Sunand waited for the hubbub to die down. Then he said, 'Gentlemen, now hear the lady's two remaining conditions. The second condition is that her residence will be guarded like a fort. The third condition is that her visitors shall not be monitored or searched by the office of the registrar.'

The supreme commander was on his feet, his faced red and shoulder muscles twitching. 'Gentlemen, this is capitulation. I cannot agree to it. If Lady Ambapali's residence is to be a fort, she will have her own army and run her own fiefdom within this city!'

The registrar rose and said, 'If we do not check who comes and goes into her fortified palace, it goes without saying that her residence will become a magnet for the enemies of Vaishali. Those who scheme against Vaishali will have safe harbour right in the heart of the city. And imagine a scenario in which one of our guards suspects someone of being an enemy agent, but Ambapali's army stands in the way of his investigation! Gentlemen, I want to pace of record that the Republic is surrounded by enemies. On the one hand, Emperor Bimbisar of Rajgrih looks at us with enmity; on the other hand, our neighbours in Matsya, Anga, Banga, Kalinga, Kosala and Avanti have nothing but hatred for us. If we succumb to Lady Ambapali's conditions, her palace will become an epicentre of subversive activity against which we will be defenceless.'

The assembly hall buzzed with animated discussion, and soon the arguments were raging in the hall and outside. Once again, Sunand quietened the gathering in the hall and waited for the commotion outside to subside. Then, he said, 'Gentlemen, we must not be paranoid. This assembly chose Lady Ambapali to be the Bride of the City, Benefactress of the Republic, for good reasons. If the Republic wants her, and we have seen that it does, the Republic will have to give to her as well. We are indeed surrounded by enemies. We must avoid internal squabbles as much as we can. I see these young men' – he gestured to the courtiers' sons – 'brandish their swords and spears, polished to perfection, time and again. I say to them: mark my words, the time is not far off when your pride, your weapons and your strength will be tested. We must conserve our energies for those testing times and not dissipate them in internal strife. I, Sunand, advise this assembly to accept Lady Ambapali's second condition. I propose an amendment to her third condition: if we wish to conduct a search of her residence and her visitors, we can do so with a week's notice.'

There was a heavy silence in the assembly hall. Sunand spoke again. 'Gentlemen, hear me. I have proposed that we accept Lady Ambapali's second condition. For her third condition, we accept it only after modification as I have outlined. Those who accept, please stay silent. Those who object, please speak now.'

The silence continued. 'All are silent', Sunand said. 'I ask a second time – does anyone have an objection? Speak now', he repeated after scanning the assembly. 'I ask for the last time. Stay silent only if you accept my proposal.

'All are quiet. So it shall be, Gentlemen. This assembly of the eight clans has accepted Lady Ambapali's conditions, subject only to the modification of the third condition that I have just outlined. I shall go to the Blue Lotus Palace to see her and convey this decision to her. Tomorrow, as per protocol, we shall issue an announcement on these proceedings. This assembly is closed.'

As Sunand rose to leave, the hall vibrated with the bedlam of thousands of heated discussions.

CHAPTER 3

THE BLUE LOTUS PALACE

he Blue Lotus Palace was named after the lake dotted with blue lotus flowers that surrounded it. Its outer walls and floors were made of the finest marble from Matsya. Intricate inlay work decorated the exterior walls. A bridge with ornate, golden-hued pillars connected the palace to the outside world. The water of the lake had sapphire tint and was always adorned with large blue lotus flowers. The plants had initially been imported at a high cost and painstaking effort from Persia. To one side of the bridge, there was an aviary that hosted many species of birds. The fluttering of the birds, the sparkling, rippled blue water, the magnificent lotus flowers, and the shimmering reflection of the palace walls were soothing to the eye.

Ambapali took in these sights. She was staying in the palace as a guest of the assembly. She sat dressed casually on a marble platform at the shore of the lake. In the far horizon, a feeble star had announced its presence. She gazed at it, as she thought about her past and her future. Many kinds of thoughts pummelled her mind. She remembered taking her first steps into the city, seven years ago, as an eleven-year-old girl holding on to her towering father's index finger. How tall the buildings had looked! And the newness of everything! A new life, with a new cadence and new ways of thinking so different from those of the village. With Commander Chandramani's help, her father had got back his old post and all that went with it. And here she was, enjoying this scented evening. The girl who had implored her father for a jacket worth six dammas and felt a pang of sorrow as his eyes grew teary now commanded a fortune others could only dream of. Today, all of Vaishali was indignant over her, and she sensed that she held the ropes that controlled the city.

The man who had jeered and insulted her father in a drunken stupor had fallen in love with her. He had been renamed Harshdev when he entered adulthood. She had accepted Harshdev's ardent desire with a flicker of her eyes and the hint of a smile on her lips. It is useless to try to surmise how much maturity there was in this acceptance, or how much ignorance. Their fathers, bound by their old friendship and grateful for this turn of events, agreed to join the families. And she lost no opportunity to tease Harshdev with eyes sparkling with acceptance, even as her lips pouted and she frowned to show rejection. She thought now of those innocent moments that did not last for long. All that was tried to hide her unparalleled beauty was of no use. It was like trying to hide the light of the morning sun. She became an object of discussion in every home in Vaishali. The courtiers' sons were ready to duel for her, and the merchants' sons to throw money to get a glimpse of her. A few people tried keeping her away from the public gaze, but that only added to her legend. Her reclusiveness added ghee to the fire.

One day, Mahanaman asked the city official for permission to marry Ambapali to Harshdev. The request should have been a formality, but it produced a flurry of activity. Instead of the permission, Mahanaman received a signed order from the chief minister to the effect that Ambapali was not to marry before she was eighteen years of age. On attaining the age of eighteen, she was to be presented in the assembly. Mahanaman had to commit his acceptance of the order in writing.

That was three years ago. In the intervening years, the people had taken it for granted that Ambapali would be declared the Benefactress of the Republic. The post was being kept vacant for her. They had built up pressure on the assembly to announce officially that she was the Bride of the City. Their desperation had been such that the chief minister had to quell it by ordering Mahanaman and Ambapali to present themselves in a special session of the assembly on the day Ambapali turned eighteen.

Ambapali's mind baulked when she tried to imagine the contours of the new life the Republic had thrust on her. For Harshdev she had at least a liking. She did not know this was the fabled phenomenon of love that had occupied so much of her discussions with her closest girlfriends. According to her father, that liking would flower into love when she became a bride. She only vaguely pictured herself as a bride in a family, let alone the bride of the entire city. Her imagination failed her equally when she thought about the two paths, of which one was closed to her. Though this thought would not have crossed the minds of those who had seen her in the assembly on that fateful day, her mind was still childlike in some ways. Like other girls her age, she had moods, she could be impulsive and stubborn; she had hopes and aspirations. She had spent many days and nights in frantic contemplation of the options she had. She had worried for her father. Finally, she had taken a leap of faith and put on an invisible armour. She had decided if that if the iron hand of the law left her no choice, she must forge her strong will on the people who had tried to pin her down, and channelise the

power they had inadvertently given her to trample them. That was how she had
arrived at her three conditions.

·

As she sat there, alone and forlorn, her emotions got the better of her. She realised that her eyes were teary, and her breasts were heaving. Her lungs almost
hurt as they pumped air like a blacksmith's bellow. She bit her lower lip and
suppressed a scream of anger. 'I shall avenge this', she said. 'I shall make the
womanising men of Vaishali pay. I shall sell my womanhood. I shall give myself
to these crazed vultures who see me as meat. But they will pay for this. They will
pay for this with their honour. I will grind them to dust.' A feeling of descended
on her as she made this resolve.

She lost track of time. The moon lit the sky, and the stars were out in full force.
Their images rippled in the waters of the lake. Ambapali took a deep breath and
wiped her teary cheeks. 'I shall not be weak. I shall not let my mind be fickle. I
shall battle. I shall win.'

As these thoughts swarmed in her mind, the night turned silvery. Ambapali
sat there motionless, in her white clothes, she seemed to have been sculpted out
of moonlight. Lost in her thoughts, she did not immediately register that someone was speaking to her. Madlekha stood, bowed and spoke with diffidence.
'Greetings to the lady. The chief minister is here and asks for an audience.'

Ambapali acknowledged the words with a delay. She knew she must live her
new persona. She raised an eyebrow and said, coldly, 'Show him in.'

She walked over to a marble seat and took it. She calmed herself by breathing
deeply.

Sunand stood before her. 'May Lady Ambapali be pleased', he said. 'I bring a
message from the Vajji Union.'

'Where are your executioners?' Ambapali replied. 'I am ready. How do
Vaishali's brutes prefer to kill me?'

'They want your body', Sunand said.

'That will be easy when I am dead.'

Sunand smiled for the first time. 'They want you alive and pleased. Lady Ambapali, the assembly has accepted your conditions. Only the last one–'

'What about the last one?' Ambapali said in a raised voice. 'My conditions
are not negotiable.'

Sunand's forehead was furrowed. 'Lady Ambapali, cleanse yourself of this
anger, this unhappiness. You will get this palace, with all its facilities running as
they do today. It will become your fort as well. You will get the money you asked
for.' He paused to let this sink in. 'But, if we need to investigate your visitors, we
will give you a week's notice. That is all we have amended in the conditions. I, the

chief minister, suggest that you accept your destiny. It will not be the first time that a great person has made a sacrifice for the common good. Save the Republic from being drowned in your blood!'

'Save this republic? Why?' Ambapali said. 'Where a woman can be trampled on like this? There is no harm in drowning a republic like this in blood. I will welcome the axe on my neck. But be clear, the conditions are not negotiable. Should Vaishali burn and riot, I don't care whether it happens today instead of tomorrow.'

Sunand recoiled. 'Don't say that, Lady Ambapali!' He spoke with urgency. 'That is a terrible thing to say. And you cannot do this, I am sure. This Republic, established by the eight clans, must live on. You are part of it. We only ask for your life to be dedicated to the Republic – on your terms.'

'And I am ready to give my life to the Republic. Send the executioners in.'

Sunand's tone was gravelly and hoarse. It was clear that he was charged with emotion. 'But we want you to live! Your name will become immortal! The defence of the Republic rests on both men and women. Men's lives are always at stake, given our situation. Women's as well. We have a protocol that has been established. This divine beauty of yours, this striking loveliness, this charisma, force, presence – why should it belong to one man? Why should an extraordinary woman like you be one man's slave? Where is the dharma in that? That is what our forefathers asked when they laid down this rule. Over time, shackles acquire the force of dharma, and ordinary folk follow them without question. An ordinary woman gives her body and mind to one man because of such shackles; she becomes his slave for life, willingly. You, you are extraordinary!'

'And that gives Vaishali the right to invade my body? Why?' asked Ambapali.

'Because', the old man said in a measured and calm way, 'Lady Ambapali, of what the Republic gives you: an unparalleled palace, its establishment, the right to run your residence as a fort, ninety million dammas in gold and the opportunity to live like an empress. All of these are signs of honour, not dishonour. The eight clans have not bestowed this prestige on anyone else. Not even to the chief minister! What more can you want?'

'So that is my price? Isn't that what you are saying? That I take my price and give myself to the Republic?'

'Yes, in short. Yes, that is my motive in coming here. But remember that it is not about the price. The price is a small part of the bigger picture. Remember, as I said, that there is a prestige that money cannot buy. The rich, the powerful, kings and emperors, will grovel before you. You will be covered not only with gold but with glory. Do not turn down this great fortune!'

'So, this is a deal, is that right? And what if I say I do not want any part of this deal? I do not want to be bought at any price. I do not want to sell my body.

I do not want a high price for my heart. What would you say to that?' Ambapali looked at Sunand with her head slanted to her right.

Sunand answered her in a composed manner. 'I am not here only to conclude a deal. I also want a sacrifice from you. Just think how Vaishali is hemmed in by enemies, each of them looking for the slightest opportunity to crush us. Look, I have given my life to the Republic. I sense that in you, we finally have a unifying figure. You will be the focal point of our lives. You will give us hope, energy, joy. I see that the young men will be falling at your feet. The eight clans and the assembly would have to exhort and admonish, struggling to convince them. In contrast, you will only have to snap your fingers.'

Sunand went down on his knees. His eyes watered. 'Lady Ambapali, I need not look deep inside you to understand you are burning with fury. All I can say is this: save us. If you do not, the city will be aflame, and our enemies will fan the fires. These fires will consume many people you know and love. I beg you to give yourself to Vaishali, on your own terms.'

Ambapali got to her feet. She stood ramrod straight, her delicate nostrils flared, her hands clasped tightly. 'Rise, Sir Chief Minister!' she said. 'Tell your assembly, and the public, I have accepted the cursed law of the Republic. Tonight, Ambapali renounces her right to become a bride of a family and accepts her destiny to become the Bride of the City.'

Sunand raised his trembling hands in homage. 'May you live long, Lady Ambapali. I think you do not appreciate it yet, but I meant every word I said. You have saved Vaishali from ruin.' He rose with some effort, pushing himself up with his wiry, muscular arms. He joined his hands again in a namaste which Ambapali reciprocated stoically. He turned towards the bridge and walked away.

Ambapali followed the receding form of the elder. Then she slumped and rested her face in the comfort of her trembling palms. On that magnificent marble slab, bathed in the soothing light of the full moon, with the scented breeze of the night caressing her, she wept her heart out.

The only witness to the plaintive cry of her heart was the shimmering reflection of the moon on the ripples of the Blue Lotus Lake.

CHAPTER 4

THE ANOINTMENT

A bath in the Holy Lake was the highest honour of the Republic of Vaishali. It was an honour granted only to those elected Licchavis who were appointed to the Legislative assembly, and even they were granted this honour only once in a lifetime. A bath in the lake was a grand celebration. The lake dated back to the foundation of Vaishali. Legend had it that the lake contained the spirits of the Licchavi ancestors who had re-established the eight clans with the might of their arms, and after being thrown out by the Aryans. The nine hundred and ninety-nine Licchavi members of the assembly were allowed to step into the Holy Lake. Many kings had mounted assaults on the Republic just to bathe in the lake, only to be beaten by the arrows of Vaishali's young men. The lake was guarded round the clock, and a copper mesh ensured that birds did not defile it. The punishment for surreptitiously bathing in it was, of course, death.

A small force of specialists kept itself busy maintaining the ecology of the Holy Lake. To those who saw the lake for the first time, the view of the still water and the lotus flowers of many colours was breathtaking, though they found it small considering its aura. On its four sides, marble steps descended into it. Pillars and canopies with exquisite carvings lined the steps. The water was so clear that the folds of silt at its bottom, framing bright shoals of fish, were visible through it. The lotus garden at the fringes of the lake was famed for its flowers of different hues.

Ambapali was a Licchavi, and she was the specially anointed Benefactress of the Republic. It was the third day of the festivities after she had accepted her position. That day she would be driven around the city as its honoured figurehead, for the common folk to see her through her delicate veil. The city seethed with excitement. The houses, streets, markets and Royal Avenue were dotted with buntings and flags. The steps of the Holy Lake were covered with floral patterns.

It had been announced that the stars were auspicious for those three days, and the city had erupted in joy.

Ambapali's chariot procession started at the crack of the spring dawn. The canopy and sides of her chariot had been polished till they gleamed softly, and its wheels were spotless. The flag of the Republic flew proudly from its mast. Ambapali sat with her eyes lowered, her face flushed red. She wore the simplest of dresses – a waistcloth and a plain cape. Without make-up or ornaments, her austerity gave her the aura of dawn without stars. Even without embellishment, her shapely neck, the swell of her breasts and her rippling, glossy black hair adorned with flowers enhanced her charisma.

The flags, buntings and banners created a riot of rainbow colours. Two caparisoned elephants bearing flags and insignia followed the procession led by a large group of musicians. Next in line came the slave girls in clean, plain attire. They carried the balms and oblations that would be used in the holy bath. Ambapali's shiny chariot followed, driven by a white horse, with Ambapali's un-bedecked beauty giving her a halo that would become folklore. The people of the city jostled on the windows and balconies, to watch and add to the showers of petals and scent. A swarm of well-dressed young men milled around behind her chariot, showering her with flowers and drops of perfume. A throng of commoners brought up the rear of the procession.

The people at the rear were stopped at the entrance to the Holy Lake. A smaller group reached the vicinity of the lotus garden. Here, there was another barrier. Only members of the assembly could go beyond, on to the marble steps bounding the Holy Lake. The crowd dispersed into smaller pockets. Those who could found shade under trees. The excitement refused to subside, and the buzz of energised voices filled the air. Rows of guards neatly lined the area just ahead of the steps to the lake, their swords unsheathed and their backs towards the lake.

Chief Minister Sunand greeted Ambapali with folded hands as her chariot slowed to a halt. He offered her his hand as she stepped down and gently guided her down the steps to the edge of the lake. Looking at the sky, he murmured a verse and bent to scoop up a handful of holy water. He emptied the water into Ambapali's cupped palms. 'Lady Ambapali,' he said gravely, 'you must say: "I am guided by the Vajji Union"'.

The crowd had turned silent. Spoken softly, Ambapali's words rang out clearly in the enclave.

Sunand guided her another step into the lake and said, 'Now, Lady Ambapali, say: "I belong to Vaishali."'

Ambapali was knee-deep in the Holy Lake. She repeated the words.

Sunand and Ambapali took another step. They were now waist-deep in the water. 'Lady Ambapali, do you vow here, in the Holy Lake, to follow the seven codes of the Licchavis?'

Ambapali replied 'I do', in her sweet voice.

Sunand folded his hands in acknowledgement. He said, 'Sirs, young men, all listen! I announce on behalf of the Vajji Union that Lady Ambapali is now our Benefactress. She is the Bride of the City.'

He reached for the perfumed oil that an aide held out for him, dipped his fourth finger in it and dabbed it on to Ambapali's forehead. He then kissed her paternally on the head, said a few words to her and stepped out of the water. The Holy Lake echoed with the cheers of the assembly, and more petals and scent were showered on Ambapali.

The Holy Lake rippled gently as Ambapali took three dips in it, and petals continued to float down onto its surface. When she stood still after her third dip, her thin, plain robe clung to her golden body. Her curves blossomed under it. The drops of water dripping from her hair appeared like pearls in the soft light. As she turned and stepped out of the water, a dozen instruments struck up a melodious fanfare. A group of slave girls surrounded her and quickly changed her clothes into dry ones. The rain of flower petals and perfumed drops from her admirers did not let up for an instant. Ambapali was guided to an ornate seat.

Then the feast started. Each of the assembly members took a piece from Ambapali's huge pattal, a plate stitched together from leaves. A retinue of servants kept her plate overflowing with blackbuck meat, pork, chicken and pheasant cooked on a slow smokeless fire. The servants took Maireya wine stored in large earthen pitchers and kept pouring it to ensure that the cups of the diners were kept brimming. The guests showed their delight at the unrestricted flow of exquisite food and drinks and the magic of Ambapali's demure, and yet, charismatic presence. They lauded the young woman and wished her well at every opportunity. It was clear that their benevolent wishes came from their hearts.

After the feast, Ambapali proceeded to the Palace of Seven Worlds in a triumphant procession. The nobles, merchants and a swelling crowd of commoners accompanied her. As her chariot reached the main gate of the palace, a hundred trumpets burst forth from its ramparts into a tumultuous greeting. The superintendent of the palace stepped forward, leading a horse and a shining sword. Following Sunand's gentle instructions, Ambapali touched the sword, mounted the horse and rode into the palace. The crowd trickled away, still animated, and with much to talk about. They knew they had witnessed a historic ceremony.

CHAPTER 5

THE FIRST GUEST

The sun had not risen. Venus glowed like a diamond in the pale light of the eastern sky. The guards of the Palace of Seven Worlds were weary and ready for their relief. The birds had not yet started chirping in full force; only a couple of them were up and about. A dusty young man with an uncertain gait, matted hair and a half-crazed look in his eyes stumbled towards the main gate.

'Halt!' the nearest guard cried out. 'Who approaches?'

'I come to see Lady Ambapali', the man said.

'The lady is still in her chamber. This is no time to meet her, anyway. Come back later.'

'I cannot go back. I will wait till she is up', the man said. He collapsed on a stone near the gate without taking the guard's permission.

The guard muttered a curse, and his eyes bristled. 'Young man, whoever you are, you cannot sit here! The hours of audience are in the evening, not now!'

'There is no harm in my waiting till the evening, is there?' the young man asked.

'Listen to me!' The guard was shouting now, and a few of his fellows started to stroll over. 'There is no audience anyway for people who are crazy!'

'You will see, I will get an audience', the seated man said calmly. 'I am not that crazy.'

The guard's jaw dropped. His hand jerked towards the hilt of his sword, but then he thought the better of it. He grabbed the man's dusty robe. The man drew a sword from the depths of his robe in a fluid motion. The guard stepped back with alacrity, and four other guards started running towards them.

A woman's shout echoed in the yard. 'It is all right! Let him enter!' The guard looked fearfully back over his shoulder. It was Ambapali herself, standing imperiously on the rampart with a hand on one hip. The guards cowered and saluted her.

The young man saluted the guards without malice and walked past the three courtyards to reach the inner building. He was shown to Ambapali's bedroom by a pair of slave girls.

'You didn't sleep at all, did you, Harshdev?' Ambapali asked him.

'Perhaps you did not either…Lady Ambapali?' he replied.

'Let that be', she said. 'Have you been walking about all night?'

'My heart burns, Ambapali!' Harshdev spoke with anguish. 'I do not know how I will find peace.'

'Is yours the only heart that burns, Harshdev?' Ambapali said. 'If it is, then ignite Vaishali with this flame! Let it burn to ashes! What use is it if you burn alone?'

'But Ambapali, will you close your doors to me? Can you be so cruel? How will I live…how will I survive without you?'

'And you – will you come here, Harshdev? Will you be so brave? Will you watch the nobles and merchants express their love to your promised bride? Will you be able to stand and watch it? Can you imagine it now? Can you see them buying every part of my heart?

'Who bars you from entering? This is a public building, by State decree. All are welcome, and so are you – but not in this manner! Not like a poor, besotted man. The poor and the deprived are forbidden here.

'Do not forget – this is the palace of the Bride of Vaishali. Come like the others. Come well-groomed, oiled, perfumed. Come showering diamonds, pearls and gold coins. Come with an assured smile, with lust dancing in your eyes. Watch the rich and the powerful show their…love for me. And don't hesitate to show the same kind of love. Laugh, speak, pay the price – and then go home with empty hands, empty wallet and empty heart. Oh, and come again to go back the same way. As long as you have your position, and long as you have gold and jewels, do come. Throw your weight, throw your money. This is the life the Bride of the City will lead. Do not forget that.'

The uncontrived torrent of words poured forth. Ambapali's face had turned white as snow. Harshdev stared at her, wide-eyed and distraught. He opened his mouth to speak, but words failed him.

'So, will you do it? Will you enjoy it?' Ambapali asked softly.

'No!' Harshdev said hoarsely. 'No, I cannot see that happening.'

'Then go. Go away. Do not stray here, ever. Do not dare to enter the house of the Bride of the City. Ambapali, the girl who was betrothed to you is dead! Now I, Lady Ambapali, the mistress of this public building, stand before you. And I am wedded to all Vaishali. If you have any humanity in you, burn Vaishali! Raze it to the ground.'

'Yes!' Harshdev shouted like a complete madman. 'Yes, I will do that. I must. And you will see it, Ambapali…you will see Vaishali reduced to ashes. This palace, its towers, the eight clans, and the cursed law of this republic…I shall burn them all along with this building.' He knelt on the ground, overcome and trembling.

'Go now', Ambapali said, her voice breaking. 'Go right away. I shall wait to see the fires.'

Harshdev drew himself up to his full height. He joined his hands in a namaste and walked away without a word.

Ambapali stood where she was. The first sunrise of her life as the Bride of the City bathed her in soft, warm light.

CHAPTER 6

THE HOLY TOWN OF URUBELA

In those days, near the holy town of Urubela, the banks of the Niranjana river drew many ascetics. Their austere thatched huts dotted the riverside and columns of smoke that issued from their ceremonial fires. The ascetics followed different sects and organised themselves in groups with their disciples. They lived off alms from begging in the city, rearing animals, and donations from believers. Some of them were quite prosperous.

Their practices varied between sects. Some were famous for the very harsh regimes of penance they followed, others because they reduced or increased their frugal food intake with the waxing and waning of the moon. The maximum food intake they allowed themselves was fourteen mouthfuls on the day following a full moon. A visitor would find some of them standing on a single leg, while others hung upside-down from trees, stood steadfast in neck-deep water, or lay on beds of thorns. They tortured their bodies in many ways – they might lie naked in the cold open air or bask in fires of five kinds in peak summer. Some of them stayed naked as a habit – they called themselves the digambar, or the sky clad – while others had matted locks, and others still shaved their heads.

There were mountain caves a small distance away from the riverbank. Some ascetics shut themselves off from the outside world and stayed in them for weeks and months on end. They would lie there naked and motionless, oblivious of hunger, thirst, heat, cold, fear or any other sensation. They had detached themselves from their bodies. Many of them had given up all connection to the physical and biological world. Many carried skull garlands around their necks, and animal skins still dripping with blood around their waists. They roamed around chanting Tantric verses, spending their nights in cremation grounds and performing acts that would horrify ordinary folks. They claimed that they had mastered their senses and desires and achieved godliness. They practised sending death to their enemies by chanting Tantric verses that killed or numbed the minds of their victims. They inspired awe and fear.

Of all these ascetics, three with matted locks were very well known. The disciples, who did not shave their heads, were called the dreadlocked ones. One of their leaders was Urubela Kashyap. He had five hundred celibate disciples. The second one, Nadi Kashyap, had three hundred followers and the third, Gaya Kashyap, two hundred. The three leaders were collectively called the Mahakashyaps. They were renowned for their mastery of the scriptures, their austerity and their powers. Kings, nobles and merchants from near and far offered gold, jewels and grain to them to get their blessings. People spoke of them in hushed tones and said they were all-powerful great minds. They encouraged these beliefs. They often performed great yagyas for which people from the kingdoms of Vatsa, Magadha, Kosala and Anga donated grain, ghee, jewels, cloth and honey. It was common for a large fair to last fortnights on such occasions.

Today, Urubela is known as Bodh Gaya[1] and the Niranjana river as the Phalgu. Devout Hindus from all over India go there make offerings to their ancestors. This is the site of the famous Bodhi Tree and of an unequalled statue of the Buddha. Even today, the visitor who imbibes the atmosphere of the town will sense that it has been a holy place since the dawn of time.

---

1 Or the city where Siddhartha became the Buddha.

CHAPTER 7

GAUTAM, SON OF THE SHAKYA KING

In that very Urubela town, by the side of that Niranjana river, a young ascetic sat in a trance under a huge banyan tree. His frail body exuded a glow that a burnished golden statue would match with difficulty. All he wore was a loincloth. His whole body, his eyes, even his breath, were still.

This was Gautam, prince of Kapilvastu, son of a Shakya king. He had renounced the choicest pleasures in search of bliss.

Gautam opened his eyes. In front of him, children were grazing their goats. The black, white and brown goats frolicked in the green pastures. Gautam looked at the scene with steadfast eyes. The morning was beautiful on that second day after the full moon in the month of Baisakhi. The play of the amber sun rays on the lush grass, the scent of dew, the refreshing coolness of the air and birdsong combined to create a magical effect. Gautam's heart was pierced by the realisation that this world was cocooned in hope and bliss. He felt warmth and light emanate from within him and diffuse to envelop the whole world. He felt full of possibilities; he felt that the world was bright, radiant and pure. The light that was spreading was bereft of any tinges of fear or pain. That light was that of immortality, freedom, bliss. He felt that he was blessed. He felt he had become the Buddha, the one who has perceived all there is to perceive – the enlightened one, the Tathagat – the one who is beyond coming and going, the Arhat – the deserving.

At that instant, two tribal men from the distant land of Odisha passed by. They stopped of their own volition and looked at the young, lean, sage. One spoke up. 'Sir, here is some buttermilk–' He gestured towards the earthen pot he was carrying. ' – And my friend has sweets. Please accept these.' Gautam smiled at them. A tender love shone through his eyes. 'I am Tathagat, I am Buddha. I cannot take alms without a bowl.' The two men looked at each other and smiled. The one who had not spoken handed him a rough stone bowl with buttermilk and two sweets. Gautam devoured the gift with relish, while the two men spoke in hushed words to each other.

When Gautam had finished, one of them said, 'Sir, I am Bhilluk, and this is Tapassu. We have wandered far. We want to take shelter with you.'

Thus did the Buddha gain his first two disciples.

After they had left, much later, the Buddha gazed lovingly at the banyan tree. He closed his eyes and meditated on the origin of symbols and their attributes, positive and negative. Ignorance or avidya leaves subtle impressions on the psyche, samaskaras, that cause vigyaan, awareness. Awareness results in forms, of which there are six concrete instances. The six sense bases – eyes, nose, ears, tongue, body and mind – enable contact with objects. This contact results in vedana, or sensation. The thirst for pleasurable sensations, or trishna, arises from sensation. This thirst leads to grasping. Grasping drives one to actions that build karma, which determines one's next existence. From here on, what follows is jaati, or birth, from which ensue old age, sorrow and death. Destroying the impressions left by ignorance destroys the cluster of sorrows.

.

The Buddha opened his eyes. 'I have attained what is difficult to attain, perceived that which many have struggled in vain to perceive. I am at peace, the highest level of peace. I have understood the essence of dharma, righteousness, that one cannot reach with logic alone!' A voice rose from his inner heart. 'This world is heading for destruction if the Tathagat's enlightened consciousness does not spread this dharma.' He said to himself, in that moment of light, lightness and resolve: 'Feel this joy coursing through every pore! Get up, look at the masses drowning in sorrow, reeling from the cycle of birth and death! Vanquisher of darkness, relentless traveller, free man! Travel further and wider! Turn the wheels of dharma!'

He looked at the world around him with the new light in his eyes. Lotus flowers may bloom in the water, in the mud beside it, or high above its surface, leaving the safety of the water behind. Many humans possessed with sharp intelligence, good nature and keenness of perception hesitate to leave their havens because their will is dull.

The Buddha resolved then and there that he would give spiritual nectar to the world. His feet turned from Urubela to the greatest of cities, Kashi.

On his way, he met Upaka, a follower of the ajivik, fatalist, school of thought. Upaka looked at him with wonder and asked him, 'Young man, I see that you are specially gifted. You have attained bliss, and you have a pure glow. Who is your guru, who has brought this fortune on you?'

Gautam replied with equanimity, and without arrogance. 'I am victorious and all-knowing. I am without attachment; I have renounced all possessions. I am freed of the dissipation that thirst brings. I have no guru. I am the Buddha. I have found peace and freedom and the entirety of knowledge. I am headed to Kashi to spread righteousness.

Upaka gaped at him for a moment. Then he said. 'Young man, if that is so, you must be a djinn.'

'Since the dirt in my mind has been washed away, yes, I am a djinn', the Buddha said.

'It is possible, young man', Upaka said and went on.

In Kashi, there was a group of sages that called themselves the Group of Five. They recognised Gautam, who had practised meditation and austerity with them earlier. One of them said, 'Look, here is Sage Gautam, he who gave up spiritual seeking and deserted his wife and son. He should not be accepted back! His begging bowl and cloth should not be accepted. All we can offer him is a place to roll his mat and sit.'

But when Gautam came closer, one of the sages, propelled by an unknown force, gave up his seat for him. Another took his bowl, and another still brought a wooden vessel with water and a tripod. Gautam washed his feet and took the seat.

'Monks,' he said, 'I come to pass on to you the nectar that I have received.'

The responses from the Group of Five were mixed.

'We know that you have not achieved the highest mark of spiritual seeking and meditation on Aryan philosophical knowledge!'

'Gautam, you have deviated from the true path–'

'Monks, I, the Tathagat, have imbibed the complete, perfect wisdom. Lend me your ears so that I can share the divine nectar with you. If you only partake of it, you can attain perfection in this life itself.'

The group persisted in their rejection.

Gautam waited for the commotion to subside. 'Monks,' he said, 'did I ever make this statement earlier?'

They agreed he had not.

'Then listen to me now, Monks!' Gautam spoke with sincerity and urgency. 'A saint must not indulge in two extremes. One path is low, uncouth, coarse, lust-ridden, devoid of meaning, and full of desires. The other is full of sorrow and torture. Monks! Save yourself from these two extremes, and follow the Tathagat's Middle Path, which will lead you to salvation, nirvana. The Middle Way is eightfold. Right discernment, right resolution, right speech, right deeds, right livelihood, right conduct, right memory, right judgement – this is the Middle Path, Oh Monks!

'Sorrow is real. Birth is sorrowful. Physical ailments are sorrowful. Death is sorrowful. The company of the unpleasant is sorrowful, and separation from beloved ones is sorrowful. To be left wanting for a desired object is sorrowful.

'The causes of sorrow are real. Sorrow stems from the three great desires – that of being born again, that of being happy, and that of being attached.

'And real, also, is the cessation of this sorrow with the Eightfold Path, for it leads to freedom.

'Monks, these are the Four Great Truths! I have become the Buddha only after I perceived these Four Great Truths and the Eightfold Path. And with this, I am ordained for freedom. This will be my last birth. I shall not return to this world.'

One of the Group of Five, Kondinya, spoke up. 'Master, is it true that whoever is born is destined for death?'

'Yes', Gautam said, 'that is true, young Kondinya! You have acquired a clear view of the dharma, indeed. Young man, from this moment on, you will be known as Kondinya Pragyaat, or Kondinya the One with Pure Intellect.'

Kondinya prostrated himself before Gautam, and said, 'Master, I shall follow the mendicant's life, the monk's life on the path that you have shown me.'

Gautam said, 'Kondinya, do you swear by dharma that you become my disciple with a mind not beset by doubt, a mind beyond shallow argument? Do you want to be adept in the Buddhist dharma and do you aspire to be free?

'That is so, master', Kondinya said.

'Then you are welcome', Gautam said. 'Dharma is beautiful. Follow a life of celibacy and consider yourself initiated.

The monks Vappa and Bhadiya spoke next.

'Master, whatever is born shall die…'

'Master, please initiate the two of us.'

'Sadhu, let it be thus', Gautam said. 'You have also acquired clarity of worldview. Welcome to the peaceful fold of dharma. Stay celibate to conquer sorrow.'

At this, two more young men, Ashvajit and Mahanabh, prostrated themselves before Gautam. 'Master,' they said, 'we see the truth. Please initiate us, and include us in your sangha, your union!' Gautam initiated them graciously, as he had the others, with an instruction to stay celibate. Continuing on his theme of celibacy, he expounded, 'Monks, all physical objects are "not atman", "not soul". If they had soul, they would not inflict pain. Pain is also 'not soul'. Even science that studies non-physical objects is 'not soul'. Now tell me, monks, is form eternal or transient?'

'It is transient, Master!' said a monk.

'And that which is transient, does it bring peace? Or does it bring sorrow?'

'It brings sorrow, Master!'

'For that which is not lasting, which causes sorrow, should one develop a feeling of attachment – should one think that this is mine, I am this, this is connected to my soul?'

'No, Master!'

'Monks, now think carefully. Do you believe whatever is associated with the past, present or future, whatever is inside or outdoors, gross or subtle, good or bad, distant or near, as long as it has form, is not mine? I am not of it? All that I am one with is my soul? Shall we understand that?'

'True! We shall!' The monks replied.

'And can we extend this understanding to rejection of pain, objects, traditions and external knowledge? That we are not attached to them?'

'Truly we can, Master. We have understood this truth.'

'Then, monks, a learnt Aryan should be indifferent to form, pain, objects and external knowledge. Being indifferent to these will lead to detachment, detachment will lead to freedom, and this freedom will be your escape from the cycle of life and death. With this escape, with adherence to your code of celibacy, nothing remains to be done.'

At the end of this brief but profound discourse, the Group of Five prostrated themselves devoutly before Gautam Buddha, the Tathagat. In one voice, they said, 'Master! Our consciousness has been freed from all blemishes.'

Gautam said, 'Then, monks, the six of us have attained perfection.' He leant against the tree trunk behind him and slipped into a trance. The monks prostrated themselves again and stepped out to get alms. Thus ended the sermon which entered the annals of history as the Buddha's first sermon at Sarnath.

CHAPTER 8

YASH, THE SCION

Yash, the only son of a wealthy merchant family of Kashi, was a handsome, well-built but tender-hearted young man. He had three palaces, one each for winter, summer and the rainy season. He was ensconced in the comfort of the rainy season palace, served by an army of eunuchs and slave women.

Yash had heard of Sage Gautam's visit to Sarnath, the suburb of Kashi, where his palace stood. Gautam had renounced the fabulous wealth and the lineage of the Shakya clan, abandoned his beautiful wife and newborn son, given up all physical amenities, and given up his shiny chariot. He walked the streets of Kashi begging for alms at the doors of Kashi's mansions with downcast but radiant eyes and a calm face. He was known to have turned the famous Group of Five sages into disciples.

Yash could not help thinking about Gautam. What wealth could Gautam have now? Did he own a nectar that kept him satiated or a hidden treasure? The sage's story intrigued Yash, and his mind kept returning to these questions.

A soft rain fell in the dark night, stirring up a cool breeze and enhancing the scents of the jasmine flowers. Yash's Rain Palace was lit with fragrant lamps. As the night sky darkened, Yash's thoughts turned more fervently to Gautam. The strains of music and the tinkle of the dancers' anklets did not engage his mind. Some slave girls came forward, knelt before him and pleaded with him.

'Sir, it is time for you to sleep. Your favourite is ready to massage your back. The others are waiting for you. You must go to bed now. If you like, we can continue the dance there. Kashi's most beautiful courtesan, Kadambari, awaits your orders. We can rub your feet if you are still tired.'

Yash sighed. 'Wait for a while, please, I need to think. This is all I do. The dance of beauties, the beauty of lovely women, the nightingale-like song of the singer, the melody of the lute… I am now bored with these. No, they do not satiate me. Who is that sage? What does he have that gives him peace of mind? He had all that I have, and even more, and walked away! People say he is free from worry, excitement, flaws. He walks on foot, trudges the streets, takes alms from households and moves on… with his calm gaze on the ground… peaceful, mute, at ease!

'No, no! Not now. Let the dance be, tell the masseuse, the courtesan and the others to sleep. And you, dear, can go to sleep as well. I am not in the mood… I keep thinking about this sage, this son of the Shakyas…'

The slave girls left, and the night deepened. The strains of music and anklets tapered off, and the hum of the cicadas took over. The lamps continued to glow and spread a soft scented glow. The sky was covered with dark clouds that poured a gentle drizzle.

A flash of lightning interrupted Yash's thoughts. He started and strolled to his bedroom. He looked at the scene of his retinue sleeping in their spread-out beds in the vast room. One slave girl had a lute by her side, another a drum. Some girls had loose hair, others drooled in their sleep, and others still slept with wide-open mouths. It was a far cry from the shimmering, glamorous forms they had displayed only a few hours earlier. He felt a shiver of revulsion.

'So, this is what that Gautam sacrificed. The pleasures of the flesh, of company, of entertainment. But what did he gain?' Once again, he scanned the sleeping forms in the room, where someone had started snoring. He sighed and said, 'Oh, I am possessed. I am troubled. I just cannot get over this lingering thought.'

He picked up his gold-inlaid shoes and let his feet propel him, first towards the gate of his mansion, and then towards that of the city. The sky was overcast, the night, dark and windy. The town was asleep. Unaccustomed as he was to walk these streets, Yash kept going, struggling as his shoes sank into the wet mud. He headed for the deer park.

•

Gautam rose early, before the crack of dawn, walked away from his mat, and strolled there, awaiting sunrise. He saw a distant speck on the road that led to the enclave. Yash was walking towards him. The sky had started to lighten. Gautam walked to the stone he used as a seat and assumed the Lotus position to receive the visitor striding in his direction.

Yash drew close, and said without prostrating himself, or greeting Gautam with a Namaste, 'I am tormented! I am agonising!'

Gautam said, 'Yash, this Tathagat is not in agony or torment. Come, sit down. I shall bring nectar to your lips that will be a balm to your soul.'

Yash felt a burden lift from his shoulders. He took off his shoes, prostrated himself before Gautam and sat down on the ground. 'Is it true, Sir, that you are at peace with yourself?' he asked.

'Indeed, it is', Gautam said. 'Now listen to me.' Gautam proceeded to explain his philosophy to Yash. As he spoke, he sensed Yash's mind ease. Gautam spoke of sorrow and the ways to end it. As an unblemished, pure cloth, gains a colour fast, so did Yash's troubled soul find solace in Gautam's calm exposition. In that one sermon, centred around the impermanence of all that is born, Yash acquired a clear world-view that would guide him for life.

.

It was morning. Yash's mother was beside herself with worry. Dawn had brought her the news that Yash had not slept at home and was not to be found. She fretted for a while and tried to get more information. When she could hold herself no longer, she went to her husband and apprised him of the matter.

Yash's father, Grihapati, went straight to the Rain Palace and asked about the incidents of the night. He diligently traced Yash's footsteps all the way to the Deer Park. He saw Gautam seated in the Lotus position.

He asked, 'Master, have you seen a young man named Yash?'

'Sit down, Sir. Not only have I seen him, but you will also see your son soon', Gautam said. The father felt a load lift from his heart. He sat with a smile on his lips. Gautam repeated his sermon, and Grihapati immediately became a convert.

'Astounding! Astonishing! Master, just as one turns the right side up over-turned, reveals that which is hidden, shows the path to the lost, lights a lamp on a dark night…so that those with eyes can see shapes, you have outlined the world for me in a new light. I seek shelter with you, Oh Buddha! I pledge to follow the dharma, to be one with the sangha. Please accept this worshipper sitting before you with folded hands!'

Gautam spoke in a grave voice: 'I bless you, Merchant! You are the first wor-shipper to make this three-pronged promise. From now on, all who join my fold must make this pledge. They must take shelter in the Buddha, in dharma, and in the sangha.'

At that moment, Yash came and stood in front of his father. His face was flushed and radiant, and he had the composure of one who is at peace with himself.

'Yash! Son!' The father cried out in relief. 'Your mother is worried! She has worked herself up into a frenzy! And your companions and friends are listless. The household is nothing without you…'

Gautam spoke in a soft tone. 'Merchant, your son has seen the dharma just as you saw it in all its simplicity and power. He has meditated further on what was revealed to him, and I see now that his consciousness has elevated itself to a higher level, erasing all blemishes. So, is Yash now fit to be sent back to his earlier life of domesticity?'

Grihapati's reply was quick. 'No, Master!'

'Then tell me, Merchant, what do you think of this recent turn of events?'

Grihapati thought for a while, with his forehead furrowed. 'It is a gain, Master. Yash has gained. His consciousness has detached itself from the quagmire of the physical world. Please accept Yash as your monk and please, visit my home for a meal after this.'

Gautam conveyed his silent consent with a smile. The merchant prostrated himself before Gautam, walked a circuit around him as a mark of respect, and left for his palace.

Yash stepped closer to Gautam and said, 'Lord Master, please initiate me.'

Gautam replied, 'Come, monk! The path of dharma is well known. Follow celibacy to end sorrow in every way. You are now a monk – the seventh of the sangha of perfect beings.'

CHAPTER 9

THE WHEEL OF DHARMA

The streets of Kashi were choked with onlookers. The roar of their whispers subsided into a hush as they saw Gautam, son of the Shakyas. Clad in the most rudimentary of garments, begging bowl in hand, his face radiant but looking at the ground, he walked the street on foot. Right behind him, presenting the same confident but stark presence, walked Yash, son of the elder and merchant of the city whose name inspired awe.

Someone in the crowd said, 'Look at that Yash! Until yesterday, he wore shoes of gold and had diamond earrings. His chariot's golden bells used to echo in the streets of Kashi. And now he walks bare feet behind this Gautam, in that dress, with a bowl in his hands…towards his own home!'

'Indeed', the one next to him said. 'And you would never guess his feet were not used to the gravel. They say he has gained the ultimate wealth and achieved immortality.'

More than one bride who peeped from their windows wondered, 'Ah, with this golden body, this strong gait, these looks like Kama, Cupid, why did he leave the world to become a monk?'

A woman said, 'Look at Yash! Look at the glow on his face! He has shaved off his glossy mane of curly, black hair. And those clothes…but he looks so brilliant!' Her friends agreed. 'He looks like he has tasted an elixir', one said.

Her wide-eyed neighbour agreed. 'Just look at him', she said. 'The high-bred beggar…He has shaved his head, but see how he shines without his gold chain and bracelets! He walks barefoot, but has a majestic glow on his face.'

A wizened old man at a street corner had a small crowd hanging on to every word of his. 'Sage Gautam has conquered Kashi without a single arrow…and Ambapali has taken over Vaishali. Now, mark my words, no one will stay at home in these cities.' He chuckled. 'This Buddha will draw the wealthy into monkhood, and that Ambapali will spin a web around the merchants and nobles of Vaishali.'

The Seven Celestials, the Buddha and his followers walked on, silent and composed. Their gazes were on the earth. Each of them was different, but they all had a few things in common: the cloth bags on their shoulders, the begging bowls in their hands, the eyes shining with a new vision of hope, the serenity on their faces and the purposeful strides. The crowds swirled, bowing, worshipfully circling around them, pointing to each of them and respectfully discussing their lives and greatness.

Grihapati, Yash's father, was waiting at the head of a large group in front of his mansion. He stepped forward to welcome the seven. There were footrests for each of them, and small tubs to wash their feet. When the Buddha took his seat, Yash's mother and his wife paid their respects and sat on the ground before him. When the Buddha started his sermon, his words were like honey; his gaze was compassionate and compelling. Once again, his words had the effect they had had earlier. Yash's mother and his wife asked with folded hands to be accepted into the way of the Buddha, the dharma, the sangha. The Buddha took them into his fold, and thus it happened that the sangha got its first two nuns.

The Seven Celestials then enjoyed a satisfying meal. Then, they gathered again, and the Buddha spoke of the importance of the right vision, communication, motivation and happiness.

Tathagat Buddha led the procession on the way back, with his six followers, Yash walking at the end. As they walked to the Deer Park, four of Yash's friends joined the rear.

One said, 'How did it come about that this Yash of ours shaved his head and beard, exchanged his clothes for this ochre robe, and went from prince to pauper overnight?'

A second said, 'For sure, it cannot be a small change of heart, a small movement that brought about this change in our Yash!'

Guided by an unknown force, they followed the procession to the Deer Park. Before any of the seven members of the sangha had taken their seats, the four friends surrounded Yash. 'Yash, we want to join the sangha. We want to taste the magic potion that makes you glow!'

Without a word, Yash took them to the Buddha, who was seated on a flat stone in the lotus position. Yash said, 'Lord Master, these four are my steadfast friends. This here is Subal, this is Subahu, this one is Poornajit and here is Gavampati. They are the sons of high officials and merchants. They wish to become your disciples.'

The Buddha preached his sermon to them, emphasising the four great truths and explicating them. The four new disciples heard this exposition with rapture. In one voice, they said, 'Lord Master, please initiate us into the order!'

The Buddha said, 'Monks, you are welcome. May you find peace in dharma. To destroy sorrow, you must follow the path of celibacy.' Thus, the Buddha accepted Yash's four friends into the sangha, and there were then eleven monks and two nuns in the world.

The news spread over Kashi like wildfire. When it reached Yash's village, a full fifty young men came forward to become monks of the sangha, multiplying its strength manifold.

The Buddha addressed his followers. 'Monks, you are free of human and divine bondage. Use this freedom to roam the world! But travel with a mission. Roam far and wide for the welfare of the people, for their happiness, to spread kindness. Do work that benefits the people and the gods. And go alone, do not go in twos. Preach this dharma, which is beneficial in its beginning, middle, and end. Follow the path of celibacy. In this world, some people are flawed. If they do not absorb your teachings, it will be their loss. If they do, they will experience the joys of dharma. Monks, fan out in all ten directions! I grant you permission to spread the dharma!'

CHAPTER 10

PARADISE IN VAISHALI

In those times, the Palace of Seven Worlds was heaven on earth. Emperors coveted its splendour. The entire palace was built of marble. It had seven courtyards and seven storeys. At its highest point, a gold-plated heptagonal parapet glittered to become a beacon of allure at sunset and sunrise. Every evening, each of its hundreds of doors was tastefully adorned with garlands of scented and ornamental flowers. These garlands were, in fact, gifts from the powerful and the rich from far and wide. The network of courtyards and atria was inhabited by peacocks, swans, cranes and doves. The first courtyard was sprinkled with perfumed water every afternoon. By evening it was crowded with vehicles of the notables of the city. There would be a sea of chariots, elephants, horses and palanquins. The second courtyard housed Ambapali's active army, with divisions of infantry, cavalry, chariots and war elephants. It also had a zoo full of animals gifted by fawning emperors, kings, nobles and merchants of Anga, Banga, Kalinga, Champa, Tamralipta and Rajgrih. The third courtyard had space for goldsmiths, jewellers, sculptors and other artists to hone their skills. Motivated by prestige, and by generous commissions, the best artists in the land outdid each other to ensure that their produce enhanced the beauty of the Palace of Seven Worlds. The fourth courtyard and the halls it led to made up the granary. It had vast stores of grain, cloth, fresh and dry fruits, and sweets. Many kingdoms from near and far were represented through master chefs who could prepare an endless range of delicacies. Here too were the expert physicians who prepared extracts, juices, medicines and wines that made the air heavy with their scents. There were also specialists who prepared perfumes, fragrance, essences and body lotions. The fifth ring of open space and halls housed the treasury. Here, a large and diverse force of workers made entries in ledgers, counted the gold and gifts in kind that flowed in and disbursed payments under the alert gazes of guards who were armed to the teeth. The sixth courtyard was the one where Ambapali, with her army of companions and slave girls, welcomed and entertained the citizens of Vaishali and visiting dignitaries. The fortunate men who entered the courtyard experienced the finest of food, wine, music and dance. There were special corners where the visitors could play high-stakes games of dice. With its pulsating rhythms, its play of bright lights and shadowed spots, intoxication in the air and its sensuous atmosphere, it seemed like a parallel enclave of the Gandharvs, heavenly beings, while its activities lasted, till midnight. Finally, there was the seventh, inner circle, where the sole denizen was Ambapali herself. Entry was forbidden to others. In the halls inside, the walls and pillars glittered with delicate inlaid gold patterns. Emperors and Kings had felt, and expressed, the keenest desire to see this part of the palace once, but this wish had never been granted.

The main door had been thrown open. Inside the palace and outside it, the thousands of lamps bathed the complex in light and perfume. The palace teemed with maids, slave girls, guards carrying staffs. Merchants and nobles started arriving in droves, dismounting their vehicles casually to leave them to the flocks of attendants, greeting their friends and coalescing into groups as they walked towards the inner courtyards. At the door to the sixth courtyard, they were welcomed by maids who ushered them into the hall of entertainment. Here, the talented Madlekha and her team of assistants would accompany and direct them to seats in keeping with their ranks. It was said of the cots there that their mattresses and pillows were as soft as the foam of milk. A tastefully arranged collection of cots with deerskin covers, silk curtains, paintings, fountains and statues created an atmosphere that was enchanting and sensuous, but subtle. The pleasure seekers who had flocked there sank into their couches and lay back lazily, to be supplied with an unending stream of wine, betel and delicacies by women who understood their needs without communication. Soon there were golden dice and boards at strategic places, and games of dice were under way. Conversations became more animated as good spirit flowed. Some of the men preferred to sit by themselves, sipping on their wine glasses. The slave girls kept glasses brimming. Soon, some of the palace staff took their positions and started playing their lutes, flutes and drums. The music made the air vibrant. A bevy of dancers appeared, covered with studded necklaces, flower dust on their cheeks, gold girdles on their comely waists, gem-studded anklets on their red-painted feet. Their feet danced in rhythm to the music as their tender young bodies sway in sinuous movements. The jingles of the bells on their anklets rippled through the air, and the soft curves of their breasts and hips heightened the effect of the wine. As the dancers whirled, their slender, naked arms snaked in the soft light; their ruby-red lips pouted, and their large black eyes shone. Red dots glistened on their fair foreheads, and their lustrous dark hair weaved patterns in the bright light. A charged, primitive, animal spirit seemed to take over the gathering.

Midnight passed. Lady Ambapali entered the hall without any fanfare. She wore a simple, flimsy gossamer cloth over her breasts, leaving their soft, fair, blemishless tops exposed. She had on a dazzling diamond necklace and matching earrings. Around her waist, she wore a tight skirt bedecked with gold and gems inlaid in intricate patterns. She had toned and shapely legs and her delicate, red-painted feet looked pretty in dark sandals. Much more than the sum of her parts and attire, and heightened by her leonine poise, her swan-like fluidity and the light in her eyes, her aura was such that she could slay any one of the haughty men in the hall, the cream of the city, with a glance. She moved through the crowd with regal ease, smiling at the merrymakers, heading towards a cluster of well-decorated couches in the centre. Three young courtiers were resting on their pillows. One of them looked besotted and was chanting under his breath. Madlekha herself was tendering to them, keeping their glasses full.

Madlekha was a sixteen-year-old girl. Her wide, grey, shy eyes gave her an innocent look that contrasted with the firmness of her young body. She was charming, and knowing it, carried her allure with practised ease. She gave one of the courtiers a glass of wine. He took it and held her wrist gently.

'How will you walk the path of life if you are so shy, Madlekha?' he said in a slurred voice. 'Come here.' He held her fingers in his and steered her closer.

Madlekha gave the man with an inscrutable glance. 'The Lady approaches. Leave me please.'

The young man turned his head and looked with soft, emotive eyes to behold Ambapali in all her splendour. She gave him a sly smile, and he rose at once, almost at attention. 'Ah, it rains nectar, finally!'

'Finally', Ambapali nodded. 'Young Prince, did you not strike a deal?'

'What deal?' The man asked, flustered like an adolescent boy.

Ambapali looked at Madlekha, and Madlekha quietly walked away from the courtyard.

'Weren't you discussing some business with Madlekha? An arrangement?' Ambapali asked with mock sternness. She sat on the couch, her back as straight as a rod.

'Arrangement? No, no – you don't think…', the prince trailed off.

'Oh, I know what to think', Ambapali said, with a smile now. 'And these friends of mine will bear witness to that.' She smiled sweetly at the other two men and seemed to turn them into jelly. 'Friends Jayaraj, Suryamall, do tell – was Prince Swarnasen discussing an arrangement, or not?'

Jayaraj chucked. 'Well, who am I to argue with Lady Ambapali, but I have heard a deal becomes a deal only when it is concluded.' He bowed, and Ambapali laughed aloud. 'Aha, I see', she said. She poured wine into the three glasses with her own hands and then continued. 'These three tumblers full of wine are tokens of my wishes for the well-being of my three best friends.' The three men took their glasses with evident pleasure, hanging on to every word she uttered.

She edged closer to Swarnasen and spoke to him. 'Prince, isn't there something I can do for you? Something that you want very much?'

Swarnasen looked at her with greedy eyes. 'Oh, yes – take this life, this broken heart, closer to yours!'

Ambapali's smile was inscrutable. 'I shall consider this an expression of love – both for Madlekha and for me', she said.

She stood up and took one hand each of the three men in her two hands. 'Princes, it will soon be time for you to go', she said, her smile as radiant as ever. 'May your sleep and dreams be sweet!'

Scattering her smiles, waving out to some visitors, stopping briefly to converse and extricating herself with practised ease, Ambapali continued to the innermost hall. The three friends rose, and so did many other men. The music and dance had stopped, and the hall emptied as the visitors trickled out, some of them helped by friends and palace staff. They left behind the remnants of the merrymaking – empty wine bowls rolling about, misplaced and crumpled bolsters, wilted and crushed flowers, scattered dice. The servants had started restoring order already, and the guards were snuffing out the lamps carefully, leaving a few burning.

From the inner hall of the Palace of Seven Worlds, coloured light streamed through a few open windows and played on Royal Avenue.

CHAPTER 11

RAJGRIH

The Sadanira river cut a crescent across verdant mountains covered with lush tropical forest. The best architects of the land had carved out Rajgrih, capital of the Magadha Empire, on the left bank of the river. Rugged and beautiful barriers bounded the city. There were insurmountable mountain ranges to the north and east, and around the south, and thick, unconquerable walls of enormous boulders to the west. The mountain air was bracing and healthy, and hot springs dotted the area. The splendour of the city was fabled, and its treasury was rich with the accumulated wealth of many generations of prosperity, fostered by the invincibility of its barriers. A remarkable feature of the city was that some of the caves surrounding it had been built, painted and decorated to rival palaces.

Many Buddhist monasteries dotted the outskirts of the city. Emperor Bimbisar himself was a worshipper of Tathagat Gautam. The Buddha lived in Rajgrih at the emperor's request. The University of Rajgrih was renowned. Here, students satisfied their thirst for knowledge at the feet of teachers, monks and sages. There were Chinese with ponytails, pale-faced Mongols, Tibetans and stock young Bhutanese reputed to be very emotional. There were Persians and Greeks with blue eyes and golden hair and Sri Lankans standing out because of their dark and glowing complexions. Others had crossed the eastern seas from Java, Sumatra, Cambodia and Burma, or came from the corners of the Greater Himalayan region: Kashmir and Kushan, the land of the Nagas. Nalanda University had yet to achieve the fame that it gained later. Rajgrih had a central role in producing intellectual discourse and new knowledge, and intellectuals flocked there to prove and hone their minds.

The king of Kosala, Prasenjit had married his sister Kaushala Devi to Emperor Bimbisar, giving the holy city of Kashi as dowry. Brahmadutt ruled Kashi as Bimbisar's vassal. The emperor's other queen, Kukina, princess of Videha, was famous for her knowledge of the Hindu scriptures and her spiritual prowess.

The major powers in India, the four kingdoms of Magadha, Vatsa, Kosala and Avanti, were in a constant state of conflict. Emperor Bimbisar's vaulting ambition ensured that even the bond between Kosala and Magadha did not engender friendly relations between the two realms.

Emperor Bimbisar mounted a campaign against Kosala, his great army chief Chandrabhadrik attacking its capital, Champa. The siege had already lasted eight months. Bimbisar's goal was to get a firm and lasting control of the east-west route of commerce. Champa was the doorway to the trade with the eastern island archipelagos of the Javanese and Sumatran kingdoms. The Chief Minister of Magadha, Varshkar, a master strategist, had gained fame for his intellect. People compared him to both Brihaspati, minister of the gods, and Shukracharya, minister of the demons.

The Magadha clan was a product of mingling between the Aryan and the so-called Asur races. Three clans had resulted from the refusal of the Aryan Brahman – priest, and Kshatriya – warrior, castes to give their lineage to the off-spring of their unions with women of other castes. The Magadhans were the predominant clan. They established a capital at Rajgrih. The legendary Jarasandha, who features in the great epic Mahabharata, invaded Mathura eighteen times to avenge the assassination of his son-in-law Kansa at the hands of Krishna. The kings of a dozen kingdoms fought under his flag, including Duryodhan of Hastinapur. Among his vassals, Bhagdatta and Kalayvan were fearsome warriors. Bhagdatta's elephant was famous for having descended from Airavat, the celestial elephant of the god Indra, and his army included many Tartar and Hun contingents.

Jarasandha's might was such that even Lord Krishna and his Yadav tribe had to wander in the wilderness for eighteen years to escape his wrath. Finally, Krishna established a kingdom in Dwarka, far from his beloved region of Brij. Jarasandha's reign and life ended when Bhim, the strongest of the Pandav brothers, killed him in a duel before the decisive war of the Mahabharata. Bimbisar was a descendant of this mixed breed heritage of Jarasandha, and his dynasty was called the Shishunaga dynasty.

Emperor Bimbisar was fifty years old. He was taller than average, fair in complexion, and his lustrous black eyes and firm bearing gave him an imposing physical presence. His manner was firm, but not his character. He was soft-hearted and could be stubborn. Still, he had gained respect as a thoughtful and brave man who had amassed wealth and created the conditions for prosperity for himself and his empire. Magadha had eighty thousand villages, bounded by the Vindhyachal, Ganga, Champa and Son rivers. The merchants and travellers who had seen the world reckoned Rajgrih as one of the six great metropolises of the time.

CHAPTER 12

A MYSTERIOUS MEETING

It was past midnight, and Rajgrih was deserted. A horse rider strode its dark and quiet side alleys. He wore a shapeless black overcoat that had gathered layers of dust. His horse was an uncommon breed, one from Sindh. Both rider and horse were tired, but the man rode at a steady gallop towards the eastern side of the city. The moonlight flashing on him revealed his youth; his glowing face and sparkling eyes could only mean that his mission was of extreme importance. The man's robe occasionally shifted, showing he was armed to the teeth. He was searching for a spot and did not know his path well, but he knew when he had strayed from it, and he turned around fast to correct his course. Repeating this procedure, he crossed into sections of the city where the streets were narrower and less organised. Soon, he was on the outskirts. This section offered a real contrast with the lantern-lined Royal Avenue. There was no soul in sight. He pulled up to a halt at a small crossroads.

He discerned the shape of a sleeping man on the steps, in front of an old house. The rider went closer and called out to the man. Woken from his slumber, the man blinked at the apparition before him. Then he spoke in a trembling, reedy voice, 'Have mercy on me. I do not have a coin on me! I am a beggar! Why else would I sleep here? I got nothing in alms today – nothing! I was exhausted, and I am just sleeping here… It is no crime, isn't it?'

The rider laughed. 'It is not. But if you slept hungry today, here is something you could use. Come forward, have no fear. Touch it.'

The old beggar got up, trembling. Closing his palm around a cold round object, he felt his breath quicken. He had never seen one, but even by the moonlight, he knew it was a gold coin. He gulped and blurted, 'Forgive me for doubting you, Sir. I am a Brahman, and I bless you! I thought…' He trailed off as he struggled to find the right words.

'Brahman, I think you will find useful getting one more of these, no?' The rider said. 'I have a minor task for you.'

'Well, well', the old man said, in a more composed tone. 'You must be a prince. Tell me what you want, Sir! May victory be yours!'

'Come with me', the rider said, 'and show me Acharya Shambhavyakashyap's abbey.'

The old man started as if the rider had threatened him with a sword. 'At…at this time, Sir?' The fear crept back into his voice. His jaw dropped at the extent of the task expected of him.

The rider said, 'Oh, have no fear, Brahman. Just point me to the place from a distance, and you can leave without getting near it.'

'But Prince, it is…not advisable to go there at this time…ghosts and vampires…dance there. It is not–'

'So, you don't need the reward? Is that what you are saying?' The rider kept his voice low.

'Oh, do not say that Sir, I do need it! But the acharya, he is a master of evil spirits and vampires!'

'Don't worry about that, Brahman', the rider said. 'Here, take this.' He slipped another coin into the beggar's hand. 'Just show me the way, and you can turn back from as far away as you want.' He spoke in the tone of someone used to command others but gives sensible orders. The old man started at a brisk pace, the rider ambling behind him.

They left the houses of the city behind them, and the road became a mud path just large enough for a chariot. After a while, amidst a cluster of trees, a house loomed into sight. The building had something inauspicious, even at first sight. The old man trembled. 'Sir, there it is. I shall not get any closer, and I suggest you avoid doing so as well.' The rider had surged past even before he finished.

The rider went around the vast abbey once. There was no sign of life – ghostly or otherwise. Nor was there any sign of a gate. He started on a slower circum-navigation, peering at the wall as he rode by. This time, he saw a small door in a corner. He dismounted, strode to it and knocked hard. When there was no response, he punctuated his knocks with calls to open up. A glimmer of light showed in a window. A head peeked out, and a man spoke in a harsh voice.

'Who is there?'

'I am a guest. I have work with Acharya Shambhavyakashyap.'

'Where from?'

'Gandhar.'

'Where in Gandhar?'

'From Acharya Bahulashavya of Takshila.'

'Are you Somprabh?'

'Indeed, I am.'

'Very well.'

The head withdrew. There was the sound of approaching footsteps, and the door swung open, revealing a man with a lamp in his hand. Although he did not know fear, Somprabh blanched at the sight. The man was tall and spindly, with a face that seemed to have no flesh at all. Two blazing eyes gaped at him from their sockets. An unruly beard and moustache, and a mop of gnarled hair enhanced his fierce aura. He had high cheekbones and a nose that jutted out in a bow shape. The hand carrying the lamp could have belonged to a skeleton.

The man raised the lamp and peered at the young visitor. Then his thin, pale lips stretched into a faint smile that also glinted in his eyes. 'Tie your horse in the shed out there', he said, pointing. 'A boy is sleeping in there. Wake him up. He will see to the horse. Come back right away.'

Somprabh did as he was told. When he stepped across the threshold into the house, a shiver ran down his spine. The air had a strange smell, and the place, an unsettling atmosphere. A few steps in the hall took him to a door that opened on to a vast open space plunged into darkness. There was no sign of life apart from the tall skeletal man who had received him. The man led the way, and Somprabh followed him with his heartbeat racing even as he tried to show no sign of fear. Soon, he saw houses looming on the western side of the abbey. They walked towards the dwellings. The ghost man stopped in front of the first and said, in a loud whisper, 'Beauty!'

A handsome young monk came out of the house, rubbing his eyes. He wore a saffron cloth around his waist and a sacred thread around his right shoulder. His hair was shaved in front and tied in a long ponytail at the back. The tall man gave the lamp to the young monk and said, 'Give this gentleman a place to sleep near the altar.' Then he turned to Somprabh, and said, 'We shall talk in the morning. I am too busy now.' He turned away without a further sign or word and melted into the darkness.

'Friend, follow me', the monk said.

Somprabh followed the monk, and they entered a large hall which appeared to be the hall of ceremonies. The monk pointed to a deerskin placed on a raised platform. 'Will this be all right?'

'Indeed, it will!' Somprabh replied.

The monk motioned for Somprabh to wait. He returned in a few moments, carefully balancing the lamp, a glass of milk and a bowl with a sweet. He placed them before Somprabh, who had seated himself, and pointed to a pitcher. 'There is water there', he said. 'You can use it to wash up, and feel free to undress, eat, and rest. Oh, and if you would like sacrificial meat, I can get you some.'

'No, friend', Somprabh said, 'this will suffice. I do not eat meat.'

'Then, friend, do you need anything else?' the monk asked.

'No, nothing, thank you', Somprabh said.

The monk left, leaving the lamp behind. Somprabh undressed and hung his weapons on pegs in the wall. He sat on his bed and helped himself to the sweet and the milk. Then, he snuffed out the lamp and sat still in the dark. His thoughts went back to the time he was eight years old. He had left for Takshila with a merchant, little knowing what the future held in store for him. During the following eighteen years, he had toiled to master the scriptures and the sciences at the world-famous Takshila University. During these challenging years, he had learnt the use of weapons and the study of tomes. His journeys had taken him to Parshpur, a land ruled by the Greeks, and to north Kuru. He had taken part in the war between the Devs and the Asurs. On the banks of the Indus, he had fought against the rulers of Parshpur. Then, fate took him to the remote corners of India until there was no region he had not seen.

Now he sat in this old abbey in Rajgrih. After his journeys around the world, it seemed petty and dismal. As if the very form of the acharya, the Master, had changed fundamentally.

A sudden wail startled him. It was loud and sounded like a cry coming from the choked throat of someone in agony. Somprabh controlled his breath with difficulty. He jumped up and grabbed his sword from the peg. He placed his ear against the wall and realised something was happening on the other side. A sixth sense told him it was something immoral. He groped around with caution, and soon enough, he made out the outlines of a door. A gentle push and it opened without effort on to a room with no light. Darkness surrounded him. Gripping his sword tighter, he stood still. He could hear voices, though he could not understand the words. He moved towards the sound. As he groped around, Somprabh sensed he was in a narrow gallery that turned as he moved further. As he rounded a bend, he saw a narrow beam of light in the distance. He walked faster now, though still softly. He made out a flight of steps descending into an inner room. The voices came from that room, and light and sound filtered out from a gap in its old door. When he looked through the opening, his eyes widened.

The door opened into a small inner sanctum, where a soft light glowed. The acharya sat, still as a rock, on a tiger-skin. Another man, clearly a royal personage, sat opposite him on another tiger skin. He had a stout, stocky body, and was clean-shaven. His eyes glowed with vigour, and his lips were firm-set. He looked about sixty years old.

Near him sat a very beautiful girl with a downcast face. She was almost naked. Her slender arms glowed in the soft light, and her locks of black hair stood out against a sliver forehead. Her hair was tied in a neat plait that kissed her feet. A slender saffron band covered her nipples but left most of her firm breasts exposed. At the waist, she wore a small, glittering, jewel-studded cloth. Her eyes had a lost, intoxicated look, and looking at her long enough would clearly be in-toxicating. Her sensuous red lips were so inviting that they would kindle desire in any man. Fearful and cowed, she pressed her lips tight.

Somprabh could hear the words now. 'No, Father', the girl said. Her lips quiv-ered. 'Not now. I cannot take any more.'

The acharya threw at her an inflamed look. 'Be warned, Kundani!' he said. 'Do not try my patience.' He cracked a leather whip with his hands, and hissed, 'Accept the sting!'

The girl looked at the acharya, beseeching him with her eyes but unable to speak, and at the nobleman. Then she stiffened, and in a single jerky motion reached out to a basket near her and flipped its lid open. A giant, hissing black cobra raised its hood high, its fangs darting in and out. The nobleman's face did not betray emotion, but he gulped and shifted backwards.

Somprabh caught his breath at what happened next. The girl held the neck of the cobra and wrapped it around her neck. She then brought its hood near her lips, stuck out her tongue and released her grip on the snake. The snake hissed, and its hood moved lightning fast towards the girl's tongue. It must have bitten her. Somprabh shivered at the thought, though he did not see the actual act. The girl threw the snake away, and it slid to the ground.

The acharya nodded, and his shoulders eased. He gave the nobleman a satis-fied look. The young woman now glared at the acharya, hatred smouldering in her eyes. The snake seemed lifeless. Large beads of sweat appeared on the young woman's forehead. Somprabh felt his heart racing. His throat was parched.

The acharya picked up a long iron rod and used it to put the comatose snake back in the basket. Then he took a bowl of wine. Now he spoke tenderly, with a smile, to the girl. 'Here, drink this, Kundani.' He raised it to the young woman's lips, and she gulped it down in one go.

The nobleman opened his mouth for the first time. 'Very well, Acharya…I shall arrange to send Kundani to Champa first thing tomorrow morning. Of course, if you also went–'

'No, no', the acharya interrupted. 'Governance is for those who govern. It is not my sphere.' His tone was abrupt. He then turned to the young woman. 'Kundani', he said softly, 'you will train your new powers on Dadhivahan, king of Anga.'

The poison made Kundani sway. Her tongue flickered like that of a she-serpent as she licked her lips. Her wide eyes were glassy. 'I won't go, father', she said. 'Take pity on me.'

'Foolish girl!' The acharya said in a harsh voice. 'Will you oppose the state?'

'Why don't you just kill me?' Kundani said.

The acharya lifted the whip. The young man, who had been too stunned to react, could not hold himself any longer. Before he knew it, he burst into the room, his sword raised. 'Acharya, Sir, this is injustice! I cannot let this happen!'

Shock was writ large on the acharya's and the nobleman's faces.

The nobleman was quick to recover. 'And who are you, Eavesdropper? Anyway, it does not matter. If you heard us, you must die.' He clapped his hands, and in an instant, four armed guards had charged in. 'Arrest this man', the noble said, pointing to Somprabh.

Somprabh kept his grip on his sword, and took his stance, making it clear the arrest would not be a formality.

The acharya looked at the flushed young man, and said in a steely voice, 'Lower your sword! That is an order!'

It was as if Somprabh was powerless in the face of that authority. He lowered his gaze and his sword. The guards disarmed him and took him away.

'Take him out', the nobleman said to the chief guard. 'And execute him, now.'

The acharya spoke up. 'No, just imprison him.'

The nobleman nodded to show the guards the acharya's command superseded his. The acharya whispered in the nobleman's ear. What he said made the other man start, his face turning very grave.

'Do not worry', the acharya said with a smile. 'I will manage him. I think he should be the one to escort Kundani to Champa.'

The nobleman was deep in thought for some time. The acharya said, 'There is no cause for worry. Leave it to me.'

'As you say. But I do not want him to be introduced to Kundani yet.'

'Yet, he will have to meet Aryaa Matangi.'

'Why is that?'

'That is how it must be. I gave my word to Aryaa Matangi.'

'No, no! Acharya, we cannot do that!'

The acharya looked hard at the nobleman. 'Whatever happens, I am a detached, disinterested scientist. Still, I cannot stand by and see the lady's distress anymore. You nobles seem even more heartless than me.'

'But until the lady does not unravel the secret…'

'It is not your prerogative to force her.'

'By the emperor's order…'

'I cannot wait for it. I will explain to the emperor. I suggest you go. Kundani will come to you.'

'And…that young man as well?'

The acharya laughed. 'Yes, the young man as well. His name is Somprabh. He will report for duty.'

The nobleman lowered his head. Worry furrowed his forehead, and anguish showed in his eyes.

Now the acharya spoke with compassion. 'Go now. Rest. It is no use remembering your nightmares.'

The nobleman sighed. He nodded and walked away, disappearing into the darkness. The footsteps of his guards accompanied his.

CHAPTER 13

THE PRISONER IS FREED

Unseen by anyone, the strange scientist of Rajgrih paced his lonely lair for a long time. Unheard by anyone, his lips hummed a tuneless melody. At times, his fists clenched into tight balls. An observer might have surmised that he was trying to forget some bitter and painful memories. After he had gained control of himself, he strode towards a tiger skin, on which he took his seat. He sat still for a long time, lost in meditation.

Then he got up and left the room, carefully locking behind him. He took a few measured steps in the dark and gripped a torch that he lit with a flint. The flickering light revealed a crooked tunnel, and he followed its winding path to the door of another room. The light was bright here, and two guards stood by the door. They folded their hands and bowed to him.

'Is he asleep?' The acharya asked.

'No, Sir, he is awake', a guard replied.

'All right, open the door.'

The door creaked as it opened. The acharya bent to enter. Straightening himself, he took a moment to adjust to the relative darkness. He spoke in a soft, kind tone. 'Why the disrespect, young man?' He smiled at Somprabh.

'But I–'

'Quiet!' The acharya said. 'Not a word! Follow me.' He signalled with a motion of his head. He stepped out of the room without looking back, picked up the torch, and retraced his steps into the tunnel. This time he took a different path that led to a large, well-lit room. The bodies and body parts of dead animals and birds, bags full of herbs and plants, and row upon row of boxes and jars filled with chemicals crowded the room.

The young man, so reckless and brave only a short while ago, was tense now. Beads of sweat glowed on his forehead. The acharya sat on a smooth stone

slab and gestured for Somprabh to sit on another one. The acharya held Somprabh's gaze for some time. Then he sighed and asked, 'Do you remember your
childhood?'

'Very little, Sir', Somprabh said.

'You stayed here with me until you were eight. Do you recall that at least?'

'Yes, Sir, I do.'

'And when you set out from Takshila, did the venerable Bahulashavya tell you
something about me?'

'He did, Sir. He said, "Som, I have taught you the scriptures and the use of
arms. I have sharpened your brain. You are now an invincible warrior, an eminent strategist and a wise scholar. Now, the great Shabhavya Kashyap will tell you
how to use the knowledge and skills you have acquired."'

'Is that all he said?'

'No. He said, "Go straight to him, do what he says without question. You have
a part to play in creating the greatest empire of eastern India. It is a great responsibility, a heavy burden."'

'I am glad to hear that. But what have you done after getting here? Not only
have you been discourteous, but you have committed a great crime – one punishable by death! I saved you this time, but I am now wondering if my friend
Bahulashavya overestimated your potential. It is extremely foolish to get so excited and oppose a guru's acts.'

The young one's face fell. 'Sir,' he said, 'forgive me. I thought a helpless woman
was being oppressed, and I could not stand by…' He did not look into the acharya's eyes.

The acharya's eyes flared. 'Only stupid fools like you oppress people! Not men
detached, inspiring fear, hatred, worry and curses in others like me. You still
have a few things to learn. You need to learn that kingdoms do not run only
on arms and brains. If they did, warriors would become kings. Son, the warp
and weave of the empire are complex, sometimes just ugly, sometimes, horrendous. Serving the empire implies bowing to its demands. Not all that is true and
auspicious is beautiful, young man! Else, why would the human race consider
shedding blood to be one of its ultimate goals?'

The acharya now trembled with excitement. His pale, awe-inspiring, skeleton-
like body had taken on the aura of a spirit, and his voice had taken on a gravelly,
ghostly undertone.

The youth was so overwhelmed by the acharya's persona that he remained
silent.

The acharya stood up suddenly. He said, 'Go now. Rest. Early morning tomorrow, you will present yourself in the service of Acharya Varshkar. You will
report to him whatever you have learnt till now.' He looked at Somprabh with

a slanted, sharp gaze and gestured with a trembling, slender finger for him to leave.

Somprabh bowed with folded hands before the acharya. 'Sir,' he said, 'I have one more favour to ask. I do not know the names of my father and mother. I do not know my lineage, caste and clan…Can the acharya not enlighten me about these?'

'What did Acharya Bahulashavya say about that?'

'He said, "Only three people on this earth know about your origins. One of them is Acharya Varshkar." He never disclosed the other two names. That is why I ask you.'

The acharya sighed. 'When the time is right, I shall tell you.' He turned around and walked into the darkness.

Somprabh dared not stay on in that spot for a single moment longer. He hastened to the sacrificial hall where a guard helped him trace his steps back to the room where he had been sleeping. He was tired, but sleep did not come. The scenes that had haunted him kept returning to haunt him – those extraordinary scenes of the deranged scientist, the alluring beauty and the vicious bites of the cobra.

CHAPTER 14

THE SCIENTIST OF RAJGRIH

Your eyes are heavy. Did you not sleep well, young man?'

'No, I did not, Acharya.'

'I see. I am not surprised. You had to see sights you did not expect – some incontrovertible truths. Did you see my laboratory?'

'Only a small part, Sir. What friend Sundaram showed me.'

'Som, you shall see more when the time is right. What we have stored in our laboratory is much more than the sum of its parts. The parts you see stored there – the spirits, the blood, the intestines and body parts, enzymes, the herbs – are a means to an end. What we have mastered is the essence of life and death!'

'Life and death?' What does that mean, Acharya?'

'Oh, that means much. That is the key to power. You have learnt the art of war. You know that waging and winning the war are two different things. Both are costly; they cost wealth, and they cost lives.'

'That, I have seen myself, Acharya', Somprabh said.

'What the jars of the laboratory contain reduces this cost. Not only does our prowess save vast wealth and large numbers of lives, but it makes victory more certain.'

'And how do you achieve that, Sir?'

'It is simple. We have poisons, different types of poisons. If we use them on wells, ponds and reservoirs, the contaminated water will spread epidemics among the enemy. We can poison the air in which their armies move to bring them down in a few moments. We can change the seasons! We can blind their horses and elephants, we can make their soldiers mute, deaf or paralysed.'

'But this…this chemical war…is dreadful, Acharya!'

'Yes, but not worse than war itself! Isn't war the unavoidable reality of life? The chronicle of human civilisation till now? The evolution of humanity? Haven't you learnt this yourself?'

'I have also learnt something else, Sir.'

'What is that, young man?'

'War symbolises the animal, not the human, instinct. As a man gets rid of his animal nature and evolves towards humanity, he will forsake war. When he reaches perfection, warring will become extinct. Then, he will no longer be prone to disease and will be contented.'

'Ah, I see. Now, this you have learnt from that wandering Shakya sage, Gautam, that staunch opponent of the Aryan dharma. He does not believe in caste, which the Vedas have ordained. He refuses to distinguish between the Aryan and the non-Aryan. He opposes the prominence of the Brahmans. He criticises our yagyas and proposes liberation for women!'

'But, Sir, man is not divided into class by birth. He attains perfection by developing his conduct and intellect. The yagyas are soaked in the blood of mute animals. They are frauds committed in the names of fake deities.' Somprabh spoke with a quiet passion.

'May your sins be absolved!' The acharya said. 'Your words are a revolt against the Brahmans, young man! The emperor also speaks like that these days. He has become a disciple of that Gautam. Some big luminaries – Shari's son Moudgalayan, Ashvajit, Mahakashyap and his brother…have become Gautam's disciples. The merchant of Magadha, Yash, joined him and turned over a vast fortune to him, and so did his four friends. And now, I find you too…Blessed one!'

'But, Acharya, all this fraud and deceit…'

'Young man, this is skill. I am not for fraud and deceit, but I do stand for destroying the enemy without harm to oneself. Hmm, let's see…you say that animal instinct places us in danger of direct war. I say that human instinct makes us destroy the enemy and keep ourselves safe. This is what politics is about.'

'Are those glass jars and their chemicals, reservoirs of skill?'

'Yes, you can say that. Why not? Simply put, they have the power to blind, deafen, drive mad, make impotent, kill…'

'Oh, my apologies, but that is unbearable to hear, Acharya!'

'Not more than piercing a healthy man's heart with a sword without mercy! Your arrows cut through the ribs of a helpless man. The youth whom you behead with your sword has a heart full of hope. You do this in the madness of war.'

'But that is a pitched battle, Sir.'

'And so is this, dear one. It requires valour and intelligence. Palaces' towers and splendid mansions of power are conquered by such means. Your army is lauded for victories achieved with the powers of those glass jars. Enough argument, now! You must go to meet Acharya Varshkar. Remember he is a great soul, a renowned personality of India. Two ministers in the world have exalted stature: Yogandharayan of Kaushambhi, and Acharya Varshkar of Rajgrih.'

'I have seen Yogandharayan, Sir. I helped Kaushambhi in the war between the Devs and Asurs, and I got a chance to work closely with that famous man.'

'You were lucky. You will be blessed a second time when you see Acharya Varshkar. But remember to be loyal to the Magadha Empire. Be steadfast and focused in your loyalty. Remember not to be discourteous to two people: the emperor himself, and Acharya Varshkar.'

'And you, Sir?'

The acharya smiled. 'I grant you permission to be fearless. You have already exhibited this trait, have you not? For me, you are still the eight-year-old boy I once knew.'

Somprabh's eyes were moist. 'I shall remember the respected Acharya's command. And your kindness.'

'Very well. Now, you will take Kundani, go quickly to Varshkar and follow his orders.'

'Kundani?'

'You saw her yesterday.'

'Who is she?'

'Your sister.'

'So, the unfortunate man that I am, ignorant of his lineage, has a sister?'

'Yes. That is what I said. But do not try to find out more. It is not right to talk back to your gurus. Som, I ask you for a promise.'

'What is your command?'

'If the great Varshkar sends you on an expedition with Kundani…'

'Expedition? With Kundani?'

'Oh, shame on you. I just said that you should not–'

'My humble apologies, Sir. Forgive me.'

The acharya sighed. 'I was saying, if you travel with her, save her life at the cost of your own.'

'Your wish is my command, Sir. But I have heard talk of the king of Malwa, Chandamahasena, mounting a campaign against Rajgrih. I thought you would need my services in that sphere.'

'Now that is a matter for the chief minister, Acharya Varshkar, to decide, young man', the acharya said. Then he called out to Kundani.

The girl he had seen that fearful night stood in front of Somprabh within a few moments. She had covered herself with long, flowing clothes. Her pale, flower-like face, sensuous lips, and her slanting and delicate eyebrows still produced an intoxicating effect. Somprabh greeted her with folded handed and lowered his gaze.

The acharya said, 'So, are you completely ready? This is your brother, and your guard, Som. Daughter, trust him! Here, take this and use it very carefully.' He gave her a small, delicate knife with an ivory handle. He raised both hands and said, 'Farewell, you two, and may fortune favour you on your path!' He stayed quiet for a while, lost in thought.

Som was surprised to see the acharya's eyes become moist, and his tone turned hoarse with emotion. 'Som, Dear One, there is one thing you must do. When you set out from Rajgrih, take approval from the chief minister and go to see Lady Matangi before leaving.'

'Who is Lady Matangi?' Somprabh asked.

The acharya's eyes blazed with fury. 'Did I not say you should not talk back? Can you not just do–'

Somprabh lowered his head. 'Excuse me, Sir. I erred again.'

The acharya sighed. 'Your horses are outside. Go now', he said in a dry tone.

Kundani hid the knife in her plait. Then she prostrated herself before the acharya, lying on the ground before him. Then she got up and said firmly, 'Let us go, Som.'

Som prostrated himself as well before the acharya, who stood stony-faced and distant. Then, as if spellbound, he followed Kundani.

CHAPTER 15

THE CHIEF MINISTER OF MAGADHA

The Magadhan chief minister's establishment awed Somprabh. He had travelled far and wide, from Greece through Persia to the Eastern Islands. But when he passed through the imposing interiors of the chief minister's palace, he felt as if he had entered a dreamland.

He and Kundani entered a hushed waiting room hosting people dressed as if they were extraordinarily rich, powerful, or both. An army of guards and ushers buzzed around them, carrying messages and controlling the people flowing in and out of the room.

They had only been in the room shortly when a guard walked up to them and spoke to Somprabh. 'Sir, if Acharya Shambhavyakashyap has sent you, the chief minister is waiting for you.'

'Indeed, he has. I am Somprabh.'

'Then please follow me, Sir', the guard said, politely motioning Kundani to wait.

The guard led Somprabh through a maze of halls and courtyards. They reached a brightly lit room in which an old man sat, bent on a silver table, his quill moving in decisive strokes as he wrote out a document. No introduction was needed. The man was the famed chief minister of Magadha. The guard left without a word after motioning for Somprabh to stand and wait.

When the chief minister raised his head, Somprabh flinched and took a step back before he could get a grip on himself. The chief minister was the nobleman he had seen with Acharya Shambhavyakashyap, the one who had demanded his death.

The chief minister was clearly troubled as well. He stood up, eyes blazing, as soon as he got a good glimpse of Somprabh. It only took him a moment to check himself and sit back, very still.

Somprabh's heartbeat was steady by then. He drew his sword from the sheath and touched it to his turban, saluting the chief minister in the military tradition. The chief minister gave him a steely look for a few more moments without speaking.

Raising his eyebrow, he spoke in a soft, menacing tone. 'So, you are the brash young man with the habit of spying.'

'Arya, I was brash indeed. It was a great crime, though I did not intend to do wrong.'

'Have you not learnt all you need at Takshila? Arms, scriptures, diplomacy?' The chief minister asked.

'That is right, Sir', Somprabh said.

'Then, the gravity of your crime increases manifold.'

'But the acharya forgave my crime, keeping in mind that my intentions were honourable. I now ask your forgiveness.'

The chief minister seemed to go into a trance. He frowned and pressed his lips together, flexed the fingers of both hands, and gazed at his palms. Then he looked straight into Somprabh's eyes. 'Granted. But do you understand the responsibility you are asked to take?'

'I do, and I am your servant.'

'What did you say?'

'I, Somprabh, am a humble servant of the chief minister of Magadha.'

'And of the Magadha Empire as well?'

'Indeed, Chief Minister. I also swear loyalty to the emperor.'

The chief minister lips reshaped themselves into a barely perceptible curl. His eyes bored into Somprabh's. 'I do not recall asking that question. But since you volunteered this answer. Now, let me ask you whose side you would take if there was a conflict of interest between the emperor and the empire?'

'The empire's, Chief Minister.'

The old man's eyes lost their hostility. 'And between the chief minister and the empire?'

Somprabh gulped but spoke in a soft and humble tone. 'The empire's, Sir.'

The chief minister digested this without reacting. Then, his forehead furrowed as if he was thinking about something else. 'But I do not know your lineage', he said drily.

'If that is a concern, the chief minister may reject my services, and free me from the pledges I have made to Acharya Bahulashavya and Acharya Shambhavyakashyap.'

'And what are those pledges?'

'They are the same pledge, Sir. To live to serve Magadha with single-minded devotion.'

'And why?'

'Because I belong to Magadha. When I left Takshila, Acharya Bahulashavya instructed me to be prepared to give my life for Magadha. Further, Acharya Shambhavyakashyap asked me to follow your orders at any cost.'

'Did he, indeed?' The chief minister smiled for the first time. He spoke after thinking for a few moments. 'It suffices that you are Magadhan. Never forget that you must live for Magadha. You are the empire's servant. And my servant.'

'That is understood, Sir.'

'All right. Did you meet Kundani?'

'Yes, Sir. She is my sister.'

'And Acharya Shambhavyakashyap has appointed you her guard.'

'Yes, he has, Sir.'

'I shall now place a great responsibility on you. You will have to start a confidential and perilous journey right away.'

'I am ready.'

'You will go to Champa this moment, with Kundani. Only five warriors will accompany you. I have personally chosen them. They are waiting outside. Your journey must be a secret outside this small group. You will protect Kundani. But more than her, you must protect one thing.'

'What is that, Sir?'

The chief minister produced a sealed letter from a compartment in his table. 'This. Get it to army chief Chandrabhadrik. This letter must reach him without misfortune.'

'Do not fear, Sir. It shall.'

'It will not be easy. The journey is fraught with danger. There will be Dasyu and Asur areas along the way. But I cannot make you visible by giving you more soldiers.'

'I promise I shall get Kundani and this letter to Chief Chandrabhadrik.'

'No – not Kundani. Only the letter. Kundani does not go to the chief. He should not even know about her.'

Somprabh thought about that for a while before voicing his confusion. 'I see, Sir. But whom do I take Kundani to?'

'You will get to know when you reach Champa.'

'As you say, Sir.'

The chief minister gestured to an unseen guard, and soon, Kundani walked in. She prostrated herself before the chief minister's feet. He laid his right palm on her head as she got up and stood before him, and then gently rested it on her shoulder.

'Kundani.' He said her name softly.

She looked at him with anxious eyes.

He said, 'For the emperor.'

She did not reply.

'For the empire', he said.

She remained quiet and downcast.

'For the people!' he said.

She was still unmoved.

He sighed. 'Give me your hands', he said gently.

She placed her left hand in his.

'Why do you tremble, Kundani?' he asked.

He stroked her head with his right hand. 'Protect Som. He will protect you. Go now.'

Kundani prostrated herself again, still without having said a word.

The chief minister motioned to a guard, who brought him a jewel-studded sword. The chief minister gave it to Somprabh without ceremony. 'From this moment on, Somprabh, you are the head of the chief minister's bodyguards.'

Somprabh did not know how to react. He felt the thudding in his chest as he took the sword and bowed deep. Kundani joined him in bowing, and they left the chamber.

After their departure, the chief minister paced his room for a while. He was lost in thought, his forehead creased, and his lips pursed.

Outside, Somprabh said, 'Kundani, we were told to leave right away, but I have one errand to run before we go.'

Kundani nodded. 'Aryaa Matangi?' She asked.

'Yes', Somprabh said. 'So, you knew?'

'Yes.'

'Then do you know who he is?'

'Have you forgotten, Som? There is no place for curiosity in diplomacy.'

'Oh, I go wrong again and again. But will you come with me?'

'No. Not everyone goes there – access is very restricted.'

'How do I know I won't be barred?'

'Father will have made arrangements.'

'Wait for me at the South Gate with the soldiers. I will join you there after my meeting.'

They mounted their horses and went their ways.

CHAPTER 16

ARYAA MATANGI

Outside the city stood a run-down, lonely monastery. It was famous as Govind Swami's abode. Govind Swami had passed away, but the people of Rajgrih still worshipped the seat that had been his. It had become an object of veneration, elders passing on the practice to their children. Govind Swami's fame as a scholar of the Vedas was great, and tales of his wisdom were still told in the city and outside it. The monastery was spread over a vast area and was believed to be the centre of learning before the university was established, drawing scholars from near and far to study the scriptures. People said that it was Govind Swami who had organised the Ashwamedha Yagya, the ritual horse sacrifice, that anointed the current Emperor Bimbisar's father as emperor. There were whispers that the ruling dynasty of Rajgrih traced its antecedents to Asurs – demons. It was Govind Swami, who granted them the status of Devs, gods, after which the emperor came to be called Dev. Emperor Bimbisar's father had been a staunch and loyal follower of Govind Swami. As a mark of respect, the emperor always visited the sage on foot.

When Govind Swami knew his time had come, he asked the emperor to take his eight-year-old daughter under his fold. The emperor said, 'Besides my son Bimbisar, this girl will be my daughter. She will be brought up as a princess.'

'No, Emperor!' Govind Swami said. 'Matangi must be brought up as a Brahman's daughter. Her lifestyle and her education should be in keeping with my ethos.'

Apart from Matangi, Govind Swami had a young boy under his care. No one knew whose son he was, but it was clear that he was very close to Govind Swami's heart and had been so since he was a baby. His name was Varshkar. Varshkar and Matangi had been together since they were toddlers.

Govind Swami said, 'The Boy Varshkar is the son of someone to whom I am especially beholden. He has the traits of a nobleman. He is capable of holding the reins of your empire. Train him well, educate him with care and groom him to become chief minister of Magadha.'

Finally, Govind Swami extracted from Bimbisar the promise that the two would stay in the monastery until the time was ripe to marry them to suitable matches. He specified that they could not marry each other. Apart from this constraint, Matangi's marriage was to be arranged with her consent. Govind Swami died peacefully soon after this handing over of his responsibilities. The emperor arranged for attendants and teachers to take care of Matangi and Varshkar.

·

In the busy streets of Rajgrih, people occasionally spotted a madman who was never there long enough to be caught. He would shout, 'Look at that hypocrite Govind Swami! How much that child's face resembles his!' And then, he would roar with laughter, duck away and slink into the crowd. Govind Swami was uncharacteristically reticent about the madman and seemed to go out of his way to avoid a confrontation. His assistants sensed that he was disturbed whenever he heard the madman had been seen in the city. People speculated he was connected to Varshkar. The speculation fuelled gossip. An imaginative rumour had it that the madman's wife had had the child Varshkar by Govind Swami, and that the madman had killed her in a fit of rage when he discovered the truth. Of course, no one knew the truth. That Govind Swami forbade a union between Varshkar and Matangi fuelled the speculation.

The children themselves had not heard Govind Swami's instructions to Bimbisar. They grew into adolescence under the tutelage of their teachers, with the emperor taking a personal interest in their well-being. Govind Swami's assessment of Varshkar's potential was not unfounded. Varshkar developed into a young man with a sharp intellect, capable of great focus and diligence. Scriptures and arms proved easy for him. Excelling in martial skills, he grew strong and athletic and commanded affection and respect. The emperor treated him like a second son, and his courtiers held him in high esteem and saw a future statesman and soldier in him. Prince Bimbisar became his closest friend. The two of them often trained, hunted and played games together.

As the days flew, and Matangi blossomed into womanhood, it was only natural for the god of love to come and command the young men's hearts. The emperor sensed the onset of love. He did not mouth his concern, but he ordered Varshkar to move into the palace, ostensibly to learn the art and science of royal administration better. Varshkar followed the emperor's diktat, but he was lovelorn.

Matangi's beauty was not ordinary. She clothed herself in the most austere and plain attire, but her body was as alluring as burning gold. Bimbisar was besotted with her and became a frequent visitor to the monastery. What happened next was fate. One day, unable to control himself, Varshkar stood trembling before Bimbisar, knowing he may be tempting death, and unsheathed his sword. 'Prince,' he said, 'all Magadha is yours. But Matangi is mine. If you forget that ever, this sword will come between you and me.'

Bimbisar looked straight into Varshkar's eyes and held his gaze. Then his face creased into a smile, and he gently pushed the sword away with his thumb. 'Friend,' he said. 'Do not worry. I will not try to come between you two. She is yours.'

Bimbisar still met Matangi often, while Varshkar was in the palace. Though he was forbidden to do so, Varshkar also went to see her in secret.

•

Matangi discovered that she was pregnant and panicked, her mind reeling. She did not let Varshkar and Bimbisar know whose child she was carrying. On their part, the two men kept her pregnancy a secret from the emperor. When the child was born, Varshkar doubted he was the boy's father and ordered the child to be abandoned. The exhausted Matangi pleaded and cried, but Varshkar, hurt by what he saw as a betrayal, steeled himself and refused to budge.

On his way to his abbey, Acharya Shambhavyakashyap saw a bundle wrapped in a red cloth, with a group of crows hovering near it. His instinct guided him closer, and he saw, in the bundle, a newborn baby sucking on his thumb contentedly, unworried by his dire circumstances. Next to the bundle lay a leather purse bursting with gold coins.

Acharya Shambhavyakashyap did not care for the gold, but he picked up both the baby and the gold. He covered the baby with his saffron-coloured top cloth and nurtured the baby personally over the next few days. It did not take him long to use his network and trace the child to Aryaa Matangi. He reached out to both Matangi and Prince Bimbisar. The prince was fearful when he learnt that Acharya Shambhavyakashyap had discovered the secret. The acharya reassured him he would keep the secret and that the child would be safe with him. Bimbisar gifted Acharya Shambhavyakashyap more money.

Varshkar's cruelty, which Matangi had not expected, broke her heart. She withdrew from the world and became a recluse. Prince Bimbisar also distanced himself from Varshkar. In fact, he was afraid of Varshkar and his suspicious nature.

When the emperor knew his time had come, he called the two former friends to his deathbed. As he lay dying, with his last breath, he issued two edicts. Firstly, Varshkar would become Bimbisar's chief minister. Secondly, after the third year of his reign, Bimbisar must arrange Matangi's marriage to a man of her choice and give her eight villages for her maintenance. He handed over a letter to the prince, directing him to open it only three years after his ascension to the throne, and before Matangi's marriage.

The wheels had been set in motion. When his father died, Bimbisar became emperor and Varshkar, chief minister of Magadha. With his formal power, Varshkar did not need to cloak his visits to Matangi in secrecy anymore. When Matangi asked him to marry her, Varshkar quoted her father's and the late emperor's orders to her. Matangi stopped talking about marriage after a few such discussions and became even more withdrawn.

When Bimbisar opened the sealed letter on the scheduled day, his hands trembled, and he passed it to Varshkar with a choked throat. Apart from the order to arrange her marriage and provide for her with a grant for eighty villages, it revealed that Matangi was Varshkar's sister. That was why they were forbidden to marry.

The usually energetic Varshkar sat slumped for a long time, listlessly holding on the letter. Bimbisar and Varshkar both knew that Matangi was expecting a child again, clearly Varshkar's, this time. Emperor Bimbisar took the lead in deciding not to tell Matangi about the disclosure in the letter. He convinced Matangi to spend some time at Vaishali and enjoy the change of air. When she came back with a daughter, and he sensed she had fully recovered from the rigours of childbirth, he and Varshkar told her the truth with bowed heads.

They saw Matangi rock slightly and then step quickly to a seat near her. She sat without a word and remained silent. She was deaf to their hesitant words. Soon after they left her, planning to return to share her grief, they learnt that she had dismissed all her servants except one. She also forbade Varshkar and Bimbisar to enter the monastery and announced she would not marry. Matangi became an unseen character, one whom everyone knew of, but almost no one sighted. She adopted the path of celibacy and austerity, and over the years became a respected figure of legend. Varshkar was filled with self-loathing. He did not marry.

Varshkar's vigour and might had made him a household name. The great chief minister of Magadha was famous for his valour and was an undisputed leader among the diplomats and soldier statesmen of the world. Not a soul doubted the purity of his celibacy, but no one knew of the troubled past shared by Acharya Varshkar, the emperor and the lady now known as Aryaa Matangi. This was a secret only the three of them held in their hearts. And there was one innermost secret – that of Somprabh's paternity – that only Aryaa Matangi knew. As to where Aryaa Matangi's and Acharya Varshkar's daughter was, only her father knew that. Acharya Varshkar suggested through messages that she meet her daughter, but she refused to break out of her shell even for that. Acharya Varshkar gave up trying after a while and avoided from intruding into her life. She gave the proceeds from her land to charity, retaining the smallest fraction that she needed for her austere life.

·

As Somprabh walked past the crumbling gates of the monastery, he sensed that he was stepping on a ground that was not much trodden by human feet. He felt a pang of unease. He crossed slanting and crooked alleys, lined by walls encroached by creepers and reached a still, clear pond. A single hundred-petal Lotus bloomed at its centre, and a delicate scented wafted over the rippled water. Two trees thick with foliage shaded the sides of the pond. Somprabh stood there for a while, savouring the fragrant, cool breeze. Once again, he pondered why he had bent sent here.

The sound of soft footsteps behind him broke his reverie. He turned around to see an elderly woman of erect bearing walking towards him, carrying a pitcher. The woman's eyes widened. 'Who are you?' she asked, clearly shocked at the sight of Somprabh standing there, armed. 'Do you know that entry here is forbidden to men, by Aryaa Matangi's order?'

'I am aware of that order, Lady', Somprabh said. 'I came knowingly to see Aryaa Matangi.'

'That is not possible! She does not see anyone!'

'But I understand she will see me. I come on Acharya Shambhavyakashyap's orders, and I am given to understand that she will see me', he spoke in a friendly and disarming manner.

The woman peered at him, and a smile played on her lips. 'Acharya Kashyap! Wait here, young man. I will tell her about you.' She lowered the pitcher on the ground and hastened back.

Somprabh wandered to a boulder and sat on it. There was so much in his life that was a mystery to him, he thought.

The woman was back very soon, slightly breathless. 'The lady will see you. Follow me', she said. Somprabh found it easy to match her speed, though she visibly strained to walk as fast as she could.

He followed her into the doorway of a small, clean hut, bending as he crossed the threshold. An old lady, dressed in white, sat on a thin floor mat. Her face was downcast. She seemed to be talking to herself in her mind. When she sensed Somprabh's presence, she looked up, her lips quivered, and she wiped her eyes with her hands. She took a deep breath and looked at him with a fixed gaze.

'Yes, it is you indeed', she said. 'Som! So many years have passed, and you have changed. But I know you. You are the same, my child.'

She stood up with surprising agility and rushed to him. Then she had gripped him in her arms. Somprabh smelled a faint perfume of sandalwood. He felt the thudding of her heart and the trembling of her hands and instinctively returned her embrace. He was surprised to feel his eyes turning teary. He felt an emotion he had not felt before. No one had ever given him this sense of pure affection.

'This insignificant Somprabh salutes Aryaa Matangi', he said.

'No, don't talk like that', the lady said. She stepped back and looked at from head to toe. A teardrop ran down her cheek. 'Call me Mother.'

'Lady, I thank you for your kindness', Somprabh said. 'Unfortunately, I do not know of which family I am, or which caste.'

'Call me Mother', Matangi said softly. There was entreaty in her voice.

Somprabh looked at her and knew he could not refuse her. 'Mother…' he said.

Matangi stepped forward and embraced him again. He put his arm around her shoulders. She was calm now. 'I am satiated. My life is fulfilled. I have been dying to hear this word…I have waited twenty-four years for this.'

'But Aryaa Matangi…' Somprabh stopped as he searched for the right words.

'Who am I? Is that what you want to know, young one? You said you were unfortunate. Well, this unfortunate woman is your mother!'

Somprabh stepped back. 'You, Aryaa Matangi? The divine Govind Swami's fortunate daughter, the revered Aryaa Matangi, you are my mother?'

'You look astonished', Matangi continued. 'I see. Did the acharya not tell you?'

'No. He only ordered me to see you before executing my mission.'

'He works in strange ways. He just sent me a message that my son was in these parts, and would come to see me. So, Som, let me see you!' She patted his shoulders and stepped back. Her eyes filled with tears again as she looked at him. Like an innocent child, she ran her hand over his torso.

Somprabh bowed and touched his fingers to her feet. He stood and looked into her eyes. His resolute gaze was that of a man who has found a deep peace. 'Mother, I am blessed. I used to think of myself as an orphan, but now I have you. I shall treasure this moment. But Mother, I must leave for a difficult journey, one full of peril.' He gulped. 'Tell me, who is my father?'

'Your father…' Matangi's eyes turned colder, and she lowered her gaze. It took some time before she could bring herself to speak. 'It is forbidden to take his name', she said in a low voice.

'Why is that, Mother?' Somprabh asked.

'Do you not know that I live in solitude?'

'I know, mother.'

'Then that is all there is.' She sighed.

'May I not know anything about him?'

'And what do you want to know, Son?'

'Perhaps if he is famous if he has a title?'

'He is world-famous.'

'And is he alive?'

'Yes!'

'For now, I will not ask more questions, Mother. I will use my skill to put together the rest.'

'Do not do that, Son. Do not. Trust me, follow me. Going down that path will do you no good.'

Somprabh looked at her fondly. 'As you command, my mother. I only wish that I could stay here, but I must go.'

'Why? Why so soon?' Matangi asked.

'I must go, mother. I shall return soon.'

'But stay longer!'

'I wish I could. But I have orders.'

'From whom?'

'From the one who sent me here. Arya Varshkar.'

Aryaa Matangi took two steps back. 'I see. So, Arya Varshkar sees this as his prerogative?' Her fists were clenched.

'Yes, Lady. I had the honour to meet him today.'

'And where does your journey take you to?'

'Champa.'

'Do you travel alone?'

'No, with my sister. A sister I never knew I had! But you must know, mother.'

Matangi gasped. 'Who said that?'

'The acharya.'

'And who is she?'

'Kundani.'

'Kundani? And you go with her! Never! It will lead to ruin! No. That cannot happen.'

'But why, mother?'

'I cannot say why. I would rather kill myself first. It cannot happen…Who told you to go with Kundani?'

'Arya Varshkar.'

'Refuse him. Tell him it is my order.'

Somprabh's jaw dropped. 'But will he…will the chief minister follow your order, Mother?'

She gripped his hand. 'He shall listen. Or I…after twenty-eight years, I shall cross that pond and –'

'Lady Matangi!' Someone called out urgently from across the small pond. They both swivelled to see Acharya Varshkar standing there. 'Do not be afraid. Let him go on his journey.'

'You, Acharya, have handed him to Kundani?'

'No, Aryaa Matangi. Kundani has a mission to complete, and she travels under Somprabh's protection.'

'Does Som know who Kundani is?'

'Yes. He knows she is his sister.'

'And does that suffice?'

'Yes. Do not worry.' Acharya Varshkar looked turned to focus his gaze on Som. 'Go now', he said, gently. 'Don't delay any more.'

'Wait!' Matangi said. Her forehead was creased with worry. 'Did you make any promise to the chief minister?'

'Yes, I did, Mother.'

'What did you promise?'

'Loyalty.'

'To whom?'

'To the empire.'

'And?'

'To the chief minister.'

'And to whom else?'

'To no one else.'

'Are you sure?'

'Yes.'

The flicker of fear in Matangi's eyes faded away. She took a deep breath and released Somprabh's hand. The acharya's dry lips formed a smile. He moved a few steps closer to them. 'That is enough. No more. Lady Matangi, do not fear for him. And you, Som – go now.'

CHAPTER 17

THE GREAT UNION

Ambapali reclined on a swing in one of her favourite spots in the Palace of Seven Worlds. It was in an orchard by the lake, fragrant with the scents of flowers. Lost in thought, she wondered about the meaning of life. Since she had moved, a new world of luxury, a cocoon of conveniences had absorbed her. Evenings saw the palace flooded by young men professing their ardour for the women living there, in an environment rich with sensuality. In the face of all this, she could not forget Harshdev's declarations of love, and her resolve to make Vaishali pay for the so-called honour it had bestowed on her.

She had realised that the fine trappings of power, which she had loathed when freshly anointed Bride of the City, had become an almost compulsory part of her life. Her beauty was at its zenith, but it was a mixture of her beauty, charisma, communicative skills and her intelligence that had quickly propelled her to become a celebrity in the country and abroad.

She often remembered the time when she had cried for a simple jacket or for other small comforts. The memory of her father's pure love for her brought tears to her eyes. Today, her physical aura was so strong that hordes of males were ready to fight to get a glimpse of her. Boys whose voice had not broken and men who bent with age, downtrodden who ran the cremation grounds and members of the assembly, chariots drivers, ambassadors, kings. She admitted that this was a source of pride. Her travelling along Royal Avenue in her palanquin became a festival for the crowds to celebrate. Every evening, garlands of the choicest flowers offered by citizens and visitors, each wanting to outdo the others in their display of amour festooned the gates of the Palace of Seven Worlds. The wealth that her lovers showered on her could not be counted, and the weighing scales of the treasurers of the Palace of Seven Worlds worked incessantly to weigh gold. White-haired merchants and courtiers let large portions of the accumulated wealth of decades flow into her coffers. She would not have found a moment's rest if she had actually paid heed to the unending messages of love that her lovers sent her way.

It was at times like this when she sought out a few moments to be alone that she pondered how far she had travelled on a path that her destiny had propelled her on to. These were also times when, thinking of all her amorous, fawning lovers, she realised with a pang that none of them had attracted her.

She had heard of deities, spirits, yogis and tantrics. She talked with her companions about their powers and ways of life. She wondered about their ability to control others, project themselves into other dimensions, take and give life. A throng of godmen and spiritual men of different hues had visited her by now and made their prophecies. She herself had travelled to see some renowned sages. Many suggested to her that there was no higher aim in life than to completely slake one's sensual appetites. All there was to this life was to be experienced in the physical world. The physical world was that of truth, satya. All else was an illusion, mithya. But she soon tired of these thoughts and of the people who were driven by them. She ended up dismissing them.

She had found the time to read philosophy, but reading did not lead to peace either. She often withdrew to be alone and seek a meaning to her existence and a path for the future. The memories she cherished the most, those of her childhood, dimmed with each passing day, though their sweetness did not fade. It was also true she could not repress her smouldering sensuality, and her lips could be burning like fire and sweet like honey at the same time. She rambled incoherently as if to convince herself: 'No! I do not love any of them! I cannot! I hate them, I hate all those who are here to appease their need for pleasure! This Palace of Seven Worlds is a burden on my life…These rich men who crawl before me are pitiful creatures, insects. They are caricatures of men. Those who flaunt their manliness are the falsest of men…'

Sometimes, she interrupted this train of thought when she looked at herself in the still water of the lake. The clear, pure water could not lie. She felt at ease with the world when she saw how much beauty she had been gifted. The passions her circumstances had accustomed her to slowly took hold of her limbs and her body. She would take a deep breath and think, 'There is no harm in this. I shall burn this crooked world in the fire of my beauty. This beauty shall remain untouched, even as its worshippers pay obeisance to it. The world does not consume but worship it.' Her heart would soar with pride and radiance. She would remember the poets, painters, craftsmen who sought out inspiration in her form and whose work had been influenced by her. Often, she found peace in these thoughts and drifted off to sleep on the marble slab, in the reassuring, fragrant, caressing breeze.

The garden was a famous asset of the Palace of Seven Worlds. It had trees from nearby and distant lands. Much effort and money had been spent in creating a suitable environment for the imported trees. A canal with a system of locks irrigated the garden with sweet water from the lake. The area had been landscaped many decades before, and sculptors had enhanced its beauty with ornamental pillars and statues. The reflections of the foliage and the sculptures in the lake and canal added to the grandeur of the setting. The many hues of the light playing in the orchard where Ambapali slept were dim as if filtered through a thin film of water. The milky-white crescent-shaped slab she lay on was one of her favourite resting places. Gem-inlaid holders were used to burn incense sticks that subtly heightened the scents of the flowers and repelled insects. The flowers around Ambapali exhibited all the colours of the rainbow. Such was the magic of that garden.

An instinct woke Ambapali up with a start. She saw an imposing man standing right in front of her, in the garden that she considered the most private of spaces. He had crossed the stage of youth and entered that of manhood. His fair face glistened in the soft light. His thick black hair, tied neatly at the back, gleamed like a crow's wings. The precious shawl covering his torso did not hide the broadness of his chest and muscularity of his arms. His wore a pale silk cloth around his waist. His flowing moustache sat well on his face, his lips forming a disarming smile that exuded confidence. He had earrings that seemed to be of diamonds and wore a necklace of pink pearls. His eyes shone with amusement.

Ambapali scrambled hastily to a sitting position, checking that her clothes were in place. Men did not impress her, but this one had created a flutter in her heart.

He spoke first. 'Greetings to the Benefactress of Vaishali! Have I offended you by disturbing your rest?' His voice was deep, measured and calm.

'No, you have disturbed, but not offended me', she said. 'How did you reach this prohibited spot? Were the guards sleeping, or did you use a charm on them?'

The man laughed. 'No, Lady Ambapali, your guards did not get the chance to question me. I came from the sky, in invisible form.'

Ambapali did not show her surprise. 'Are you a Gandharv, then?'

'No, my lady, I am human.'

'And yet you say you arrived in invisible form?'

'I have acquired some special skills, Lady. I have the power of becoming invisible, and of taking animal forms.'

Ambapali got up. 'You are not an ordinary man. Definitely not. You are a god, demon or spirit...And you have come to cheat me.'

'No, no, Dear Lady. I heard of your beauty and persona of your intelligence and radiance. I have come from far away, in disguise, just to see you. And now I know the truth is superior to the legend. I do not say this to flatter you. I am not an unctuous man. I say it from my heart.' He looked into her eyes with a sincerity that she knew to be true.

Ambapali had heard such words before. 'Sir, you are as good at praising women and expressing your secret love for them as you are at transporting yourself across barriers in invisible form, but –'

'But Ambapali, in my heart a deep love for you had taken root before I set out to see you. I thought you would be more precious to me than my life and soul, and I was right.'

Ambapali raised her voice a notch but still spoke softly. 'Tread cautiously on the path of love! Your skills at becoming invisible or changing into an animal form will not help you on this path.'

The man laughed good-naturedly. 'Lady, all acquired powers come to nought on the path of true love. But lust does not fuel my love. Ambapali, I…I see you as a being to treasure forever, not as a material pleasure to slake my thirst…I may have declared my love for you, but I do not think of you as one would think of the finest of aromatic wines.'

Ambapali knew there was something to what he said, but she wanted to test him. 'Your love seems somewhat otherworldly, I must say. What do I gain from your love and your high praise?'

'Love?'

'I am new to the business of love, Sir. Still, I do not hope to find any novelty in it. That would be too much to hope for. You talk like a philosopher, and I like it, but lovers are perhaps better at love than philosophers?'

'I had expected this kind of reply from the Benefactress of the Republic, and I am not disappointed. But I have something that I think may help to win you over.' He patted an object that had been lying next to him, covered in a silken shroud.

'And what is that, Sir?'

He removed the shroud to reveal a lute that looked very special. Its wooden body, adorned with ivory inlay work, gleamed in the filtered light.

Ambapali was struck with wonder, but she spoke with some acerbity. 'I am sure this lute is unique, but do not dare to assume that means much to me.'

'Oh, I make no such assumption, Lady Ambapali. It is not the instrument itself. This lute has value because when I play it, you will dance.'

'You do realise that I may not want to?'

'But you will. It is decided. You will not stop yourself.'

Ambapali was astounded. 'Is that so? Are you sure?'

'Indeed, I am, Lady!'

Without another word, the man sat on the marble slab, away from Ambapali. He took the lute and held it with practised ease. He obviously wasted no effort as he quickly turned its ivory knobs with his ears placed close to it. Then he sat very still, upright and legs crossed, cradling the lute in his lap.

His fingers strummed the strings, softly, each note ringing as clear as crystal, and then the notes fused into a simple melody. After a few repetitions of the basic scale, his fingers were dancing, and there were layers of melody. Ambapali no longer saw the man. Music had been part of her life as a courtesan. But now, she experienced something higher, a divine sensation flowing through every pore of her body and making it tingle with pleasure beyond the physical. The music had started with a few notes and now filled the garden, making its colours appear more vivid, and its scents more intense. She felt a flush, a warmth, permeate her. Later, she would recall it as a kind of drunkenness, but of a higher order, a feeling that she had transcended to another plane. Her eyes had been wide when her visitor had, without a hint of false modesty, started his performance. They were now closed as if she tried to maximise the pleasure the music gave her.

The nature of the vibrations in the air changed. They throbbed faster, but there was more to it than that. She opened her eyes to see that the lute player was now playing three simultaneous melodies. It was a feat she had not only never experienced, but never imagined. She breathed deeply, and the air smelled sweeter. She felt a burning desire to move to the music.

She was on her feet, composing herself, feeling the soft grass on her soles. And then her limbs moved of their own accord. She danced to please not the man, but herself and felt peace descend on her as her feet delicately drummed on the earth, and her arms traced intricate patterns in the air. She danced because she could not stop herself. She felt no signs of her energy being spent; it was as if her energy had become boundless. She felt as if her body itself was the instrument that the musician's fingers were playing and there was no barrier between them. The tempo grew faster, and faster, and though her feet strained to keep pace with his fingers, they had attained the perfect union, and there was no question of missing a beat. She reached a stage of bliss in which the lines between them blurred, and it became unclear who lead and who followed. The pleasure heightened to a moment of almost unbearable joy, in which the whirling world around her seemed to come to a halt. From that moment on, the music – and her dance – came to rest in a gentle pattern. She held on to a tree for some time after she stopped dancing. A pleasant tingling sensation buzzed in the spot between her eyes. She felt a shiver of delight as the man lifted her off her feet gently and laid her to rest on the marble couch. She kept her eyes closed for her long time.

When she opened them slowly, the visitor was looking at her with an unassuming smile, eyes twinkling. 'Victory to Lady Ambapali', he said.

'I have been defeated, Sir', she said, without a hint of malice.

'There is no winner or loser in love. Love destroys schisms, it unites.'

'What I have just experienced, I could never even have dreamt of. Are you the king of Gandharvs, Chitraratha himself? Did you come down from your capital Alkapuri to win me?'

He smiled. 'I am no Gandharv. I am Udayan.'

'I see. So, you are King Udayan of Kaushambhi? Pardon me for not knowing you. I do know of you, of course.'

'We should not stand on courtesy in love', he said.

'How can you play three melodies together, Sir? I have never seen, nor heard, of such an accomplished artist, in the three worlds!'

'On the other hand, none in the three worlds could have danced to what I just played, except the Benefactress of the Republic of Vaishali.'

'Oh, I was in a trance. I do not think I could do it again. Can I?'

'Yes – if there is such a lute performance again.' Udayan smiled.

'This lute of yours casts a spell on the living, and the non-living.'

'And so does your dance!'

'Can anyone else play like you do?'

'As you might guess, the king of Gandharvs, who gifted me this lute, and his skills.'

'King of Kaushambhi, may I ask you for another performance?'

'Not now, please, Lady. But you know that you will never forget this episode, and your admirer will never forget the dance you performed.'

'I see. Will you be my guest? Your disciple's guest?'

'No, Lady. I will depart as I came.'

'And is there something I can do to please you?'

'Nothing more than what you have already done.'

'But Sir…'

'As I had told you, my love is not fuelled by lust. I have drunk in your beauty with these eyes and fused with you when your dance and my music mingled.'

'Is there nothing more I can do for you, King of Kaushambhi? This Republic grovels at my feet. In their obsession for me, its men have created feelings of desire, envy and competition that are heavy enough to flatten mountains. Is there indeed no favour I can grant you?'

'Perhaps there is. Lady Ambapali. Can you accept this ordinary gift that you once refused?' He reached behind his neck to unclasp his pearl necklace and tied it around Ambapali's neck. His closeness increased her flush, and his. Then he stepped back.

'I am grateful. But may I ask you a question?'

'Of course, Lady.'

'Have you ever seen another woman like me?'

'Honestly, I have. But she was not superior to you.'

'And who is she?'

'Kalingasena, the daughter of the king of Gandhar.'

'And what is missing in her?'

'Nothing, except that she cannot dance to the three simultaneous melodies.'

'I see. And have you known her?'

'Yes and no, Lady. I have loved her, but not made love to her.'

'How did that happen?'

'It just happened.'

'That is puzzling, Sir. How could she not love King Udayan, who seems to be an avatar of Kamadeva, the god of love?' Ambapali smiled. 'Or did the king of Gandhar have such high standards that he would have rejected all the gods? Perhaps even Sahasranik, Indra's friend, for whom Indra, the king of gods, used to send his own chariot?'

'Lady, what can I say, except that fate came in the way.'

'I am too curious to let this go now. Can you tell me how?'

'Here is how it happened. The king of Kosala, Prasenjit, whose youth was behind him, had asked the king of Gandhar, for his daughter's hand in marriage. Refusing him would have been undiplomatic, so he accepted Prasenjit's request. Now, by chance, Kalingasena was very friendly with one Somaprabha.

'Somaprabha said, "You are beautiful like a lily in autumn, and Prasenjit is a withered jasmine in winter. You do not deserve this match." She told Kalingasena about me, in flattering terms, and I hope she spoke the truth.' He smiled. 'Kalingasena became attracted to me. We could have been united, but I had my own constraints. At that point, I did not want to offend the king of Avanti, another player in this drama involved in the political manoeuvring between these kingdoms. I knew that Kalingasena would have been happier with me, but I could not ask for her hand.'

Ambapali said, 'There are many such stories in our lore, and you must also have kept Queen Vasavadatta's courage in mind. After all, she took quite a bold step. Anyway, is Lady Kalingasena very beautiful?'

'Lady, among all the women in the world, only you can compete with her. And when it comes to dancing, you have no match – as I have already said. As it happened, her friend Somaprabha, an Asur, had great magical abilities. She took Kalingasena to Mayapuri, their famed capital city and a centre of sorcery, deep in the Vindhya mountains. She gave her heavenly herbs and magical implements. One day, Kalingasena used a flying vehicle to come to my abode in Kaushambhi.'

'It was as if the holy Ganga river had turned and flowed to your abode', Ambapali said.

'Yes, it was, but kings' ways are strange.'

'And how did those ways obstruct you?'

'The moment I heard of her arrival to marry me, I asked my aide Yogandharayan to welcome her suitably, and select an auspicious hour for the wedding. But Yogandharayan concluded I would be besotted with her and make my queen Vasavadatta pine away with grief. The chain of reactions could lead to destroying the kingdom. So, he did welcome Kalingasena but delayed the wedding without alerting me to his scheme.

'He sent news to both Prasenjit and Kalingasena's father. Prasenjit sent his army to subdue Gandhar, who did not have the strength to antagonise such a powerful foe. Neither could Kalingasena's father enter the battle with a hope of success, nor did he want to be locked in a conflict that would block his access to the far-east trade. He reached out to his daughter with a plea for mercy. And Kalingasena responded the only way she could, by yielding and giving herself to Prasenjit.'

'I am sorry to hear that. But I have to say Lady Kalingasena deserves praise.'

'That she does. But she is not the only one who sacrificed herself for her peo-ple. Lady Ambapali did so, as well.'

'I am happy to hear these words of praise from King Kaushambhi.'

'And on that note, Dear Lady, let me depart. But do promise me one thing.'

'If it is within my means, I shall.'

'Never dance for any man the way you danced for me.'

'I promise.'

Udayan disappeared into the garden. Ambapali sat there long, reliving the memories of their great union.

CHAPTER 18

SINGH, SON OF GYATI

Singh, son of Gyati, returned to Vaishali after ten years, having graduated from Takshila University. He had studied military strategy and political science from Acharya Bahulashavya, a towering intellect in these fields. During his time at the university, he had acquitted himself very well in the harrowing wars with the Persians. Acharya Bahulashavya gave him his only daughter Rohini's hand in marriage. Thus it was that Singh returned to Vaishali with fame, wealth and a wife whose beauty was delicate as that of a moon-ray. He was welcomed with much fanfare.

Five other Licchavi youths, who had also recently graduated from the university with flying colours, returned to Vaishali at the same time as Singh. The king of Gandhar, of which Takshila University was a part, had also sent ten citizens in a goodwill delegation. This delegation brought ten extraordinary horses for the royal stables. They carried sumptuous gifts and a clear message that Gandhar wanted to cement a strong friendship with Vaishali. The delegation leader was a young brave who had accepted King Indra's invitation to join his Devs in their battle against the Asurs. He had fought well and hard, and in return for his outstanding contributions to the victory, Indra had gifted him a garland of jasmine flowers that never withered.

Chief Minister Sunand had arranged a large garden party in honour of all these distinguished guests. The venue was a large public garden, which had been lavishly decorated with buntings, garlands and swastikas. Lamps lit with special scented oils, and large torches on high pillars added a heady mix of perfume and play of light to the atmosphere.

Singh looked radiant in a Greek choga, gifted to him personally by the king of Athens after he had led a valiant action with the Greeks against the Persians. His feet were encased in red coloured strapped shoes, and on his head, crowing his glossy black hair, was a band of small lotus flowers tied in the Greek fashion. He resembled a fashionable Greek noble.

His wife Rohini, who stood out with her golden hair, wore a two-piece dress made of the finest Kashi silk, covered with a striking saffron-coloured jacket. She had tiny flowers carefully embedded in an intricate pattern in her hair. She wore the lightest of make-up, and by way of jewellery, she had just two exquisite diamond earrings and a pearl necklace. She stood a head taller than most women. With her height, slender and confident bearing and the glow in her eyes, her presence made her stand out one among millions of women. The way the guests deferred to and looked upon her showed she was one of the celebrities in that gathering. The other graduates from Takshila University were also made to feel welcome and honoured.

Among the citizens of Vaishali was the chief of staff of the Army, Suman, with his flowing white beard and a grave demeanour, was mixing with the crowd and giving his attention to the guests. Chandrabhadra, commander of the Navy, was another of the luminaries. He was older than sixty and white-haired, but his twinkling eyes, brightly coloured dress and jovial tone marked him out as a completely different personality from Suman. He had the aura of a born commander, but an unaffected, smiling, nature and the people near him often burst into laughter.

Ashvalayan the wise, the famed Brahman who had composed the Grihasutras, the household code of conduct, was in the crowd. He donned an ochre silk shawl, and his long ponytail wagged as he spoke, to anyone prepared to listen, of the many aspects of the code. The sacred thread he wore, the janeu, marked his caste. With his bald head, decayed teeth and a body that seemed to be a skeleton encased in a sheath of skin, he was by no means a glamorous figure. From the way he gazed at them, he seemed to enjoy the sight of the beautiful women of the party.

By his side was Shursen, the second-in-command of the army. With a small and rotund, but muscular, body almost completely covered with weapons of various types, he looked every bit as theatrical as Ashvalayan. He was known to be jovial, with a great passion for singing. It was a poorly kept secret that the way to extract a favour from him was to praise his song.

Acharya Bhardwaj, the learned head of the Brahman Abbey, was entangled with the renowned philosopher Gopal in what seemed to be a heated discussion, given the light mood of the party. Bhardwaj's ponytail fluttered faster as his volume increased, while Gopal countered him with resigned amusement and a raised eyebrow. While he talked, Gopal's eyes wandered to the beauties in the room. Some of the subjects of his attentions were cold to him, while other women responded with knowing smiles.

One man would have stood out to a distant observer of the crowd. He scrutinised the others, and something in his demeanour showed he considered himself lucky to have been invited to this party. His rather fine clothes were worn in a somewhat dishevelled way. It was difficult to guess his age. He was plainly as strong as a bull. He was not discourteous, but when people talked to him, the conversation did not last. As the party went on, he increasingly gave rise to speculation. More and more fingers pointed discreetly towards him, and men and women turned their gazes at him. This mysterious character was a genius alchemist named Gaurpad. There were wild rumours about his capabilities, including speculations that he was hundreds of years old and could turn mountains into gold.

In a separate coterie stood Crown Prince Swarnasen, his friend and master of treaty-making Jayaraj, and the head of the inner-city guard, Suryamall. They were deeply engrossed in comparing the relative merits of the known beauties of the land, particularly Rohini and Ambapali. The mayor, Subhadra and his assistant Ajeet, also part of the small group, had splintered away into a parallel, whispered discussion.

Among the women, Sauliki's wife Rambha was one attracted attention. She had a brightness about her as intense as the radiance of a spring afternoon. Her smiling lips, playful eyes and seductive figure were enough to captivate men. But her quick wit and sharp tongue really enslaved them. As an informal and natural leader of Vaishali women, she had gravitated towards becoming Rohini's conversation partner in the party. The group she headed broke out with raucous laughter now and then, making heads turn their way.

In that group, a woman different from Rohini and Rambha sat close to them. Her exquisite beauty was more understated than theirs. Her eyes had a deep, piercing look, and her thick, long hair was pitch-black. Her shyness stood out. She was Army Chief Suman's only daughter.

A quarter of the night had passed, and the tumult showed no signs of abiding. It was time for dinner already, but dinner could not be served before an all-important guest had joined the gathering. That guest was Ambapali, and the assembly was looking forward to the reunion of exquisite beauties.

•

Navy Chief Chandrabhadra walked towards Singh with both hands outstretched in a gesture of warm welcome. 'Welcome, welcome to Vaishali, Singh! And a special welcome to your wife from Gandhar!'

Singh bowed and greeted Chandrabhadra with a namaste.

'Seeing you today, young man, reminds of something that happened a long time ago', Chandrabhadra said. 'It happened...twenty years ago! Your father, the great man Arjun was the chief of the Army, and I, his second-in-command. That was the time when he had humbled the Magadhan army and made them lay down their arms, after a particularly hard battle. A lowly Magadhan soldier, who owed his life to your father, sneaked into the camp and killed him by deceit.' Chandrabhadra's face clouded. 'And now Magadha is at it again – they have designs on the Republic.'

'Sir, I vow to avenge my father's death', Singh said. 'It is my sacred duty. I shall shed every last drop my blood to fulfil my duty. I shall be a true Licchavi.' His words rang sincere and true.

'Just as I expected, young man, just as I had hoped. Now I have no regrets at being an old man. But…'

'But what, Sir?'

'Your dress today – it is completely foreign?'

'Sir, Acharya Bahulashavya gave me two precious gifts. One, of course, was Rohini. The other was his injunction to be open, to have an international outlook.'

'Well, between the two gifts, I prefer Rohini!' Rambha said with a smile.

'And I do appreciate the second, as well. Wise words indeed', Chandrabhadra said. 'Young man, I will leave you to straighten it out with Rambha. I will meet the other guests.' He chuckled and moved towards another guest from Takshila.

On the way, he caught sight of Ashvalayan. 'Ashvalayan!' He called out. 'Welcome, friend! We don't meet often enough! How are you, how have you been?'

'Ah, Chief, where is the time?' Ashvalayan said. 'I am so deeply engrossed in the Grihasutras. It is hard work to establish the rules, to convince the people who will enshrine them…And I know how important it is for civilisation. This knowledge keeps me going –'

'That is good, friend', Chandrabhadra said, 'but do you give all your days and nights to work? Do you not get time for yourself? To rest and turn to other things?'

'Oh sometimes, I do, Chief, but…' – here, he lowered his voice and looked around before continuing – 'but when I do get free time, my wife clings to me like a coiled snake! She grows more and more attached, and more desirous, as she grows older!'

Chandrabhadra's face broke into a broad grin. 'Ah, I understand, friend, I see. So how did you manage today?'

'Ah, I slipped out. I came to see that Ambapali, the sinner. Her doors are open only to those who throw diamonds and gold, of course, not to poor men like me. This is a chance to see her up close.' He nodded sagely.

'I see', Chandrabhadra pursed his lips in complete empathy. 'But does the wife know you are here?'

'Oh no, not at all! Would I be here if I had told her? Oh, Chief, you don't know how paranoid, how jealous she is. I can't even begin to describe it. If I so much as smile at a maid, she dismisses her. Just a few days ago, she sold one maid away for only forty coins…That maid used to give this old Brahman a little care once in a while. Oh, she can be cruel, so cruel.' Ashvalayan's face fell.

'Friend, why do you want to see Ambapali so much?' Chandrabhadra asked.

'Oh, just like that', Ashvalayan said. 'One should – one must – see both the holy and the profane in this world.'

'Well, friend, I hope you will enjoy yourself today, without the wife hovering over you.' Chandrabhadra patted Ashvalayan's shoulder.

The Brahman laughed, showing his rotting teeth. 'Bless you, Chief! But will that woman come here?'

'Oh, she will. She is keen to meet Singh, and even more keen to meet his wife, Rohini.'

'Why is that, Chief?'

'She has heard of Singh, but not seen him grovelling. Of course, she is jealous of Rohini.'

'If that is so, I must get a good look at the woman from Gandhar as well!'

'Yes, take a good look, friend', Chandrabhadra said with a smile. 'This is a rare meeting of beauties. And I see two great men coming this way. Welcome, Shursen and Bhardwaj! Let me introduce you to the scholar Ashvalayan –'

'It's a pleasure', Shursen nodded. 'But, Chief, do you know why Ambapali is not here?'

'No, Sir.'

'Will she come?'

'I believe she will. May I ask why you are so eager to see her here, Chief?'

'Oh, I just want to see her once. I have heard that she turned down the king of Kosala, Prasenjit.'

Bhardwaj theatrically raised his hand. 'She is the spirit of Vaishali. I shall cast a spell on her with a mantra.'

'I see that my learned friend has been haunted by this spirit for many past lives!' The great mathematician and astrologer, Suryabhatta, jutted in, swaying his back as he spoke. The group turned to Suryabhatta and his friend the philosopher Gopal, who had joined them.

Gopal put on a mock-serious face. 'Well, that may have happened. It may also not have happened. It is not as if it could not have happened.' The group dissolved into laughter.

A short distance away was a group consisting of Prince Swarnasen, Suryamall, Jayaraj, Subhadra. They sat on a crystal slab.

Prince Swarnasen said to Subhadra, 'Friend, how is it that you did not attend my dinner party yesterday, but have been here since the early evening.'

'The reason is clear, Sir. Ambapali will be here, and she was not there.'

'Ah, I see! And since when have you become a beggar for her grace?'

'Who, me? Oh, for many births!'

'Well said', Swarnasen said. 'Suryabhatta, what do you say? We are not following protocol. We should pay our respects to Singh and his wife, Rohini.'

'We should, but where is the time, Sir? Look, Lady Ambapali has arrived.'

'No, no, there is still time. The diner has not yet started. Let us go to Singh.'

The group walked over to where Singh, surrounded by young men and women, answered their questions and satisfied their curiosity.

Ambapali had come with two maids. She wore her favourite white satin wrap over a red attire and the pearl necklace Udayan had gifted her. A hush descended on the crowd as her presence made itself felt.

Drinks were served. A team of bustling maids and servants brought different kinds of wines – Maireya, Madhvik and Dakha.

Ambapali wandered through the gathering with a graciousness that now came to her naturally. 'Friends, I welcome you', she said. 'Enjoy yourselves and please, have your heart's fill!'

Soon she had reached Singh and his companions. She greeted them. 'A warm welcome to the lady from Gandhar on Vajji soil!' she said. 'Singh, son of Gyati, I welcome you. And your friends, of course.'

She turned to Rohini. 'How do you find Vaishali, Sister?'

'Blessed Lady, what can I say?' Rohini answered. 'I have not even been here twelve hours yet, and I have found so much goodwill and closeness that I am overcome. Sister-in-law Rambha's touch was enough to wipe out the exhaustion of my three-month journey.'

'I wish you well again. And Rambha, this praise makes me jealous.'

'And I am delighted to hear that', Rambha said. 'Your jealousy is a matter of pride!'

'Friend Singh', Ambapali said, 'I congratulate you for bringing such an exquisite treasure here from Takshila.' She asked Rohini, 'Do you find our Vajji land like Gandhar in some ways? Or is it very novel?'

'I have to say there is one thing I cannot tolerate here.'

'What is that, Sister?'

'These slaves', she pointed to the two Ambapali had brought. They stood, bowed and meek, in a corner. 'How can people buy and sell humans like sheep and goats? And how can you have unlimited rights over them?'

She walked to Ambapali's Greek maid Madlekha and pulled her closer. Madlekha was dressed in plain white clothes. As Rohini lifted her chin, Madlekha closed her eyes and flushed a deep pink out of shyness. Rohini's eyes were teary. 'How do you bear all this, Sister? When we laugh, talk and joke, how can you stand mutely? Have you been taught this false humility?' She hugged the trembling maid and asked her name.

Madlekha went down on her knees. 'Lady, this slave's name is Madlekha', she said.

'Not slave, but friend', Rohini said. 'Well, Ambapali, as long as we are here, Madlekha and her companion…What is her name?'

'It is Chandrabhaga, Lady!'

'Good. May we grant Madlekha and Chandrabhaga independence to participate freely in the enjoyments today?'

'It has to be as the princess of Gandhar wishes!' Ambapali laughed. 'But Prince Swarnasen,' she gestured towards the prince 'is it not possible to free all slaves, not just these two?'

'Can the prince to take such a step?' Rohini seconded the request.

'No, My Lady', the prince said. 'It is beyond my powers. The slaves are too many in number. And then, there are many non-Licchavis in Vaishali.'

'Non-Licchavis in Vaishali?' Rohini asked, frowning.

'Yes, Lady. We Licchavis are the largest in number, but there are other clans. They are only slightly fewer than us and include, apart from workers, Brahmans and traders. They do not rule, but they can be as prosperous as the richest Licchavis. They have land, and their trading networks spread all over the world. They do not carry any burdens of statecraft or war. They lead free lives and have all the rights of citizens. They have solid slave-owning traditions, and they state they cannot live without slaves. A steady stream of slaves to Vajji lands stems from the kingdoms governed by the Greeks and from Kamboj, Kosala and Magadha.'

'But Prince, they can get their work done by workers, for a fee', Rohini said.

'You certainly have the right intentions, Lady, but you do not know how difficult it is for us to engage with the non-Licchavis. Acharya Ashvalayan is here – he is a learned and wise man, and one of their statesmen. You can ask him about it', the prince said with a smile.

During the discussion, Ashvalayan had been greedily drinking in the beauty of the women. Now he found Rohini's and Ambapali's eyes turning to him. 'May God forgive your sins! Indeed…what can I say? Slaves are slaves, and Aryans are Aryans. It is as fundamental as that. I have spent a life in letters. I know the six branches of the Vedas, I have authored commentaries on the philosophical tracts, and I have laid down the Grihasutras. This is our common heritage, that of the Aryans. Can these slaves ever equal us?'

Eyes wide and lips pressed and trembling, he looked at the women and the men around him. He turned to glare at a dark young man refilling a pitcher with wine next to them. The man's hands trembled, and he kept his eyes on the flowing liquid.

An unpleasant hush descended on the group.

Ambapali broke the silence with a gentle laugh. 'Sir, what do you think about my friend, this delicious Greek lady?' She gestured towards Madlekha.

The fire in Ashvalayan's eyes went out in an instant. 'Well, she – she is different, I agree. But the point still is that a slave is a slave, and an Aryan, an Aryan.'

'That is – it is cruel, it is unjust. How can you say this, and how can they bear listening to it? Look at this lady. To me, she personifies humility, culture, beauty and goodness. I can tell just from the few minutes I have been with her. How can you address her as a slave?' Rohini was clearly distraught.

'Well, we treat our slaves well. Our laws are, in fact, relatively liberal. We do not sell our slaves outside of the Vajji union.'

'But does equality for all mean nothing here?'

'No. It does not, Lady! I am the controller of social mores, and I can say from the bottom of my heart that humans are not equal. They cannot be. In this Vajji union, we have the Licchavis with their eight clans. Each clan is different. Collectively, they do not consider the offspring of non-Licchavi mothers or fathers as members of their clans. Only those with Licchavi fathers and mothers can bathe in the Holy Pond. These rules are strict. The Brahmans and the trading classes, both pure Aryans, follow the sixteen Vedic rituals and perform the five yagyas. The working classes and the slaves support these higher layers of society. The slaves come here from all over the world, from neighbouring Magadha to far off Greece. How could there be equality in this complex mixture? Some are destined to rule. And the languages, colours, cultures and bloodlines are different.'

'Oh, but in Gandhar, we have complete unity. One language, one blood. One nation. At least, that is how we see it.'

'That cannot happen here, Sister', Ambapali said with a smile. 'Now that you are in Vaishali, you should feel at home and forget the ways of Gandhar. Here, you will find more young braves like Swarnasen and wise old men like Ashvalayan who must remain bigger men than others. They want their slaves. And they want slave women. They need their pleasures. But enough talk. Let us get you a drink. Slave Madlekha, get Lady Rohini some wine.'

'No, no, come and sit next to me, Madlekha!' Rohini said.

Ambapali smiled. 'Well, do as she says.' She ignored the silent protests of the men.

'How can I, a –'

Rohini signed and smiled. She patted the space next to her. 'Come and sit down here, my friend', she said. 'Prince Swarnasen, I trust you do not object?'

'Indeed, I do not, Lady', Swarnasen said. 'I only feel that you cannot really do her good with this.'

'That is sad, Sir. When I travelled east, I saw much material progress, almost enough to justify the legend that the streets are paved with gold...and it made me happy. I accept that in Gandhar, we do not have such wealth. But I am saddened by the traditions of slavery and untouchability here. When I first saw their crumbling huts and the way the Aryans treated them, it broke my heart. Who do you think is responsible for this poverty, Dear?' She addressed the last question to Singh.

Singh thought for a moment before saying, 'Perhaps it is the old king you saw at Kalmashdava – do you remember him? The man with a wrinkled face, an ugly beard, whose head doddered under the weight of a heavy gold and diamonds crown?'

Rohini had a bemused look. 'But why him, Dear?'

'Because he considers rights very important – the rights of the ruling classes. And he is the wealthiest and most powerful man in his kingdom. The land's riches – which flow to him without his having to lift a finger – and subjects are his property. Not only the slaves but the citizens and farmers have to bend before his will as well. He can, at will, summon their daughters to his palace for his pleasure and their sons to their deaths in battle. The sweat of his subjects turns into ever more ostentatious palaces.'

'Oh, that sounds horrible.' Rohini said with a shudder. 'How do people tolerate such tyranny?'

'It is a matter of accepting the way of the world. As you know, western Gandhar accepts the Persian rule. The king sent a lady such as Kalingasena to Prasenjit. It is all about guarding territory and keeping control.'

Ambapali placed a hand on Rohini's shoulder. 'Perhaps the princess of Gandhar does not know that until someone has tasted his drinking water, betel leaves and food, the king of Kalmashdava will not touch them.'

'And why is that?' Rohini asked.

'Out of fear for his life, of course.'

'Ah, so it is not only the crown that sits heavy on his head. His very life has become a burden for him? And yet the poor man must bear these burdens. These rulers – they live in fear and yet dream of annexing more land. It is such a shame.'

'Indeed, it is. And that is the difference between imperial and republican systems. Here, we follow the rule of the people. That rule is more about duties than rights. The idea is to foster harmony and efficiency. The kings thrive in a world of conflict and division. Look at the Aryans. Wherever they have established their kingdoms – think of Kanauj, Kosala, Hastinapur – there is division by class. We are part of this larger organisation. In Vaishali, the Licchavis are united, but the others are Aryans and slaves. There is nothing much we can do about it.'

Rambha yawned. The discussion had dragged on too long for her. 'Dear Lady, Daughter of Gandhar, this deep discussion will leave you hungry. Come with me and feed yourself.' She tugged Rohini's hand, and the group moved towards the dining area.

The flow of food and drink started. Wine, pork, venison, beef and sweets were served in copious amounts. Ambapali engaged in conversation with the religious scholars, enjoying their company for a change. She laughed often and freely. Rohini kept the maids with her all the time, and they stayed with a group of women.

The festivities continued till late night, the party breaking up into smaller groups, some entertained by musicians and dancers, while others joined in the dancing. It was long after midnight when the guests' chariots took them towards their homes.

CHAPTER 19

THE MALLA COUPLE

Spring was in the air. The fragrance of the white flowers on the tall Sal trees wafted through the forest. A young couple rode side-by-side at a leisurely pace on the forest trail, talking to each other. The woman's knee-length skirt billowed in the wind, and her coal-black tresses swayed like serpents.

The man pulled his reins and pointed a spot out to his companion. 'Look, what a target we have there. Near that pond. See that pig? See how it enjoys eating the roots, with its nostrils in the mud?'

'Indeed. Shall I ready my bow and arrow, Dear?'

'Wait, Dear. Look – there comes a boar. Yes, now aim at the boar's heart.'

The woman steadied and stopped her horse, and readied her bow and an arrow in a fluid series of moves.

The man followed suit. 'Be careful', he said. 'If you miss, the boar will be upon you. Yes, let go now.'

The woman pulled her bow up to her ear and let go. A twang and the arrow planted itself between the animal's ribs. The boar roared and charged the woman's horse. The man let loose with his arrow, which pierced the boar's eye and emerged on the other side of its neck. The boar collapsed into a heap, writhing in pain.

The woman cried out in exultation, raising her fist. While her companion dragged the boar to a spot below a tree, she dismounted and tied the two horses. She got a fire going. Meanwhile, sweating from his labours, the young man had skinned the boar and cut up pieces of meat. Once the fire gave off less smoke, they put the pieces of meat to roast.

The woman raised a small pitcher of wine to the young man's lips, and they shared the drink. A short time later, as the meat started sizzling, she picked up a piece, let it cool and gave it to the man. 'Try this. Tell me what you think.'

He took a bite and chewed on it. He smiled. 'It's tasty. But more importantly, this is the taste of freedom.'

'That is true', she said. 'But it breaks my heart to leave Kushinara. Does Kushinara not need Bandhul Malla?'

He sighed and looked at the swaying treetops. 'It seems it was so…so many years ago that I graduated from Takshila. The guru had said, "Here is a man who understands arms and mind craft. He will bring glory to the Mallas." He said it with conviction. And did Kushinara not need my skills? Did they not depend on them for four years? The head of the Republic gave me ever more arduous tasks, and I did not shirk back from them. I went beyond the call of duty. But they never wanted me to grow. They even refused to make me deputy chief of the army. There was always someone lurking behind my back to make me stumble.' His face fell.

Mallika, who had been turning the chunks of meat, gave her husband more. They continued to sip the wine. 'Let it be', she said, stroking his shoulder. 'Being unhappy does not help. But Kushinara is our birthplace…'

'Birthplace?' Bandhul said. 'It is my homeland! My body is made of its earth. But I shall no longer look back. It has no need of me. The nobles are jealous of me. They fear my popularity.'

'That's a shame. They know all about your strengths, and they realise you will use them for the common good. Did any other Malla attain so much distinction at Takshila?'

'No.' Bandhul drained the pitcher and set it aside. He gave Mallika a sad look. 'All I wanted was to protect Kushinara from the greedy clutches of the Magadha Empire…But enough of that. No more.'

'But, Dear, why the imperialist Sravasti? Why not Vaishali of the Licchavis? Mahali of the Licchavis is your close friend and well-wisher. He is your classmate at Takshila. When he came over the other day, he never tired of praising you.' She smiled. 'I have heard he is the Head of the Fortress Guards at Vaishali.'

'I know, I know. But Mahali has always been the one to grovel before me for favours. I shall not bend before him. It is not right. Then again, today's Vaishali is decadent. The young men lust after Ambapali. Wine and women are all they care about. They are hollow. Their demise is impending.'

'Do not say that. We do not know for sure. And among the small republics, Vaishali still has the most power.'

'Yes, but this power will not last. Sravasti has better prospects. King Prasenjit of Kosala has sent me many letters. He will give us respect. We were together at Takshila! He knows my skills and my capabilities, and he needs me.'

'I am still worried. You say the Mallas ruined you with their jealousy. Will you avoid jealousy where we are going? What makes you popular also arouses envy and we, republicans, never had any faith in imperialist states.'

'True enough', Bandhul said. 'This sword is a remedy for jealousy.' He patted its hilt. 'All things considered, I think our future beckons us in Sravasti. Prasenjit heads a federation of five kingdoms, including Sravasti. He is not the wisest of men, and his desire for the good things of life blinds him. But he is surrounded by enemies, and their tribe only increases. He needs a stalwart man by his side. Me. I hope he will honour us.'

Mallika patted his hand. 'Then let it be so. We have rested enough. Let us continue.'

They mounted their horses after finishing their meal. In the meantime, the sun had mellowed, and they felt its mild warmth on their backs.

'Where will we spend the night, dear?' Mallika asked.

'In Malligram', Bandhul said. 'It is a village of Brahmans. I have a friend there, Sankritya. He is a renowned warrior. I know they will welcome us. Look! Do you see that white riverbank up ahead? The river is the Achiravati. The thick forest there covers Malligram. Let us hasten. We can reach in an hour.'

The horses that had been cantering until then got the message from their masters. They broke into graceful gallops, kicking up a whirlwind and drowning out the birdsong as the evening air stroked their backs.

At the riverbank, the couple slowed and stopped. They guided the horses to the river and let them take in the cool water. The clear waters flowed languidly along a white-sandy bank. The village was in sight.

•

A young woman came into sight. She was carrying a leather water bag. Her pale hair blew in the wind, and she wore a white woollen shawl and a red skirt. She stopped short when she saw the riders.

'Where have you come from, Guests?'

'From Kushinara.'

'Hmm. I know the place. Bandhul Malla lives there.'

Mallika smiled. Bandhul said, 'I am he.'

'I see!' The girl grinned. 'Then you are Mallika. Welcome, Sister. I am Sankritya Gautam's daughter.'

'Then you are Gopa, the fox!' Bandhul laughed and dismounted.

'Let me fill this with water, and then we can go!' Gopa was elated. 'They will be happy to see you.'

Bandhul said, 'Here, hold the horse. Let me fill that.' Gopa gave him the leather bag, and Mallika stayed on her horse.

.

'How did you manage to stray here, Bandhul?' Sankritya's wife, Ahalya, asked.

'I did not stray, friend. I intended to come.' Bandhul said.

'It has been so long!' Gopa interjected.

'Yes, it has. You were very young then', Bandhul said.

'But I remembered you! Lady Mallika, how long will you stay this time?'

'Just tonight, Gopa. But I promise I will not let you sleep. We will talk away. Isn't it?'

'And what does our friend do these days?' Bandhul asked.

'Oh, he composes. And if he adds so much as a letter to his composition, he feels on top of the world.' Ahalya laughed.

'And does Ahalya not stop him from dreaming?' Bandhul asked.

'Oh, what are the chances that he would obey her?' Gopa interjected. 'And there he is! Look, Father, whom I brought!'

Sankritya looked, and his face broke into a broad grin. 'Oh my, Bandhul! What brings you...Welcome, welcome!'

'Thank you, and may you be well. How is your treatise on justice and philosophy progressing? Is it complete?'

'Oh no, friend! That fool Bodhayan – that crook. He impedes my progress. But I will crush him, and I will get to the end.'

'Ah, that is great. Then you will become a warrior, philosopher and a priest.'

'Oh, but the Dravidians create so many problems! They want to push non-Aryan culture into ours. And that Mahavir – oh dear, I forgot to even welcome Lady Mallika!'

'It is our own home, isn't it?' Mallika said with a smile. 'Gopa gave us a royal welcome by the river.'

'Oh, Gopa remembers you so much, Bandhul! She recounted how you killed that boar with one arrow so many times! And it gets grander each time...Where is Jaymini?'

'He has gone for firewood. He should be back soon', Gopa said.

.

They had made themselves comfortable when Jaymini entered. He looked at the visitors shyly. He greeted them with a namaste.

'Jaymini, these are my friends Bandhul and Mallika. They come from far away. You weren't born when Bandhul was last here. Can you bring a duck in honour of our guests? Friends, how would you like to eat duck meat, stew and honey?'

'That would be very good, and kind of you, friend Sankritya.'

'Gopa, take Mallika inside. But can you first get them a basin to wash their feet? Friend, where shall we sit? Under this cedar?'

'Yes, this is fine, thank you', Bandhul said. 'What did you say about Bodhayan?'

'I was talking about him, but that can wait. Let us get our arrangements in place. Gopa, can you get us roasted pork and the old Maireya wine? My friend must be tired.'

'Yes father, the fire is ready, I shall bring the meat, and ask for wine.'

'So, that's all taken care of', Sankritya said. 'Well, come on, sit down and stretch yourself. So, where were we – yes, Bodhayan. The atheist. What about him? Here are a few things he says. There is no harm in having meals with women or eating leftover food. It is not wrong for children not to wear the sacred thread. Oh, and it is acceptable for a man to marry his maternal or paternal uncle's daughter. He divides India into three parts. The middle basin of the Ganga and the Yamuna rivers is the best, according to him. He has the temerity to include tribals from the south, Vanga and Kalinga in the representation of society!'

'Well, friend, with so many disputed topics, it looks like you have a problem on your hands. But you will never complete your treatise.'

'And why is that?' Sankritya looked surprised.

'Have you not heard of the Gautam, son of the Shakyas?'

'Why would I not have heard of him, friend? Is he in Kashi these days?'

'No, in Rajgrih. But his faith spreads like wildfire. Your treatise on what is just and what is not will not find many takers today. Unfortunately, that is how things are.'

Sankritya sighed. 'Time will tell, friend. Let us see. Here, take a drink. Yes, Gopa, that smells wonderful. Friend, help yourself to this soft pork. How is it?'

Bandhul took a bite and closed his eyes in appreciation. 'Wonderful', he pronounced. 'I love the taste of roasted meat with salt.'

'Eat as much as you can!'

'That I will. But, friend, I think what you hold sacred, that Brahmans are superior to others…that is not correct.'

'Oh, isn't it! And why not? Don't you see that the leaders have already established a council to look into the matter and taken leadership positions in the council? They want to reduce the stature of Brahmans. Do you know, the horse-owner Kaikeya insulted me in front of my son? He said to me, "Sit down, Sankritya. Today I shall reveal the true knowledge. You will be the first Brahman to imbibe it."'

'And did you learn that true knowledge?'

'Hardly! It was neither true nor knowledge. It is all deceit! Fraud! Hypocrisy! They state there is a universal and absolute Brahma. Kings and emperors need not perform yagya to receive their titles! The tricksters! I understand them all too well!'

'Well, help me understand them too, friend', Bandhul said.

'At one level, it is elementary. In the yagya, we place offerings in the name of the gods. We offer fragrant rice, duck meat, silk, slaves, gold and chariots. The offerings aim at securing the grace of the gods. Who has ever seen gods? No one. But people can dream of seeing them. But this brahma – people will imagine something like a sky, an abstraction.' Sankritya chuckled in disbelief.

'And this has also deluded the famous scholar Aruni?' Bandhul said.

'It is the wonder of it all. The new movement explains the concept of brahma and denigrates our rituals with such earnestness it makes me laugh.'

'Then keep laughing, friend. But let me tell you, you are a fool. If they did not do what they do, if they did not proselytise, how would they get thousands of gold coins and thousands of cows? If you join them, perhaps Ahalya will wear silk.'

'But I do not need that, friend! Material accumulation is what the nobles need. The guiding principle of power play is that those who raise doubts must be dulled with the world of senses: the best delicacies to eat, luxurious living and the pleasures of slave women. They will lose their vitality. They will sing to the tunes of the powers that be.'

'Well said.'

'Friend, there are in my treatise concepts you will find difficult to refute. For example, if a Shudra beats a Brahman, cut off the limb he uses. If he hears the Vedas, fill his ears with molten lead. If he recites them, his tongue must be severed.'

'Ugh! I cannot hear this, friend. Those poor souls…'

'But what else is the remedy? Tell me that. Don't you see that the Brahmans are getting worse with each passing day?'

'Well…Let me rest today. And when your book is complete, let me know.'

Sankritya kept his disappointment to himself. 'Of course, you must rest if you have had your fill. Your bed is ready.'

CHAPTER 20

SAKET

King Prasenjit of Kosala was visiting Saket. The merchant Mragal had invited Prasenjit to grace his son's wedding. The capital of Sravasti was about fifty miles away. Saket was a bustling city on the banks of the Sarayu river. It was a critical node where the river and land roads intersected playing a commanding role in the trade along the northern route. The Sarayu of those times was not the thin stream of a river that it is today. At Saket, its span in the monsoon season stretched to one-and-a-half miles. It was navigable by large ships all year round. Saket was one of the six large metropolises of India. Prasenjit had a palace surrounded by a fort here.

The mango trees had bloomed, and the hum of intoxicated bees filled the orchards. The trees were attired in young russet leaves. With the mango harvest, nature declared the cold had finally beaten a retreat. It was a pleasant evening, and the red sun scattered its glow on the flowering trees.

Young men and women thronged the banks of the Sarayu. Some of them walked bare feet on the silvery river sand, away from the paved promenade. Young men were engaged in loud swimming contests in the river, waist-deep or neck-deep in the water that they turned frothy. The crowd was a mix of races and colours. Some of the young were obviously Greeks. Many couples, having hired boats, crossed the river to the other side. Often, a couple dived off one of the hundreds of ships into the river, shrieking and calling out to others. Vendors had set up a supply of roasted meat and wine. Some frolickers were enjoying their food and drink while swimming in the water. It was a teeming, seething mass of people.

This was the panorama that awaited Bandhul and Mallika when they reached the city. Their backs were hurting, and their horses were tired. Mallika took a deep breath of the exhilarating air. She said, 'It is so lively! Look how they enjoy themselves! I never thought people could be so happy under the nobles.'

'Come, dear, let us get into the water', Bandhul said. 'It will wash away our tiredness. Isn't this air refreshing?'

'It's wonderful!' She said.

He jumped off his horse and helped her down, beckoning a slave standing close by. 'Friend, take care of our horses and give them a good rub. Here are four nishkas for your wine.' He winked.

The couple stripped and jumped into the water. Soon, they became the centre of attention, as the crowd watched them display their swimming skills. Mallika shouted out to the onlookers, 'Friends! Join us in a race! Whoever gets to that bank first gets unlimited wine! And your friends are invited as well!'

In an instant, the race started. The waters became choppy with the swimmers who had jumped into the fray. People on the bank began cheering the swimmers, and their shouts increased in volume as the swimmers neared the far bank. The Malla couple, Bandhul and Mallika were the first to touch it. They lay spent on the sand for a while. Mallika was laughing even as she panted from exhaustion. A prosperous-looking young man rowed his boat to the bank and called out to Bandhul. 'Friend! You are new here. Welcome! Come on board – all of you. Come on!'

Bandhul climbed on to the boat and helped Mallika on board. The others followed them. 'Thank you, friend', Bandhul said. 'We are, indeed, newcomers.'

'Where from?'

'Kushinara.'

'Ah, we know only one name from there – Bandhul Malla.'

Bandhul smiled consciously as Mallika poked him. 'Friend, I am Bandhul Malla.'

'Are you? You are doubly welcome!' The man held Bandhul's hand and raised it joyfully. 'Friends, welcome our new friend – Bandhul Malla of Kushinara!'

The Malla couple became the centre of attention once again, on a larger scale. A few people showered them with flowers. Bandhul and Mallika bowed and received the greetings with namastes. The owner of the boat said with a please smile, 'I am Hiranyanabh Kaushalya. You may not have heard of me, but I am the Satrap of Saket. And I know all about you.'

'On the contrary, the fame of Hiranyanabh Kaushalya has reached my ears', Bandhul said. 'I heard the name a long time back – in Takshila.'

'And I heard about you from the emperor. So, what brings you here?'

'A wish to see the emperor.'

The satrap nodded as if that made sense. 'Good! The emperor is here, you can meet him tomorrow. But today, you must be my guest.'

Bandhul turned to Mallika. 'Wife, we are lucky to meet Hiranyanabh. When I was at Takshila, I often heard he was the leading scholar from the Avanti school, and in the sphere of knowledge he excels all the kings of Kashi.'

'I congratulate my husband on winning such a friend', Mallika said.

'And Mallika, we shall be this friend's guests.'

'We are lucky', Mallika said, and Hiranyanabh smiled. 'But Sir, does the emperor remember my husband? He says that they spent ten years together at Takshila.'

'And he does not exaggerate. The emperor often praises Bandhul and wishes for a friend like him.'

'Is that so? That is good to know.'

'Oh, yes. Lady Mallika, your husband is no ordinary man. I heard, since my days at the Avanti school, before I went to Takshila, that no one comes close to Bandhul in political or military science.'

'And how about the science of swimming?' Mallika asked, slanting her head.

'Ah, there he does have a match', Hiranyanabh said and guffawed.

'Our horses are here', Bandhul said. 'Shall we?'

'No, don't worry', Hiranyanabh said. 'We will take the boat to my garden. The horses will follow. He turned to a deputy who nodded and signalled to another man.'

He pointed to a garden at a bend in the river. 'Do you see that garden, Lady Mallika? That is where we are going.'

'I see it, Sir. And I hope I do not sound too presumptuous, but I sense we are heading for home.'

'Indeed, it is your home, friends', Hiranyanabh said with a grin. 'Please wait here for a while. I will make arrangements and be back soon.'

CHAPTER 21

PRASENJIT, KING OF KOSALA

King Prasenjit sat on a soft indigo-coloured mattress. Two Greek slave women stood behind, fanning him. Older than sixty-five, Prasenjit had a very fair complexion and grey-black hair, parted in the middle and tied into two small plaits. His carefully groomed and imposing moustaches reached his ears. He wore a glistening silk robe and jewel-inlaid ornaments laded his neck, arms and waist.

His furrowed forehead showed that he was not happy. A guard informed him that Prince Vidudhab had arrived.

The king looked up and motioned for the prince to be called in.

Prince Vidudhab walked in and said, without saluting the king, 'The king sent for me?'

'Yes, I did', Prasenjit said.

'May I know why?'

'For advice.'

'And are your ministers and Acharya Mandavya not competent to advise you?'

'Ah, that they are. I want to advise you.'

The prince stiffened. 'I do not need advice.' His tone was harsh.

'But the patient's wish is not what decides the medicine.'

'So, I am the patient, and you, King, the healer?'

'Yes, that is so. Youth and indiscretion have made you impertinent.'

'Perhaps the king would do well not to create opportunities for me to act with impertinence.'

'Remember who you talk to! This is Kosala, and I am King here!' Prasenjit sat bolt upright and flexed his biceps.

'And I the future king.' Vidudhab met Prasenjit's gaze without flinching.

Prasenjit rolled his eyes and closed them for a few moments. He sighed and spoke in a softer tone. 'Think it over, Son. Did you have to be this indiscreet? You have dispatched the army against the Shakyas! Without my approval!'

'I shall free Kapilvastu of Shakyas, as I have pledged.'

'Why, may I ask?'

'To wash away your sin.'

'My sin! Watch your mouth!'

'I do not need advice on my choice of words, Sir. I will wipe away the blot of your sin with the warm blood of the Shakyas.'

'My sin again! And what is my sin? Tell me right now.'

'I shall. As it happens, there is no end to your sins. I shall mention only one: Why did you produce me with a slave? And does my life have less value because you did? Do I not deserve a place in society?'

'What is all this? Who has insulted you?'

'Why did you send me to the Shakyas?'

'I do not understand you. You are my son and heir, and the Shakyas' grandson. We live in times of peril. In the west, King Udayan of Vatsa is preparing his army for war. In the east, Emperor Bimbisar is readying for, and Vaishali Licchavis are on the warpath as well. All this we know from our spies. We need the Shakyas on our side. And that is why I sent you to them.'

Vidudhab laughed sullenly. 'Grandson of the Shakyas? Or son of a slave woman? Do you know what happened there?'

'No. Tell me.'

'Here is what happened. They received me with no feeling, and after I had left, they washed the assembly hall with milk!' Vidudhab's fists were clenched, and his eyes blazed.

Prasenjit pounded a fist into his palm. 'Curse them!'

'But for one of my aides who forgot something there, I would not have known. When he went back, a group of slaves was washing the hall. One woman said, 'Look at the cheek of the slave woman's son! He comes dressed as a noble and desecrates the place.'

Prasenjit stood up, erect and fuming. 'I cannot forgive that. I shall finish them.'

'Why you, Sir? They have not harmed you. You were eager to marry the Shakya princess, driven by your sovereign ambitions. But the Shakyas did not want to give their daughter to a weak and sick old man. You had no high-bred princess in your harem then, and they did not want to be the first to give you one. Your chief queen was a gardener's daughter. The Shakyas were arrogant, but they feared your sword. They sent you a slave's daughter.'

Prasenjit stood with his arms folded. His eyes were glaring. 'That was a lowly trick, indeed, but –'

'But not a sin. Which is what you committed. You produced me when you coupled with that slave, my mother, who at least gives me love. Now you do not dare to give me what a father should – you will not proclaim me heir to the throne. This is the mean Aryan tradition: to collect a bevy of women to fulfil your desires, to buy them, win them over with deceit, to use force where needed. To abduct weeping maidens, to rob unconscious, intoxicated virgins of their innocence. And there is no bar to having them without marrying them. You so-called brave Kshatriyas collect beauties by fighting, winning, bribing…and these so-called Brahmans, those cowards, conduct yagyas for you and grovel before you to collect the slave girls that your unions produce.'

Vidudhab's eyes were red by now, and his chest was heaving. His voice qua-vered. But he continued the tirade. 'You Aryans are wicked beyond belief! The king of Videha called a council. One old Brahman received thousands of cows with gold coins tied to their horns and two hundred slave women wearing golden ornaments. It makes me sick! The Brahman sold the cows and took the gold and the women home. If those women have children, you will gleefully declare them mixed breeds.

'I too am a mixed breed. I am the son of a slave. My stepping into the assem-bly hall makes it impure. I am a blot on my family.

'Hear this. I can bear it no more. I shall wipe out the Shakyas and take the throne of Kosala with this sword. The days of the Aryans are numbered, and with them, those of the fraudulent Brahmans. There are not that many Aryan kingdoms left in this land you call Aryavarta. We, whom you call mixed breeds, have taken over most of them.

'I declare that I shall annex Kashi, Shakya and Magadha if I am the true slave-son Vidudhab.'

Prasenjit closed his eyes in anguish. His lips quivered. In a low voice, he said, 'There are traditions. And you are no stranger to royal luxury…'

'Maybe, but I want honour. Honour! I want the throne! And if you don't give it to me, I shall take it!'

Prasenjit sat on his throne. 'This is rebellious talk', he said.

'I am a rebel.'

'The punishment for rebellion is death. You do know that the regal code is harsh?'

'The demands of self-respect are even harder!'

'That is a personal view, not a universal code.'

'Not anymore, not if I can help it. All of us sons of slaves, mixed breeds, the objects of hatred of the so-called high-born – we shall make it a public cause. We will take over your kingdoms and end your robber rule.'

Prasenjit clapped his hands. 'I order you to be taken prisoner. Guards!'

Two Greek women rushed in with their swords drawn.

'And I declare you deserve to be beheaded!' Vidudhab raised his sword.

His son's manner of speech and the sword he drew at him made Prasenjit's eyes teary. He stood and unsheathed his sword.

At that instant, Vidudhab's sword fell to the ground with a loud clang.

Prasenjit peered at the visitor responsible for the deed. 'Whom do I owe this?'

There were two visitors. One of them stepped forward, sheathing his sword. Hiranyanabh said, 'None other than Bandhul Malla of Kushinara, Your Majesty.'

Prasenjit extended both his hands in a wide embrace. 'My friend, Bandhul! Is it really you?'

'It is me, Sir', Bandhul said. 'Victory to the king. And I am glad I timed my entry well.'

'Oh, yes, you did. Else this slave's son would have killed me. Satrap Hiranyanabh, arrest him!'

Before Hiranyanabh could move, Bandhul joined his hands in prayer. 'King, I ask you to forgive the prince this once. We overheard part of your conversation, which was loud enough. The prince will realise how wrong he has been.'

The king frowned and sighed. 'Friend Bandhul, you are welcome here. And I pray to God that your words about Vidudhab hold true.'

'I am obliged, Sir', Bandhul said. 'Prince, you are free to go.' The prince left without a word.

Bandhul continued. 'I am not sure you remember, Your Majesty…long ago, at Takshila, you had said that if you became king, I should be your army chief.'

'How could I forget? Kosala needs you. And so do I! Have you not heard of King Udayan's machinations? Since Gandhar gave his daughter Kalingasena to me, he has determined to campaign against Sravasti. And Emperor Bimbisar, forgetting our traditional ties, is ready to swallow my empire as well, while others still covet our peace and wealth. Friend Bandhul, I need you here.'

'And I am here, King. But I have conditions, if I may be so bold as to state them.'

'Speak freely, friend!'

'I am a Malla.'

'I hear you. You will not fight the Mallas. Have no fear, you will not have to, I do not wish to expand my empire. I just want to keep it. What else?'

Bandhul thought for a moment. 'In fact, there is nothing else, Sir.'

'In that case, Satrap, make all the necessary arrangements for my friend Bandhul. While I am here in Saket, he should settle in Kosala.'

'It shall be done, Your Majesty', Hiranyanabh said.

'And as soon as I reach Sravasti, he will be anointed chief of staff of the army. Bless you, my friend, Bandhul', Prasenjit said. 'Now go and rest while you can.'

CHAPTER 22

MANDAVYA UPARICHAR

Prasenjit sat on one of the white marble steps of a pool. Brightly coloured fish played in its clear water. The morning breeze gently rustled through the trees around the pool. The king's eyes were sleep-laden, and his body languid. He watched the ripples and the shimmer of light in the water.

A guard bowed before him and said, 'Your Majesty, Acharya Mandavya is here.'

'Bring him in.'

Acharya Mandavya's face was emotionless, his eyes slanted, eyebrows bushy, earlobes dangling and his dark, muscular body was very hairy. His persona was such that it defied all attempts to guess his age. He wore a red silk cloth around his waist, his feet were encased in deerskin shoes, and his back and chest were bare. He wore a swab of sandalwood on his forehead. His teeth were perfect. An unusual light glinted in his eyes, and a luxuriant moustache covered much of his face. He wore the sacred thread of the Brahmans and carried a silver staff in his hand. He swaggered like a slightly intoxicated man.

Raising the staff, he blessed the king in a hard, grating voice.

'Acharya, I have waited long for you', Prasenjit said.

'Why, King? Do you sleep well at night?'

'Do not talk about nights anymore. My life is worn out. I think I should meditate on the next world.'

'Ah, how you talk, King. This world and the other sorrow, virtue and sin, moral and immoral, deities and demons…These are all figments of children's imagination. Or have you fallen for the fool Pravahan's web of lies? Do you believe his talk of the cycle of rebirth and the liberation of the soul?'

'But life is not a lie, Acharya.'

'Life is truth. Why hanker after a loan when you have money?'

'Does he who has money to guard not worry?'

The acharya laughed and sat on a rocky slab next to the king. He said, 'Are things so bad?'

Prasenjit sighed. 'You could say that, Acharya. Naked, young beauty does not arouse my jaded senses anymore. The fragrance of aged wine, which gave the world a cheerful hue in my days of action, does not colour my eyes.'

'In that case, the king has become a yogi.'

'And what should the yogi do with his host of beauties from around the world?'

Acharya Mandavya chuckled. 'Give them away. Young men will want them. Perform a great yagya and gift them to deserving Brahmans.'

'Oh, but many of those Brahmans take the gifted girls, keep their ornaments, and sell them over to old men for five nishkas each.'

Now the acharya laughed. 'Well, Your Majesty, such is life. Those old men benefit from the exchange. They are in dire need of young women.'

'Well, then, what about this old man? Why does the acharya not pay attention to him? Do you not know that Kalingasena is about to adorn our great capital? Do you not see a pressing need to use your powers of chemistry? To make her beauty flower?'

'I see what you mean, but was the treatment of that young physician from Magadha not helpful?'

'Are you talking of Jeevak Kaumarbhritya, Acharya?'

'None other.'

'Not helpful. Not at all. Acharya you had praised him, I had heard great things about his laurels at Takshila. I had hopes…'

'But you don't any longer?'

'Well, while you are there I do have hope, if nothing else. What use would be your being a disciple of the great Brihaspati if I could not hope your powers would rescue me?'

The acharya nodded and smiled. 'In that case, here you are, King.' He reached into the folds of his dress and placed a small fruit in Prasenjit's palm. 'This has only one active medicine. It works equally well for health and potency. You can use it to convert that hillock to gold or turn this rotting body into a thunderbolt and empower it to strike deep into the very being of your new bride.'

'The acharya has obliged me indeed! I have no need for more gold. I only wish for my body to continue to serve my mind.'

'In that case, King, rest assured, you shall enjoy the mastery that you seek. I bless you with that power.'

The acharya laughed and walked away.

CHAPTER 23

JEEVAK KAUMARBHRITYA

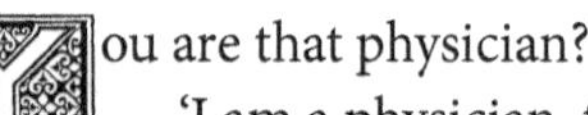ou are that physician?'

'I am a physician, true enough. I have no comment on whether I am "that" physician.'

'From where do you come?'

'Rajgrih. Educated at Takshila.'

'Under Acharya Atreya?'

'Yes.'

'Then you really are that physician.' Vidudhab's tone was gentler. 'Sit down, friend.'

The young physician sat down without a word. He must have been about twenty-six and was fair, dark-eyed, with a broad forehead, thick curly hair and a thickening chin. A golden belt tied his oversized robe at the waist, and a precious stole lay casually draped on his shoulder. His shoes had intricate golden embroidery.

Vidudhab stared at him for some time. Then he said, 'So your birthplace is Rajgrih?'

'Yes, as far as I know.'

'It is a pleasant city. But you left your hometown long ago?'

'Since I was about sixteen.'

'And in Takshila you were Lord Atreya's chief disciple?'

'There is no such thing, in my opinion. I was just one of his petty disciples. I am Kaumarbhritya. That is my identity.'

'Your name has travelled, friend. And your praise. You are young, but youth does not suggest a lack of merit.'

'Does the prince need my services?'

'I am above the services of physicians, friend. I am fortunate to have a robust constitution. But I do wish to be your friend.'

'I am at your service.'

'Friend, are you attached to jewels and gold?'

'Far from it. I never have been.'

'That is good. And do you look for a true friend?'

'I do need true friends, very much, Prince.'

'From this moment onwards, consider that you have found a friend to fulfil that need. Will you be my confidant and guide?'

'I am just a poor physician, unaware of the ways of kings.'

'You are a great man and have all the qualities of one.' Vidudhab took off his necklace of pearls and gave it to the physician to wear. 'Take this as a token of love, friend.'

Kaumarbhritya took it slowly, pondering this turn of events. 'This is a bribe, Prince. I will be happy with a modest gift.'

'No, no, don't return it, friend! It is quite ordinary.'

The young man took a deep breath. 'As the prince commands', he said.

'Now, friend, tell me, could you do my father any good?'

'Not a bit. I told him right away that his glands and organs have atrophied. His heart no longer has the pumping power it had. If he uses a potion to stimulate his flesh, it may risk his life.'

'And he still does?'

'He has tried it. Thrice, Prince.'

'Without effect?'

'That was expected. Medicine cannot always overturn nature. We have to accept we have limits, compared with the divine.'

'In fact, Acharya Mandavya has blinded him and made him a slave to lust. But does that chemical of his have a semblance of truth?'

'Prince, I have not studied such esoteric sciences. There is some truth to them. Acharya Mandavya is a disciple of Sage Brihaspati, whose Charvaka system has gained fame recently. Much of it is justified. His principle is that the body must not be tortured, that value-based actions matter more than fate. He stresses self-dependence and propounds there is no Almighty and no next world. He considers the Vedas as a web of deceit, and for him, intelligence is paramount. Of the five elements composing the soul, visibility is sufficient proof of truth. He opposes the justice of Gautam Buddha and the Brahmans' yagyas. The Shudras and the mixed breeds have taken to his beliefs. The Brahmans' supremacy has suffered, which may be a good thing. But misconduct has increased. In particular, instances of people declared mixed breeds by the Aryans in retaliation have soared.'

'It is true, but the Vaishyas, the merchants, suffer the worst impact. They can only marry within their community or lower, but they come into contact with the lower castes in their trades of agriculture, livestock breeding and commerce. Each year, more of them become lower in status because of mixed blood.'

'But is there a remedy, short of uprooting the Aryans?'

'The time is ripe for that cure, Prince. The all-conquering, elemental forces of Mahavir and Gautam, son of the Shakyas, have started that process. They have set in motion new faiths that have no Vedas, no god who created the Vedas, and no Brahmans condoning the sins of kings in return for donations. There is no hypocritical talk of brahma and atman. They have seen the essence of life, and they are propagating it. Two non-Aryan kings, Hiranyakashyapu and Ashva-greeva have announced the death penalty for performing yagyas and reading or listening to the Vedas.'

'The sooner the Aryans are destroyed, the better, Sir.'

'The Shudras face an immense problem.'

'And what is that?'

'They cannot take women from higher castes. The Aryans buy or kidnap the prettiest of their girls before they even come of age. They get women from the Dravidians, Asurs and slaves. Many of their young men stay unmarried, while Aryan houses have bevies of women. The gender imbalance in the Shudra caste often causes bloodshed as men compete for a shrinking pool of women.'

'Doctor, do you think the demise of the Aryans will cause any great misfortune?'

'Nothing of the sort, Prince. Their pride is mostly empty bragging. Their belief in blood purity is hypocritical. They have the same blood vessels as others, and they also carry the blood of non-Aryans and so-called lower castes. The truth is simple. There should be one caste – mankind. Nothing good can come of all the divisions that have shackled society.'

'But, friend, the traditions have lasted for centuries. And the rulers and the Brahmans draw enviable benefits from the tradition.'

'That is so, Prince, and that is why the Tathagat has struck first at the caste system. His assault bears fruit because he attacked the establishment with a sword of logic rather than steel. Don't you see that the foreigners, Greeks, Gur-jars, Shaks, Abhirs – remember they are called malechha, the dirty – have been welcomed into the sangha as equals? You will see that the caste differences will soon be erased. Some Brahmans have responded to the Tathagat's movement by giving posts to people from the lower castes, but that is too little, too late.'

As Vidudhab pondered that subject, one very close to his heart, the physician continued. 'Just think about it, Prince. See how the Brahmans have sold them-selves to the kings. There was a time when I was deluded and firmly believed in the caste system. When I studied medicine at Ujjain, I immersed myself in the Vedas, the Nirukta system of philosophy, and the traditional literature. The Brahmans among us used to taunt the others and wear them down with constant reminders of their superiority. That was sanctioned by the teachers, of course. But when I ventured out to Bharukaccha, I saw the Greeks' splendour, the Shaks, and Abhir satraps opulence and military prowess, and the fierce Huns with their cheeks like oranges, hairless faces. My eyes opened, and I realised the Brahman-Kshatriya had numbed our society with their talk of brahma and rebirth.

'Here in Kosala, Prince, see the soaring, golden mansions of the merchants and nobles, and the miserable huts of the workers, sculptors and farmers. Is the wealth of those mansions not sucked out of the lives of the poor struggling to make ends meet? And Magadha is no different. In the cities, towns and villages, the vast community of artisans, weavers, goldsmiths, blacksmiths, chariot makers, potters…creates value with their skills. But it is the creamy layer of society – the kings, nobles, Brahmans, merchants – that reap the benefit of their manufactures. Their goods reach Egypt and the eastern islands, but what good does it do them?'

The prince's eyes shone as he reflected. 'You have a sharp mind, friend, and much insight. I want to meet the Gautam Buddha once. Although by blood, I am in part one of the Shakyas, I am their greatest enemy. But I do want to meet this illustrious son of the Shakyas.'

'He treats friend and foe alike. You will realise that when you see him. Do you, by any chance, know the old monk of Kalandak?'

'His name is Dharmabandhu Mahasthir, isn't it? I know he established a sangha here, in Saket, after returning from Kashi.'

'He is the one. He comes from a family of Chandals – about as low as it gets. Today, he heads the sangha here. Bhardwaj and Sumant, sons of the highest order of Brahmans, have to genuflect before him. He initiated them. Such is the power of the Shakya sage!'

'I have heard of Mahasthir. He is also a renowned scholar.'

'That he is! But if the Brahmans had had their way, do you think you have heard about it? The Tathagat calls his sangha an ocean that absorbs all rivers, a place where all lose their past.'

'I see. But outside that idyllic world, here in Saket, there is great injustice,' Vidudhab said.

'That is so, Prince. As long as Brahmans feed on fattened calves, accepting young women for gifts, and nobles protect them in return for their blessings, that is how it shall be. Don't you see how Katyayan, Varuchi, Shaunak and Vasishta have composed ever more profound treatises in which they document the rights of the rulers, their masters?'

'Well, friend, I am happy to have found you. I see a kindred spirit in you.'

'I am honoured, Prince. But I may not live long in Kosala.'

'And why is that, My Friend?'

Kaumarbhritya smiled a wan smile. 'The king is unhappy with the failure of the potion I gave him. I have asked his leave to proceed to Rajgrih. I must leave before things get worse for me.'

'Oh, if that is on your mind, do not leave yet. Wait till I tell you to go. Stay on at my request and leave things to me.'

'As the prince wishes.'

CHAPTER 24

THE APPOINTED SON

Harshdev's aimless wanderings took him across many borders. One day, he reached the city of Veetibhay, ruled by Udayan. By this time, Harshdev was no longer the handsome, confident man he had once been. He wore tattered rags and had matted hair. His eyes had the gleam of a lunatic. He was possessed by thoughts of revenge on the city of Vaishali. He wanted to win Ambapali back. But he had lost his self-esteem. He no longer believed in his own strength of character and arms. He was just another tramp.

Harshdev found shelter in an abbey on the outskirts of the city. As soon as he got to a corner under a thick tree, he sank into a deep, exhausted sleep. By chance, an elderly woman noticed him at that instant. She was looking for an orphan, and something told her this man was one. She sat down, waiting for him to wake up.

When Harshdev woke up, his eyes fell on the old woman staring at him. He sat up, and said in a parched voice, 'Mother, are you…Is there something I can do for you?'

'Yes, become Kritpunya.'

Harshdev was confused after waking up in a strange place. He was polite to the kind woman, though, and kept his irritation in check. 'Who is Kritpunya?' He asked.

'He was my only son.'

'Where is he now?'

'He is lost forever. He sailed down the sea to Tamraparni with three loaded ships, in partnership with other merchants. The others came back, telling of a storm in which my son's ship sank. Kritpunya was the only son of the late Dhanavah, the famous merchant. And I am his unfortunate mother.'

'I share your grief, Mother. I cannot become your son, but if thinking of me as your son does you some good, then I am your son.'

'It does me some good! If the king's men get wind of my situation – me being a woman without an heir – they will usurp my assets. One look told me you are the one. Become my son.'

'Mother, I have taken an oath I need to act on. It comes in the way of my accepting your request.'

'Do not let it. First, fulfil my wish, then act on your oath.'

'What is your wish, Mother?'

'My son has left behind four wives. Each of them is high-born, beautiful and young. I would like to appoint you my son's inheritor. You will stay with us as my son and produce a son with each of them. I shall pay you for that.'

Harshdev blinked as he took in her words. She was silhouetted against the pale rays of light which broke through the thick canopy of the trees. He let his instinct guide him. 'The gods work in mysterious ways', he said. 'I shall do as you ask, but ask for my reward as I please.'

'My husband, Dhanavah, the merchant, owned more than a thousand gold coins. Seven of his ships plied the oceans. Do not worry about asking me too much money.'

'Mother, I am your son Kritpunya.'

The woman took him with her. As soon as they had reached the threshold, she shouted out aloud, 'Look what the gods have wrought! My son is back! The light of my house is back. Oh, Kritpunya, how we waited for you!'

The neighbours came out to see what was happening. When they were near, she took his hands in hers, and said, 'Look what the ravages of time have done to him! See how worn down he is, the only son of Dhanavah. How he has suffered!'

The neighbours consoled her and reminded her to be thankful more than sorrowful. They stared at Harshdev's bedraggled form. The old woman set about ordering her servants one by one. 'Call the barber to give my son a shave. Heat water for him to get a bath. Add perfume to it. Call a physician and masseur to see him later.'

·

With a flurry of activity from the slaves, the maids, and those called to restore the so-called Kritpunya to his former self, Harshdev became a transformed person. Shaven, clad in silk with perfumed, clean hair, he sat, chewing scented betel, against soft velvet bolsters surrounded by the neighbours. He thought about his past, his present and his future. The house was full of the aromas of fragrant cooking. The old woman had ordered her four daughters-in-law to get good herbal scrubs, put on their finest jewels and wear their best silk dresses.

Prabhavati, the eldest of the wives, took a good look at Harshdev from a window, and her heart sank. She called the other three wives into a conference, and whispered, 'My, my! Do you know what is up? That man is not our Kritpunya!'

They shrank back in horror. The youngest said, 'Then we must tell Mother!'

The four of them trooped to their mother-in-law.

'What is this?' The old woman cried. 'You have not finished getting ready! It is already evening. My son –'

'But mother, that is not your son. He is an impostor!' Prabhavati interrupted her.

The old woman raised her eyebrow and lowered her voice to a threatening tone. 'Do you know my son better than me?' She asked.

'He is not him!' The four wives spoke as one.

'My saying so makes him my son!'

'But we have seen through this man!' Prabhavati said.

'Quiet! I, Kritpunya's mother, have appointed him. I have my reasons!'

The wives were struck dumb.

The old woman said, in a quiet, determined tone, 'Each one of you is intelligent. You should know where your welfare lies. Do not trip me. You and I have one thing in common – we do not have male heirs. You know how greedy the king is. His men will only be too ready to pounce on our possessions and confiscate them for the treasury. And do not think it will be only the gold and jewels that will go. We can lose the house. But if we continue our lives as if Kritpunya had returned, if you have sons with him, we will secure our collective future.

'I know what I ask is strange. But it is not unique in the Aryan tradition. Shantanu's son Bhishma followed this principle to protect the Kurus. So, if you value your happiness, do as I say.'

The mother-in-law's words convinced the four wives. Thus, Harshdev lived as Kritpunya. The old lady maintained the pretence, drawing on every available resource she had. She used the four time-tested means of saama, daama, danda and bheda – pleading, bribery, force and trickery – to steer her family's path to survival. She quelled every doubt that was raised.

Harshdev lost his resolve and lost himself in a world of luxury and domestic pleasures.

CHAPTER 25

THE APPOINTED SON'S FEE

Three years later, Harshdev was the father of three sons and two daughters. The old woman rejoiced in hearing the house echo with the peals and cries of the toddlers. The children were hale and hearty, and as is natural for children of mixed-race parentage, they were bright and intelligent. For a long time, Harshdev remained haunted by images of Ambapali, even as he played out Kritpunya's role. He gradually found he was taking root in his immediate environment. His four wives loved him, and the third wife, in particular, was devoted to him. Her father was a famous merchant of Champa, and she stood out for both her looks and her brains.

The old woman had a very calculating and orthodox nature. It often crossed her mind that she had met her aim. The family's fortunes were safe in the hands of its heirs, and the lineage would not be extinguished. It was time for the appointed son, the saviour, to depart. She started looking for an opportunity to suggest this to Harshdev. While this thought festered in her mind, she grew resentful of Harshdev's manner. He lorded it over her daughters-in-law, had a free-and-easy deportment as the master of the household, and treated the family wealth as his own. Even before she could voice her thoughts to Harshdev, she started plotting to remove him.

One day, fortune smiled on her. Harshdev bought a horse from a group of itinerant merchants for a thousand gold coins. The son of a courtier, he used to ride and to carry and use weapons. He had often longed to go out deer hunting and to enjoy the taste of freshly roasted meat. Kritpunya's family were vegetarians.

He rode the horse home, humming and imagining the pressure of the bow on his thumb. At the threshold, he called out to his third wife to pay his fellow rider, one of the merchants, a thousand coins. The mother-in-law came out instead, eyes blazing in anger. 'One thousand coins! What for?'

'I have bought this horse, Mother.'

'And what for?'

'To go riding in the forest once in a while.'

'Then you can go riding forever. Consider yourself a free man.'

The merchant looked away in embarrassment. Harshdev was stunned. 'What does that mean?'

'Ah, Innocent One, you ask what it means? I appointed you, remember? Now your appointment is over. I have met my aims. And you – you have a resolution to fulfil. Go ahead and do it now.'

Harshdev closed his eyes for a moment. Then he gaped at her. 'Then I am no longer your son Kritpunya?'

'That is right, young man.'

The merchant had withdrawn to a corner of the street, out of courtesy. Harshdev waved to thank him. 'I see. Then I shall go to the court and say that you deprive me of my rights. Everyone knows that I am Kritpunya.'

'Yes, you can do that, and I shall say that you are an impostor who deceived me and polluted my family's honour. You will hang. When were you ever my Kritpunya?'

The third wife stepped out and whispered, 'Mother, this is not right. This argument will make my son illegitimate and disqualify our heirs from inheriting the property. Do we want that?'

'But what do you want me to do? Shall we bear with this cunning man's whims all our lives? And let him do as he pleases with my husband's and son's money?'

'If you must, send him away but pay his fee.'

'What fee?'

Harshdev was angry now. 'Did you not promise a fee?'

'And did you not eat, drink and make merry here?' The old woman asked. 'Remember how you were, lean, dirty, with your ribs showing when I selected you. How have you eaten and drunk? Look at your belly now!'

'Foolish woman! How dare you!' Harshdev unsheathed his sword, and it glinted in the afternoon sun. 'You measure my belly now, don't you? I shall behead you!'

The old woman's jaw dropped, and she burst into tears. 'Mother, do not do this', the wife said. 'The neighbours will soon come and ask questions. Our secret will be revealed, and our name ruined.'

'Tell him to go away', the old woman said, sobbing.

'I will go now!' Harshdev said. 'Not because of you, Villainous Woman, but to save my honour.' He rode the horse to the end of the street. Dismounting, he said to the merchant, 'My friend, I am sorry. I cannot buy your horse now. You have seen enough. Take this horse away, and for your trouble…here, take this ring.' He pulled a ring off his finger, and the merchant accepted it with a salute.

Harshdev strode back to the doorway and threw away his costly ornaments and layers of clothing, trembling with rage. He undressed until he only had a simple cloak around him.

The four wives were out now. They were all teary-eyed but dared not rebel against the old lady. The third wife said, with a catch in her voice, 'If you must go, do not leave empty-handed. This is not the way. Wait a minute. Let me prepare something for your journey.'

The mother-in-law did not object. When the wife came back, she brought a packet with two large sweets, fragrant with ghee. She also slid a handful of gems into Harshdev's hand. She smiled through her tears and whispered, 'Go to Champa, dear. Wait for me at my father's place. You know where it is.'

She broke down and ran into the house. Harshdev looked at the road ahead. He was a wanderer again.

CHAPTER 26

IN THE FORESTS OF CHAMPA

The sun was past its zenith. On the distant horizon, dark shadows were visible at the foot of the thickly wooded hills. The trees on the hilltops bathed in a golden light. In front of the seven riders was a deep valley. The uneven ground made the tired horses slow down. Somprabh and Kundani led in silence, the five guards following them with their eyes darting around.

At the mouth of the valley, Somprabh said, 'Kundani, let us speed up. If what they said is true, beyond the green meadow at the end of this valley, we will see the gates of Champa.'

'Yes, Som, but this valley has a reputation. I am sure you know it is the base of the Asur King. There are enough horror stories about him. Death is certain for anyone getting caught in his web. Legend has it he is hundreds of years old, and he sacrifices a man to his deity every day. He is a sorcerer and has the strength of ten elephants.'

'Well, we have to survive him, as we have survived the others before him. Let us hope our luck will hold, and we will get past the valley without trouble. Let us try to cross it before the sun has set.'

'Yes, let us try. I just feel uneasy. There is something about the air here.'

'Do you not trust me, Kundani?'

'It is not that, Som. I am just warning you. If we come up against the Asurs here, do not try to use your strength. We will need to use our brains to survive.'

Somprabh smiled. 'Show me the way, Kundani!'

She did not smile back. 'Follow me', she said.

Somprabh drew his horse next to hers. 'Kundani, the acharya said you are my sister. Is it true?'

'Do you think Father would lie?'

'Why not, if he thinks it necessary?'

'And you?'

'Me too. Only fools shirk lies, like the untrained who fear weapons.'

'So, in your opinion falsehood is a weapon?'

'And a very effective one.'

This time Kundani laughed. 'Well, your argument is not worth refuting. But as it happens, Father did not lie.'

'But Aryaa Matangi said I have a sister, and it is not you.'

'Well, Som, barring the enemy, I am every man's sister.'

'I see you are not joking. But I can't understand you.'

'Don't try. Just as you cannot understand my father, you can't understand me. Let's leave it at that.'

'But, Kundani, I –'

An arrow swished past Kundani ear.

'Watch out', she shouted, 'enemies!'

Before she finished, Somprabh had thrown his heavy spear into the bush in front of them. The shrub moved violently, and someone shouted. Somprabh drew his sword and charged towards the bush. They had all drawn their swords, and they surrounded the bush before riding into it cautiously.

They saw a dark man, as dark as kohl, writhing in a clearing. The spear had pierced his ribs and reached into his lung. The man's head was small and flat-topped, his short and stocky body bare, except for a golden girdle around his waist, and his wound and his mouth were bleeding. On the ground next to him, another man sat dazed. The man raised his hands and said some words which could only mean that he was begging for his life.

Som signalled he would spare him. Then he pointed to the wounded man, and asked, stumbling on the Asur words, whether the wounded one was an Asur.

Visibly elated at hearing his language, the other man replied in the affirmative. 'Check whether he is dead or alive', Somprabh said.

The Asur looked at his comrade and felt his vein at his neck. 'He is alive, but will not survive this', he said.

Somprabh ordered the wounded man some water. As soon as the guard followed his order, the man hiccoughed for the last time, and then his eyes closed.

Somprabh looked carefully at the second Asur. His girdle was solid gold, and his eyes had a shine in them. He spoke again, searching for the right words. 'Was he King Shambhar's man? The Asur King?'

At the mention of Shambhar, the Asur nodded vigorously.

'I have spared your life. Will you guide us to Champa?'

The Asur nodded. But he said something Somprabh did not understand. He paused, pointed his arm to the depths of the valley, and said 'Shambhar' twice.

'Is there danger there?' Somprabh asked.

'Yes', the Asur said.

'Is there another way?' Somprabh had to repeat the question before the Asur understood him.

'Yes, but very long.' The Asur counted on his fingers. 'Seven days.'

'And this way?' Somprabh pointed to the valley.

'One day.' The Asur lifted a finger.

Somprabh looked at Kundani. She shrugged. 'We cannot afford a week', he said. She nodded.

'Take us from the valley', he ordered the Asur.

The Asur ran a finger across his throat. Somprabh raised his sword. 'Do not worry! You are with me', he said.

'The sword will not save you', the Asur said. This time Somprabh understood him, and – he suspected – so did Kundani.

Somprabh sighed. He had cleaned his spear and pointed it at the Asur. 'If you betray us, you will die.'

The Asur prostrated himself, and when he got up, he touched a mark on his girdle. It seemed to bear a special significance. 'I will protect you till my death', he said.

The party followed on their horses as the Asur led them on foot. As they descended into the valley, the air became oppressive with strange fragrances.

'We are walking right into the mouth of danger, Kundani!' Somprabh said.

'Yes, it seems so.'

'Do you want to return?'

'That is not an option.'

'And are you afraid, Kundani?'

'No, Som, not anymore. It is useless.'

Somprabh smiled at her, and they marched on without talking. Darkness was descending on the valley. The Asur pointed to a waterfall, some distance away. 'For today we should stop there', he said.

Somprabh looked around. The approach to the place was visible on all sides. Soon it would be very dark. He nodded his assent. The party dismounted and stretched their tired limbs.

'Is there hunting here?' Somprabh asked the Asur.

The Asur shook his head and smiled. He motioned for Somprabh to wait. In a short while, he returned with his arms full of roots and fruits. They made a meal of the Asur's harvest. Later, they agreed on a sequence of guard duties and went to sleep. Sleep descended on them at once.

CHAPTER 27

IN SHAMBHAR'S LAIR

Somprabh woke with a start. At first, he thought it was a nightmare. The Asur was trussing him up. Through his bleary eyes, in the darkness, he could distinguish another one tying Kundani's hands and feet. She lay unconscious, like the five guards. He tried to crane his neck and look around him. Some ten yards away, a bright blue and purple flame burnt, giving out a strange smell. Somprabh felt that inhaling the air sucked out the energy from his body. His weapons were right beside him, but he could not so much as lift a finger. He tried to call out to Kundani, but he could not utter a syllable.

Suddenly, he felt a desire and an energy course through him. He was on his feet and started walking away. He looked back and saw Kundani following him, taking small steps, and walking like someone in a trance. Then, they formed a procession – Somprabh, Kundani, the Asur and the guards. He opened his mouth to talk to Kundani, but no words came out. Their horses joined them. It seemed as if a puppet master was manipulating the party.

The Asur was behind them, speaking to an invisible presence in halting words that Somprabh could not decipher. Now and then a strange noise pierced the crickets' songs and echoed in the hills. The Asur spoke as if he replied to the sound. His tone sounded pleading and desperate.

Paleness had diffused into the eastern sky, obscuring the stars. The strange, involuntary journey continued. Now, their feet took them towards and into the mouth of a deep dark cave. The young Asur produced a purplish-blue flame that showed the hugeness of the cave. They trudged along the path he chose for them. After an unknown time span, they saw a light at the other end of the cave. Somprabh felt as if a heavy stupor had lifted, and he was wide awake again after a long slumber.

It was a brilliant sunny day. The pleasant sunshine lit up a vast, lush green plain surrounded by low hills, at the centre of which stood a charming village. Its houses, made of mud and stone and topped with thatched roofs, were small but clean and neatly laid out. Bamboo fences marked their boundaries. The streets were broad and clean. The visible animals were well-kept and healthy, and their pens were clean. With their shiny kohl complexions, the Asur women wore red rubies and snow-white pearl necklaces, long skirts of animal skin and big gold bracelets on their wrists. They watched the helpless prisoners trudging by with curiosity. Their children, who seemed to think the party would provide entertainment, chattered and gesticulated in excitement. The young women were commenting on Kundani's looks, with blatant envy. Despite her exhaustion, she looked like a jungle goddess, with her bright clothes and regal bearing. She stepped close to Somprabh.

'Som, this is the legendary Asur City', she said. 'We heard so many stories about it. We are lucky to see it with our own eyes. Yet it is so small, clean, and pleasant. Aren't you surprised?'

'I am surprised to see Kundani enjoying herself and entering it without fear', Somprabh said, with a chuckle.

'What is there to fear, Som?'

'Ah, that we shall get to know by night when Shambhar sacrifices us to his gods.'

'Does he have so much power?'

'Have you not seen his power? Has he not brought us all the way here using no physical force?'

'If he is behind that, he is powerful, for sure. I do not know how we ended up here.'

'It must be the power of the Asurs, and perhaps it lasts only during the dark hours', Somprabh said.

'I see. Anyway, I was paralysed on the way here, but I am fully alert now. And when I am alert, I do not know fear.'

'I am thankful to have a companion like you. Perhaps this is a good time for me to say I have some regret I cannot make you my life partner.'

Kundani smiled sadly. 'Well, if we are sacrificed tonight, I will have become your life partner in a certain way. Tell me, are you terrified?'

'Should I not be?'

'Why should you be? Because you are helpless in the enemy's city? Is this what you imbibed at Takshila?'

Somprabh looked into Kundani's deep eyes and drew solace from their shine. 'You have a hidden strength, Kundani. What is it?'

Kundani said, 'Som, you too are a capable man.'

'If I weren't bound, if I had my sword in my hand, I would not worry about the enemy's numbers!'

'Oh, Som, you still think of bodily strength. Remember, here, we can only win our lives with our brains. Keep your head calm and wash away your fear. Let us enjoy the sights and the splendours of the Asur Kingdom.'

A blast of fanfare from a large group of instruments rent the air. The wind, string and percussion instruments had a pleasing harmony. They saw a massive red sandstone fort wall loom up ahead of them. Through holes in the turrets, they could discern heads peering at them. The enormous wooden doors made grinding noises as they were hauled open with rope pulleys. On the top of the fort wall, they could now see bare-chested, muscular, Asurs wearing animal skin waistcloths and golden girdles and holding large spears. Their black skins gave them the glint of polished bronze.

'Where did you learn the Asur language, Som?'

'In Gandhar. I got many opportunities during the Dev-Asur wars. When you fight a race over a long time, you end up learning their language. I talked to many Asur prisoners.'

'Then, Som, remember what I said. We must use our minds here. Join these Asurs and chant for their king, in their language!'

Somprabh looked at her with new respect. 'Victory to King Shambhar!' He shouted a few times in the Asur language. The crowd around them and the soldiers on the fort walls received his shouts with smiles and applause. They increased their tempo.

They crossed the main gate and walked along a cobbled street to a large hall. It seemed carved out of a mountain, and baked bricks strengthened it. Somprabh noted the excellence that had gone into the construction.

In the geometric centre of the hall was a raised stone throne. A large tiger skin covered the throne, and the tiger's fierce face had been preserved. Its teeth and claws added dramatic effect.

On the throne sat Shambhar. Large and very dark, he sat erect in the Lotus position, legs crossed. His age was difficult to guess, but his body was taut and muscular. Pearl and ruby necklaces of different sizes adorned his neck, and bands of gold-plated boars' tusks his arms. Instead of a crown, he wore a headdress that had two large gold-plated horns fixed on it. His very thick and curly hair had a reddish tinge and his moustache, streaks of grey. He had red sandalwood smeared on his forehead, and a golden plate covered his chest. Two massive spears were planted on either side of his throne. Four young Asur women freshened him with fans made of large feathers. One of them also held a wine pitcher, and two had incense lamps in hand. At an altar in front of the throne, they saw a purple and blue flame like the one they had seen earlier. The stone wall behind the throne displayed a carving of a terribly fierce animal. Shambhar wore bracelets of gold, and in his hand, held a thick sceptre that also looked like solid gold.

He had a deep, penetrating glance. Two older Asurs sat on tiger skins below the throne, one on either side of Shambhar.

Somprabh had seen many courts in his life, but none like this one. 'This Asur king appears to have a lot of gold', Somprabh muttered to Kundani.

'Hush! Greet him in his language!' Kundani said.

Somprabh nodded. He addressed King Shambhar and articulated in the Asur language. 'Greetings, King of Asurs, King Shambhar! Your fame has travelled everywhere, and today, humans and Gandharvs do not tire of retelling the stories of your feats. I, Somprabh, salute you!'

Shambhar smiled and said something to one of his ministers. Then he turned to Somprabh and roared. 'And are you human or Gandharv?'

'Human.'

'Where from?'

'Magadha.'

'Hmm. I know the chief of Magadha, Bimbisar. He is no friend of mine. Why did you trespass into my kingdom? Do you know this is punishable by death, without exception?'

'The all-powerful Shambhar has laid down this rule for enemies, not for friends. The great Bimbisar wishes to establish a friendship with Shambhar.'

After conferring in whispers with his two ministers, the Asur King pronounced his view. 'Bimbisar has Asur origins, but he is no longer my friend as he chose to defect to the Devs. He now is my sworn enemy.'

'He specifically wishes to establish a friendship with you! I am his emissary, and I bring you the message of friendship.'

Shambhar stroked his chin and again consulted his ministers. He said, 'What is the proof of it?'

'I am here without our mighty army. What bigger proof can there be?'

Shambhar spoke to his ministers for a longer time. 'Who is that beautiful woman?' He asked, pointing to Kundani.

'She is with me and is from Magadha.'

'Bimbisar should send me a hundred such beauties, and I would be his friend.'

Somprabh's face turned red, and he clenched his biceps. Kundani noticed his reaction right away. 'Do not do or say anything stupid', she said in a whisper. 'What is he saying?'

'He is asking for a hundred girls like you in tribute.'

'I see. Well, tell him that Magadhan women have lightning in their bodies. Touching one means instant death for Asurs.'

Shambhar said, 'What is the beautiful girl saying?'

The turn of events troubled Somprabh. Pushed on by Kundani, he said, 'She says Emperor Bimbisar can meet the condition Your Majesty suggests. However, because of the lightning in their bodies, Magadhan women can only unite with their own men. Asurs who unite with them will die on contact.'

Shambhar grunted. 'I have travelled the world in my youth. Gandhar, Persia, the realm of the Gandharvs – I have seen them all. I have kidnapped Dev and Gandharv women. The code of the Asurs allows it. We have enjoyed these Dev and Gandharv girls – what would stop us from enjoying the Magadhans?'

As she saw Somprabh trembling with rage, Kundani asked him, 'What does he say now?' She heard Somprabh out and then explained he must say this is a boon granted by our goddess. 'We are protected from contact with the Asurs.'

Shambhar replied, 'I see. We shall test the truth of this statement on the one Magadhan woman before us.'

When Kundani saw Somprabh's eyes redden, she gripped his hand and asked him what Shambhar had said. He translated Shambhar's words to her.

She said, 'Remember what I said. We will get out of this in a different way. This situation demands no military or diplomatic skill. I know what it requires.' She smiled. 'Tell him we are sure of what we say. If he wants to risk lives, he can do so. Tell him the king of serpents, Vasuki, has granted me his favours.'

Shambhar raised his eyebrows, and asked in a loud voice, 'What does the woman say?'

Somprabh translated Kundani's words, and they held each other's hand in a tight grip while Shambhar conferred with his ministers. After a while, Shambhar said, 'We are in no hurry. We shall think about it. Till then, you are our guests.'

He turned to his ministers. 'We shall feast and dance today. Inform the city, beat the drums!' Then he turned to Somprabh and spoke matter-of-factly. 'You are not fearful, I see that. If the chief of Magadha does not meet my condition, I shall sacrifice this woman first, and then you and the rest of your group, to our god. Now you can go and rest.'

He made a signal with his finger, and his men swarmed over the captives to disarm and untie them. Kundani, Somprabh and the five guards were herded to their rooms to rest.

CHAPTER 28

KUNDANI'S CAMPAIGN

Somprabh made the best possible use of the little independence he had in the city of Asurs by walking back along the path they had traversed in the morning. He was aware of the watchful eyes of Shambhar's men, but they did not trouble him. When he returned, tired and listless, to the cave where he and Kundani had been put up, he screamed at the sight that awaited him. Kundani sat on a stone covered with a tiger skin in the middle of the cave. In her hand, she composedly held the snake that had horrified Somprabh when he first came across it many days before. The snake had coiled around Kundani's neck, and she calmly held its hood, wide as a hand, as if it was a mirror she was holding to herself. Only her eyes betrayed any sign that something exceptional was happening. They had a reddened, intoxicated look, and their rolling motion made Somprabh dizzy. Kundani's eyes seemed locked with the snake's.

Somprabh's scream made Kundani loosen her grip for a moment. The snake bit her, gently, on the lip. Somprabh leapt forward, grabbed the snake and threw it away.

'What have you done now, Kundani?' He cried.

'Don't be a fool, Somprabh', she said. 'What if you kill the serpent? Father brought this extremely poisonous snake of the Takshak clan all the way from the jungles of Cambodia. It has no par. Even if you hurt it…'

She stood on her feet, swaying a bit. She walked to the snake, picked it up and held it to her heart. The snake was a shadow of its former self.

'Kundani, I don't understand you. The acharya appointed me your protector. But here in this world, I don't know…'

'Then stay my protector. And don't try to understand things that are beyond you.' Kundani's eyes flashed.

'But what is all this – what were you doing?'

'I was doing what is right.'

'Do you mean suicide? I know they have disarmed me, but–'

'Does the snake's bite kill me? Did you not realise it the first time?'

'You perplex me. Who are you, really?'

'Father has already told you. I am your sister. Don't ask me anymore.'

'I have to ask. We need to get out of here, and I don't know how. I spent the day roaming the city, and there seems to be no way. Shambhar has given us notional freedom, but we are still prisoners.'

'We are prisoners', Kundani said, 'but there was no need for you to wander in search of a solution. You would have been better off resting here. It is cool, and you could have slept well.'

'I doubt it. Not that it is not a pleasant place to sleep in – it's just that in this hour of trouble I don't think I would find sleep.'

'But the hour of trouble will only come after the feast, don't you think?'

'True enough, but should I have waited, lying there with my legs stretched out?'

'I think so. You would have rested, calmed your nerves and faced the hour of crisis with renewed energy.'

'Oh Kundani, I must say I admire you. My experience and skills have been reduced to nought, but I could learn to face the Asurs without fear the way you seem to.'

'I am not who I am for nothing, Som! Remember the unusual things you have seen, and take heart from my fearlessness. My training would have been useless if I feared the Asurs today.'

'What do you aim to do?' Somprabh asked, puzzled.

'What is there to say? Either Shambhar accepts our message of friendship, or he dies with his Asurs.'

'Dies? Who will kill them?'

'Why, I shall. Who else?'

Somprabh laughed in disbelief. But he immediately stopped and, unsmiling again, said, 'You have a plan. I do not want to probe into your secrets, no doubt related to sorcery. But tell me enough that I can help you!'

'Som, you are a warrior, and you have been chosen for a great task! Take note – I am younger than you, and a woman. But I am the one developing a calm and methodical approach here. What you thought might be suicide was actually preparing to deal a death blow to the enemy.'

'But…how?'

'You will see for yourself when the times comes. I still have some work to do now. Why don't you get some rest? We will soon have to show courage. I know the Asurs do not eat before midnight.'

'So, you want me to do nothing? Is that my role?'

Kundani sighed. 'I have told you, Brother – be calm, be ready and be clever when the time comes. Where is inactivity in all this?'

'I see. But my weapons…'

'They confiscated them, true, but you have your wits about you.'

'Perhaps I do', Somprabh said with a smile. He took a deep breath and looked around. He selected a buffalo skin mattress to lie down on. When he woke up from a deep sleep, Kundani was shaking him. His bleary eyes made out the shapes of many Asur warriors at the mouth of the cave. Some of them held flaming torches, and the others, musical instruments. A middle-aged man with a gold shield strapped to his chest, and a long spear in his arm, led the group.

By the bright, flickering light of the torches, Somprabh saw that Kundani's beauty had multiplied manifold. Her thick, plaited black hair reached her knees, swaying like a she-serpent. She had interwoven pearls along the parting line of her hair, and her white forehead gleamed to give her a magical aura. She wore a red silk blouse over her full breasts, and a sapphire hung between them. A matching red skirt with a silver girdle accentuated her hourglass figure. Her anklets gave each of her steps music that added to her allure.

'Kundani, are you trying to create the look of a goddess?'

'Perhaps – the Asurs are lucky. Get dressed quickly', she said, smiling. She pointed to a tiger skin. 'Wrap that around your body, you will find it useful.'

'We have to go unarmed to the enemy', Somprabh said, as he hastened to change.

'Not unarmed. Just go with the three things I mentioned.'

'You mean I should be calm, ready and clever? Is that all?'

'Indeed!'

Somprabh inhaled and looked at the lines on his palms. 'I am ready. Kundani, you are the commander today.'

'As you say', Kundani said with a dazzling smile that radiated confidence. The guards who had accompanied them were nowhere in sight. She walked out and spoke in Magadhi to the Asur leader. She told him they should lead the way, and she and Somprabh would follow. He understood her meaning, and – such was her commanding presence – he hastened to order his men to do her bidding.

Soon, her anklets dancing bells rang on the Asur city Royal Path, and the men joined the procession as if spellbound.

•

Somprabh whispered, 'Kundani, it looks like you have mastery of all of them!'

'And of their energy', Kundani said, smiling.

CHAPTER 29

THE FEAST OF THE ASURS

The preparations for the feast were in full swing in a field at the centre of the fort. A huge, blazing fire roared on a platform. A whole buffalo was being roasted in the fire. Asurs of all generations, from toddlers to grandparents roamed around it, their faces lit with excitement and their shouts and laughter welding into a raucous commotion. As soon as Kundani and Somprabh entered the field, their hands clasped to each other, the noise reached a crescendo. A high rock slab had a tiger skin placed on it. It might have been for Shambhar, but Kundani walked towards it without hesitation and sat on it. The Asurs gasped and chattered. They seemed to ask one another whether Shambhar would tolerate this. The Asurs knew their king's might and temper. Kundani knew his weakness.

She said to Somprabh, 'Som, tell them to get the wine pitchers here.'

Somprabh spoke to the leader of the group that had escorted them to the field, and he transmitted the message. In no time, the pitchers had accumulated at Kundani's feet. The musicians struck up a loud performance. The Asurs looked with apprehension at Shambhar, who strode into the field. He had dressed for the occasion with a golden two-horned crown and a golden breastplate. He had on a new tiger-skin waistcloth and shining gold bands on his lower arms. A different set of pearl and ruby necklaces adorned his neck.

Somprabh said, 'Won't you vacate his throne, Kundani?'

'No, I will not', she said. 'And tell me fast, how do you say, "To the Great King Shambhar's health and life!"?' Somprabh helped to pronounce the syllables and make them more guttural. Immediately, she stood up and shouted out the toast in a clear voice. The Asurs, young and old, took their cups from her hands and repeated the toast.

Shambhar saw the proceedings and could not help smiling. He stepped up to the throne, and said, 'Give me a cup with your hands, woman! I like this!'

Kundani grabbed a large cup, jumped off the throne and danced around Shambhar with the cup in her hands, and then on her head. Her eyes were full of mischief. Shambhar beamed with pleasure. 'Woman, give me my cup!' He ordered.

Kundani became more playful. She took the cup to Shambhar's lips, and he leant forward, but then like a flash, she whisked it away and held it to an old minister's mouth instead. The old man guzzled it down, laughing uncontrollably. She beckoned Somprabh for another cup, and this time she repeated her act, only to give the cup to a young man, who broke into a wild dance. That set all the Asurs dancing around Shambhar and Kundani.

Now, Kundani took a whole pitcher from Somprabh and danced with the pitcher balanced on her head. The Asurs went wild. 'Tell them', she shouted, 'to toast Shambhar each time!' The cheering, the dancing, the fumes of wine and the music were making Somprabh giddy. By now, some asuras had started drinking wine straight from the pitchers. Kundani took up one pitcher, and flashing a brilliant smile, held it to Shambhar's lips. He gulped all of it down without a pause and then swayed with his eyes closed.

Kundani whispered to Somprabh, keeping her smile intact, 'We have got them the way we wanted. They will die today, each of them. We just have to keep them drinking. Make sure you always hold a cup and give me one – just take it from that pitcher over there.' She motioned with her eyes to a pitcher set at a crooked angle.

'You are incredible, Kundani', Somprabh whispered back, as he kept the flow of wine going.

The wine now produced its effect on the revellers, who laughed, danced and joked among themselves. Women and children were also inebriated. Shambhar was tottering, but still dancing with Kundani, while talking in a slurred voice.

'What is he saying?' Kundani asked Somprabh.

'Mostly that he wants to make you his queen.'

Laughingly, Kundani said, 'That is what I would have guessed. I shall take care of him. Make sure the others also drink themselves silly. Not a single one of them should be alert. Don't leave a drop of wine in the pitchers.'

'I think our problems are a lot less severe now', Somprabh said. 'You have half-slain them with your smile.'

Kundani laughed. Shambhar stepped closer to her and put an arm around her waist. 'Woman, come closer to me!' He said.

Kundani said, 'Poor Asur, you are about to embrace death.'

'What does she say?' Shambhar asked.

'She says the men don't seem to drink fast enough', Somprabh said.

'Ah, they have just got started! Drink up, fellows!' He bellowed as Kundani handed him a pitcher. He took a gulp from it and tottered.

A group of Asurs started chanting, 'Feast, feast!'

Shambhar tried to make a speech, hiccoughing as he spoke. 'In honour of this Manav woman from Magadha, all eat and drink as you can…hic…I allow you…And you, Magadhan, enjoy yourself!' Then he leant on Kundani for support.

Kundani asked Somprabh for a quick translation, as she steered Shambhar to a seated position on the rock. She sat by him and invited Somprabh to sit on the other side. Some men had now started cutting up the buffalo meat, and their haste showed they had worked up a healthy appetite.

The buffalo's head was placed on a sizeable plate, and a large group of Asur women carried it around the throne, dancing, and chanting. The plate passed on from one swaying woman to the next, the woman receiving it singing new lines of the song. Finally, one beauty knelt before Shambhar, greeted Kundani and Somprabh, and offered it to the king.

Shambhar staggered to his feet, took out a knife from a sheath and cut off the buffalo's tongue. He placed it on a small gold plate, and offered it to Kundani, talking all the time.

'What does he say?' Kundani asked.

'He says this is a mark of respect. Getting the tongue means that he grants you the highest honour.'

'Thank him on my behalf, Som', Kundani said, 'and ask them to drink a toast to me.'

Somprabh shouted out Kundani's message.

Shambhar led the Asurs in a toast, shouting: 'Magadhan beauty! Magadhan woman!' They gulped down more wine. Then they attached the food like starving animals. Kundani plied Shambhar with more wine, and Somprabh passed around another set of pitchers into the crowd.

Still chewing on the meat, with his head rocking, Shambhar said, 'Now, Magadhan beauty, dance for us!'

'Now', Kundani said to Somprabh.

Somprabh stood up and shouted loud and clear. 'The Great King Shambhar has accepted King Bimbisar's friendship. Should we not drink to this new friendship?'

Shambhar eyes were lolling. 'Ah, yes, friendship…but we will have a hundred such beauties…'

Kundani started dancing, going close to the Asurs. As if a river dam had burst, they drooled and reached out for her as she cleverly danced away from each of them, creating a trail of swooning admirers.

CHAPTER 30

THE KISS OF DEATH

Kundani nodded to Somprabh. Somprabh stood, clanged two plates for silence and shouted, 'Listen, everyone. Here is a Magadhan beauty Asurs cannot enjoy. Whoever kisses her shall die!'

The Asurs had lost their senses by then. 'Kiss her, kiss her!' They shouted.

Shambhar threw away his pitcher and stammered, 'Yes…k-kiss her!'

Somprabh's face reddened with anger, but Kundani talked to him with her eyes. He gulped his rage down. 'Whoever kisses her shall die. The great Shambhar should not forget that!'

'This Shambhar knows everything. He has known many women – Dev, Manav, Gandharv – and there is nothing like this. Yes, give…give me a hundred such women!' His eyes were wide, and his breathing ragged with excitement.

Kundani had started dancing. The Asurs gathered around her, gawking at her graceful, sinuous moves. From among the pitchers, she took out a cloth bag. Before the Asurs amazed eyes, she held a slithering black cobra and wrapped it around her neck. The Asurs jumped backwards by reflex. Kundani kept dancing, getting closer to Shambhar as if daring him to kiss her.

Shambhar's eyes narrowed. 'What – what is she doing with that snake, Manav?' He asked Somprabh.

Somprabh said, 'She is a snake's consort. The snake will kiss her first, and then whoever is ready to face death can kiss her.'

'Let the snake kiss her then! All drink a toast to the snake god!' The Asurs shouted their cheers and drank up again.

As her audience watched, spellbound, Kundani brought the snake's hood closer to her mouth, and it bit her gently. She put the snake away in the bag. When she began her dance, her forehead glistened with beads of sweat, and she swayed like a woman possessed by an animal spirit. At times, she seemed suspended in the air, hanging by invisible threads. Her eyes were intoxicated, her lips swollen.

The Asurs were beyond any control at this point. A young man stepped forward, hugged her and kissed her on the lips. He collapsed as if struck by lightning. Somprabh was dumbstruck. He had seen nothing like this in his years of travel. Kundani fixed her eyes on the next youth, and he lunged for her. He too fell in a heap. After that, the Asurs, propelled by what seemed a force of nature, reached out to kiss her and fall lifeless. The two older ministers shrank back in fear, but Kundani embraced them and reduced them to still heaps.

Shambhar was still drinking, seated on the ground.

Somprabh gulped as Kundani danced near them. 'Kundani! So, you are a snake woman?'

'This is no time to talk about that. Be careful – look, his mood is changing.'

Shambhar was no longer the jovial drunk. He had seen the havoc Kundani had wrought in a few moments. Kundani gave him an enticing smile and handed him a cup of wine. He flung it away. 'Did you lay waste my men?'

When Somprabh translated the question for her, Kundani, still smiling, told him to use the weapons by Shambhar's throne, but only if necessary.

Somprabh said, 'The all-powerful Shambhar ignored her warning, and mine – we repeated it many times! And the king gave the order to kiss her.'

'This Manava woman is dreadful – I don't know where she…' His head lolled.

'King, Magadhan men can also be dreadful when antagonised. Do you not wish to accept our chief Bimbisar's offer of friendship?'

'The woman is terrible…a snake woman.' He looked thirstily at her. He tried to stand up but staggered and fell back. Kundani gave him yet another pitcher with a smile. This time he took and drained it as if he sought energy in it. With an effort, he made it to his feet.

Meanwhile, most other Asurs had run away, terrified at the dance of death they had seen. Some of them sat dazed by what had happened. Heaped bodies lay scattered all around. The flickering flames added to the unreal atmosphere.

Shambhar's gold crown gleamed as he stood straight, looking at Kundani with longing. He gulped down the pitcher and lurched towards Kundani. 'Give me – give me a kiss, even if it means death. Ah…'

In an instant, Kundani slid out of his encircling arms, returning to him with yet another pitcher she held to his lips. She gave Somprabh a nod. Shambhar started drinking from the pitcher, but by then he had reached his limit. He threw it aside and grasped Kundani again. 'Yes, a kiss. And in return…you wanted…. Friendship for Bimbisar, yes.'

Kundani looked at Somprabh. She seemed to hesitate before condemning Shambhar to death. Somprabh intervened and pulled Shambhar away. 'No, we shall not kill Shambhar', he said. He bent and spoke into Shambhar's ear. 'You have offered your friendship to Bimbisar. You must live. Long live Shambhar.'

Shambhar's lips moved, but they did not form words. He fell like a log of wood, with a loud thump. At this, the few Asurs who remained fled the spot.

Somprabh clutched Kundani's arm. 'Shall we leave him as he is?'

'Don't be a fool', Kundani said. 'Kill him.'

'No, I don't think we should. We should just get away.'

The young Asur who had led them earlier was straggling up towards them. He prostrated himself and said, 'It is time to run. Pick up that trident, it will be useful, and let us go. I know the way to Champa.'

Kundani whisked a small knife out of her plait. 'I also have this – I have dipped it in poison, and it is far more lethal than it looks.'

'Your wonders will never cease', Somprabh muttered, as they followed their Asur friend at a slow and steady run. The Asurs in the field were in no position to stop them, but at the gate were four alert guards.

Kundani walked up to them without fear. She said, 'Fools, you have not kissed me.' She embraced one of them, who was surprised but did not resist. He tumbled as soon as Kundani's lips reached his. One of them made a hissing sound and pointed his spear at Kundani, but Somprabh killed him on the spot with the trident. Kundani's knife and Somprabh's dagger dispatched the other two.

In a few more moments, they had secured their horses, and Somprabh, Kundani and their friend were riding under the stars, glad to leave the City of Asurs behind them.

CHAPTER 31

IN CHAMPA

Chandrabhadrik, the Army Chief of Magadha, stepped into the tent. His officers were ready. He looked at the group with quiet satisfaction. 'Men, it is five days to the festival of Baisakhi. These five days will decide the fate of this army and that of the ancient Kingdom of Champa. If we breach the fort of Champa on Baisakhi Day, Magadha's empire will extend to all the eastern islands. If we fail, in my estimation, none of us will return alive to Magadha.' He waited for the reaction.

One officer said, 'Chief, we are in deplorable condition. Arya Varshkar has not sent us help. We can only do so much. If we lose, the responsibility will be Arya Varshkar's.'

'No, Sir, not so. We are responsible for the outcome. Let us step up to take complete responsibility', Chandrabhadrik said.

'We have besieged the fort for a full three months, away from our supply lines. This is no small feat, Chief.'

'No, it is not. But we will be judged on the outcome. If we can breach the fort in five days, we shall win. If we cannot, Magadha will suffer a blow that will take centuries to recover from and will forever dash our ambitions to extend our influence in the east.' He turned to one man. 'Brij, is there any hope of food supplies?'

'I am afraid not.'

'So, whatever we could do, we have done?'

'There is a slim chance – with time, we may get help from Rajgrih.'

'If that is the case…many of our men are injured, most of the horses are not useful anymore. We have suffered hunger and thirst, but…If we do not get supplies, fighting on will only mean more casualties, with the same outcome.' Chandrabhadrik crossed his arms behind his back and closed his eyes. 'What are your thoughts on accepting Champa's terms? Is it better than a grinding descent into defeat?'

'Is this Arya Chandrabhadrik speaking? The same Arya Bhadrik whose exploits the ministers of Persia never tire of repeating?' The tone was loud but polite.

'Who are you, young man?' Chandrabhadrik asked.

Somprabh stepped forward, dressed in the simple attire of a farmer. Chandrabhadrik could not recognise him.

'Who are you, and by what right do you lecture me in that tone, at such a time?' Chandrabhadrik repeated.

'Honoured Chief, I am Somprabh. I come from Rajgrih, with help from Arya Varshkar. This is his letter.'

Those in the council who had not seen Somprabh enter craned their heads to get a better glimpse of him. Chandrabhadrik took the letter and broke the seal. After reading it, he said, 'Where is the help, young man? This is just an order to enter Champa on Baisakhi Day, which we know is our last chance, anyway.' His forehead was furrowed, and his lips pursed.

'That is not obvious, Chief.'

'But the plan of action?'

'May I suggest something, Chief?'

'Surely! Arya Varshkar has written a few things about you.'

'If you trust me, on Baisakhi Day, the people of Champa will see the Magadhan flag fluttering over their city.'

'And how?'

'If you can trust me, I shall deliver that outcome with your help.'

Chandrabhadrik frowned. 'How did you get into this tent, young man?'

'I got to know today's password, Sir, by chance', Somprabh grinned.

'Hmm. That is extraordinary.'

'Sir, I am not an ordinary man.'

'We shall see, we shall see.' Chandrabhadrik smiled. 'But what do you want to do?'

'We still have four days, Sir. We shall accomplish much in this time.'

'And what will my men eat in these four days?'

'Your army will get rations tonight.'

'I see. And to get my men ready for action…We need to replenish our weaponry.'

'A hundred soldiers will reach here tonight.'

'Just a hundred!'

'You only have to check the enemy, Sir. Those soldiers will do the rest.'

'We lack armour. Ours is not good enough for the enemy's arrows.'

'That is easy to solve. I saw many broken boats. We need to fill them with sand and them for our defence. I have seen this the Gandhars use this technique to good effect in the Indus wars.'

'Are you a Gandhar officer?'

'No, I am Magadhan. I studied at Takshila, under Acharya Bahulashavya.'

'I see! You have learnt from old Bahulashavya. Well, well, then I need not question you anymore. Gentlemen, do you have questions for this young man?'

The room was silent, but Chandrabhadrik sensed quiet approval. The fire was back in his officers' eyes. He nodded. 'Your plan is good', he said.

'We will need to get the boats over and filled with sand tonight, under cover of darkness.'

'We shall arrange it. And the hundred men?'

'They will reach by the third night watch.'

'Very well. And until then, you…'

'I will walk the city and prepare its map.'

'Do you need anything from us?'

'No, Sir. I shall take your leave.' Somprabh bowed and left, amidst loud murmurs of approval.

CHAPTER 32

A FRIEND IN THE ENEMY CITY

Somprabh's feet had trodden on many streets before he reached a small alley. He knocked on the door of a run-down house. A strong middle-aged man opened it, stepped aside to let him slip past, and shut the door quietly.

Inside, a room led to a courtyard. A stove burnt bright, exuding an infernal heat, and casting a reddish light on a team of workers toiling on weapons in various stages of readiness, their bodies glistening with sweat. The air was pungent with smoke.

The one who had opened the door said, 'Well, friend, what did the chief say?'

'They were morose, but they seem charged up now. Friend Ashvajit, all depends on you now. Tell me, what is to be done?'

'It is simple. On Baisakhi Night, my brother will guard the South Tower during the third watch.'

'I see.'

'Now your task is to reach the South Tower at the right time, with the best of your men.'

'How many men will be enough?'

'Not more than twenty. But be aware, the South Tower is at the mouth of the river, and you must climb very slippery rocks. You and your men will be tempting death, make no mistake.'

'We understand', Somprabh said. 'We will be on time.'

'That is enough planning. The rest of it we will plan on the spot.'

'Very well. Anything else?'

'Well, there is a lot more. We have enough weapons. I have armed the Magadhans in the city. When the South Tower is under attack, there will be a revolt in the city.'

'That is good. But I need something more.'

'And what is that?'

'I need a hundred soldiers. And they should carry food for five days.'

'You will get them.'

'And some more rations. The chief and his men are starving.'

'That is no problem either. He will get the soldiers and the rations tonight.'

'That is great. How will you manage it, friend?'

'Leave it to me. They will come from the South Tower. A fisher friend will help to move men and rations in the third watch.'

'Very well. I shall also need to use your fisher friend.'

'When?'

'On Baisakhi Night.'

'I see. Once he has dropped the soldiers and the food, he will find a place to hide for four days. When the time comes, he will be ready to help.'

'Thank you, my friend! Can I give the good news to the chief?'

'And my salute as well.'

Somprabh embraced his friend and retraced his steps.

CHAPTER 33

THE PERSIAN JEWELLER

A famous jeweller from Persia was staying at an inn in Champa. He had been a guest for many days, and his flamboyant, luxurious lifestyle attracted much gossip. His own bodyguards and a large contingent of soldiers from the Champa army guarded him day and night. He was most conspicuous because of his invisibility – no ordinary citizen had seen him yet. This fuelled the speculation about him to feverish heights.

One observation that kept tongues wagging was that each one of his bodyguards, from the lowest to their chief, spent money lavishly. They paid gold coins instead of copper, and nonchalantly forgot to take the change due to them. Gold seemed like dust to them. Yet it was the jeweller's daughter who was the talk of the town. Every evening, she rode out on her horse, with a retinue of maids and guards, throwing out coins to the poor, laughing and brushing aside the compliments and cries of gratitude she inspired. Her youth and beauty, her confidence and her lavish generosity made the jeweller and his daughter famous within a few days.

Two days before, one of the city's wealthiest merchants had paid the jeweller and his daughter a visit and invited them to his home. Now the king of Champa, Dadhivahan Dev himself, visited the inn. The innkeepers had worked frenetically to have the building decorated with flowers and lamps. Cavalrymen were roaming the street to manage the crowds.

The king made his entry with Princess Chandrabhadra at the end of the first night watch. The jeweller welcomed the king and the princess at the doorway and guided them to high seats. He asked his daughter to wash the king's feet. The jeweller's humility and refinement charmed the king, and his daughter's beauty even more. Princess Chandrabhadra took the jeweller's daughter's hand and made her sit next to her.

King Chandrabhadra said, 'Merchant! You are most welcome in Champa! We are pleased to see you. I hear you carry many priceless jewels. The princess would like to see them.'

The jeweller bowed profusely and asked an assistant to bring the jewel box. They placed the casket on a seat covered with silk and opened. Sifting through its contents, the jeweller brought out a string of large glowing pearls.

'May the king be pleased! Here is a jewel unfit to be sold because no human can pay its price. If I have your leave, I would like to gift it to the princess, and earn a good name.'

King Dadhivahan looked wide-eyed at the necklace. The jeweller stepped forward, and with polite gestures, placed it on the princess's neck. The princess jumped in elation and clapped her hands, not bothering to hide her glee.

'Now, Sir, by your permission, I can turn to jewellery within the realm of commerce. Perhaps the princess will like some items.'

He gestured, and on cue, a few big caskets joined the jewel box on the silk-covered seat. The princess absorbed herself in trying on ornaments, liking each more than the previous one. In the meantime, the jeweller's daughter and her coquettish glances visibly smote the king.

King Dadhivahan bought many ornaments to please his daughter. When he stood up to go, he said, 'We are pleased to have you in the city. As you know, we are under siege by the army of Magadha. Your young daughter must have been inconvenienced by the situation.'

'Thank you for your concern, Sir', the jeweller said. 'Her mother is no longer alive, and I am grateful the princess has been so friendly to her.'

'Well, the princess had heard of your daughter, and we are happy to see her. She is welcome to stay in the palace, as my daughter's guest.' He glanced at the jeweller's daughter and enjoyed seeing her blush.

The jeweller said, 'She is fortunate. I can see it will delight her to be the princess' companion. She is all alone here.'

Princess Chandrabhadra clasped her newfound friend's hand. 'Come, friend, I have been looking for a close friend. We will have fun, I promise you.'

The girl smiled shyly. The merchant's assistant placed a veil on her shoulder. While he arranged it with the fuss typical of an old-time servant, he whispered in her ear, unheard by anyone else, 'On Baisakhi Night, at the end of the fourth watch.' He bowed away.

The young woman touched her father's feet, and their eyes seemed to speak to each other.

The girl was Kundani.

After the king had departed with the princess and Kundani, the jeweller ordered the door to be closed. Once the others had gone, he removed his wig and mask with extreme care. He stretched and yawned like an actor exhausted after a long performance.

'My friend Somprabh, all went well', he said.

'Yes, Arya.'

'Will the army chief Bhadrik do his part?'

'I have seen to it.'

'And Ashvajit will do his work?'

'Yes, Sir. He has become a blacksmith. He has armed all the Magadhans in the city.'

'Perfect. And how many are they?'

'More than a thousand and two hundred.'

'Good. The merchant Dhanik has bought many promissory notes issued by Champa from other merchants on my order. On the morning of Baisakhi Day, he will trigger their demand for encashment. I know how much gold there is in the treasury – almost none. King Dadhivahan will need to borrow money even to pay me for the jewels he has bought. He will be in no position to honour the promissory notes.'

'The Magadhans will revolt, and the default will be one of the stated causes of the uprising. But Kundani?'

'She will find her path. By the fourth watch of Baisakhi Night, Dadhivahan shall be dead.'

'At that moment, at the West Tower, the guards shall have been subdued, and a Magadhan trumpet will sound. That will be the signal for the Magadhan army to storm into the open doors and take control of the fort.'

'The plan will work, yes. I will slip away. Announce that I have taken ill and maintain this until Baisakhi Day. I will not be available for socialising. Your line will be that I do not want to infect anyone.'

'As you command, Arya. But –'

'Wait. You, Som, will leave for Sravasti by the fourth watch of the night. Do not wait until morning to see the Magadhan flag fluttering over Champa. The emperor is miserable.' Acharya Varshkar, for that is who the jeweller was, turned pensive for a moment. Then he stood and clapped his hands.

A servant appeared.

'How much of the night has passed?' Acharya Varshkar asked the servant.

'The second watch has begun, Sir.'

'And my horse?'

'It is ready, Sir.'

'Where?'

'Close by, in the hills, as you ordered, Sir. You can get to it from the back alley.'

Acharya Varshkar nodded to Somprabh and walked towards the back door.

'Shall I ask my Asur friend to guide you?' Somprabh asked.

'No, I have my arrangements', Varshkar said. The next instant, he had melted into the darkness.

CHAPTER 34

MATCHLESS COURAGE

'So, young man, your plans have failed?' Chandrabhadrik asked Somprabh. There was no complaint or taunt in his tone.

'Why do you suggest that, Chief?' Somprabh asked.

'Because tomorrow is Baisakhi Day, and we have nothing of what we were promised.'

'Sir, we have a full five watches to go for Baisakhi to dawn.'

'And what we will do in these five watches? Will we mount an assault with my beaten down army?'

'But Sir, are you not satisfied with what we have done in the four days since we met?'

'Perhaps I am, but what we did matters less than what we shall do. Shall we win or lose? I think we cannot win tomorrow. Are you sure you do not want to surrender? I hate the thought –'

'Sir, it is ruled out, in my humble opinion', Somprabh interjected politely, but firmly.

'Then we will be wiped out by morning.'

'Trust me, Sir. By sunrise, the fort will have succumbed.'

'Are you expecting divine intervention, Som?'

'No, Sir, I am counting on human actions.'

'I see. And you are still hopeful?'

'I am more than that, Sir. I am confident.'

Chandrabhadrik sighed. 'What do you want to do?'

'Sir, please wait till sunrise.'

'Som, I hope you are not contemplating anything foolishly courageous.'

'Sir, our task is vital, and my approach is serious and contemplative. I am bound by Acharya Varshkar's orders, and cannot divulge as much as I would like to. I assure you of the result. The Magadhan flag will flutter over the fort of Champa at sunrise…Sir, I do need one help from you. What is today's password?'

'Let it be "Matchless Courage".' Chandrabhadrik smiled for the first time.

'Very well, Sir. I suggest you rest. The night is young. Let me get my men ready.'

'May you have fortune on your side. Anything else?'

'Nothing else, Sir. When you hear the Magadhan trumpet at the West Tower, at the end of tomorrow night fourth watch, that will be the signal for you to lead your army into the fort. The gate shall be open for you and your men.'

Somprabh bowed to the chief and marched out of the tent. Chandrabhadrik stared for a long time at the place where he had disappeared from his sight.

Ashvajit was waiting outside for Som. He stepped closer, identified himself and said, 'Everything is all right, friend.'

'The boatman?'

'He is hiding with his boat in the cluster of sandalwood trees, at the spot we had agreed.'

'Can we trust him?'

'Completely.'

Somprabh chuckled. 'Remember, friend, the fortunes of the Magadhan empire rest on this one boatman.'

'He deserves complete trust.'

'Then let us go to him.'

Ashvajit guided Somprabh through a wet, rocky path to the forest on the bank of the Chandana river where the boatman sat quietly, his boat tied to a tree. The boat bobbed on the gentle waves of the river.

Ashvajit made a sound like a shrill bird call. The boatman immediately looked at them, and having made out their shapes, jumped into the water and walked to them.

Somprabh looked at boatman long and hard. 'What is your name, friend?'

'I am Somak, Arya.'

'Friend Somak, do you know you how important your task is? And are you clear about every step?'

'Sir, we are used to risking our lives to catch fish. I am sure for you, Gentlemen, the stakes are higher. Have no fear, I will get you and your men to South Tower.'

'I have faith in you, friend. What will be the right time?'

'The fourth watch of the night', Sir. The river will be in high tide.'

'No, friend Somak. We will leave during the third watch. That will be better.'

'That will also work, Sir. As you say.'

Somprabh handed him a bag full of gold coins. 'And as I mentioned, there will be twenty of us. Here is your wage, friend.'

Somak saluted and thanked him.

Somprabh nodded and turning back to Ashvajit, told him a few words in urgent whispers. Ashvajit nodded and walked away briskly. Somprabh traced his steps back to the camp.

CHAPTER 35

THE ASUR'S COURAGE

ear the south tower of Champa fort, a short distance from the bank of the Chandana river was an abandoned abbey. The massive edifice was in ruins, except for two crumbling buildings. In one of them, twenty soldiers had assembled in a hidden hall. They were having fun with Shambh. This was the name they had given to Somprabh's Asur friend. He seemed to like his new name. The Magadhan soldiers had become friends with him, and as they plied him with wine, meat and sweets, and he had every reason to like them.

Shambh was acting out Kundani's dance and her kisses of death in the Asur City. He wiggled his solid waist, poured out make-believe wine from imaginary pitchers, and held them to the soldiers' lips. Now and then, he offered one of them a kiss. Shambh and the soldiers seemingly enjoyed the charade, although no one had yet taken up his offer of a kiss on his thick lips.

Bemused, Somprabh watched the spectacle for a while. Then he shouted, 'Shambh! have you had too much to drink again?'

Startled, and suddenly very stiff, Shambh looked for Somprabh and bowed to him. His expression eased as he realised that Somprabh was not really angry.

'Not too much, no, Sir!' He said.

'Men, you know what you have to do. Tonight, we risk our lives for the empire. I know what I am doing. Are you with me?'

'Yes, Sir!' They shouted in unison.

'We do this because we know it is crucial for the empire.'

'We are ready!' The man said.

'My mind is at ease. One watch of the night is gone, we have two more watches to go before we launch the operation. Till then, I suggest you sleep.'

Then Somprabh turned to Shambh. 'Shambh, I have a hard task for you.'

Shambh nodded with pleasure and stroked his girdle.

Somprabh took a long coil of rope from a corner of the hall and motioned for Shambh to follow him. When they were near the South Tower, but still under-cover, he asked in Asur language, 'Shambh, how long can you stay in the water?'

Shambh signalled it was a very long time.

Somprabh stripped, and so did Shambh. The river was in spate now, and its waves crashed on the boulders at the bank with some ferocity. They held the rope tight, entered the water and swam towards a large boulder right below the South Tower. Swimming against the current was strenuous, but they managed to reach the boulder and hold on to it. Somprabh said, 'Shambh, here is what you have to do. Dive down and tell me how deep the water is here.' He held an end of the rope between his teeth.

Shambh tied the other end of the rope to the girdle at his waist and dove. Soon, the cold made Somprabh shiver. His muscles ached from holding on to the rock, and his teeth from clenching the rope. Time seemed to slow down as he strived to ignore the pain and the cold. When he thought he had reached the limit of his endurance, thankfully, the tension in the rope eased, giving him a huge relief. A few moments later, Shambh's head burst out of the water. He handed the rope to Somprabh. Somprabh estimated the depth and recalled that Ashvajit had told him the surface would rise by six feet by the time they attacked. He tied the rope around the boulder and gave the other end to Shambh.

'Shambh, be very careful. You must stay here. When the boat reaches, throw us the rope. The river should not carry us away when we disembark. We shall have to be very quick. Do not show any light. You will see a rope thrown down from the tower. Hold on to that as well.'

Shambh did not say a word. He smiled to show everything was under control and sat down, looking like a man settling in for the long haul. Somprabh dived deep into the water and disappeared living Shambh alone, shivering in the dark night.

CHAPTER 36

THE SECRET LETTER

Chandrabhadrik paced up and down in his tent, frowning, sometimes closing his eyes and occasionally shaking his head. He was alone. An observer would have inferred that he was torn by conflicting thoughts. At one point in his reflection, he paused. He strode purposefully to his seat. He righted the lamp which had dimmed to near extinction. He took out a Bhoj leaf and a quill. He was poised to put pen to paper when he heard footsteps. He looked up, startled.

It was Somprabh. He said, 'Som, you? At this time?'

'Arya, a slave has brought this letter from Rajgrih.'

'From the emperor?'

'No, Sir. From Army Commander Udayi.'

'Bring it here. Have the slave taken care of.' Chandrabhadrik went back to writing. After a few strokes, he noticed that Somprabh had not moved.

'Well?' He said, eyebrows raised. Then he smiled. 'All right. Open the seal and read the letter out.'

Som looked at it. He said, 'It is coded, Sir.'

Chandrabhadrik nodded. He took a scroll from a box and handed it to Somprabh. 'Use this key to decode it. I believe you will find it quite easy.'

Somprabh started reading it, but his eyes grew wider, and he could barely bring himself to say some of its words. 'I trust that I will soon address you as Emperor…'

Chandrabhadrik smiled, but his eyes were cold. 'Go on, young man, read it. This is not sedition, it is politics. Magadha is not the only empire. There are others. Anyway, since you have given me so much hope, perhaps this Chandrabhadrik instead of Dadhivahan on the throne of Champa would not cut an unusual figure? Magadha had absorbed the Kasis, and I have subdued the emperors of Anga, Vanga and Kalinga. The Mallas are tottering. I have fifty thousand men at my disposal. And the emperor of Kalinga has promised me twenty thousand infantry and a hundred ships…Think about it.'

'But Chief!'

'Read the letter, Som!'

Som's hands were unsteady. He read aloud now, stopping to decode the words. 'I would like to point out three factors. First, the emperor has mounted a campaign against Sravasti. King Prasenjit of Sravasti is engaged in battle with King Udayan of Kaushambhi. The emperor sees this as the moment to make a decisive strike against King Prasenjit. I hear King Chandamahasena of Avanti urged the emperor to take this step.

'But I have also come to know from reliable sources that Chandamahasena, having precipitated the emperor's attack on Prasenjit, has planned to attack Magadha. Arya Varshkar obviously knows this, but he is bogged down in Champa, and with the emperor advancing against Prasenjit, Magadha's defence is no longer what it used to be.

'Finally, the chief minister has left on a secret mission, and I control the city. There is a clear and present danger from Chandamahasena, though as usual, Arya Varshkar has prepared secret emergency plans.'

Chief Chandrabhadrik stood up, stretched and resumed his pacing. He said, 'Well, it seems the emperor has lost his mind, and so has the great Varshkar. Do they not know of Bandhul Malla? Som, keep reading.'

Somprabh read on. 'The emperor sent a gift to Ambapali, but she returned it. He is very anxious on this count. Arya Varshkar has encouraged him to give vent to his hurt pride. Varshkar seems to want a total war to annex Vaishali. In truth, his aim is to get the emperor closer to Ambapali and insert Acharya Varshkar's snake woman into Ambapali's establishment. But the emperor specifically ordered to use her against Champa. It will be no surprise if she infiltrates Champa before this letter gets to you.'

Beads of sweat had broken out on Somprabh's forehead. The Chief's shoulder shook, and he sat down again, slapping his thigh. 'Now, I understand. This is why that scheming Brahman did not allow us reinforcements. Go on.'

Som continued. 'To complicate matters, Avantivarman of Mathura thinks of attacking Magadha. That has led the emperor to send me to the border districts. But Acharya Varshkar nullified the emperor's order and had me pull back to Rajgrih, to run the capital.'

Chandrabhadrik shook his head and held up his hand. He drew a deep breath. 'Wait, Som', he said. 'Let me clear my head. Where might that crooked Brahman be now?'

Somprabh held his tongue.

'Couldn't Arya Varshkar be here, in Champa?' Chandrabhadrik pondered aloud. He looked at Somprabh.

'If he is, it will only help us, Sir', Somprabh said.

'Help – perhaps. But will we get credit for the victory?' His eyebrows were raised, and his forehead furrowed.

Somprabh had found this whole discussion awkward. He could not help feeling disappointed at the narrow-mindedness of the famous soldier of the empire.

Chandrabhadrik breathed and exhaled deeply. 'Somprabh, whatever happens here, the emperor's attack on Sravasti shall be repulsed. Vaishali is truly a thorn in our flesh. So, why not focus attention on Ambapali and make her the target of our political strategy? Let the emperor fulfil his wish to bond with her. It will help us. Young man, I have two vital messages for you to convey. We might not meet soon if I understood you rightly. It will be for the best if your plan works, and we shall not meet anyway if it does not. Meet Commander Udayi as soon as you can after your exit from here. Tell him he should not hurry. Let us hold our horses for now and focus our efforts as I have just explained.'

Somprabh felt the old man looking at him and trying to read his mind. He said, 'Your message shall reach Arya Udayi word for word, Sir.'

'Good. Here is the second message.' He stood up again, stepped closer and leant forward. He whispered, 'Make my great opponent, the wily Brahman, your friend. The emperor, the wily Brahman, and I have only agreed on one thing, destroying Vaishali. We have different motives. The emperor wants Ambapali. The Brahman wants to root out republicanism. I…I have a different reason…Here is what I suggest you do: tell Udayi to manoeuvre the Brahman into Vaishali, and the emperor back into the capital.'

Somprabh saw that Chief's eyes were now lustrous. His manner was energetic.

'Listen', Chandrabhadrik said, 'there is more.' He paused for effect. 'You may know that I have a reserve army of fifty thousand. I appoint you my second-in-command. Use that critical force sparingly, when needed, and use it for the good of the empire.'

Somprabh's mind reeled. He bowed and accepted the order silently.

'Now, Som', Chandrabhadrik said, 'it looks like the time is near. You have prepared to strike the blow, now go and do it. I shall wait here. I will not drop my eyelids for a moment and will wait for the call of the trumpet.'

Somprabh saluted the chief with a namaste and prepared to take leave. 'Not this way, Som', Chandrabhadrik said. He stepped forward and embraced Som. 'Go with my blessings. The empire's fate rides on your shoulders. You are the chief today, not I.'

Somprabh felt the chief's racing heartbeat and found solace in the pat on his shoulder as they unlocked from the embrace. Somprabh saluted the chief again, still without a word, and walked into the dark night.

CHAPTER 37

INTO THE FORT

The Chandana river was in high tide. The boat stopped below the South Tower, dancing on the river's waves. The sounds of the night drowned the slapping of waves against the hull. Trained for riverine assaults and mountain warfare, the soldiers on the boat remained still and silent. Somprabh lowered himself into the water, and Ashvajit followed him. They stepped onto the bank and found Shambh guarding a thick rope that seemed to descend all the way from the sky.

Somprabh gestured to the soldiers to start climbing the rope. They kept their swords in sheaths strapped to their shoulders. The distance to climb exceeded one hundred feet. Shambh led, followed by Ashvajit and Somprabh brought up the rear. They had worked out the details – there would be no more than five men at a time on the rope. Not looking down, they would climb at a slow and steady pace, to avoid injuring or exhausting themselves. When the men lined up on their stomachs at the tower wall, Somprabh used the coded touch system to ensure each of them was accounted for and fit to fight.

Ashavjit's brother was the guard on duty at that point of the tower. He raised his sword twice and turned inwards, the signal that the guard was about to change. There would be four new guards at different spots on the tower. Somprabh and his men had drawn their swords but kept lowered to prevent them from glinting, even in the moonless night.

The invaders waited until the retiring guards had long gone before moving with stealth and speed. They knocked down the four guards with ferocious skill, two men attacking each guard from behind without giving him a chance to alert the others.

It was now time to put down the sixteen guards at the main gate. This would be the turning point of the attack. Apart from these, another two hundred soldiers stationed in the nearby barracks would come charging at the first sign of trouble.

'What time is it?' Somprabh whispered to Ashvajit.

Ashvajit looked at the stars. 'Three watches are gone.'

'Hmm. We have a watch to go', Somprabh said.

Ashavjit's brother Bahuk had joined them. Somprabh turned to him and said, 'Friend, we need you to do more for us.'

'I am Magadha's servant', Bahuk said.

'Did you get a pitcher of wine ready?'

'Yes, it is in the corner there.'

'All right. I think you know what to do. Take it to the gate, say you are celebrating something. Drink from it and pass it around. Make sure you act as if you have drunk yourself to a faint. Lie in a corner and wait for us. At the end of the fourth watch, the Magadhan army will storm the fort.'

'They will find the four guards less than ready and the door open', Bahuk said.

Somprabh gave the signal to his men. They crouched closer to the main gate but stayed in the shadows.

Bahuk rubbed his eyes and rinsed his mouth with the wine, to appear drunk. He walked to the main gate and called out the password.

'Ah, it's you Bahuk?' One guard said. 'What, not sleeping? Is there a reason to celebrate?'

'Bless you, friend', Bahuk said. 'I am afraid you don't have a share. This is special!' He pretended to take a large mouthful.

'Where are you coming from?' Another guard asked, smiling.

'From the palace. They have a big celebration. There is a Persian nymph there!'

The other two guards came closer. 'Who is she?' One asked.

'Oh, you men, spending lonely nights here…Her name – what does it matter? I think it is Rambha. The king enjoys himself and has given wine to the guards there. I got just this one pitcher. It is a really high-quality wine. How fragrant it is!'

'Well, why not share it with us, Bahuk?'

'Go get it yourself! This is all mine!' He took a gulp and sat down on a stone. He put the pitcher down, swaying and pretending to fall in a heap.

'Bless him!' One guard said. 'There is still a lot left here. It looks like our friend can't stand liquor well.'

'Or maybe he was tired after the shift', another said. 'I wonder why he came this way, though.'

'Who cares? Let us share this. It is not too much', the third said.

'And let us finish it quickly', said the fourth one.

As they passed the pitcher around, they saw Bahuk sitting with his back against the stone. Eyes lolling, he launched into a slurred but still melodious song, encouraged by the guards.

'Did you see the woman, Bahuk?' One guard asked.

'Did I indeed! Ah, how she dances as she pours wine! I think…I think I can show you.' He tried to stand but fell back.

The guards laughed. In the distance, there was some movement at the barrack door. The soldiers there must have come out to see what was happening and realised it was just the guards having a good time.

The four guards and Bahuk were singing together now. Bahuk lay down on the ground and looked at the stars. The end of the fourth watch was approaching.

CHAPTER 38

THE EMBRACE OF DEATH

Kundani had captivated King Dadhivahan. Her manner of speaking, intoxicating eyes, pouting lips, shapely body and her cloying mix of self-confidence and flirting drove him mad with desire. Bringing her to the palace as Chandrabhadra's friend was a pretext. He had assessed the jeweller as a man richer than some emperors. In his mind, he had already decided to take Kundani as a wife.

On Baisakhi Day, Princess Chandrabhadra needed little prompting to arrange a celebration with drink and dance to officially welcome her friend – and also a state guest – Kundani. King Dadhivahan was very much part of the festivities. The cream of Champa attended the reception, and Kundani was the centre of attraction. According to the rumour, the Magadhan army, running out of supplies, had no choice but to lift the siege asking for favourable terms to be allowed to retreat without harassment. The way the people of Champa drank and enjoyed themselves reflected the lifting of this oppressive burden from their minds.

By midnight, Chandrabhadra had retired to bed, and the guests had finally left, but Kundani and the king showed no signs of tiring. Kundani took every opportunity to keep Dadhivahan imbibing fragrant wine, as she had been doing all evening.

When the last guest had left, Dadhivahan dismissed all the slaves and servants. He had a glint in his eyes as he said, 'Kundani, there is something different about you. You have…a grace.'

'Lord, you embarrass me by giving so much courtesy to a merchant's daughter.'

'No, Young Lady! Your father is a very important man, a wealthy man. But you have what money cannot buy!'

'Sir, you have the choicest jewels in your palace', Kundani said, fluttering her eyelashes.

'No, Dear Girl, let me speak my mind', Dadhivahan said. 'I want to ask you something.'

'What is your wish, Sir?' Kundani asked in her innocent tone.

'Will you be my queen?'

Kundani laughed. 'The King wishes me to become the chief queen's enemy! I could never have imagined that', she said wide-eyed. 'Let me fill your cup.' She poured wine into his gold cup.

Dadhivahan swayed. 'I have a much smaller request as well.'

'And what is that?'

'Drink from my cups first. Touch it with your rosy lips!'

'Oh dear, that would be against the throne's dignity! Let me show you my most accomplished dance. It is a dance to die for! And look, there is no one else here – I dance only for you!'

'Show me!'

Kundani pushed the cup's rim on to the king's lips and stepped away. She started dancing, building up the tempo of her footfalls, her anklets producing music. Dadhivahan set his glass aside and sat at a mridang, a drum. He was an accomplished player. Kundani's eyes were transfixed on his. Her hands flowed gracefully, her fingers expressive, her hips and breasts accentuated by her fluid movements. Dadhivahan was beside himself by now. He called out to Kundani to come to him, but she tormented him by stepping closer and quickly dancing out of reach.

And then, before his bleary, shocked eyes, Kundani reached for a bag behind a seat, opened it – and from it sprang a cobra! The serpent raised its hood and danced on Kundani's arm. Dadhivahan's jaw dropped, but he kept playing the mridang. For an instant, he wondered if he was hallucinating. But he quickly concluded that the snake's hiss was real. As he looked on wide-eyed, the snake's hood darted forward and bit Kundani on her tongue. Kundani accepted the bite gently, almost as if it were a kiss.

She put the snake back in the bag, and her dance took an even more magical quality. She had slowed down, and with slow, controlled movements such as Dadhivahan had never seen, she danced as if propelled towards the king by a force beyond her will. Her eyes had a new luminosity, and as she drew nearer, her lips opened, the fragrance of her body driving Dadhivahan wild.

He threw aside the mridang and clutched Kundani tight. She bent down to kiss him. The moment seemed to last an age.

He crushed her and felt the softness of her lips on his. The heavenly sensation was his last. He fell lifeless on the ground that very instant. Still and stony-faced, Kundani stood straight.

CHAPTER 39

THE ESCAPE

At that moment, a flaming arrow spewing red sparks landed on a mattress which, in an instant, burst into flames. The silk and cotton fabric and the wooden furniture were quick to catch fire. A dozen arrows followed the first, spreading the heat and the crackling of fire all over the palace. Soon, shrieks from the palace's inmates rent the air, and the palace guards swung into action. But in the utter commotion, they were no match for the well-trained attackers who benefited from the element of surprise. The war cries of the Magadhan soldiers demoralised the guards. The defence was short-lived and feeble, and the clashing sounds of swords striking each other did not last long.

Kundani picked up Dadhivahan's sword, blanketed herself in a cloth she had dipped in water, and strode towards the inner rooms. A figure came charging through the smoke, a bloodied sword in his hand. She smiled with relief when she recognised Somprabh.

Relief showed on Somprabh's face as well. 'Kundani, we meet again! All went well, but there isn't a single moment to lose. Take the princess to the stables through the secret path, she knows the path. Shambh is waiting there with horses. Head straight for Sravasti and do not wait for me. My work is almost done, I will catch up with you.'

Kundani flew to the princess's room. Chandrabhadra stood by her bed, awoken from her sleep, half-dressed, and looking frail and cowed. Her servants had run away, and she was confused. She ran to Kundani and hugged her. 'Kundani, what is happening?'

'The fort is lost, friend!' Kundani said. 'The enemy has entered the palace. Your father is dead. You must run and save your life.'

Chandrabhadra stood rooted. She tried to speak, but no words formed. Her grip on Kundani tightened. Kundani freed herself with an effort and rushed to the princess's wardrobe. She helped Chandrabhadra dress and pulled her away from the room, which was filling with smoke.

'Be brave now, my friend', Kundani said. I don't think the enemy has reached the secret door. Come, lead me to it. Every moment matters now. We must be quick!'

She pushed Chandrabhadra to move. Like a puppet, Chandrabhadra led Kundani behind the wardrobe, down a stairway, through a long tunnel, and finally, into the open – away from the palace. Kundani saw her tears streaming when she looked back and saw the palace in flames. Kundani knew where the stables were, and she led her towards them. They were running now. In the distance, she saw a dark figure riding a horse, and leading two others. It was Shambh, waving to them.

Kundani gave Chandrabhadra a hand, helped her mount and leapt up onto another horse. 'Now you must sit tight, Princess, we will have to gallop hard.'

Chandrabhadra said, downcast, 'Where shall we go?'

'To your friends.'

'Will your father not help us?'

'I do not know how safe he is, Princess.'

'But I took you from him, under my family's protection…and now…'

Kundani patted her. 'The shock has been too hard for you. Do not ponder now. It is time to flee.'

'Will you put yourself in danger for me, my dear friend?' Chandrabhadra bit her lip but could not hold back her tears.

'I shall give my life for you. Just be brave, all right?'

'But I am just a girl…'

'I am more than just a girl. I am with you. We have Shambh, and we shall meet another man, a good friend and a brave warrior. Do not worry.'

They started riding towards a forest path. The two women rode together, Shambh behind them, looking over his shoulder.

'Where is your friend?' Chandrabhadra asked.

'He is committed to meeting us. Where he is, I know not.'

'Can we trust him, friend?'

Kundani's eyes watered as she saw how broken Chandrabhadra was. She handed her sword over to her. 'Take this, and use it when you need', she said.

'And you?'

'I am armed. Shall we go to Sravasti?'

'Yes, Lord Mahavir is there. He is a great soul and my guru. I will go to him.'

'That is an excellent idea. You will find solace there.' She stroked her horse, and it broke into a gallop. The other horses followed.

The morning sun had broken, and soon the sun rays cast a comforting warmth on the three riders. Chandrabhadra was more composed now that she had a sense of purpose. Shambh shouted to them and pointed to a hilltop where Somprabh was waving a cloth tied to a pole. Shambh showed the path to the hilltop and took the lead. The young women followed him.

CHAPTER 40

THE FALL OF CHAMPA

The Magadhan army attacked as soon as the trumpet sounded at the South Tower. Most of the fort guards lay unconscious by then. As one of the hidden men blew the trumpet, Bahuk attacked the only guard was still half-awake with his bare hands. Before he realised it, a shadowy figure coming from behind dispatched the guard with a swift sword blow. The infiltrators searched the guard's clothes with haste. After a few agonising moments, one of them exulted as he held up a huge key.

The rumbling of the gate awoke a few guards, but they had no strength left, and the attackers made quick work of them. At that moment, the thudding of the Magadhan cavalry burst into earshot, and the ground shook. Chief Chandrabhadrik, flanked by two bodyguards, burst through the gate, followed by a swarm of soldiers with their swords drawn.

By the time the Champa army barracks started moving, the Magadhans had unfurled their flag on the South Tower. They blew their trumpets again, louder this time, and the Champa soldiers faced a flushed, victorious, and charged enemy who had the advantage on that ground.

They grouped quickly to fight off the invaders, but the Magadhans laid King Dadhivahan's body in the square. That ended the battle before it had flared up into full-scale man-to-man combat. flare lit up the eastern part of town. The rebellion had started. Hundreds of men, who had been waiting for the signal, attacked the city with fire torches and swords. The rebel action was short and effective. The rebels took over the markets and the city hall in short order.

By early morning, Chief Chandrabhadrik's men fanned the city with news of the takeover and assuring its citizens that military actions were over and there would be no sack. The men told Chandrabhadrik they could not trace Somprabh, Kundani and the princess. Chandrabhadrik gave orders for the women in the place to be given security, and gave Dadhivahan a dignified cremation.

CHAPTER 41

VADRAYAN VYAS

The ancient Vadrayan Abbey stood on the Ganga river, about midway between Vaishali and Rajgrih. It had a hoary past. Kings, courtiers and merchants from many countries had lavished it with grants. A steady stream of visitors – kings and commoners – reached it every day to pay their respects.

Vadrayan Vyas, to whom the abbey owed its reputation and standing, headed the place. For years, scholars of many countries had stayed in the abbey to study under his tutelage. Rumour had it that Vadrayan Vyas had been at his post since time immemorial. No one knew when he had become head of the abbey. Nor would anyone hazard to guess his age. In popular memory, he had always looked the way he did.

Vadrayan Vyas wore white clothes. The flowing hair on his head and in his beard was silvery, and his perfect teeth looked like a string of pearls. His serene smile was like an autumnal moonlight. He slept little, and took his main meal of the day about noon, from the leftovers of the yagya. No one had ever seen him angry. His students said that his knowledge was limitless, his thought clear, and his philosophical outlook considerable. The unanimous opinion was that his ability to look at the past, present and future, was unique. Although tall and lean, he exuded a quiet strength. He had a high nose, a broad forehead and bright eyes. From him emanated an aura of personified kindness, wisdom and equanimity. Such was his god-like following that people respectfully moved a few steps back or prostrated themselves on the ground in his presence.

He would leave his bed two watches into the night and then walk to the inner sanctum to sit in samadhi, a state of deep meditation. At the crack of dawn, he would walk to the class hall and give lectures until the first day watch. Next, he would take his seat on a tiger-skin covered slab and receive visitors. In his unassuming manner, he would hold court and commoners and kings would seek his audience to find solace from him. Midday was the time when he ended the session and looked into administrative matters. Later, he would retire to his room to write, study and perform astronomical calculations.

No one had seen or heard of an exception to this schedule. Nor had anyone ever seen Vadrayan Vyas sick, tired, or sorrowful. Such was the persona of this great man, whose fame had spread everywhere.

It was an autumn evening, and dark monsoon clouds overcast the sky. The Ganga river in spate resembled a sea. One could not see the far bank from the abbey. The river had swallowed up much of the foliage and creepers along its banks. The bushes-like objects that jutted out of the fast-flowing waters were the tops of immense trees. A faint, warm twilight lent its glow to the land and water.

The disciples had completed the evening yagya. Vadrayan Vyas stood erect on a high rock, gazing at the river. A disciple who looked in his early thirties stood beside the guru. His neat, small beard heightened the brightness of his face. He had a muscular and imposing build, but his body suggested he had much energy coiled up in him. His posture suggested a deep reverence for his teacher.

'Dear Madhu, the Ganga's span increases every instant', Vadrayan Vyas said. 'Has help reached the flooded villages on the other bank?'

'Yes, Lord', Madhu the disciple bowed and said, 'Two hundred boats went over following your command yesterday. They carried food, water and medicine. They first took children, women, the elderly, and the unfit, to safer places.'

'Was it sufficient?'

'Not entirely, Lord. We did what we could. The current swept away some boats, and we struggled to find enough boatmen. But we shall press a hundred more boats into service by tomorrow morning.'

'That is good. Do we have enough supplies?'

'Yes, Sir, we think so. We lack physicians, but the safe areas have good facilities.'

'We should ensure enough facilities in the affected areas too, Madhu. The villagers are helpless – the deluge swept away all they had.' Vadrayan Vyas's eyes were moist.

'That is true, Sir. We have followed your orders and called physicians from Rajgrih and Vaishali. We are ready to swing into action as soon as they arrive. As the floodwater recedes, we shall be ready to help in rebuilding houses and sowing seeds for next season.'

'That is well. Tell me, did you not write to the head of the Republic? The villages are of the Vajjis, are they not?'

'We wrote at once, Lord. We should hear from him soon.'

The guru gazed at the rushing, murmuring waters and sighing, said, 'That is well, Madhu. It is time for prayer. Listen, a very important person should arrive today. Because of the floods, I do not know whether this guest will follow the

Ganga, or travel along the road. Make suitable arrangements and wait for our honoured guest. Bring the guest to me at dawn, before the daily class.'

Madhu listened to the guru with a bowed head. Then they went back to the abbey's main building, the lean Vadrayan Vyas leading the way, and the stocky disciple following him.

CHAPTER 42

THE IMPORTANT GUEST

The evening prayers were finished. Lord Vadrayan retired to the inner sanctum and Madhu accompanied him to the door, bowing and touching his feet, before returning to the courtyard. While the other students retired to their dormitories, the staff carried out their end-of-day duties. As they left, they snuffed the unnecessary lamps out. Only Madhu remained awake. He sat on a tiger-skin, with his back erect against a cool marble pillar, his eyes closed in concentration, his mind sharp.

Clouds overcast the sky. The faint moon on the fourth day of the month peeped through, lightening the sky when the cloud cover thinned. At times, stars made hesitant, brief entries. Madhu thought of the important guest. Who might it be? He had to be someone who mattered, for the guru to take such interest and wanting to meet him before the class. He resolved to make sure the visitor would not find him asleep.

After two watches of the night, he was weary, but he had stayed alert. He sensed a barely perceptible change in the environment as if an unclear, intermittent, thudding sound was filtering through from the distant hills. Soon, the sound became more persistent. The thudding stemmed from the hoofs of more than one horse. He stood up and hastened to the rear gate of the abbey. It was dark, but he knew his way well enough to walk even blindfolded. When he peered through the open doorway, he could distinguish the outlines of a man and two horses behind him.

He raised his hands in welcome and then joined them in a namaste. 'Welcome, Sir!' He said. 'Lord Vadrayan commanded me to wait for you. We are honoured to have you here.'

The shadowy figure stepped forward. It was a wizened old soldier whose weapons glistened in the starlight. He bowed with respect, and said, 'Excuse our late hour of arrival, Young Sir. We ended up arriving at this untimely hour because the rain held us.'

'It does not matter, the Lord has issued his command to me, and receiving you is my duty. You are welcome.' Madhu was puzzled. Was this ordinary-looking soldier the important guest? He, who had bowed so low, and addressed Madhu as 'Sir'? He peered at the soldier, unable to hide his curiosity.

The visitor said, 'Lord Vadrayan can see beyond us, ordinary mortals. I am honoured to be here.'

Madhu saw a second shadow looming behind the soldier. Madhu remained stunned when he realised the shadow was a woman, a young woman. This, he had not expected. In the faint glimmer of light, he could see that she was no ordinary woman. Her beauty and form were exceptional.

The woman stepped forward and spoke in a voice that was music to Madhu's ears. 'Young Sir, you must be a student here. Our greetings. We are tired and bedraggled, and we have not fed our horses. Can you kindly help us rest for a while? We shall seek the honour of the Lord's audience in the morning. We are sorry for the inconvenience we have caused you.'

Nonplussed by these surprising developments, Madhu reasoned that if the guru himself considered the guest important, he should not question the order, even mentally. He said, 'We are honoured. Please follow me.'

'The horses?' The soldier asked.

'You can leave them there. I will take care of them later, do not worry', Madhu said with a smile.

He led the guests to a set of two rooms he had furnished with the best means available in the abbey. The guests were visibly surprised at the comforts that awaited them. The woman harboured a sweet smile, sans malice and said, 'So the Lord Vadrayan is very prosperous?'

Madhu hesitated now. 'I did the best I could. Lord Vadrayan only told me about this in the evening. If you see anything lacking, please let me know.'

'Oh, no, far from it. We need nothing. All we need, and urgently, is rest.'

'Very well. I will arrange some warm milk and offerings from the evening's yagya.'

'We are grateful. Can you also inform the Lord that we are here?'

'I will, of course. His command is that you shall meet him at dawn. I will take you to him.'

'That will be well. We shall rest now.'

Madhu bowed humbly and proceeded towards the outer courtyard. It was still and quiet. He had to cross the vast enclosure to reach his hut in a secluded corner of the northern side. He intended to first pick up the refreshments for the guests.

Two flickering lamps were lighting the large area. As he neared the northern gate, he thought he saw, in front of the door and below one pillar supporting a lamp, the image of a man. His tired eyes assumed it must be an image. It took him time to register that this was a live flesh and blood figure. He quelled his fear, stepped forward and said, 'Who is there?'

'A guest', was the brief reply.

Madhu walked closer. This guest was exceptional as well. He was a tall man with a heavy build, exuding energy and strength. His biceps bulged, and his eyes were steadfast. He had a certain gravitas. He wore expensive clothes, and a jewel glittered in his turban, like a bright star of Venus. His sword was huge, and his spear heavy. Fine gems inlaid the sheath that covered his sword.

The sight astounded Madhu. He held his ground, but asked in a hesitant tone, 'Sir, how may I help you?'

'I need a small place to rest. And I would be very fortunate if I could get warm milk.'

Madhu was undecided. 'Sir, at this time, a place suitable for you…'

'No, no, young man, do not bother with formalities. This is Lord Vadrayan's establishment. Every corner of the abbey is blessed.'

'Then, Sir, I can offer you my hut.'

They talked no more. Madhu led the man to his hut and lit its small lamp. He looked again at this imposing man and gulped at the thought of having him stay in the meagre hut. It was very small. In the middle stood a wooden cot with a deerskin spread over it. A small stool held a pitcher of water. Along a wall, on makeshift shelves, were scattered books, and below them were Madhu's weapons – two well-made bows, a massive spear and some swords.

The guest did a quick survey of the hut. Then he smiled at Madhu. 'So, this is your abode?'

'Yes, Sir.'

'And these books, this deerskin?'

'They are for my use.'

'I see. And these weapons?' Picking up a bow, the man tightened its string.

The fluidity of the soldier's moves impressed Madhu. 'The guru makes us all practice with arms.'

'That is well. You will need these skills in these times.' He put the bow back. 'Well', he said. 'I will sleep on this cot. It looks inviting.' He smiled. 'But how about you?'

'Please rest here, Sir. I will find a place for myself. There is milk in this vessel. I will leave it for you after taking some for other guests. And you will find dry clothes here if you wish to use them to sleep.'

'Very well, young man. What is your name?'

'It is Madhav, Sir, but the Guru calls me Madhu.'

'Then that is what I shall call you. Now, Madhu, young man, I must fall asleep.'

'Shall I inform the Lord of your arrival? What shall I say?'

'Do not worry about it. I will think about it tomorrow.'

Madhu took milk and food for other guests. He wondered who that man was, and what was the secret of his authority? He was clearly someone who was used to being obeyed. And the unusually lovely lady? Which of them was the important guest?

The thoughts continued to hover in his mind as he finished the last of his errands. When he finally laid himself to rest on a clean slab in the courtyard, his bones aching, sleep descended on him and smothered his thoughts.

CHAPTER 43

IN THE INNER SANCTUM

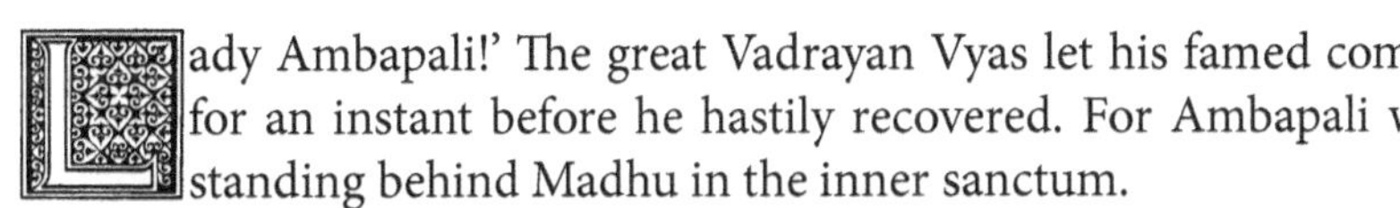

ady Ambapali!' The great Vadrayan Vyas let his famed composure slip for an instant before he hastily recovered. For Ambapali was the one standing behind Madhu in the inner sanctum.

Madhu's eyes widened, and he turned to gape at Ambapali, who smiled back at him and then prostrated herself before Lord Vyas.

Vadrayan Vyas blessed her, asked her to rise and then spoke. 'I am honoured by your visit, Benefactress of the Republic...but...why this sudden arrival?'

'Please forgive my trespass, Sir. I came uninvited, but thanks to your all-knowing nature, this undeserving servant of yours was received at an unearthly hour with excellent arrangements. Your student has been very kind.' Madhu blushed.

Vadrayan Vyas gave Madhu a questioning, bemused look.

'I did what I could, Lord, to follow your orders', Madhu said, with a sinking feeling that something had gone wrong.

Vadrayan Vyas sighed. 'Did no other guest arrive at night?'

Madhu gulped. 'Indeed, there is another guest. A nobleman is also here. He slept in my –'

A shadow flickered behind him, and he noticed, with a shock, that Lord Vyas had raised both hands first, and then joined them in a namaste.

'Victory to the emperor of Magadha', Vadrayan Vyas said simply.

By the time he had finished, the emperor of Magadha had prostrated himself, and his head was at Vadrayan Vyas's feet.

Madhu's mind reeled. He had hardly had time to digest the reality of what was happening before his eyes when Vadrayan Vyas signalled to him with a smile to arrange seats for the visitors.

After making himself comfortable, Emperor Bimbisar said nonchalantly, 'Lord Vyas's blessings are late. Prasenjit has trounced my army. I did not take your blessings before I started my campaign. Vidudhab caused my downfall.' He smiled ruefully and shook his head. 'He wrote that the old, besotted, lusty Prasenjit, tied down by his conflict with King Udayan, could not fend off my attack. And he said he would align with army chief Karayan to stage a mutiny and make things easy for me.'

'And the emperor attacked Sravasti on this assurance?' A slight smile played on Vadrayan Vyas's lips.

Bimbisar lowered his head in what seemed to be a mock shame.

'And you did not take into account Bandhul Malla and his twelve men', Vadrayan Vyas continued.

'That is right', Bimbisar said. 'In fact, Varshkar did not approve of the idea. He wanted to take Champa before thinking about other campaigns.'

Vadrayan Vyas held his counsel. After a few moments, he said, 'And when did you arrive?'

'After midnight. My horse died on the way. I walked and later took a boat. It was just my luck – the boat capsized. I swam some distance. Young Madhu here was kind enough to lend me his hut, and I recovered strength with good sleep.'

Vadrayan Vyas looked at Madhu, who reddened in shame. 'Forgive me, Sir, I did not recognise the emperor, as I have never…Your orders were for…' He trailed off, as he looked towards Ambapali.

The emperor had not yet seen her. Now, all eyes turned on her. She looked statuesque in the soft light of the ghee lamp.

Vadrayan Vyas laughed and shook his head. He smacked his forehead playfully. 'What a strange turn of events', he said. 'Lady Ambapali usurped the emperor's bed, and the emperor spent the night in dear Madhu's cot!'

Ambapali stepped forward and joined her hands in a namaste, to greet Bimbisar. 'Victory to the emperor!' She said. 'Perhaps you can pardon me? I am guilty, but I claim ignorance.'

Bimbisar laughed. 'Well, what can I say? I am content to know that the one and only Lady Ambapali spent the night in a room prepared for me. No, I am more than content – I am thrilled!'

'And I am honoured by that response', Ambapali said.

'Well, Lady Ambapali has at least accepted one of my suggestions. Ah, what pleasure', Bimbisar grinned. 'I think I have overcome my disappointment at my defeat.' Bimbisar's shoulders shook this time as he laughed, with his palms wide open.

'All is well, then. I am glad you did not find us wanting in our hospitality', Vadrayan Vyas said. 'Lady Ambapali, we shall talk tonight.'

Ambapali stood up at once, saluted the sage and the emperor, and left the inner sanctum.

When they were alone, Vadrayan Vyas said to Bimbisar, 'So, emperor, your ambition made you override your great advisor, Acharya Varshkar?'

'And I led my army to a disaster. But…'

'But with Vaishali, it will be different. It will be different this time. Is that what you want to hear?'

'I see that you, Sir, are aware of the tugging of my heart. I hope you will also grant me your blessings this time.'

'But what need does the emperor have of my blessing? Does not victory in battle derive from one's army, and from diplomacy?'

'Respected Guru, you say this out of anger, though you do not raise your voice. You chide me, Sir, as you have every right to do.'

Vadrayan Vyas smiled. 'Not so, emperor. I do not speak in anger. But an emperor's viewpoint and that of an indifferent man necessarily differ.'

'Sir, surely you are not indifferent to the welfare of the people.'

'Maybe not. I meant indifferent as in one who thinks of duties, while an emperor thinks of rights. These rights, and differences in the perception of these rights, lead to bloodshed, disquiet and a general lack of peace. Though, of course, these rights are always exercised in the interest of welfare.'

The emperor received these words with humility. 'Pardon my discourtesy, Lord Vyas, but these battles, the bloodshed, the lack of peace, do sometimes derive from the welfare motive. Small, warring states do not know what peace means. A large, stable empire brings peace and prosperity. National strength lies in empires, not in small republics. We know the empire to be the superior system of organisation for society.'

Vadrayan Vyas smiled and raised his eyebrows, fixing his gaze straight into the emperor's eyes. Madhu shrank back from this display of understated sarcasm. 'And that leads the emperor to conclude that Vaishali's fortunes will improve with its absorption into Magadha?'

Bimbisar had the ashamed look of a chastised student. 'Sir, freedom is generally good, but perhaps not always? And freedom may sometimes be cloaked in a different kind of slavery? In such cases, it is accompanied by restlessness and troubles.'

'I see the emperor has a firm mindset. Incidentally, did King Udayan of Kaushambhi not help you in your campaign?'

'That is so! Vidudhab completely misled me! He told me that Udayan had mobilised and was ready, at the head of his army, waiting for me to attack Vaishali and that he would cross the border as soon as I did.'

'And did Bandhul Malla have anything to do with the foiling of this design?'

'No, Sir! King Udayan could not refuse the slightest suggestion from Princess Kalingasena of Gandhar, Prasenjit's latest acquisition. Udayan stood ready to charge into battle for Kalingasena's sake, but she sent word that she had given herself to Prasenjit, that she was his, and that Udayan's campaign was not in keeping with dharma. Udayan lost his fervour.'

Vadrayan Vyas pursed his lips. 'I suggest the emperor rest after completing his daily chores. We shall converse more later. I must not keep my class waiting.' He joined hands in a namaste and stood. He turned to Madhu and smiled. 'Young man, for the emperor –'

'No, Sir! I shall not hear of it. I appreciate Madhu's hut too much. And this man as well. He is clearly a promising young man.'

'He may be a soldier more than a saint. I sense that in him', Vadrayan Vyas said.

'Lord Vyas, I need soldiers like him.'

'I will not come in the way of your wish, and his', Vadrayan Vyas said.

The three of them left the small room.

CHAPTER 44

THE HARD BARGAIN

mbapali invited the emperor to her room. When the emperor arrived, she welcomed him as an honoured guest, by giving him the higher seat and washing his feet with holy water.

'May I now hope the emperor has forgiven me?'

'For what charge? You have to explain that first', Bimbisar said.

Ambapali displayed the hint of a smile. With mock seriousness, she said, 'The charge should be clear, Majesty. I usurped the room and the hospitality that were yours.'

'Ah, now that is not a crime. It is pleasing. I would like you to be a continuous offender on this charge.'

'Does the emperor usually dispense justice with such emotion?'

'When the accused personifies the fanciful imagination of a poet in her beauty, the emperor's and the executioner's hearts will be swayed.'

'Sir, this does not do justice to the reputation of the emperor of Magadha.'

'Ah, maybe so. It comes from the heart of a besotted lover.'

'Victory to the emperor, but I must submit that you do injustice to the empress!'

'And peace be on you, Ambapali, but you do injustice to me.'

'How so, Sir?'

'By standing so far from me. Come and sit by me, and let me tell you a fact.'

Ambapali sat next to him. 'Sir, I am all ears.'

'Lady Ambapali, take pity on this emperor', Bimbisar said. 'This man in front of you has not only lost to Prasenjit...'

'Did another misfortune strike you, Majesty?'

'Yes, but it goes back far in time. This unlucky Bimbisar has been spectacularly unlucky in one field – that of love. I have lost in love.'

'You, Your Majesty? What are you saying?'

'Ah, I am saying what I can only say to Lady Ambapali. My old heart hides a tucked-away treasure of love…I have longed to give it but never found the one. I still search for the woman who can own it.'

'That is astounding, Emperor. Have you not found her yet?'

'I have. Today.' Bimbisar looked at Ambapali, and a softness came over his steely gaze. 'Now, take a drop of love and let it fall in this dry, lonely Emperor Bimbisar's life. Dear Ambapali, I have been waiting for you, not since you became the Bride of the City of Vaishali, but since time immemorial. You have returned my gifts, you have denied me permission to see you. But – such are the ways of fate – today, we meet without my making any effort.

'And see how the wheel of time turns to shape events in ways we could never imagine. I owe my good fortune today to my crushing defeat at Prasenjit's hands!'

The emperor stood up and walk towards Ambapali with his hands outstretched.

Ambapali stood up and stepped back. She was no longer smiling and pliant. 'Your Majesty, you must control yourself. I expect good thought and good conduct from the emperor.'

'I shall not disappoint you, Ambapali', Bimbisar said and lowered his hands.

'I have to inform the emperor I understand his declaration of love, but I am afraid I cannot reciprocate.'

'You crush the flower of hope with these words.' The emperor still stood erect, but his face had fallen.

'It can be no other way, Sir. You are an emperor, I, a courtesan. We have both lost the right to follow our loves.'

'But we are human! And we have the rights of humans.'

'You know well we have lost them, Your Majesty.'

'I hear you say that we should just let it be. Can we not enjoy courtship like insects, moths, birds? Not even like those forms of life?'

'No, Your Majesty. My fate was to live a courtesan's life – some say a prostitute's life – , your fate was to be an emperor. The kingdom of love is forbidden to us. We cannot taste its sweet rewards.'

'Then let us cast our fates aside. I shall give up my throne. And you, you…'

'Cast aside this despicable courtesan's life? I see that you want to say. You falter because that is impossible. I did not choose this life. I did not become a courtesan of my own will, just as you did not become emperor of your own accord. We are burdened with our roles. There is no way out.'

'Is that so?' Bimbisar closed his eyes and sat down, stroking his biceps. 'Is that so?' He said again. 'It is a dreadful fact. Dear Ambapali, my honest friend, there is no hope, then?'

Ambapali's face was a mask as she looked at the sight of the mighty emperor sitting forlornly. She spoke in a hollow voice with downcast eyes. 'Perhaps there is, Your Majesty!'

Bimbisar looked at her with new excitement. 'Is there? Explain yourself!'

Ambapali sat next to him, still as a statue. 'Our hope arises from the facts. I am a courtesan, you an emperor.'

'You keep repeating that, dear Ambapali! That is our misfortune!'

'It could also be our good fortune.'

Bimbisar exhaled. 'How so, Ambapali?'

'Well, it is our misfortune because, as I said earlier, we have lost the right to love.'

'Yes, I have heard that.'

'But we have the right to bargain. That is what we do.'

'Bargain!'

'Yes, Emperor Bimbisar. Bargain. I am a prostitute. As I mentioned, I did not choose this life. This life chose me. I can sell myself, and you, Emperor, can pay any price I name.'

The emperor looked away from her and pondered this statement. He unsheathed his sword, and Ambapali felt alarmed before he laid it at her feet.

Ambapali had a wan smile. 'What will this petty, blemished woman do with your emperor's sword?' She held the sword with caution in both hands and put it back in its sheath.

'What else can I offer you, Ambapali? You refuse my heart and my wealth. My body? My youth is behind me, as you can see.' His tone was harsh now.

'The emperor's body is a boon. It has the power to unite this land.'

'What do you want?' Bimbisar asked, puzzled.

'I want one thing, Lord.'

'Speak!'

'The throne of Magadha for the child born of your seed in my womb.'

'I, Bimbisar of the Shishunaga dynasty, give my word that the son born of our union will be the future emperor of Magadha.'

Ambapali's eyes were moist. She said nothing. She looked around the lavishly furnished room and picked up the most attractive garland of flowers. Eyes closed, she placed it around Bimbisar's neck. Then she bent to touch his feet.

Bimbisar held her by her shoulders and guided her up. He took off a necklace of pearl – the only one he wore – and put it around Ambapali's neck. 'This is all I have left now, after the debacle at Prasenjit's hands.'

'And now you have lost it to me!' Ambapali laughed affectionately.

'No, no, it is in a good place. Now it does not have to fear robbery.' He clasped Ambapali's hands.

Ambapali withdrew her hands from his with grace. 'Your Majesty, the emperor must behave like one, and so must the future emperor's mother.'

'Do not say that, Dear. Not now!'

'I must, Lord. You have to remove a thorn in the heart of the future emperor's mother. Else your son will have to bear a burden of shame.'

The emperor mulled over these words. He sat again. 'I think I know what you mean. But tell me in plain words.'

'You know the Licchavi Republic, with its cursed law, made me Bride of the City. I did not apply for the position, nor was I born to it.'

The emperor closed his eyes, and his face reddened.

'Master, my fault was that I was exceptionally beautiful.' Ambapali swallowed and held back her tears. Her shoulders shook, and her breasts heaved. She composed herself with an effort. 'Vaishali must be punished', she said, her eyes moist, her voice hoarse.

Bimbisar raised his hand. 'Vaishali shall burn.'

'And in the polluted atmosphere of the Palace of Seven Worlds…' Ambapali sighed.

'No, Lady Ambapali, you shall come to Rajgrih, to the palace, and shall be formally anointed.'

'I am grateful. I feel like a woman today. Now, I still have one thing to bring to your knowledge.'

'Speak freely.'

'Lord, I am a virgin, and I shall wait till the end of my days for you to consummate our marriage.'

'I am fortunate', Bimbisar said. He stood. Ambapali touched his feet again. Bimbisar placed his hand on her forehead and left the room without a word.

A teardrop streaked Ambapali's right cheek.

CHAPTER 45

THE FORECAST

Vadrayan Vyas sat next to a lamp, writing something on a scroll. He tore himself away from his task with some reluctance to look at the intruder. It was Madhu, who prostrated himself to greet his master, and announced Ambapali's arrival. Ambapali entered and prostrated herself before the guru.

'Rise, dear Ambapali', Vadrayan Vyas said. 'What can I do for you?'

Ambapali stayed quiet. Without a word from his master or from the guest, Madhu understood that he must leave. He did so. After his departure, Ambapali said, 'Is the Lord busy with important work?'

'Well, perhaps. I was counting your stars', Vadrayan Vyas said.

'What lies waiting for this unfortunate one, Lord?'

'Much lies ahead of you, Benefactress. Your bargain will be successful. You will be the mother of the emperor of Magadha. But…'

Ambapali could not control herself. 'Lord Vyas is omniscient. Why the "but"?'

Vadrayan Vyas sighed. 'But your destiny is not to be Empress.'

Ambapali's lips quivered, but she did not speak.

'And there is yet another thing', Vadrayan Vyas said.

'What is that, Lord?'

'You are a citizen of Vaishali. Don't harm it.'

Ambapali trembled and her fists clenched on their own.

Vadrayan Vyas sighed and smiled at her. 'I know you hate the idea of Vaishali, because of that cursed law.'

'Yes', Ambapali said.

'That is now past. The city granted you all you asked. Has your rage not subsided?'

'No, Lord, no!'

'And your recent good fortune? Does that not quell your rage?'

'Being the future emperor's mother without being Empress?' Ambapali's nostrils flared.

Vadrayan Vyas was unmoved. He sat still, with the hint of a calming smile. Ambapali stared fixedly at him, noticing the furrow of worry on his forehead. 'There is more…'

'Still more?'

'Much more.'

'What is it?'

Vadrayan Vyas closed his eyes for a moment and then smiled as he looked deep into Ambapali's eyes. 'Dear Ambapali, you will be famous forever in the world. Famous as a sage.'

Silence reigned for a long time. 'I see, Lord, that you are serious', Ambapali said. Vadrayan Vyas smiled and nodded. 'Lord, you know what I am', she said.

'Do not indulge in self-degradation', he said. 'Remember, the wheels of a mighty empire shall turn at your bidding.' He raised both hands in blessing. 'May fortune smile on you, and may you bring only good fortune to your city. Now, do not burn the city with your rage. Once upon a time, you gave yourself and saved Vaishali from self-destructing. Much water has flowed since then. Your anger is a basic instinct, just like the one that created the cursed law. We must value the social fabric over the thread of an individual's life. The selfishness of society is useful, while that of individuals seldom is.'

Lost in thought, the guru frowned. After a while, he said, 'Sacrifice is the greatest act. Sacrifice acts as a barrier to ills and misfortunes. If, and when, you become the instrument of destruction of Vaishali, the only republic of this Uttarakhand, northern India, look for a path to sacrifice. It will steer Vaishali away from misfortune. Whatever happens, remember these words of mine. Value them, for they form the key to your good fortune.'

'I shall remember, Lord!'

'Bless you, dear Ambapali.'

The meeting was over. Ambapali prostrated herself again, and lay still for some time, basking in the positive energy the great sage exuded. Then she stood up and walked backwards, head bowed, to leave the room. Her heart felt lighter.

CHAPTER 46

THE EMPIRE

Now?'

'When you say, My Lord!'

'The creators of empires are not intellectuals, Emperor, they are iron machines. They move on at their own pace until they shatter into pieces. Whoever comes in their way gets crushed', Vadrayan Vyas said.

'But, Lord, the purpose of life is to create, not to destroy. What if those who come in the way do not get crushed?' Bimbisar said.

'emperor, excess of creation is also a curse. What if destruction were creative?'

'No, Sir, I think creation is born of need.'

'If that is so, what is the need to frighten the Republic with an army? Constant wars spread hatred, doubt and enmity', Vadrayan Vyas said.

'They also establish the order for the long-term', Bimbisar said.

'Where might establishes order, people do not get welfare', Vadrayan Vyas said. 'This sort of order is meant for individuals to assert their rights and garner benefits for themselves. Those individuals expand their needs beyond all reason. They suck up the energy, wealth and labour of the people, leaving them hungry and thirsty.'

'But, Sir, a large-scale organisation of power contributes to the welfare of populations', Bimbisar said. 'It brings stability.'

'Where? In the greatest display of organised might, the Mahabharata war, the Aryans, and mixed breeds put in a vast amount of military power. But even with the great Krishna steering the course of events, the people gained no benefit from the rivers of blood that flowed in that war. All they achieved was total destruction.'

'Where was the fault in this?' Bimbisar asked.

'The fault was inherent. Why were eighteen million soldiers killed? Why did the youth of the land attack one another with a ferocity we would call animal-like, but animals do not display? Why did the people pay such a terrible penalty to allow the Pandavs obtaining their share of the kingdom? Emperor, try that experiment today. Mobilise new armies, make them loot people, and let the foolish louts – those who think heroism lies in slaughtering the weak – of the armies keep a minor part of the booty. Give a little gold to Brahmans to circulate tales of your glory. They will sing hymns to you, your divine right to rule, the gods' sanction of your acts. Keep the main part of the wealth and enjoy it as you like. You will discover that society bears this experiment meekly.'

Vadrayan Vyas fell silent after speaking at length without passion, in a calm, measured manner. He stared at the stars as if trying to fathom a pattern. Then he turned back to Bimbisar. 'emperor, The Aryans have paid the price for their sins. They committed mistake after mistake. They came to this land, fertile enough to give to all, and waged wars of destruction. The Kuru-Panchalas who crossed over the Himalayas could have formed a joint clan with North India Kurus. But their military victories intoxicated the northern Kurus, the Devs. They did not even spread all over the north.

'The Pauravs went south and mixed with the Dravidians. This was the first, fundamental mistake. Then, they started stratifying society into rulers, Brahmans and traders. The southern Brahmans and the northern Kshatriyas accumulated slave beauties. First, they kept the offspring from such unions in the paternal clans and gave them their due share in the inheritance. In time, these offspring became outcasts, and they excluded them from inheritance. This was their second mistake.'

Bimbisar listened, rapt with attention. Vadrayan Vyas stroked his chin. 'The separate caste the offspring formed tended to be intelligent, hard-working and enterprising. The Aryans, living off the land's cream, became decadent. As you know, they are obsessed with yagyas, rituals and fake beliefs centred on brahma. Is it surprising these hard-working mixed breeds now hold the reins of power? Just think about Prasenjit, from the old guard – will it surprise you if he soon breathes his last in pitiable circumstances?'

'But Lord, will my dream come true?' Bimbisar asked.

'Of an undivided empire across India?' Vadrayan Vyas smiled. 'You have begun work on this in the east, I see. And the Persian emperor has similar projects in the west.'

'But the Aryans will never accept him, Lord!'

'Why not? He has accepted the position of Indra many times. And the Aryans accepted him then.'

'On the whole, yes, but Krishna opposed him.'

'Yes, I know.'

'And I, Bimbisar, am of the Shishunaga dynasty – not an Aryan. I shall also counter him.'

'I am aware of your inclinations.'

'Then, Lord, what is your command for me?'

'You should proceed to Rajgrih.'

'And why is that, Lord?'

'Important events are going to take place there, Emperor.'

'May I ask, Lord, if they are good or bad?'

'emperor, you will get to know soon enough, but I suggest you prepare for both.'

'Is that your sole command, Sir?'

'Yes, it is. Gautam Buddha will reach Rajgrih soon, and he will tell you the rest.'

Vadrayan Vyas stopped talking. When Bimbisar looked at him, he had already slipped into a trance. Bimbisar stood there for some time, pondering over the discussion he just had with the great soul who spoke without fear or favour. He heard a noise behind him. Madhu had crept up to tell him his soldiers were at the main door, ready for his command.

Emperor Bimbisar prostrated himself on the ground before the silent sage and left the inner sanctum.

CHAPTER 47

THE GUARDIAN

The four riders spent the entire day on the move. They skirted every city, town and hamlet, and stuck to the forest trails. They encountered a few wild animals on the way, and Shambh slung a deer he had hunted on his horse. Somprabh rode at the head of the small group, silent and despondent. The campaign had been exhausting, and he was too drained to even talk. Kundani rode with the princess, keeping her to the right. Tears streaked the princess's cheeks, and her shoulders slumped. Her eyes were listless and dazed. Often, she signalled she could not go on, and they stopped for her sake.

Shambh brought up the rear, scanning the surrounding forest. Kundani tried to talk to Princess Chandrabhadra once in a while. The riders mostly travelled in silence, sunk in their thoughts. Descending from the hilltops, the wind lashed through the thick foliage around them. The hissing it made pierced through the drone of cicadas and sounded like whispered threats. Somprabh looked back and saw that Chandrabhadra's face had turned to stone, and her eyes were lifeless.

Somprabh asked her twice if she wanted to rest. Both times, she had replied in the negative, looking at Kundani as if to seek her support. She said her horse did not feel tired and claimed she did not either.

The bright midday sunlight had dimmed. The strain of the relentless ride was now telling on the travellers. When they reached a high spot, Som surveyed the lay of the land. He saw huts in the next valley, columns of smoke rising from a few of them. The place looked like the outskirts of a town. He said to Kundani, 'This is as far as we will get today. We must stop there.'

Without waiting for a reply, he went towards the settlement. The others followed him. The sun had disappeared below the treetops by the time they reached the huts. Somprabh made a quick inspection of the layout and exchanged a few hasty words with Kundani when he returned. They decided to take shelter in a nearby ruined abbey instead of venturing into the city. The sanctuary was ancient and run-down, but they found a corner with a roof and an even floor. There was a pond next to it. Both riders and horses drank their fill.

Kundani and Somprabh showed Chandrabhadra to her resting place before taking stock of their situation. Somprabh gestured to the deer Shambh had hunted, and said, 'We do not have food fit for the princess.'

'Yes, but what can we do?' Kundani said. 'We will find milk in the city, perhaps, but for today we have to do with Shambh's hunting.'

The deer was heavy, and his success at hunting it had delighted Shambh. He arranged for the princess and Kundani to rest. Using a flint stone, he got a fire going, and soon, meat was roasting on it, stirring their appetites. Shambh hummed with pleasure as the fire crackled and the flavours wafted in the air. Somprabh stepped out to see if he could get milk nearby.

The warmth of the fire and the sight of the unaffected, cheerful Asur appeared to lighten Chandrabhadra's mood. Kundani thought she should reach out to her. 'Princess, you have experienced too much in too short a time. Life has its trials and sometimes brings extremes. We cannot do much about it. Do not despair – you are with friends.'

'I am not in despair anymore', Chandrabhadra said. 'What happened is past. I am worried about the debt I have accumulated. I do not know how I shall repay you and your very well-behaved slave Som.'

'Think of us all as your slaves. We shall be happy if you can be', Kundani said choking. She felt sorry for this innocent girl who had shown her nothing but kindness and naivety.

'But Friend, is that brave man really your slave?' Her eyes turned towards Somprabh.

'He is your slave, friend', Kundani said with a smile.

'He has a noble appearance, and he is polite and capable', Chandrabhadra said.

'That is how he was brought up, friend.'

'His name – what is it, Som?'

'Yes, Somprabh, and everyone calls him Som.'

'And the slave's slave, he is Shambh?'

'That is right.' Kundani laughed.

Chandrabhadra said, 'In these circumstances, I suppose I have no right to think of them as slaves. They are friends.'

'Well, Princess, slaves are slaves', Kundani said. 'Doing what they do is their duty. Feeling obliged to them or giving them the impression that you are indebted is spoiling them.'

'I don't know', the princess said. 'I have always thought of…I think of my servants as humans, and this man has a certain character.'

'You have a large heart, Princess', Kundani said. She was glad to see Chandrabhadra show signs of getting over her trauma. Chandrabhadra was blushing, and her eyes filled with tears.

They saw Somprabh striding towards them, a bag on his shoulder. He was carrying pouches of milk and fruits. As he laid them on Lotus leaves for the two women, Shambh brought the first few pieces of venison.

The princess helped them lay the food. She shyly raised her eyes towards Somprabh and said, 'Sir, please enjoy your meal.'

'It is a poor meal we have rustled up, Princess', Somprabh said. 'We men will eat after you two.'

'No, we cannot –'

'But this slave requests –'

'Not slave, guardian. You are my guardian angel.' Her eyes filled with tears again, and she lowered her head as she tried to hold them back.

Somprabh would have reached out to soothe her, but he restrained himself as he did not want to embarrass her.

'Let us all eat together', he said. He called Shambh, who laughed when he understood what they suggested as if he considered the idea ridiculous. He helped himself to a generous helping of food and took his cupped and heaped Lotus leaf to a corner, humming.

The three friends ate in silence.

CHAPTER 48

SOM'S DILEMMA

The night air was fresh as a balm. Som basked in the serenity outside the abbey. He walked to an old, imposing banyan tree that straddled the surrounding walls, and sat leaning against its trunk. It felt like an eternity since he had last enjoyed a genuine moment of leisure. A moment not fraught with making trade-offs, risking his life, or taking responsibility for many others' lives. The cloudy night sky was an inky black without a single star.

He thought of the princess, of her face once as fresh as a dewy rose. He had turned the princess of a thriving kingdom into this shattered wreck who spoke, when she did, with diffidence, and was reduced to eating off leaves in godforsaken, abandoned ruins. Was this what a young patriot aspired to at his life prime? He thought of his discussions with Acharya Varshkar. He had never been so instrumental in implementing a political strategy. Was he going to inflict pain, sorrow and suffering for the rest of his life?

He thought of his experiences in the Asur capital and in Champa, and of Kundani's extraordinary courage and capabilities. He remembered how many times she had driven him, a seasoned, trained soldier, to action. The acharya was not exaggerating when he had said Kundani alone was equal to a regular army.

Som could not stop his mind from wandering back to Princess Chandrabhadra. For days, he had struggled against himself, using all his willpower to strangle the slightest desire for Kundani, beautiful as she was. The assertion that she was his sister and the knowledge that she was a snake woman had helped. For the innocent, exquisitely feminine princess, he had no way of controlling his febrile, young mind. He had reduced her to this state. Their togetherness could only arouse him. Now, he must become her protector. He must make it right by her.

'What are you thinking, Som?'

Somprabh had lowered his guard. His heart thudded as he absorbed what had happened. Kundani, standing beside him, had spoken. He had no idea how long she had been near him.

When he spoke, he did not show any signs of trouble or surprise. He said, 'We have brought the princess to this state, haven't we?'

'Do not be a fool, Som. We are tools of Magadhan policy. There is nothing else to it.'

Som gazed at the thick darkness of the sky. 'You must be right, Kundani. But I am spent. I have nothing more to offer to politics.'

'What? Do you know what you are saying?' Kundani said. 'You are…The chief minister has great hopes for you! I know that! You are the chosen one. You cannot just step back now.'

'I made up my mind', Somprabh said. 'Your path leads you back to Rajgrih. My way is different.'

'No! We have one goal!'

'Perhaps not. You will serve the nation.'

'And you?'

'I will serve the princess.'

Surprise and anger had clouded Kundani's face. Now she relaxed, nodded and laughed as she collected her thoughts. She laid a hand on Somprabh head. She whispered, 'Som, you know I am your sister. Don't you?'

'I know.'

'Who else but I will think of your good?'

'Then do me good.'

'What do you want?'

'Stop serving the kingdom.'

Kundani laughed again. 'And serve the princess? With you?'

'What is so amusing?' Somprabh said. He felt anger welling up in him. 'Is that not a good idea?'

'It is', Kundani said.

'So why do you laugh as if the idea were ridiculous?'

'We have served her well.'

'I see. So, forcing her from royalty to poverty, and orphaning her, is a service to her?' Somprabh hissed.

'That was not our doing. That was statecraft. We stood by her in her hour of need. She is alive and well, remember?'

'Well? What will become of her?'

'Something will work out. We need not know now. We are heading for Sravasti. There will be possibilities.'

'She will not go there. I will not take her there.'

'Where will you take her, Som?'

'To that end of the earth where the two of us will live together?'

Kundani stroked his head. It was feverish. 'And what about your sister, Som? Where will you leave her? Here?' She paused for a while, choosing her words. 'This is not right.'

'Then what is?'

'Think, Som, think about it. Will the princess accept you?'

'I will tell her I am not a slave. I will –'

'Tell her you are a Magadhan agent and the destroyer of Champa?'

'But…' Som stood up and paced the cracked platform. He nodded to himself, hands clenched behind his back. 'I know. I know! I shall make her the queen of Champa. And I shall revolt against Magadha! Yes! For once, I shall do the right thing!'

Somprabh could not see Kundani's moist eyes. 'That is a good plan, Som. Or you think that is a good plan. You become king of Champa, let's forget it will not be easy, but will the princess forgive you?'

Somprabh folded his hands. 'Won't she?' He lowered his head again. 'Will she not…after even…'

'Paying back interest after you stole her principal, do you think you do her a favour by making her your slave?'

'My slave? That is not what I have in mind!'

'Yet, you did not even ask her what she wants, whether she can even consider going back to the city that saw her grow up and now burns. You assume she is yours for the taking. Is that not sad?'

'It is…It is', Somprabh said. He rotated his head, and his shoulders slumped. 'I will die for her.'

Kundani restrained herself from reaching out to Somprabh. She sensed that he was suffering from battle shock. She said, 'That is an option. You can do that, you will not lack occasions. For now, remember you are committed to taking her to Sravasti safely. We are disguised infiltrators in enemy land. We took the capital and won a battle, but the war is not over. You know that well. We have a duty we promised to fulfil. We cannot even think of keeping the princess with us. What right do you have to even harbour the thought? Do not forget, your clan is unknown. You do not belong to this land. Where can you take the princess? Champa is no longer hers!'

Somprabh turned away from her. His shoulders were clenched.

Kundani continued. 'Are you thinking of taking advantage of her distressed state? Or taking her by force? But Som, I am sure you are not that kind of man?'

Somprabh walked towards Kundani, and she wondered whether she had gone too far. He bent and touched her feet. She felt tears drop on her toes.

When Somprabh stood up, she could not see his eyes in the dark, but she sensed a new poise in him. 'You are right, as usual, Kundani. I was wrong. I was not…in possession of my senses. I was wrong. We must get her to safety. That is what I must focus on, it is my first duty.'

Kundani held his strong shoulders. 'Well, now you are the Som I know. It is late. We must leave at the end of the first watch. We are lucky to have rested and eaten with no disturbance. Let us sleep for a while. I will wake up Shambh for him to take guard.'

Somprabh did not say a word. He lay down on the ground and fell into a deep sleep. His last memory was of Kundani covering him with a cloth and patting his forehead.

CHAPTER 49

ATTACKED

The travellers had ridden relentlessly for three days. They had switched to riding by night and taking shelter during the day. They ensured they were in mountain caves when the sun came out. They lived off the land, surviving mainly on the roasted meat of animals they had hunted. Sravasti was still far.

On the fourth night of their flight, they had started riding after the first watch. It was breezy, and a few wispy clouds sailed across the clear, bright sky. On the sixth day of the lunar month, the moon was a brilliant thin slice. The path was stony and uneven, and the horses, slow.

Somprabh tensed as he saw riders in the distance. He raised his hand. 'Riders', he called out. 'Friends or foes, we don't know.' He pulled his sword out of the sheath but did not raise it. Kundani and Shambh put arrows to their bows, and the group rode in tight formation. An arrow whizzed past Som's ear and buried itself with a soft thud in a tree behind him. Kundani raised her bow to let fly, but Somprabh stopped her with his hand. Instead, they quickly took shelter behind a large rock to their left. Somprabh directed Kundani and the princess to a crevice, telling Shambh to guard them.

When he rode out, bent low, he could make out the enemy was a large group. They were clearly surrounding the rock. Ahead of them, perpendicular to the path they rode, was a valley and at its end, he could make out a broad path through the forest. A long and narrow valley led to the track. He motioned to Kundani, and she drew near.

'There are more than fifty of them, and they have seen us', he said.

'What do we do?' she asked.

Somprabh mulled the alternatives. 'We must protect the princess at any cost. See that valley? It looks like the only way out of here. You go first with the princess. Shambh and I will bring up the rear. Whoever survives must lead the princess to Sravasti. If none of us survives…we shall have done our duty. Fly like an arrow, go now. Wait at that point–' Somprabh pointed to a hollow – 'They can't see it from where they stand. I shall hold them. Go when I shoot my first arrow, and the princess and Shambh will start at my second and third arrows. Tell them.'

He squeezed her hand. There was no time for farewells. He chose a spot where a large crack in the rocky surface gave him an opening from which he could survey the low land around him. The shapes were still circling the rock, not ready to mount an assault. He pulled the bowstring to his ear and let fly an arrow. It found its target. One attacker screamed as he fell to the ground. Kundani rode off towards the valley and waved to the princess when she reached the spot Somprabh had pointed out to her.

The attackers had taken cover, but Somprabh's eyes had become used to the darkness. He scanned the ground below and waited for them to move. He whispered to the princess to keep ready, and she nodded. He let fly two arrows wide apart, towards two shadow areas where he sensed movements. There was no cry this time, but he knew his arrows would have deterred the enemy. Behind him, he heard the hoofs of the princess's horse. He turned and was relieved to see the two women safe together. He waved to Shambh, who joined his palms in a long salute.

Somprabh waited for the next move from the attackers. For what felt like an eternity, he only heard the breeze rustling through the forest. He held his fire, keeping the bowstring taut. He kept his breath regular and deep. He had trained to shoot an arrow blindfolded, guided by the sound of a moving target. When the sounds came, he realised a whole group was moving. He shot five arrows in quick succession. The fourth drew a cry, and the shuffling sounds of the attackers stopped. Somprabh shot two more arrows leapt up to his horse and galloped towards his friends.

An arrow plunged into his neck and Som silently fell, the muffled sound of his fall echoing all the way to the mouth of the valley. Shambh sprang to his master. The princess screamed and meant to follow him, but Kundani grabbed her reins. 'Stop right here', she said in a choked voice. 'Shambh will do what he can.'

Shambh had let off half a dozen arrows high in the sky, so they would fall on the men if they chose to charge the rock. He picked Somprabh up and staggered with him to the safe spot. He lowered Somprabh on to his own horse.

'What about his horse?' Kundani whispered.

Shambh shook his head as he plucked out an arrow that had stuck to his back. He winced in pain but made no sound. He shot off three more arrows. Now the enemy's arrows flew thick and fast.

Kundani said, 'Shambh, get him on the princess' horse. Give her yours and jump on mine. Quick!'

'Kundani, take the princess and fly. We shall hold them here.' It took them a few moments to realise that Somprabh was speaking. The words were more like croaks.

Chandrabhadra said, 'No, I shall not go. Take my horse.'

'Do not argue. We will all die. My time has come anyway. Go!' Somprabh said.

Shambh, groaning in pain, was shooting at the attackers. Two of his arrows found their targets and the men leading the attack fell. They were dragged into cover by their comrades, who stayed back, unsure of their opposition's strength.

Som dragged the arrow out of his throat. He was shivering, but he did not make a sound. Blood spurted from the wound, and he sat down, dazed. The princess leapt to him and tied her scarf around his throat. 'Get up, Sir, and go! You must go!'

'No Princess', Somprabh said. He was barely audible. 'Each instant counts. Go!' He glanced at Kundani, who, for once, looked torn and confused.

'I shall not leave you!' the princess cried, embracing Somprabh.

'Many of them have crossed over', Shambh said. He was shooting arrows even as he spoke.

'For God's sake, Princess, run. Save your life and your honour.'

'Let us die together', Chandrabhadra said.

'You don't know me, Princess. Don't be so attached to this lowly man. Save yourself.'

'But I –'

'Do not say it, Princess! If we live, we shall meet. And then…'

'I can't leave you', Chandrabhadra insisted. Dark blood covered her, and she embraced Somprabh again. Shambh looked helplessly at Kundani. His arrows were running out.

'Listen, Princess', Som said. 'I said you don't know me. Let this be a lesson for the rest of your life…I am a Magadhan. I am your enemy.'

Chandrabhadra shrieked as if she had seen a snake. She stepped back, her hands trembling as they smacked her head. She looked at Som for some time, dazed.

Somprabh signalled to Kundani and dragged himself to a boulder kneeling with his bow. Shambh had picked him up with his bow and his quiver of arrows. 'Shambh! We fight until the end! I take this side, you that one.'

But his arrow did not reach the rock. His neck rolled, and he remained still.

Shambh ran to his master and felt for a pulse. His shoulders shook. Then he resumed his barrage of arrows at the shadowy figures darting from the rock, sending them scurrying back.

Behind him, Kundani was calling out to him while she dragged the stunned, passive princess onto a horse. He gestured to her to gallop. He picked up Somprabh one more time and ran into the foliage. He found a cave and laid Somprabh to rest there.

When he scrambled to a vantage point to survey the scene below, he saw they had fought in vain. The attackers had surrounded the women within a few moments. Kundani started attending to the unconscious princess.

The attackers were Dasyus. One approached, his teeth gleaming in the moonlight. 'Both women. Good, very good.'

Right behind him, another said, 'And both beauties. The Master was looking for a slave like this, and now we have two. We must inform him.'

A third one lit a flame so they could admire their catch. 'Who are you?' He asked Kundani.

'Don't you see we are travellers?'

'We see that. And your companions who killed so many of us? Where are they?'

'Find them yourself.'

The man smiled coolly, twirling his moustache. 'Perhaps we shall', he said. 'Where were you headed?'

'Sravasti.' Kundani said flatly.

'It is still many hundred miles away', he said.

'What is that to you? Let us continue', Kundani said.

'Well, we are going to Sravasti. You will join us', he said.

'Are you… Are you forcing us?'

The man laughed now. 'No. Consider it a request', he said. There was no sign of malice in his voice. Kundani did not know what to make of this group. She felt for Chandrabhadra's pulse and felt relieved to find her alive.

Kundani led Chandrabhadra on her horse while she walked with the men surrounding them. The events of the last hour had drained Kundani, and she had no fight left in her. Anyway, she did not see a way out.

.

They reached a clearing in the forest, where more men, most of them armed, had gathered. In a huddled group, surrounded by men, were some women. Some slept while others looked dazed.

The two newly captive women quickly attracted the attention of the men. Two torches were lit to examine them. The princess, even though she still lay unconscious on her horse, drew her share of attention.

'What a catch!'

'The Master must know right away!'

An elder stepped forward, and the hubbub died down. He was a fat man with a thick neck and a grizzly beard. He wore a red waist cloth that marked him out. The master was there. He looked at the two women, sizing them up, and then his wizened face broke into a smile. He rubbed his hands. He did not utter a word, but Kundani noticed that pride overwhelmed the men who had led the attack.

'So, you are a slave trader', Kundani hissed.

'Indeed. Have no fear, you will not be molested. You are better off with us than with others. We shall give you to the king.' The man's voice was a deep baritone. 'You shall get good positions in his palace, I think. You seem troubled. You have come a long way, and I see your companion is not well. We shall make sure we keep you hale and hearty.' He smiled. 'Now, you shall rest. I see you are not commoners, but you must join those women there. There is only one class here.' His brown teeth flashed in the firelight. 'We shall talk in the morning. I shall not harm you, but…I must collect what is due to me', he smirked.

He lowered the princess down from her horse. She had sat up but did not seem in her right mind. The master signalled to an aide to lead their horses away.

Kundani had kept her strength for one last effort. When the man reached her, he stumbled back. It took the men a long time to realise a dagger had cut down their master. Their captive sprinted into the forest, and by the time some of them ran in hot pursuit, Kundani was out of reach.

The princess collapsed in a heap.

CHAPTER 50

A NEW FACE IN SRAVASTI

Although it had rivals like Saket and Kashi, Sravasti was acknowledged as the largest metropolis in India. Kosala's capital had moved from Saket to Sravasti many years before. Saket's significance arose from its location on the northern route, where the north-south and east-west roads and waterways crossed. But Sravasti held the key to countless treasures. Men like Sudatta and Mrigar had become legends for their fabled wealth. Their ships plied not only in India but from Egypt to China, and their wealth multiplied day by day.

On the east-west routes, the rivers provided faster and more efficient transport. On the north-south routes leading to major centres such as Rajgrih, Vaishali and Nalanda, the hilly roads passed through Sravasti. Traders who travelled through Sravasti went on to China, Burma, Gandhar and Babylon.

Nine types of armies guarded Sravasti's wealth, including cavalry, elephants' divisions, chariots and archers. Kosala army employed Greeks, Tartars, Huns and Shakas. Some Greeks had risen to the rank of general.

Sravasti had a vibrant commercial sector, with many trades. Stone-cutting, woodwork, ivory work, jewellery, textiles and dyes, fisheries, pharmacies and precious metals were the artisans' main trades.

As usual, Brahmans and Kshatriyas were the highest castes. After these came the merchant class. Brahmans and Kshatriyas held one tenth of the nation's wealth while merchants owned the rest. Among the population, one tenth were higher castes, two tenths were slaves. The rest were commoners, whose sons were fodder for wars and daughters, if desirable enough, concubines or secondary wives in rich and powerful households. The Brahmans declared the rulers were divine beings to whom wealth and women had accrued because of their good deeds in previous births. In return, the Brahmans received gifts of gold, and of bejewelled beauties.

The old King Prasenjit had demolished Bimbisar's military campaign against him, and gained by force the beautiful Kalingasena, who had given her heart to King Udayan of Kaushambhi. King Prasenjit was celebrating these victories, and his head had swollen with pride. He had organised a Rajsuya Yagya, a grand ritual in which the sponsor gained divine status. Emperor Bimbisar was still in Saket, but preparations for the Rajsuya Yagya and the wedding were in full swing in Sravasti. Gifts had poured in from kings and emperors eager to register their homage, and groups of merchants, Brahmans and other guests had swarmed into the capital, expecting rich rewards.

Kalingasena was welcomed into the palace complex at Sravasti with the pomp and show expected on such an occasion. An army of workers made sure to deck out the entire city like a bride to receive her. She received a palace of her own. Each of the over one hundred queens in King Prasenjit's bevy was a beauty in her own right. When they saw Kalingasena, however, they knew she would be the jewel in Prasenjit's crown. As it happened, apart from being physically alluring, Kalingasena was also wise and free-thinking. She had grown up in Gandhar, among more liberal values, and had studied at Takshila. Not only had she studied the Vedas, astronomy, and the fourteen sciences. She was also an expert rider and proficient in the use of weaponry, archery in particular. She had ridden horseback from Gandhar to Sravasti, refusing to sit in a palanquin.

A vibrant city at all times, Sravasti had swollen with crowds. This only added to Kalingasena's discomfiture. She had not seen her husband, but had, of course, heard he was well past his youth and eccentric. She had given her heart to King Udayan but consented to marry Prasenjit. She saw the union as a duty to her people, one many women before her had performed, but had no feelings for Prasenjit. She witnessed the preparations and waited for the consummation of her marriage like an animal for sacrifice. She took heart from knowing her sacrifice had a greater purpose. In this frame of mind, she waited for her old husband-to-be and kept interactions with the other queen at a minimum level.

Sitting alone on a swing, in an ornate room with a large window, Kalingasena gazed through the window at the clear blue sky. She had dismissed her attendants and sat huddled, feet up on the swing, arms crossing her legs, and chin resting on her arms. She had a vacant, distant look. In the corner of her eye, she noticed a movement and turned to see the middle-aged woman who had entered the room.

What she saw surprised Kalingasena. The woman had something about her, an almost blinding presence. Her young days were behind her, but she still had a grace, a charm and an aura. Kalingasena stood up and welcomed her with a namaste, asking her to take a seat. She did so. Kalingasena noticed her elegant movements and poised manner.

Kalingasena adopted her most polite tone. 'May I know who has done me the honour of granting me her presence today?'

The lady smiled, and her eyes twinkled. 'You will know of the one whom the Council of Ministers of Kosala calls the Greatest of the Great, His Divinity, Lord Emperor. I am his slave. I was born when Mahanam Shakya planted his seed in his slave Vasavakhattiya, or so I am told.'

Kalingasena rose to her feet. 'Then you, Lady, are the chief queen Lady Nandini. I salute you.'

'So, you know my name and my position. That is excellent', the lady said.

'I have heard much about you, Lady, even in Gandhar. I have heard of your energy, persona and your wisdom.'

'You flatter me. You are a graduate of Takshila. You must know so much!'

'I am your unimportant little sister, Lady. I shall need your support in this strange place', Kalingasena said. She tried to fight back her tears and trepidation, but her eyes were moist.

The next instant, Nandini was with her and held her in a light embrace. Kalingasena eyes dropped to Nandini's shoulder.

'Do you feel lonely here, in spite of being the centre of attraction, Sister?' Nandini asked.

'Not anymore', Kalingasena whispered.

Nandini took a deep breath. She seemed to weigh her words. She took Kalingasena's chin in her thumb and index finger and raised it to meet her eyes. 'That is right. Do not think you are alone. You will feel lonely at first. It cannot be helped. A woman knows how to make a stranger her own. You will have to give your purity to a lowly entity.'

'I cannot do that!' Kalingasena said.

'But that is how you will become a queen.' Nandini said.

'I do not want to be one.'

'What made you ride over eight hundred miles to come here then? Surely, you are not serious', Nandini said. Her eyes bored into Kalingasena's, and she pursed her lips.

Kalingasena laughed. 'I came to see you.'

Now it was Nandini's turn to laugh. 'Well, you have achieved that goal. Next, you will see your lord and master.'

'That, I have no desire for.'

'You realise you were born a woman?'

'What of it?'

Nandini shook her head and looked askance at Kalingasena. 'What of it, you ask? Well, it means you were born to give yourself to a man.'

'I thought nature had in mind a mutual giving to each other.'

'Friend Kalingasena, it may be so in Gandhar. Here, the woman gives herself, not the man. The man gives shelter to the woman.'

'Shelter! Fie on shelter! I do not need shelter!' Kalingasena said. She realised that she had raised her voice.

Nandini's poise asserted itself. 'Are you going to declare war, friend?'

'Whatever you think', Kalingasena said softly.

'I see. You will fight the king of Kosala?'

'I do not know. Perhaps not. I could not bear the sight of my father's fear and my mother's tears. Kosala massed its army on the border and threatened to cut off the trade routes. It would have ruined Gandhar and harmed the trade revenues of north Kuru and Persia. Gandhar's sword could have decided this dispute, but I surrendered myself to save the blood of my loved ones.'

Nandini nodded in sympathy without saying a word. She knew Kalingasena had much pent-up feeling.

'In Gandhar, we believe in equality', Kalingasena continued, 'nobles and subjects are closer to one another, and the nobles do not consider the people as their slaves. Nor do we think their blood expendable for the slightest of causes. We have our wars, of course, but waging war is the last resort and a decision we do not take lightly. One daughter of Gandhar giving herself to save a war is a just sacrifice. That is what I thought and told my father. I saved thousands of lives.'

Now Nandini patted Kalingasena's shoulder and said in a soft voice. 'And it saved what remains of Kosala's honour. It is even possible that for all its much-vaunted might, Kosala could have floundered in front of Gandhar's righteous fury. Big houses can have gaping holes. Our dear king is weak and old, and so is our army. Our might is brittle.'

'We are aware of that in Gandhar, Lady', Kalingasena said. 'Where soldiers are mercenaries, where the king treats his subjects like slaves, there are always holes. But winning wars is of lesser interest to us than ensuring stability and avoiding mayhem. We do not aspire to set up empires, we want good lives for ourselves. We have more equality. The rulers and the people are, in fact, not bound to master-slave relationships... And yet, we wonder how Kosala trounced Magadha.'

'Well, that is a question I can answer. I know Emperor Bimbisar ignored Acharya Varshkar's advice and launched the offensive when Chief Chandrabhadrik and most of Magadhan army were pinned down in Champa. I have heard the emperor was counting on King Udayan attacking Kosala at the same time – out of his love for you.' Nandini smiled. 'But that was not to be.'

'No', Kalingasena said, 'that was not to be. I sent word to him I had given myself to King Prasenjit.' She sighed.

'In fact, King Udayan's army has still not retreated. But they did not cross the border. I have heard Arya Yogandharayan has something to do with it, apart from your message to King Udayan. It turned out to be Emperor Bimbisar's undoing. And then, Bandhul Malla and his group had organised the Hun units very well. The emperor had no inkling, or he would have waited for Chandrabhadrik. Be that as may be, friend, I congratulate you on your husband's great victory.'

'Surely you are not serious, Lady', Kalingasena said.

Nandini had, in fact, put on a severe mask. Now she burst out laughing. The peals echoed in the hall. 'Perhaps I am not, Dear Friend. But you know being a queen of Kosala is a great privilege.'

'I am not so sure, Lady', Kalingasena said. 'In Gandhar, while a man has a wife, he cannot get another. We are used to a shared life with our husbands, without further…'

'Well, here among the Aryans, you see how it is. The woman is handed over to a man who can be the master of many women. So, you still follow the northern Kuru tradition?'

'Yes, we do. Like the Persians and Greeks. Kings will be men, but the queen is the king's life partner.'

'Let us just agree, Sister, that in these parts the ways are different. From Kosala to Kalinga, the man has absolute rights over his women's body and soul.'

'I shall fight this, Lady Nandini. I have given myself to King Prasenjit, but I keep my right to think, have opinions and state them. I shall claim my rights.'

'I feel…I understand you, Sister. But I do not see what you can do, and I do not wish you to come to grief. Here we use the word pati, master, for husband.'

'I shall change this, Lady!' Kalingasena said.

'Here? It will be an arduous battle, Young Sister', Nandini said. Worry for her new friend now lined her forehead.

'I shall not battle, Elder Sister', Kalingasena said. 'Gandhar promised to give me to King Prasenjit and has kept its word. Now, I shall ask for a say on the terms on which I shall be part of his life.'

Nandini squeezed Kalingasena's hand as she said, 'Younger Sister, I want you to be happy here. All this talk of equality…I am a slave woman's daughter. I shall help you as much as I can.'

A maid called out from the door. 'My Lady, the prince asks for an audience.'

'He may enter', Nandini said.

Prince Vidudhab came into the room and bowed low before his mother.

Nandini smiled. 'No doubt you want to see your new mother', she said. 'Here she is.'

Vidudhab bowed deeply and joined hands in a namaste. 'Respected Lady, I welcome you, and salute you.'

Nandini said, 'Well, you now have a son older than you, but he is old only in looks. He is still a child!' She laughed as Vidudhab coloured at this description.

Kalingasena said, 'I have heard much about the prince's qualities on the way here. I wish him all success.'

'I am honoured, Lady', Vidudhab said. 'My mother and I were relegated to an inferior status. Perhaps, though I do not wish it, we shall have you join our group.'

'I already feel I am not alone here. I am glad', Kalingasena said.

Nandini stood up to leave. 'It is time for me to go, Younger Sister. Remember this, the eldest queen here is Queen Mallika – the first of the queens. She is but a gardener's daughter, but she has carved out a different place for herself. She is famous for her great austerities and devout prayers. Her patience and magnanimity have no end. You must show her the respect, as we all do. It will come naturally, but I thought I should let you know.'

'I am not careless in respecting elders, Elder Sister. I met her earlier, and it is as you said; she inspires respect.'

'Peace be on you, Younger Sister', Nandini said. Vidudhab bowed again as they both left.

CHAPTER 51

VARSHKAR'S PLAN

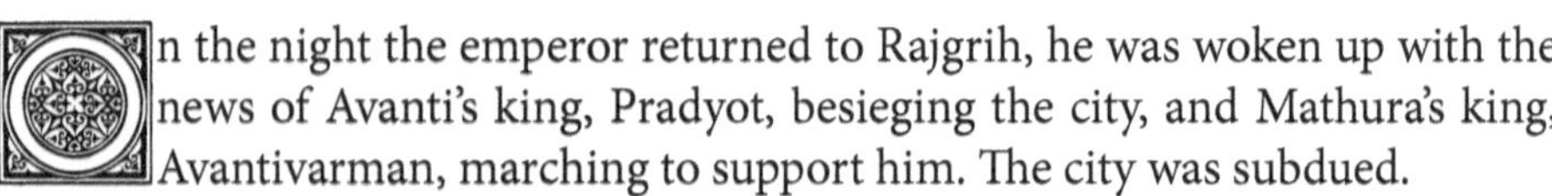n the night the emperor returned to Rajgrih, he was woken up with the news of Avanti's king, Pradyot, besieging the city, and Mathura's king, Avantivarman, marching to support him. The city was subdued.

The emperor was spent after his disastrous war. The chief minister, Arya Varshkar, was not in the city, neither was the army chief Chandrabhadrik. The army division that had conquered Champa was still stationed there. Another division had been smashed during the debacle at Sravasti.

The emperor summoned the deputy chief of the army, Udayi. He said to Udayi, 'General, we are in poor shape. We have no resources. And we have two enemies at our gates.'

'That is so, Majesty.'

'General, Sir, make sure these two armies do not combine.'

'I am afraid the chief minister has forbidden any action.'

'Did you say – on what basis has he issued that order?' In another time, Emperor Bimbisar would have raged at the insolence of his chief minister. Now, he was a wiser and more cautious man.

'Based on his plan, Your Majesty.'

'Did you say plan? What plan is that?'

'I cannot say, Your Majesty. It has been kept a secret.'

'And who is this secret plan's inventor and operator?'

'It is Acharya Shambhavyakashyap.'

'Get him to me', Bimbisar said.

'But he is not in the city, Your Majesty', Udayi said.

Bimbisar frowned. 'Where is he?'

'The chief minister has sent him in disguise to a place I am not privy to, Your Majesty.'

The emperor rolled his eyes. He could see his general was not uncooperative – it was just that the man did not know. 'What is the chief minister up to? Does he have a method, or is this just madness?'

'I suspect, and I hope there is a calculated method, Your Majesty.'

'And what method do we follow here, General?'

'With all respect, Your Majesty, we wait for Arya Varshkar.'

'So, we are nothing! The chief minister…' The emperor's breath had quickened, but he controlled himself. He was stroking his biceps.

'Does the emperor wish to attack the enemy?'

'I do not know how to answer that question, General. Our army here is pitifully small, and we cannot take on two armies. Those two would never have dreamt of crossing the border if they had not known what shape we are in.' The emperor let out a long breath and closed his eyes in concentration.

'Your Majesty, I am hoping for something unprecedented.'

'I see. And when do you think this remarkable thing will happen?'

'Now', Udayi said.

A guard came running and shouted at the door. 'Permission to enter, My Lord!' He stepped in without waiting for an answer. He was panting. 'Your Majesty! The siege has been lifted. The invaders are on the run!'

The emperor frowned and smiled at the same time. A burden had been lifted from him. 'What miracle is this, man? Tell me more!'

'Your Majesty, Acharya Shambhavyakashyap has sent word in a coded message there is no need to worry about King Pradyot's army. However, Acharya Varshkar is battling King Avantivarman at the border with Mathura, and he is outnumbered. He should be reinforced immediately.'

'Is that all, or is there more?'

'Your Majesty, King Pradyot has lost faith in his generals and has fled the field on his elephant, Nilgiri. His army is retreating in complete disarray. The acharya suggests this is a good time to capture the king.'

The emperor spoke with resolve now. 'General, you will capture King Pradyot, and your men will scatter his army. Send your scouts out now. I will take the Royal Bodyguards and ride to the border to reinforce the chief minister's men.'

'At your command, Your Majesty. I shall leave now and bring you king Pradyot. May I say, My Lord, that I do know the chief minister's plan?'

'What! You said it was a secret.'

'Your Majesty, I was ordered to keep it secret until King Pradyot's retreat. I was bound by that order.'

The emperor shook his head, but he was evidently not angered. 'The chief minister and his ways…So, what was his plan?'

'When Arya Varshkar heard of King Pradyot's campaign, he got Magadhan gold coins buried in spots that could be military camps on the way to Rajgrih.'

'What?'

'Yes, Your Majesty. And then he sent word to King Pradyot through double agents that the king's generals had received money from you to kill him during the siege. He received information on the places where the coins were buried, and when he ordered his agents to check, they found Magadhan coins in their camps.'

The emperor laughed. 'General, Sir, Magadha is lucky to have two great generals but equally fortunate to have these two cunning Brahmans.'

'That is hard to argue, Your Majesty. Now I shall take your leave and bring King Pradyot to you.'

'Issue orders for the guards to be ready for a lightning march. I shall lead them myself.'

'As you command, Majesty.'

CHAPTER 52

SON KOTIVINSH

Gautam Buddha's sangha had swollen to one thousand and two hundred members when he reached Rajgrih. The sangha camped at Ghrihakoot Mountain outside the city. Arya Varshkar made a stirring speech to Bimbisar and his ministers. He said, 'Your Majesty, the son of the Shakyas, Gautam Buddha and his huge sangha of monks, has visited the city for the sixth time. His fame has spread far and wide, and he is revered as the perfect being. He preaches pure and total celibacy and has conquered his senses. His sermons, with their deep meanings and their simple parables, have melted hearts. It will be a good policy to show the emperor's humility and visit this perfect being.'

Emperor Bimbisar was quick to make a decision, as he knew his chief minister's recommendation would be based on a holistic view. 'Sir, we seek an audience with him. Inform our Brahmans, and our village chiefs this shall be an official visit, and they will go with us.' The information minister sent the messages out.

At that point, Son Kotivinsh, a young merchant from Champa, was a guest of the emperor. He was known for an unusual feature – he had hair on the soles of his feet. When he heard of it, the emperor invited him to the palace on a whim. Son Kotivinsh asked the emperor to allow him to join the entourage heading to Gautam Buddha's camp. The emperor consented, and asked him, as an honoured guest, to lead the procession.

When the procession reached the camp, Gautam Buddha, a young assistant named Swagat, was at the entrance. The information minister explained the background to him and pointed out the emperor, who had travelled on foot, as well as the chief minister and other dignitaries, including Son Kotivinsh.

'Sir, please wait here. I shall inform the master of your arrival.' Swagat ran inside, and in a breathless voice, told Gautam Buddha, the emperor himself and other important men had arrived. He said they were waiting for the Buddha to pronounce a suitable time for his meeting them. The Buddha said the visitors should take their seats in the shade of the trees first.

The great Tathagat, Gautam Buddha, stepped out soon and sat on the stone slab he used for public audiences. The emperor himself went first to the Buddha, bowed to him, and sat by his side. The others bowed and sat as well. While some sat silent and solemn, hands folded, others performed a circumambulation around him in homage before taking their seats.

The Buddha started speaking in his compelling, melodious way. He talked with conviction and simplicity of the fourth great truths, the noble Eightfold Path, and the virtues of triumphing over the senses. He spoke of sorrow, of its nature, causes, and of the means of eliminating it at the root.

As his audience listened to him spellbound, they realised the profundity and the essence of what he was saying. He explained that all they saw created would be destroyed. He expounded on the various facets of dharma, the righteous path.

At the end of this sermon, the assembled nobles, village chiefs and other luminaries led by Emperor Bimbisar entered the ranks of the followers of the Tathagat, Gautam Buddha.

Son Kotivinsh had listened in rapt silence through the Buddha's talk. At the end of it, he mulled over the idea that dharma, as explained by the great sage, highlighted what is perfect and whole in every respect, and what rests on celibacy. At that instant, he felt a strong inner urge to become a monk.

When the emperor and the leaders of Magadhan society felicitated the Buddha, and left, having performed their homage by turning around him, Son Kotivinsh sat alone in one corner. When the Tathagat's gaze turned to him, he prostrated himself and said, 'Lord, from what I have understood of your sermon, I realise I cannot practise celibacy at home and in the material world. I wish to become one with the sangha – please initiate me!'

Son Kotivinsh won his initiation on the strength of his shining sincerity. His head and beard were shaved, and he forsook his finery to put on the ochre robes of a monk. He was given a place to stay with the other monks. But the tender young man, who had been brought up in luxury, had never walked on his feet. This was why he had hair on his soles. Now, as he walked, his feet bled profusely, and the ground was covered in red.

Gautam Buddha saw the footprints of blood and followed them to Son Kotivinsh's vihar, his spartan quarter. Son Kotivinsh was alone in his quarter, lost in thought. He was reflecting on the fact that although he had become a monk, he could not free himself from the memories of his family and friends. 'At home', he thought, 'I have access to objects of pleasure. I can sink myself in the delights of the world, but also perform good deeds. Why should I not return home, enjoy the amenities that are mine for the taking, and do charitable deeds from that haven?'

He looked up to see the Tathagat himself at his door, with monks behind him. He jumped to his feet and greeted the sage. He offered his only chair to Gautam Buddha and sat on the floor.

When he had seated himself, the Buddha said, 'Son, what were you thinking of, all by yourself?'

Son Kotivinsh unhesitatingly spoke his mind because he knew nothing was hidden from the sage.

The Buddha said, 'Tell me, Son, before you joined us, were you proficient at playing the veena?'

'Yes, Lord!'

'So, when you tuned your veena, you must have made sure the strings had the right tension? And that must have been necessary to produce music?'

'Yes, Lord!'

'Did your veena produce music when the strings were too tight?'

'No, Lord!'

'And when they were too loose?'

'No, Master.'

'So, the harmony, the melody, the scales – they all flow only when the tension is right?'

'Yes, Master.'

'In the same way, Son Kotivinsh, overzealousness creates an excess of anxiety. Be industrious in your new vocation. But be composed. In matters of senses, be aware of the conflicts that can arise if you are not balanced in your thoughts.'

'Very well, Lord.'

'And Son, you are very tender. I permit you to wear shoes.'

'Master, people will say Son Kotivinsh left behind eighty cartloads of gold coins and seven herds of elephants to become a monk but is attached to his shoes. I shall wear them if you allow them for all monks.'

The other monks were aghast to hear this new initiate's challenging tone. The Buddha smiled and issued orders that all monks were allowed simple shoes with soles of a single ply.

CHAPTER 53

ANATHAPINDIK, THE LANDLORD

Anathapindik of Sravasti was a visitor in Rajgrih. His brother-in-law, Grihapati, was a prominent merchant in the city. Grihapati was so busy with preparations for the welcome of Gautam Buddha he was unmindful of his duties as a host to Anathapindik. He scurried between errands, haranguing the servants, and reminding aides of what they should do to ensure that the gargantuan but straightforward feast and the welcome ceremony went well.

Anathapindik could not help thinking that this man, who used to leave all his work to welcome his brother-in-law in earlier times, had not a moment to spare today. Who might be the guest who had induced this frenzy? Even the emperor did not produce this reaction.

Grihapati chose that moment to rush to Anathapindik, greet him and sit next to him. Anathapindik noticed his brother-in-law was drenched in sweat and breathing raggedly. Grihapati had sat down because he was exhausted.

Anathapindik said, 'Dear Grihapati, what is the occasion today? It must be something out of the ordinary, but I struggle to understand what it might be. Is the emperor attending a feast here?'

Grihapati said, wiping his forehead, 'No, brother. I am preparing for something more important. The Buddha and his monks will be here tomorrow.'

'The Buddha?' Anathapindik gasped.

'Yes, friend.'

'Do you mean…Tathagat, Gautam Buddha?'

'Yes, I do mean him.'

'Did you say the Buddha will be here? Here?'

Grihapati nodded without rancour. 'Indeed.'

Anathapindik eyes were still wide. 'May I go and see him? He must be nearby!'

'Now, I do not think so. I believe this is not the time to visit him. I do believe you can go at dawn tomorrow when the perfect one receives visitors.'

Grihapati realised he had failed in his duties towards his brother-in-law. He made up for the lapse quickly. He arranged for his guest a room to rest, food and drink. Then he went back to prepare for the great event of the next day.

While his brother-in-law was in this frenetic state, Anathapindik was excited. He could not sleep all night. Thrice, he left his bed in a panic, afraid he had missed the crack of dawn, only to realise from the stars outside it was still too early. Finally, he could take it no more. It was still pitch dark when he got up and strode towards the city gates, oblivious to the time of the night. The guards opened the doors as they knew him to be a prominent man.

Only when he crossed the gates into the darkness outside did he realise he was alone on a dark path. He felt a shiver run through him. The distant cry of a strange animal gave him goosebumps. He almost turned on his heels, but a voice from an unknown source spoke to him.

'Keep walking, Anathapindik, keep on walking! A hundred elephants, a hundred horses, a hundred chariots and a thousand virgins bedecked with the costliest jewels – all together are not worth even a sixteenth of one sentence of his! Move ahead, do not turn back!'

Anathapindik steeled his trembling heart and kept walking. He thought he saw shapes hanging from the trees by the path, but they turned out to be illusions. The wind whispering through the trees on both sides of the starlit track encouraged him. 'Go, go!' It seemed to say.

As the trail sloped up to the summit of Ghrihakoot Mountain, his feet felt less tired, as if by magic. He entered the sangha's unguarded camp when the sky, inky black a few moments earlier, took on a lighter shade. A figure ambled on a level patch of grassy land, bare feet on the dewy grass, while the others slept. Anathapindik needed only a glance to know, from his demeanour and intensity, that the man was the one whose call he had answered.

'Come, Anathapindik', the Buddha said.

Anathapindik prostrated himself at the Tathagat's feet. He felt new energy coursing through his veins. He searched for something to say, but words failed him. 'Did the Lord sleep well?' He asked.

'One who has attained nirvana has no trouble sleeping well. Unmet desires do not torment him, and he has no emotional attachments, no fear of losses. He has peace of mind. So, he sleeps well.'

Then, the Tathagat told Anathapindik a story from an earlier life. As he listened to this great being, who unadorned, without raising his voice, had such a towering presence, the most significant realisation of his life dawned on Anathapindik. 'Please accept me as your devotee, Lord', he said. 'And please honour me with a visit tomorrow, with the sangha, to make your acceptance.'

The Buddha indicated his acceptance without saying a word. Anathapindik stood up, circled around the Buddha in obeisance and walked away with a light heart and an indelible image of the smiling sage in his mind.

When he told Grihapati of the events of the dawn, Grihapati said he felt happy for his brother-in-law. He offered him money for the feast he would host and the alms he would give to the monks. Anathapindik turned down the offer politely, saying he had the money. As word spread, the mayor and then the emperor offered the visitor money in case he did not carry enough to travel. He turned down these offers.

Anathapindik served the sangha during their visit to Grihapati's house, and the next morning, sent a man to remind the Buddha the sangha was awaited again. The sage himself, wearing his usual ochre robes and carrying a bowl and a fluffy brush to wave insects away, led a long procession of monks. Welcoming crowds lining both sides of Rajgrih streets received them. Once again, Anathapindik and Grihapati, and their friends and families, bursting with pride, served the monks.

When the sage politely signalled the end of the meal, the banana leaves were carried away. 'Lord, make Sravasti your centre during the rainy season. We shall be blessed to have you among us', Anathapindik said. The sangha monks were known to be itinerant, except during the monsoon months, when they took shelter in one place.

'Good Sir, we reside in a solitary place. We are humbled by the invitations of men such as yourself, but we need quiet for our way of life', the Buddha said.

'I shall set up a suitable place', Anathapindik said.

Anathapindik had an extensive social network. He was efficient at getting things done. When he completed his business at Rajgrih and returned to Sravasti, he became an evangelist for the cause of the sangha. 'Friends, make build rooms, build abbeys. The Buddha is a gift to humanity. We are lucky to have him with us. I have invited him, and I have sent word to him we shall build vihars for his sangha. I know he shall bless our land!'

People listened to him because they saw he was selfless in his motivation. Those who had wealth used it. Anathapindik freely gave money to those who did not. Anathapindik led a large and diverse group that ensured they established a vihar for the use of the sangha every eight miles along the path from Rajgrih to Sravasti.

When he achieved this great goal, he started thinking about his next mission. Where should the Tathagat stay? It should not be too far from a city, but not too close either. It should be accessible to the sea of humanity that would travel to see him. It should provide an environment for meditation and contemplation. After dwelling on this problem, he decided the ideal place was a garden belonging to a prince.

He strode to the garden and said to the prince, 'Gentleman, I need to build a shelter here. I wish to buy this garden from you.'

'Sir, it is not for sale', the prince said. 'Not at any price unless you cover it in gold coins.'

'Gentleman, it is sold.'

'No, Sir, it is not!'

Anathapindik and the prince took their dispute to a minister of law. The lawyer opined that since the owner had named his price, and the buyer accepted it, the garden was sold at that price.

Before an officer of the court, Anathapindik had his men cover the garden with gold coins. When they ran short of coins to cover one corner, he told them to empty his coffers and get more.

The prince stopped him. By now, he had realised Anathapindik was not a man on an ordinary mission. Anathapindik did not want the land for himself but was willing to give everything all he had for a higher purpose. He said, 'Enough, I do not need more. Leave this small pocket of land for me. I shall live here.'

Anathapindik, in turn, reflected that the prince was an influential man. His becoming part of the establishment they were building would help the sangha. He gave the parcel of land back to the prince.

On the land he had purchased, Anathapindik built a simple but large monastery, with dwelling halls, huts, wells, lawns, toilets, ponds and canopies. He named the complex Jetavan, to honour its former owner, Prince Jeta.

Thus, the first large monastery of the sangha came into being.

CHAPTER 54

ARYA VARSHKAR'S STRATEGY

Emperor Bimbisar ordered a large monastery for the Tathagat to be built at the Trikoot mountain. Thousands of artisans started work on it, guided by a master architect. The emperor and the empire worshipped the Buddha. The sacrifices of many wealthy men, Son Kotivinsh and Anathapindik among them, impressed the common people. Even more admirable was the stream of renowned intellectuals who joined the sangha, drawn by its egalitarianism and its spirit of reform. Purnakashyap, Makkhali Goshaal, Prakrudh Katyayan, Sanjay Velaathaputa, Sariputra and Pindot Bhardwaj were among the luminaries who adorned the sangha.

Masses of people flocked to hear the great sage. In those days, Rajgrih people had two topics of conversation. The first was the attack and sudden retreat of King Pradyot. The second was the living sage Gautam Buddha, whose newly created religion had captured the hearts of the nobility and the masses. Many princes and merchants, forsaking their luxurious lives, became monks, adding to the mystique of the Buddha. The ochre-clad monks with their begging bowls had become a usual sight. The new, egalitarian religion held a quiet appeal to the non-Brahmans, people of mixed blood, and sects such as the Vratyas, living outside the fold of Vedic society. Up to that point in social evolution, the Brahmans had forced a doctrine of religion on the masses. But that religious order did not satisfy the people. It had become regressive and excluded the multitudes of lower castes from social and economic progress. The wealthiest layer of society – the nobles, Brahmans and merchants – were the ones benefiting from the setup. Ever grander yagyas turned rajas – kings – , into maharajas – great kings – , and maharajas into samrats – emperors. The Brahmans received lavish donations, proclaimed the kings to be divine beings, and drummed ideas of fate and destiny into the people.

The fate of lower-class people was to give their young sons to serve the causes of the nobles, and their daughters to feed their desires. The land's wealth was channelled into the affluent layer, while the masses sweated in penury.

While this decadent form of Brahmanism was the imperial attire, the Tathagat brought a new, republican fashion. He vigorously sought means of smashing the forces of inequality and extortion, which now dominated society. He emphasised simple, introspective meditation over overwhelming and grandiose rituals and sacrifices. He liberated the downtrodden from exploitation by the rich and the powerful, and his monks became respected emblems of celibacy, simplicity and virtue. His own conduct, and his credentials as a former prince who had walked away from luxury, helped to inspire many young men. Rattled by the Buddha's meteoric rise, several Brahmans established monasteries and propagated the view that men should first marry and lead a domestic life, becoming ascetics only in their old age.

·

The Tathagat's face displayed unusual signs of paleness and exhaustion. His body was lean and wiry, and his voice mellow, as always. He had started his day early, as the moon still shone in the sky. He sat on his mat in the Lotus position and talked to the monks in a blend of high philosophy, homespun wisdom and simple parables. His disciples listened in rapt silence. His gaze was steady and mesmerised those on whom he laid eyes.

Arya Varshkar entered the gathering without fanfare. He circled around the Buddha, prostrated himself at the sage's feet, and sat in a corner, mixing with the others. Lines of worry were writ large on his forehead. The Buddha ended his oration and looked at the chief minister of Magadha with a smile.

'Master', Arya Varshkar said, 'is the empire the highest organisation in the land?'

The Tathagat's smile deepened. 'Indeed, it is', he said, 'if it serves the people.'

The chief minister mulled this reply in silence. 'And the Vajji Republic, Master? Is it well-to-do, in your opinion?'

Gautam Buddha turned to his disciple Anand. 'Anand, do the Vajjis take every decision in a joint assembly?'

'That is so, Sir', Anand said.

'And is it true that their leaders meet often, and as equals, share advice, and eat, drink, and work together?'

'Yes, Master, it is true.'

'And is it not true that they do not break their own laws?'

'It is true, indeed, Lord.'

'Do they have high standards regarding respect for elders and family traditions?'

'Yes, Master.'

'Are kidnappings and rapes of women common?'

'No, Master!'

'Do they maintain their places of worship well?'

'They do, Master.'

'Are their scholars respected and happy?'

'They are, Lord.'

The sage nodded. 'In that case, they will progress and cannot be destroyed. Their prosperity will increase.'

The sage had not looked at the chief minister, but his words ingrained themselves in Arya Varshkar's mind. His nimble mind had already reached a swift conclusion. The only way to destroy Vaishali was to change the factors Gautam Buddha had listed as their strengths. Prime among those was their egalitarian, united, republican governance.

Arya Varshkar sent his spies to Anga, Kalinga, Avanti, Kaushambhi, Gandhar, Bharat, Andhra, Shabar, Mahishmi, Bhrigukach, Shurpartak, Ashmak, Prathisthan and Vidisha. He knew he must form a coalition of states indifferent to Vaishali's interest as a first, essential step in diplomacy.

He paid particular attention to activating his network of spies in Vaishali. Magadhan agents settled as jewellers, merchants and builders in the city. Many more infiltrated the city as prostitutes, jokers, entertainers and acrobats. These agents were to send a stream on information to their handlers on the gossip, internal power struggles and divisions in the Republic's council. While the council appeared united from the outside, Arya Varshkar knew that no human organisation was without internal conflicts. Soon, he moved a step further and instructed his agents to stir up quarrels, encourage drunkenness and debauchery, and use young beauties to provoke besotted nobles to armed fighting. The chief minister of Magadha monitored the progress of his intelligence offensive with satisfaction.

There came a time when Arya Varshkar felt he had a good idea of the pulse of the famous Vaishali Republic. He thought he had done just enough to undermine its foundations without raising the alarm at the highest levels of its council. He called a meeting of the Magadhan Royal Council. For the emperor, Vaishali was not an ordinary part of expansionary conquest. Vaishali was about his quest for Ambapali. He had kept his secret treaty with Ambapali secret from his chief minister, the prime mover of his empire and his childhood friend. But while Arya Varshkar gave no sign he knew of this treaty, he encouraged Emperor Bimbisar's love for Ambapali.

In military terms, Arya Varshkar's goal was to annex King Pradyot's Avanti. This would take Magadha's borders to the Arabian Sea and give the empire unprecedented access to the western world. The Jewish King Solomon's boats came up to Rauruk Sauveer in Avanti, laden with gold, and took away manufactured goods such as textiles, ivory work and jewels, and spices. Magadha already had a grip on the eastern trade after annexing Champa.

Arya Varshkar quickly established solid diplomatic ties with the king of Saagal, to the north-west of Avanti, and sent an ambassador bearing gifts to King Solomon. He reasoned that after the upheaval of Avanti's aborted campaign, the situation was ripe for Magadha to attack and annex Avanti before concentrating its vastly expanded power on Vaishali.

This policy became a matter of dispute between the emperor and the chief minister. Having seen the deleterious effect of ignoring Arya Varshkar's advice, the emperor was wise enough to realise he must not repeat the same mistake. He called a council of his advisors.

CHAPTER 55

CONFLICT IN MAGADHA

The chief minister's expression was stony, and his gaze distant.

Emperor Bimbisar was flushed and made no effort to hide his anger. 'By whose order was a messenger sent to Avanti?' He shouted out the question.

The Royal Council was in session, and the councillors were silent as the two arbiters of Magadha's fortune sparred in public as they had never done before.

Arya Varshkar answered the question. 'It was my order, of course, Emperor.'

'And why not mine?'

'You have no knowledge of politics, Your Majesty.'

'I had ordered a campaign to take Vaishali!' Bimbisar said.

'And I revoked the order', Arya Varshkar said.

'And how dared you do it, Sir?'

'I did it for the empire.'

'I am the emperor, Sir!'

'But you can harm the empire, Your Majesty. We have seen that.'

'I am the empire. Its harm is mine. I am free to harm myself.'

'No, Your Majesty. Harm to the empire is not harm to you.'

'Let me understand this – have I ever caused harm to the empire?'

'Yes, Your Majesty. You led your soldiers to disaster in Kosala. An avoidable disaster. A blot on our history. The responsibility is entirely yours.'

'Why not yours? Did you send support on time?'

'Your Majesty, we have discussed this. I had more important matters to tackle.'

Now, the emperor was visibly restraining himself from springing on his childhood friend. His sinews showed up, and his limbs trembled. 'What, pray, can be more important than protecting the emperor?'

'Protecting the empire, Your Majesty.'

'Without the emperor!'

'emperors come and go, Your Majesty. I must serve the empire and make it immortal.'

'Sir, you insult the emperor!' Bimbisar shouted.

'The emperor insults himself', Arya Varshkar said.

'I am the centre of the empire! Am I not?'

'No, Your Majesty. That is your misconception. You are its highest jewel.'

'Who runs the empire?'

'This Brahman.'

'I see. I declare that I take over your responsibilities.'

'Not while I hold my post, Your Majesty.'

'Then I dismiss you.'

'That is the only order of yours that I am bound to accept, Your Majesty.'

'But I have another order.'

'You can state it, Your Majesty.'

'You have mutinied again the crown. I spare you the death penalty because you are a Brahman. But the State will confiscate all your property.'

'I am a Brahman, and I accept this order as well. However, I have a statement to make, Your Majesty.'

'You can state it.'

'I am not a subject of the emperor anymore. I return this sword to you, Your Majesty.'

The chief minister's face betrayed no emotion as he laid the sword on the ground and touched his head to it. He rose erect and stood before the council. The other council members were distraught, and some were wringing their hands, but the emperor asked the opinion of none.

Emperor Bimbisar had spent his fury. He spoke softly now. 'One who is not my subject may not stay in my empire.'

Arya Varshkar spoke without drama or fuss. He said, 'I shall eat or drink only after I have left this land where I grew up.'

One councilman sank his head into his hands but still said nothing.

Arya Varshkar bowed and left the hall. His footsteps echoed for a long time in the silence that ensued.

Bimbisar did not see the desperate pleas in his councilmen's eyes. He looked at the receding form of his childhood friend and spoke in a whisper. 'Announce that anyone providing shelter to Arya Varshkar shall be sentenced to death.' He nodded towards the army chief, and said, almost casually, 'Prepare to attack Vaishali.'

CHAPTER 56

THE BARBER-GURU

A run-down hut stood at a crossroads on the outskirts of Rajgrih. The small structure was a famous establishment. Its master, Prabhanjan, was a tall, wiry, and active man of more than sixty years. His most prominent feature was the eyepatch he wore to cover his blind left eye. He was an expert in his trade, but also at tying turbans. His hut was a melting pot where Brahmans and outcasts such as the Vratyas met to buy his services. He was clever and well versed in the art of conversation. He could relate to the lowly and the noble, and his cheerful outlook helped. His customers saw him as a likeable man, but there was always an edge about him. Customers soon realised he was great company, but they could never get very close to him. A mysterious spirit lurked in him, showing glimpses of itself, hinting that it had fangs without ever really baring them.

Rumour had it that Bimbisar and Arya Varshkar had been Prabhanjan's clients since they first needed the services of a barber and he still serviced them in their palaces. There were whispers he knew enough secrets about the two nobles for them to be careful with him. Efforts to get him to talk about these special relationships got nowhere. Prabhanjan laughed off the topic. To those who persisted, the slightest glint of a threat in Prabhanjan's gaze was enough of a warning. Often, he achieved the change of topic by switching to religious discourse, which seemed to be his favourite subject. Such was his enthusiasm that his clients, even the Brahmans, did not despise this pretentious trait of the low caste. His familiarity with simplified religious treatises earned him the nickname 'Barber-Guru'.

•

Two watches of the night had passed. The hut was still full of customers. Prabhanjan was busy at work with two of his assistants. As usual, it was hard to tell which of his tongue and razor moved faster.

A man in rustic attire entered the hut. He looked ill at ease.

Prabhanjan stopped in the middle of a repartee. 'What do you want, Villager? If you need a haircut, my disciple here will do it.'

'Umm…Massage –' the man said.

'Not at this time, friend, I am afraid', Prabhanjan said. 'Come back tomorrow.'

'No, no, friend. I am a masseur. I came looking for a job. I have travelled far. You can test me.' The man spoke softly but did not hesitate. His soft tone made one pay attention to what he was saying.

Prabhanjan smiled as if to tell his client, who was eyeing him in the mirror, that wonder never ceased, and that was all right. To the man who had come in, hc said, as hc resumed nipping hair, 'I see, I see. Well, we all need people with skills. I know a noble who is looking for a masseur, indeed. Which village are you from, friend?'

'From…you have not heard the name, Sir. From near Vaishali.'

'And are you a Licchavi?'

'No, no! Are there any Licchavi masseurs? I am a Vratya.'

'Ah, I guessed when I saw the lowered tip of your turban. I still asked because Licchavis are not like they used to be.' Prabhanjan guffawed, and his customers joined in the laughter.

The visitor looked confused. 'How is that, friend?'

'I can be your friend, Villager, but the way to show it is to call me what the others call me, Barber-Guru.'

The visitor smiled for the first time. 'Well, Barber-Guru. Very well. I shall be indebted to you if you can arrange employment for me.'

'And how will you pay off your debt, Villager?'

'I shall give a month's salary, and sing the praises of the Barber-Guru, and –'

'Very good, Villager, before you go on, that's not needed. I shall test you out and then take you to the noble. But…he is a great man. Have you ever served a great man?'

'Oh yes, Barber-Guru. I have only served great men. Common men cannot afford my services.'

The Barber-Guru laughed. 'That makes sense', he said. 'All right, we shall talk more in the morning. Let me show you a place to sleep.'

Prabhanjan took the man across the courtyard to a row of cubicles. He opened one, looked into it and said, 'Here you are, Villager. Stay here. I shall get food for you when I am finished with my work. It will not take too long.' He turned away.

'Prabhanjan!' It took the Barber-guru an instant to realise the villager had called him by his name, in a somewhat peremptory tone. He wheeled around to see the man had removed his shawl and turban and stood looking somehow more imposing in front of him.

It was Chief Minister Arya Varshkar. Prabhanjan prostrated himself before his visitor.

The chief minister gave him a fleeting smile in acknowledgement. He said, 'Prabhanjan, get me a scroll and something to write with. Now. Later, when you have finished work, get ready for a long journey.'

Prabhanjan had lost his talkativeness. He dashed into another room and ran back with his arms full of material. He laid it down and sprinted to get a lamp and light it.

'Shall I come back after I have finished there?' Prabhanjan asked. He looked back over his shoulder, to check that no one had come looking for him.

'Yes, of course. It shall take me time to write. But later, you will go on a long journey. It will be a secret trip. I will stay under this thatched roof. I think I will like it here. Make sure no one talks too much about your guest.'

'I shall do so, Sir', Prabhanjan said.

Prabhanjan finished the interrupted haircut and distributed the remaining work among his assistants. He engaged the customers in conversation as he wound up his day's work and eased himself out of the hut in his usual way. The assistants would take a little time finishing to clean up and organising the place for the next day's work.

He went back to Arya Varshkar, who, using a wooden box as a table, had just finished writing the letter. He rolled the scroll and sealed it with care and gave it and a bag – it obviously had gold coins – to Prabhanjan.

'Take these', he said. 'Get to Sravasti. Give them to Army Chief Udayi. Once the men outside will have left, tell the assistants you will be away for three days, and they should leave me alone. Tell them I am here because you will not risk offending Lakshmi, the Goddess of Wealth. I think they will believe that of the Barber-Guru.' Arya Varshkar chuckled.

Prabhanjan felt a surge of pride at this indirect compliment from the great man. 'Is there anything else, Arya?'

'No. You will leave on foot and buy a horse on the way. Go in disguise. Make sure the horse does not stand out and do not attract bandits' attention. When you return from Sravasti, you will find me waiting at the usual place on the route back to Rajgrih. Go now. I am exhausted.'

The chief minister collapsed into a deep slumber on a bed that was nothing more than a wooden plank. His underling fingered his eyepatch as he thought through the discussion he would have with his assistants.

CHAPTER 57

SHALIBHADRA

Shalibhadra was a scion of an influential merchant family in Rajgrih. His father Gobhadra was one of the richest men in a city full of rich men. Shalibhadra was the darling of his parents and lived with his thirty-two wives in a mansion tastefully decorated with artefacts from every corner of the civilised world.

A group of merchants from Persia was in the city. They had carried blankets studded with jewels, but their prices were exorbitant, and Emperor Bimbisar had baulked from buying them. His mind was on the coming wars and the pressure on the royal treasury. The merchants had not imagined this outcome when they set out from their homeland – Magadha was known as a land of unlimited purchasing power.

As they walked to their inns, they crossed Subhadra's mansion, and one of them presumed to knock on his door on a whim. Subhadra's mother, Bhadra, gladly bought their blankets, and the merchants concluded a sale that lightened their thus far heavy hearts.

When the empress heard of the merchants, she asked the emperor to buy just one blanket, at any price. Now the emperor, under compulsion, asked his finance minister to visit the merchants and buy one blanket from them.

The minister hastened to what seemed an easy task but had to report to the emperor that Lady Bhadra had purchased all the blankets. The emperor thought briefly before ordering the minister to buy just one from Bhadra at any price.

When the minister sent his messenger to Bhadra, she replied she had cut the blankets into small pieces for her daughters-in-law to use as foot towels. As a result, she did not have a single one left to sell. The minister took this missive to the emperor.

The emperor's jaw dropped, and his eyes widened. 'Sir, do I have such wealthy men living in my empire?' Bimbisar asked. 'I must see this Subhadra!'

The finance minister conveyed an invitation to Bhadra. She came to the Royal Palace in a palanquin at once. She bowed politely before the emperor, and said, 'Lord, my son Subhadra does not descend from the seventh floor of his mansion, and I do not wish to ask him to break his practice. But we would be greatly honoured if the emperor blessed our abode with his presence.'

The emperor was not the type of man to fly into a rage at such a statement. He listened to Bhadra with wonder and accepted her invitation without comment. He was curious by nature and wanted to see this man who lived so close to the palace, and of whom he knew nothing.

Emperor Bimbisar reached Subhadra's mansion at the appointed hour, dressed in full regalia. He was welcomed with fanfare and taken to the fourth storey where Bhadra washed his feet. She sent word to her son through the chief slave. Since the emperor himself had come up to the fourth storey, it was proper that Subhadra should descend a few floors to meet the emperor.

Subhadra had never heard his mother use the word 'should'. His mother's suggestion, simple though it was, put him in a quandary. Was this not a lack of independence? He had all the pleasures he had sought out for himself, but he enjoyed them in a state of dependence. So, wasn't his luxurious existence a shallow life spent under the patronage of one who had all the power to usurp it?

He came down to salute the emperor in this distracted frame of mind. He greeted the emperor perfunctorily, and left in an instant, without saying a word. The thoughts that had pummelled him on his way down did not let go of him. He lay listlessly in his bed as he pondered them.

CHAPTER 58

MAHAVIR, THE ALL-VICTORIOUS ONE

The towering Kshatriya had sinewy and muscular arms that looked like they were made of iron. Pulling bowstrings had marked his wrists, and his chest was broad. His eyes were large and dignified, and he had a certain solemnity. His neck was long, and so were his arms that reached up to his thighs. The man did not wear a shred of clothing.

He often had no place to sit. He would seek shelter against a tree, leaning his back on it to rest his tired feet. In many villages, the people thought he was a madman and beat him. He did not fight them. Groups of children often followed him, mocking him. The days he had food to eat were few and far between, and on fortunate days, all he got was dry leftovers.

Sometimes, rogue village boys would set dogs on him. His shins and calves bore the marks of their bites. All these tortures and difficulties did not stop the man, who bore them with composure and quiet dignity. He trod on his path with steadfastness. Often, he walked endlessly before seeing signs of habitation. There are villages where people took him for a lunatic and threw stones, dust and dirt at him to shoo him away. In others, village ruffians sneaked up to push him to the ground when he quietly sat in meditation.

This great man, misunderstood and maligned by those ignorant villagers, was the great Tirthankar, Mahavir Jin. In keeping with the traditions of his family, he had spent his adolescence as a warrior, a Kshatriya. He was now engaged in a single-minded pursuit to deliver himself from desire and root out from his inner self the basic instincts coming in the way of a life of truth and non-violence.

Mahavir stayed in a city or village during the four months of the rainy season. At the end of the rainy season, he would again begin his journey on foot. He had travelled through many kingdoms and hundreds of miles when he entered Rajgrih from the western side.

In those days, Gautam Buddha had become a celebrity in Rajgrih. He had visited the city often and counted the emperor and the former chief minister among his followers. The monks of his sangha were a familiar sight all over the city. But Mahavir's bend of mind differed from that of Gautam Buddha and his followers. While Gautam Buddha emphasised celibacy, Mahavir believed most of all in non-violence. Through meditation and deep thinking, he realised the jiva, the soul, becomes omniscient and blissful when purified. He walked the path he preached by living a spartan, simple, and non-violent life.

His austerity, gravity and his deep sincerity led to his gathering an ever-increasing host of loyal followers. Word of his greatness reached the emperor, and the emperor went to see him.

One of Shalibhadra's wives asked him, 'Does the Arya know a monk came to Rajgrih who is pure, intellectual and free from desire? They call him Mahavir.'

'Do you mean the great sage Gautam Buddha?' Shalibhadra said. 'The one whose followers include so many luminaries?'

'No, he is Mahavir the all-conquering. He refrains from clothing himself and speaks only a little. But the emperor himself has worshipped him.'

'Can he remove my sorrow?' Shalibhadra asked.

'But what sorrow is that, Lord?' His wife asked.

'Dear, did you not see it happen? At my age, I take orders from my mother. I am bonded. I do not see the point of these achievements, this life of pleasure. I feel burdened. My heart is heavy.'

'Then, husband, shall we visit the all-conquering monk?'

'Let us do that. Let me leave this cocoon. Take Mother's permission.'

Bhadra, Shalibhadra and his thirty-two wives travelled to the spot where Mahavir sat in meditation, surrounded by his followers. Bhadra prostrated herself before the sage first and then circled him in homage. The others followed suit.

Bhadra said, 'Great sage, here is my son and his thirty-two wives. For the first time in his life, my son stepped on the ground to seek an audience with you. The emperor had wanted to see him. Since my son never descended below the seventh storey of our mansion, I requested Emperor Bimbisar to come to the fourth floor, and my son to come down to greet the emperor. I had not thought...Great Sage, genuflecting before the emperor seems to have saddened my son. His has become listless. Lord, he has trodden earth to seek solace from you. Please guide him!'

Tirthankar Mahavir remained quiet for a while. A hush descended on the audience as they waited for him to speak on this most unusual request. Mahavir adopted a conversational tone and spoke as a genuinely knowledgeable man would, without premeditation and from the heart. He did not condescend, he did not seek to overpower.

'Young man,' he said, 'you must know the five kinds of jivas, living beings. These are the earth-bodied, water-bodied, fire-bodied, air-bodied and vegetable-bodied. Do not inflict sorrow on any one of these. Do not incite others to inflict sorrow on them. Respect the environment composed of these five beings. To be true to the goal of not inflicting sorrow on them, what does one need? Five vows: non-violence, truth, purity, celibacy and the avoidance of hoarding. If you take these five great vows and follow them with mind, speech and action, you will achieve the goal.

'Now, these five great vows have twenty-five emotions associated with them. Young man, I have adopted this philosophy in my life, and I ask others to uphold it as well. Those considering others like themselves and controlling their bodily senses can live without sinning. Those who seek, find, and absorb knowledge can gain compassion. The one who has no knowledge of behaviour remains ignorant. Understanding the difference between jiva, soul and ajiva, non-soul, is fundamental to the knowledge of this world and the behaviour one must inculcate. One who understands jiva has a sound footing for life. This understanding becomes the basis for a deeper understanding of causes and sin, bondage and nirvana. The person who achieves these can renounce the so-called human and divine enjoyments. He becomes a renunciate. Giving up all sins, he follows his dharma and is untouched by the muck of accumulated karma. He achieves the supreme knowledge, and that supreme knowledge shows him the true nature of the real and the illusory world. Then, with his mind, speech and acts, he attains the strength and stability of a mountain. He destroys his karma, reaches moksha, liberation, and becomes the Siddha, the great achiever.'

Such was the great sage's charisma that the gathering hung on to each of his words. When the soft-spoken sage stopped speaking, Shalibhadra savoured the sensation of a great burden lifted from his heart. Then he, his wives, and his mother rose. One by one, they saluted the sage, circled him and left for their abode.

CHAPTER 59

SHALIBHADRA'S AUSTERITIES

In Shalibhadra's mind, the turmoil he had been in, and his deliverance at Mahavir's feet, created a keen yearning to become a monk. The more he thought about it, the more he realised the momentary pleasures his indulgent life had procured him did not lessen the searing sense of hurt he had experienced during the emperor's visit. He asked his mother for permission to enter monkhood.

Bhadra knew her son well. He had a strong will, and she realised she would fail in dissuading him. Instead, she said, 'Your thought is auspicious. Others have performed it. But to withdraw from the material world in one instant may be too much of a burden. It may drown you in a different sorrow. So, Son, gradually reduce the fulfilment of your desires, and you will know when the time has come to withdraw entirely from them.'

Shalibhadra obeyed his mother. He decided he would leave one of his wives every day. He called them to him, and said, 'My ladies, favourites of the gods, each of you is beautiful, well-spoken, loving, and affectionate. You are dearer to me than my own life, and I hope I have been a good husband to you.

'But this world, it now seems to me, is burning with the sorrow of destruction. The signs of our greatness, from which we drew pride, are transient. A man living in a burning house will try to save what is precious to him. My soul is precious to me, and I must save it. I must save it from hunger, thirst and disease before it is destroyed while I ply my body with all that is available to keep the outer shell that is my body healthy. Yes, I must save my soul. That is all I want.

'And that is why, Dear Ones, I must join the Tirthankar Mahavir's order. I have made up my mind to free one of you each day from our marriage. I would like to ask the one who loves me the most to liberate me first, and the second, and the third, and so on, and to make this decision in the order you decide.'

Padmavati, the daughter of a Videha merchant, spoke first, tears streaking her cheeks. 'Husband, this youth, this body and our wealth are not eternal. If you seek to liberate your soul from human bondage, I free you from your bond as my husband.' She removed her ornaments and the sindoor powder in the partition of her hair, which was a sign that she was a wife. She said, 'I will wear the simplest white cloth, Master. But I wish to join you in your new journey.'

Shalibhadra choked back his tears as he said, 'I am grateful, lady. I am contented. Let us both share this journey.'

Shalibhadra's other wives arranged for a simple ceremony to mark the beginning of Shalibhadra and Padmavati's new lives. Shalibhadra freed one wife from his bond each day, and the other wives, following Prabhavati's example, announced their intention to become nuns.

The news of these events shattered Shalibhadra's sister when they reached her. She burst into tears as she narrated the turn of events to her husband, a rich merchant of Rajgrih.

Her husband laughed and said, 'Do not worry about him. A man who leaves one wife a day cannot become an ascetic.'

This remark incensed her. She said, 'If you think it is that simple, why don't you become a monk yourself?'

He realised he had infuriated his wife, but her remark pricked him as well. He left his home that very instant, to receive Mahavir's initiation. He also sent word to his brother-in-law, Shalibhadra, who set off from his home to join the order the same day.

Both merchants began their process of absorbing the Tirthankar Mahavir's preaching into their daily lives. They had to go through severe austerities, much as iron being forged into a sword at red heat. Without caring for their bodies, they launched into fasts of weeks, followed by fortnights, months and two-month periods. Their hearts became lighter, and their bodies like skeletons clothed by skin.

Mahavir was spending the four monsoon months in Rajgrih. The two monks asked him to allow them to step out of the monastery and beg for alms. Mahavir ordered them to start by begging at their homes.

They walked to Shalibhadra's former mansion and presented themselves before Bhadra. She had already received the news of her son's completion of a two-month fast. She rushed to the monastery to greet her son and give him the alms that would mark the end of his initiation. In her hurry, she did not recognise the two feeble, trembling monks who stood at her door. If she had paused to speak to them, as were her habit with monks, events would have turned out differently. But she was too keen to see her son.

The two monks turned back from the mansion. On the way back, they received their first alms from a cowherd woman. When they reached back, they asked Mahavir's leave to undertake a final fast. On getting his permission, they marched to Mount Vaibhar to commence the fast.

Bhadra reached the Tirthankar after them. She was frail and took a longer, but easier route. She begged him to let her see her son and her son-in-law.

Mahavir said, 'They went to your door to beg for alms. In your hurry to come here, you did not recognise them. I have just allowed them to complete their final fasts, and they have continued to Mount Vaibhar.'

Bhadra's heart broke when she heard this. She returned to her mansion in a daze and lay senseless. Emperor Bimbisar himself heard the news and rushed to see her. He took her to the mountain in a palanquin, while he rode horseback himself, with a single guard.

When they reached the summit of the mountain, they saw the two monks lying still on a rock. Their bodies were still warm, but they were not breathing. Their faces were serene.

Bhadra broke into a loud lament. She cursed herself, and all women, for her lapse in not recognising her own son. Bimbisar laid a hand on her heaving shoulder to comfort her.

'Lady, your son and this other monk have gained immortality', he said. 'They shall be remembered forever. Do not sadden Shalibhadra's soul by crying. Come, let us go. I shall arrange for their last rites.'

They returned after paying their homage to the immortals.

CHAPTER 60

THE PANCHALA COUNCIL

The Council of the northern Panchalas was in session in Kapila, their capital. The council members included the kings of the Kuru, Assak, Kalinga, Sauvir, Videha and Kashi. In addition, the king of Madra, and the five sons of the king of Kosala were present, and so were a large number of representatives of nobles and Brahmans from a wide swathe of land from west to east. Leading intellectuals and sages had graced the occasion.

Atharva Angiras presented the new code of marriage. He spoke in a resonant voice. 'Members of the council, I now wish to present a new code of marriage for adoption in this council. I propose to abolish the current Vedic marriage system. From now on, no girl who has reached womanhood should stay unmarried. She may not herself choose her husband. She must devote herself to her husband and not envy his other wives. She must keep in mind that her purpose in marrying cannot only be to create offspring but also to be a dutiful housewife. Her elders give her to her husband, and she stays with that husband for life.'

Vaishampayan rose. 'These views, as the learned sage has clarified, are contrary to Vedic traditions. These traditions specify the woman shall choose her husband and is not compelled to follow the choice for life. She is free to stay unmarried.'

Angiras said, 'From today, we wish to promulgate Atharvangiras as the fourth Veda. The cow has four legs, so do I propose the Vedas become four instead of three. We need a new code as today's man is no longer a farmer and herder. We have large cities, kings and emperors with immense responsibilities on their shoulders. We have royal priests, who are the arbiters of social mores. We have armies to upkeep. Our properties, rights and duties have expanded. In this new order, I propose that man is the master and woman his slave. It is that simple. In yagyas, I propose that Brahmans take the wife's place. Inheritance should pass to the son instead of the wife. While these practices are already in place informally, our aim today is to codify and institutionalise them.'

Bhardwaj spoke without standing. 'Are we to understand the wife is not her husband's life partner? And that she is not inseparable from her husband for rituals?'

Angiras said, 'They stay life partners, but on the clear terms I have mentioned earlier. The husband and master has more rights.'

Vaishampayan said, 'So, men and women are not equal?'

Aitreya stood and interjected: 'No. And I wish to add here that my contribution to the code of conduct specifies a man may have many wives, but a woman may not have many husbands. I also wish to codify that for four generations from a paternal viewpoint, there may be no marriage within blood relations.'

Angiras said, 'And to whom her elders give her, the woman owes all her duties. She must be his sweet companion, give him happiness, be adept at work, uphold rules, produce brave sons, and be inclusive towards her husband's brother.'

Bhardwaj said, 'Let us be clear about the new codes of conduct we lay down today. One, the wife serves the husband and is not his equal. Inheritance flows to the son. Two, she follows the rules. Three, she is given by her elders.'

Angiras said, 'There is another practical matter. She must live with her husband and his parents. She is to become part of the husband's family and is no longer part of her father's family on marriage.'

Vaishampayan said, 'So she shall not only be a wife but a member of the husband's extended family?'

Angiras said, 'Indeed! And this code shall apply to all those in our ambit, including Aryans, non-Aryans, mixed breeds. This is the new Vedic standard. It shall preserve this land's purity, wealth, religion and polity. Once this august gathering adopts the code, it becomes incumbent on all to accept it.'

Now he raised his voice. 'Members of the council, do you adopt this resolution?'

A chorus of assent greeted him. The discussions on the code had been feverish, and much-heated debate had already preceded the council to iron out any potential differences. In cases, the new code only formalised existing practices.

Now Gautam said, 'Friends, I wish to raise a more important question. Four castes are no longer enough for us. Many non-Aryan brothers and sisters have mixed with Aryans to form ever-branching subcastes. We had reasons not to forbid mixed marriages earlier. Today, I propose to bar the offspring of such marriages from inheritance. I bar them from the traditions and name of the pure castes, either paternal or maternal.' He looked around the hall for effect. No one challenged him. 'I also wish to document the kinds of marriage', he continued. 'This scroll, submitted earlier to the council members, describes the permissible and recognised kinds of marriages.'

'I wish for an amendment in this', Aapstambha said. He spoke of the need for a distinct class of marriages for Asurs, for example, who lived in large numbers in the southern parts of his realm.

Vashishtha supported his proposal. He laid out the need to acknowledge such marriages, failing which existing alliances would be disrupted. He stressed the need to keep a clear separation between arranging formal unions and procuring slave women, to prevent slaves from seeking the limited rights of wives.

'I agree with all that was said', Gautam said. 'Finally, we need to consider, and – in my view – add two more kinds of marriages. The first is practised in the civilised northern republics, where the father gives his daughter in marriage to her husband stating the spouses are free to agree on a common code between them. This sort of marriage should be limited to those republics. The second, as essential, is the case when the woman is abducted – she may be unwilling or unconscious.'

Vashishtha said, 'That second addition is no marriage!'

'It is among the people of Kamboj', Gautam said. 'And they are within our ambit. The Nandinagar Kamboj people have joined the Aryans. And they also live in the areas adjoining Gandhar. Now, it is true they are mostly barbaric forest dwellers, but we need to include them in our larger Aryan brotherhood.'

Bodhayan said, 'I accept the need to bring them into our union, and the need for these two types of marriages.'

The discussion, arguments and counterarguments continued, by-and-large following the broad consensus fixed during the negotiations leading up to the formal council. The topics they took up next further tightened the clauses ensuring higher castes' purity and forbidding breeding within subcastes.

Then Gautam said, 'I propose that a widow desiring an heir may approach her elders, and with their permission, produce an heir with her brother-in-law. If no brother-in-law is available, she may produce the heir with another man without violating the purity of the caste. She may not produce more than two such children, and their father shall be known and shall acknowledge the children.'

Haareet said, 'I agree, except that this clause also applies when the husband is alive but cannot produce children.'

Bhardwaj then said, 'Married women who are still virgins should be treated as unmarried, and be married as per the code.'

Bodhayan said, 'That is agreed. But consider a woman who is not a virgin, though unmarried. She must also be married with proper procedure.'

Panini said, 'I agree. She may have lost her virginity, but for all official purposes, she is a virgin until she gets married.'

Vashishtha said, 'I have noted there are six kinds of women. One, unmarried virgins. Two, unmarried women who are not virgins. Three, married virgins. Four, normal women. Five, special women. Six, women committed to promiscuity.'

Gautam said, 'That is settled. Now, if a woman's husband goes to a foreign land, she may remarry after six years. But if the husband is a Brahman gone abroad to study, she must wait for twelve years.'

Katyayan said, 'Let us also decree that the woman has a right to alimony for her son's clothing from her first husband if he is impotent or a criminal.'

More discussion followed on the rights and inheritance of sons born of special arrangements, such as between a woman and her brother-in-law.

As the prominent men of the land spoke, the views they expressed became the foundation stone of what would and would not be permitted for centuries.

CHAPTER 61

THE TATHAGAT IN JETAVAN

The Tathagat travelled to Sravasti, having spent the four months of the monsoon at Kapilavastu. The monks of the sangha accompanied him. By this time, the sangha had become a more formalised and hierarchical organisation. Its higher rung included famous monks such as Saariputta, Moudgalayan and others.

Anathapindik received the news that the Tathagat and his sangha had arrived. He addressed a monk named Manavak. 'Friend Manavak', he said, 'please go to the Buddha, prostrate yourself and convey my greetings. He may remember me. Say to him that I pray for his and the sangha's wellness, health, peace and progress. Please tell him he should consider staying at Jetavan, where his followers have made arrangements for him and the sangha. And please ask him if he, with the sangha, will be kind enough to visit me for a meal tomorrow.'

The Buddha accepted the invitation, and Anathapindik swung into action, preparing for the day. Flowers decorated the path to the Olive Garden, without being too extravagant. The meal proposed was tasty, but not lavish.

Gautam Buddha, leading his sangha, reached the gates of Jetavan early in the morning. He wore his usual ochre robes and carried a begging bowl. He found Anathapindik pacing up and down in excitement, and he smiled as Anathapindik greeted him profusely.

Now Anathapindik guided the Tathagat to Jetavan entrance. He pointed to a carpet laid on the path.

'Please step this way, Lord!'

The Buddha paused and then stood still.

'Lord?' Anathapindik said, puzzled. 'Please step this way.'

When Anathapindik asked the Buddha to proceed a third time, the sage looked at his disciple Anand. Anand said politely to Anathapindik, 'Sir, you must remove the carpet. The Buddha prefers to walk on the earth.'

The Buddha and the sangha members entered Jetavan for the first time. They sat on stone seats. Anathapindik and his aides served the monks the meal with great relish. The monks ate frugally and politely, as was their habit.

At the end of the meal, Anathapindik asked the Buddha, 'Lord, you see Jetavan. It is my labour of love. What is your command?'

'Merchant, give it to the sangha. Let us use it – those of us who are here today, those who are in other places, and those who will come in future centuries.'

At this simple sanction of everything that he had worked for, Anathapindik beamed with pleasure. 'It shall be so, Lord!'

The Buddha then spoke to express his gratitude for Anathapindik's great work. He said, 'Your charity protects us from cold, heat and wild animals. And from snakes, mosquitoes, rains and wind. Of the various forms of charity, the one that creates a lasting benefit and gives monks a place for shelter, meditation and writing, the act of donating a vihar is supreme.'

One disciple, Darbha, stepped forward. 'Lord, shall I arrange for the monks to occupy cubicles?'

'Indeed, Darbha', the Buddha said. He turned to the others. 'Monks! Darbha Mallaputra will be the one to manage this establishment, including sleeping arrangements and meals. May we select him for the task?'

The monks agreed at once. Darbha discussed with Anathapindik and set to work. He grouped the monks by their study specialisations and started assigning cubicles and rooms to them. He consulted with the senior monks and assigned names to the principal buildings of the vihar. He named head monks to run the facilities and groups of cubicles. He appointed all-important officiating monks who would be in charge of stores, farming, shopping, cooking, cleaning and other essential works.

By dusk, the seed had been sown for Jetavan, the first vihar, to become a great institution of the Sangha.

CHAPTER 62

AJIT KESKAMBALI

An unusual turn of events had occurred in Sravasti. The merchant Mrigar, a rich and influential man, had a daughter-in-law named Vishakha. The Tathagat's teachings deeply moved Vishakha, and she had taken pains to understand and imbibe the philosophy of the sangha. Mrigar was so moved by her exposition of the Buddhist concepts that he converted to Buddhism. As he continued to learn from Vishakha, he declared that he accepted her as his spiritual mother. Thus, Vishakha became Mrigar-Mata or Mrigar's mother. During the construction of Jetavan, Mrigar offered all his wealth to Vishakha to promote the sangha. Vishakha used the enormous wealth at her disposal to erect a monastery at Sravasti. It had seven storeys and a thousand rooms. This monastery had no parallel in scale, not only in Sravasti but in the whole of India. However, Mrigar and Vishakha did not straightaway fulfil their wish to see the monastery become a centre for the sangha because the Buddha had accepted the invitation to stay in Jetavan.

Ajit Keskambali was sitting on a deerskin-covered slab in his abbey, his disciples seated around him. He was swarthy, had a massive body and unusually bright eyes. He wore a simple waistcloth. A spotless white sacred thread around his shoulder – the mark of a Brahman – contrasted with his dark skin. In front of him sat Mahashal Lauhitya, a thin, fair-complexioned man. He had a sacred thread as well and wore a long ponytail. His chest was muscular and broad, and his eyes wide.

Ajit Keskambali said, 'Well, Mahashal Lauhitya, I understand Gautam has arrived from Sravasti?'

'Yes, Master, he has', Mahashal Lauhitya replied. 'And this time his airs are insufferable! He has converted many pious Brahmans to his disciples.'

'Well, that was expected, Mahashal Lauhitya', Ajit Keskambali said. 'These foolish Brahmans are sunk. Did I not tell you that rescinding the traditional wisdom of Brahmans such as Yagyavalakya, Jaivili and Uddalaka, and inserting new ideas like those of rebirth would rebound on these men? You will see the efforts of Videha's king to organise grand meetings of Brahmans, hold discussions on conceptual matters of religion and give lavishly in charity shall all go waste. People are becoming freethinkers these days. Now take Gautam Buddha – the other Gautam. What a fraud he has perpetrated! And what about you, Senior Minister Payasi? You know the Buddha's father well, do you not? What does the father have to say about this son?'

Minister Payasi had a copper complexion, and his luxuriant moustaches reached his neck and sideburns. He had strong biceps he was fond of stroking. He said with folded hands, 'In fact, the Buddha's father, Suddhodhan, has become a disciple of the son. And not only Suddhodhan, but all the Shakyas have declared themselves his disciples. Suddhodhan reaps significant benefits from this, Sir. He wants to throw off the yoke of Kosala. From vassals of the Kosala Kingdom, they have grown in stature as the clan of the one to whom emperors and kings bow to, Gautam Buddha. Don't forget, Emperor Bimbisar is a disciple of his.'

'Why would he not be? Why would he let go of an opportunity to cover up for the fact that his clan is tainted with Asura blood lines?' He nodded and swayed. 'And what of chief queen Mallika?'

'Ah, she is under the spell of Vishakha, Mrigar's daughter-in-law, now a leading exponent of Buddhism.'

'Is that so? And what does King Prasenjit say?'

'He hesitates, Acharya. He fears Prince Vidudhab. In fact, even Suddhodhan dreads that Vidudhab. Both of them use the Buddha as a loving shield to protect them from that temperamental young man.'

'Hmm. Very well, Payasi. Have you heard yourself what the Shakyas' son preaches?'

'Well, Sir, he speaks much the same as you. He states there is no eternal entity such as God in this world. All that is born must come to an end. This world is not a collection of objects, but a flow of events.'

'Hear, hear. These are sweet words, coming from that young man. He has polished the truth, indeed. What say you, Mahashal Lauhitya? Will he entangle in his web those who care for worldly norms and incite people against me?' He paused to think and frowned in concentration. 'But how is this world flow of events, pray?'

'Acharya, Gautam Buddha says there is no eternal, conscious soul in the world', Mahashal Lauhitya said. 'There is a flow of consciousness spanning heaven and hell, and connecting our bodies.'

'He is a clever man, this sage!' Ajit Keskambali said. 'He holds on to my preaching, combining it with Pravahan's theories of rebirth. Clever, indeed.

Payasi, now I understand his power. If not for this simplicity, would the kings, nobles and merchants of these parts have opened their hearts and their purse strings to him?'

'Just so, Acharya! And do you know Vishakha now has a competitor in Rajgrih?'

'Who is that?'

'The merchant Anathapindik!'

'I see. And what has he done?'

'When he saw that Mrigar-Mata, as they call her, had chief queen Mallika's blessings and was out to gain the Buddha's grace, he found a way to gain it too.'

'And what was the way?'

'He bought Prince Jeta's famous garden, Jetavan, to set up a vihar for the Buddha's sangha. He has gifted it to the sangha!'

'Gifted Jetavan! Are you serious?'

'Indeed, Sir, I am!'

'And Prince Jeta sold it to Anathapindik? Even that is hard to believe.'

'It is, truly! It was not easy, Sir! Anathapindik had to cover the garden with gold coins. A hundred and eight million coins!'

'I see. So, Prince Jeta allowed himself to be bribed for a vast amount.'

'Just so, Acharya. Anathapindik has no shortage of gold coins. People say he recently received three boatloads of them. And his fame has reached every home in his land, while Vishakha's palatial monastery lies unblessed.'

'Well, that was fated. After all, Prince Jeta had blessed it', Payasi said.

'But it was not his doing alone, of course. The Buddha's blessing carries vastly more weight. See how chief queen Mallika has stopped gracing our abode with her presence. I have heard that Gautam, the Shakya, has cast a spell on her.' Ajit Keskambali said.

'Why is that surprising, Acharya? Think about it – a gardener's daughter rose to become chief queen just because of her looks, and those looks have withered. King Prasenjit has no time to spare to enjoy the pleasures of younger flesh. That young physician of Rajgrih has not been able to stoke the dying embers of his vigour. But it seems that Mandavya, Charvaka's disciple, is out to prove the efficacy of his concoctions to the valiant king', Payasi said.

'Charvaka, the rogue of Saket? Yes, I know of him, and his dodgy disciple. He is a blot on the Brahmans. Has he given the king hope?'

'Yes, Sir. He says that one must indulge his senses to the limit…'

'And he has given the king medicine?'

'Yes, he has, Sir. And like the dry wood turns quicker to ashes when the fire is fanned, the king will burn himself to exhaustion as he fuels his lust with that medicine. While the seventy-year-old king plans to marry the young Kalingas-ena, Prince Vidudhab plots regicide.'

'Is that so?' Ajit Keskambali said. 'I didn't know matters had deteriorated so much.'

'Yes, Acharya. Since the Shakyas insulted him, he burns with hatred for the king, his father. He holds against the king that the chief queen did not face discrimination while his own mother, the Shakya slave, did.'

'Well, his view cannot be rejected outright', Ajit Keskambali said. 'The truth is that these slave sons are the scourge of today's lusty old kings. Tell me, Vidudhab must hate Gautam Buddha with a passion?'

'If it were left to him, he would kill the sage!' Payasi said. 'But his young doctor friend…'

'Who?'

'The young physician of Rajgrih. He is a devout servant of the Buddha. And these days, Vidudhab is very close to the physician.'

'I see. So that scoundrel sage appears to exert his newfound influence to make sure his spies are everywhere…Do this for me, young Lauhitya. Get that fool Prince Vidudhab to me. Let us make him one of our party.'

'I shall try, Acharya! But be aware that he is no fool. He is a sharp man', Mahashal Lauhitya said.

'Even better', Ajit Keskambali said. 'These mixed breeds tend to be energetic – that is true. In any case, if he plans to stake a claim to the throne of Kosala, it makes sense to keep him close to us. And if he hates that son of the Shakyas, our alliance becomes more natural. That new sage has spread his tentacles everywhere!'

'I shall definitely try, Acharya. He respects me', Mahashal Lauhitya said.

'Then make use of respect!' Ajit Keskambali smiled in a way that made it clear he was chiding the younger man. 'Now tell me, what was it you said about the chief queen?'

'She is now an ardent devotee of the Buddha. She knows he is the one who can wipe out the stain of her lowly birth. And Lady Vishakha is very close to her.'

'Perhaps we can engender differences between them. We must urgently get the chief queen on our side. Then I can grapple with that Shakya Suddhodhan.'

'That will be difficult, Acharya! The chief queen is a gardeners' daughter, but with her pious life, she has built up quite a following among the people. Her stature is not less than that of the king.'

'But that is why she is important to us, young man! But don't you worry about it. I shall find a way. The chief queen shall again bow before me. I shall wait for this Rajsuya Yagya to end. Till the yagya goes on, anyway, I hold the king in my grip. But…another evil shadow hovers over Sravasti.'

'Whom do you mean, Sir?' Mahashal Lauhitya asked.

'Sage Mahavir Jin.'

'Yes, Acharya. I see what you mean. His reputation is formidable. His brand of asceticism is unique. My mind cannot grasp how he survives his two-month-long fasts. Like those of the Ajivika sect, he spurns clothing. He has drawn to him many Brahmans, and some have adopted his lifestyle. Like the Buddha, he sees Shudras and Brahmans as equals. And Prince Vidudhab is a fervent believer of his.'

'Yes, yes', Ajit Keskambali said. 'Yes, Lauhitya, there are many routes to fame. I know this rootless Licchavi sage well. The Licchavis calculate that their expansionism will find a channel through their own brand of fake faith and that Prince Vidudhab rather than the emperor will champion it. Their alternate plan is to hollow out the Kingdom of Kosala. Well, well, we shall see. Let me finish the Rajsuya Yagya.'

CHAPTER 63

PRINCE VIDUDHAB

Prince Vidudhab came to the acharya, saluted him and took his seat. He said, 'Acharya, you remember me?'

'Bless you, Prince!' Ajit Keskambali said. 'I sense that you need me.'

'What for, Acharya?'

'What else? To realise your greatest aim.'

'What are you hinting at, Acharya?'

'Do you really not understand me?'

'Well…perhaps you could speak your mind, Sir?'

'Ah, young man, you know, there is such injustice in Sravasti…'

'What kind of injustice, Sir?'

'Will that Shakya sage destroy the king and his subjects?'

'But how do you imagine that will transpire?'

'I take it you have heard the story of Jetavan?'

'I have, Acharya.'

'And perhaps you have also heard that of Vishakha, now called Mrigar-Mata, and of her seven-storey palace-turned-monastery?'

'Indeed, I have, Sir.'

'Is it true the chief queen is a daily visitor there?'

Vidudhab nodded as he sensed what the guru meant to say. 'She is, Sir.'

'And is it true that the gold from the merchants' safes and the State coffers of Sravasti, Saket, Kaushambhi and Rajgrih flow in streams to the Shakya sage's feet?'

'Yes, yes, Acharya. But what can I do?'

'What can you do? Young man, who is destined to be the king of Kosala? The sage or you?'

Vidudhab's eyes flared. 'But I am a slave's son. I am not in the succession line, or so I am told.'

'God forgive you!' Ajit Keskambali said. 'What about the calculations of the stars I spent so many hours scrutinising? Young man, your fate is to be the king of Kosala! But, at the rate things are going, by that time the entire wealth of India will have been placed in the Buddha's begging bowl! Treasuries and hoards will have been drained, and youths will have become monks. Son, can you be so blind as to not see? That fraud sage is accumulating a vast economic empire that will hollow out your future kingdom!'

Vidudhab gulped. 'Is that…is that true, Acharya?'

'Son, think about it. Who will perform sacrifices for you when they are banned? How will you pay a standing army? What will make the wheels of commerce turn? Remember, the youths will have become monks. All property will have been handed over to the Buddha! And then you, Sir, will have to rule without military power or economic clout. How will you do that?'

Vidudhab closed his eyes for an instant, and his eyebrows knit themselves together. Then he sighed and looked up at Ajit Keskambali. 'Your words ring true, Acharya,' he said.

'If they do, then step up to your task! Stop this from happening. Oh, and about your maternal side?'

'Call them the Shakyas, Acharya. I shall wipe out their roots.'

'Yes, you must. And your paternal side too, I presume?'

'That too. I shall destroy that too.'

'Well spoken. Your path to the throne requires wading through their blood. Now listen, since we are at the heart of the matter. I recognise the thorn in your flesh.'

'What do you mean, Acharya?'

'Bandhul Malla and his twelve men – his sons and cousins. King Prasenjit depends on him to run the kingdom. Bandhul Malla himself has become minister, and he has placed his gang of twelve in the army and treasury. As long as those stubborn men live, your hopes will remain dreams.'

'But, Acharya, I am biding my time, waiting for the right moment.'

'This is foolish talk, young man! You will spend the prime of your youth waiting! Your vigour, your strength shall fade away! And so shall your courage and ambition. Your friends shall give up on you and seek succour from those who hold the strings of power and wealth. Young man, you must learn to seize the day!'

Vidudhab sat erect now, drinking in this talk that was music to his ears, hanging on to every word. 'What must I do, Acharya?'

'I shall tell you. Listen. Destroy Bandhul and his men – except for his nephew Dirdhkarayan. That is the crux of the solution. Both King Prasenjit and Bandhul

Malla have neglected that Dirdhkarayan. He is a brave and discontented man. Just your man.'

'This sounds too difficult, Sir.'

'It is very easy, young man! King Udayan has massed his army on the border. He is a man whose love was thwarted. The king is afraid that Udayan will try to interrupt the marriage and the Rajsuya Yagya.'

'I am aware of that, Sir. I heard the king sent General Karayan to the border.'

'I shall arrange for success to elude General Karayan', Ajit Keskambali said.

'What will that achieve, Acharya?'

'Think about it. You will recommend the king to take the logical step. Which will be to order Bandhul Malla's twelve men to the border this time. And, of course, to call back General Karayan and humiliate him.'

Vidudhab frowned. 'I think I can do that, provided the king is paranoid enough.'

'Bandhul's men shall die.'

Vidudhab shrank back in horror. 'How…'

Ajit Keskambali took an exasperated breath, but in the next instant, he had put on a patient smile. 'Son, Bandhul's men shall die. Bandhul shall have to go to the border himself. Today he swells with pride, having destroyed Emperor Bimbisar's attack. But the conflict had weakened his war machine. He shall struggle to meet the Kosala attack. Both King Udayan and his minister Yogandharayan are mighty warriors.'

'I still think about the Bandhul ring…they are very well organised.'

'Do not worry about them, young man. Minister Yogandharayan has few peers in this world. He is a close friend of mine. I shall send him the message required through Payasi. Bandhul's sons and their cousins shall die before they reach the border. And death shall not announce itself to them.'

'It sounds like accomplishing an impossible mission, Sir.'

'Perhaps it does. But it shall happen. And one more thing – Payasi will return to Saket with Karayan. He will use their time together to soften him towards you. After his return to Saket and his loss of face, you must befriend him. He will be vulnerable, and you only need to show him a little sympathy.'

'Please rest assured, Acharya – I shall do that.'

'Well, then, Son, this series of steps will allow you to realise your ambition. But there is one thing still.'

'What is that, Acharya?'

'Anathapindik's Jetavan Monastery has become the Shakya Gautam's abode.'

'Yes, Acharya.'

'Go there. Become a fake disciple of his.'

Vidudhab gulped. 'Will I have to…kill him?'

'No, young man! He should live. He will suck all these kings, their sons and the merchants dry. And they are your enemies. Son, let him continue his great work.' Ajit Keskambali grinned. 'But tell me this, do you know when he will go to Vishakha's monastery?'

'Yes, I do. This full moon day.'

'That is when the Buddha will initiate chief queen Mallika, is it not?'

'Yes, Acharya, that is what I heard Vishakha has arranged.'

'Now, here is what you must do. Get Bandhul Malla's wife Mallika to join chief queen Mallika in the initiation.'

'I think it will only take some talking, Acharya. I know her well, and her eyes shine at the very mention of Gautam Buddha.'

'Can you do it without her realising you are the one encouraging her? You need to be subtle about it.'

'I shall be, Acharya! And I am also aware that the chief queen has considerable influence on her.'

'Very well, very well. And there is still another thing.'

'Your wish is my command, Sir.'

'Only do what is right.'

Vidudhab raised his eyebrows. 'I must confess I am puzzled, Acharya. What is right?'

'What is necessary is right.'

Vidudhab laughed. 'Sir, your faith is vastly better than Gautam Buddha's.'

'That it is. But keep this in mind: that, which we call faith or religion, is a great untruth. Clever people created it to grab the wealth of others and enjoy it without fearing the sword of retribution that hangs over warriors. Dear One, never fall for the chicanery of the tricksters who peddle religion. Understand the true nature of all faiths and be fearless. Use the waves of discourse to your ends.'

'I understand now, Master! The young physician of Rajgrih has many poisons, but he knows how to use them. He does what is right. He says that his selective use of those poisons turns them into nectar. They have the power to revive the flesh of those who are half dead.'

'That is so, that is so indeed. Now you speak with clarity. You are a good student. Go now and start on your auspicious mission.'

'Very well, Sir!' The prince stood and saluted. The guru blessed him with both hands raised.

As the prince walked away, his limbs showed signs of stiffness from sitting on the floor for so long. There was a spring in his steps.

CHAPTER 64

IN THE SLAVE MARKET

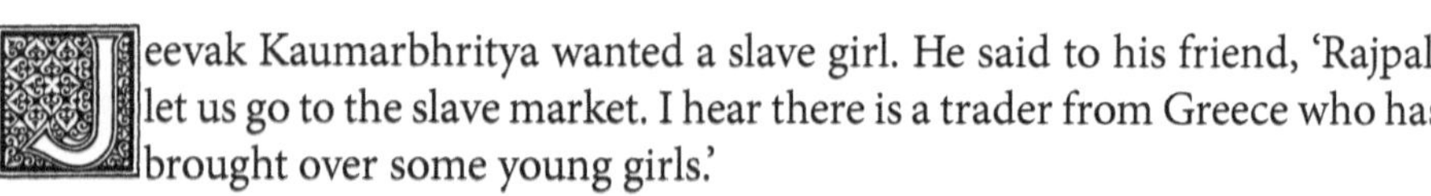eevak Kaumarbhritya wanted a slave girl. He said to his friend, 'Rajpal, let us go to the slave market. I hear there is a trader from Greece who has brought over some young girls.'

Rows of chained men and women awaited them in the market. A large, roofless enclosure bounded by iron bars stood at the centre of the market. It held the slaves, about twenty men and women, due for sale that day. All of them wore shackles. Rumour had it some of the women were Greek. They were of all ages. One of them looked about thirty years old but had not lost all her youth. Another, sitting next to her, was about twenty. Her complexion was as clear as a pearl, and her eyes were large and limpid, though they remained downcast. Both of them sat close to an old woman, arms crossed over their chests. There was a boy in his early teens. Many slaves had a dark complexion.

The slave seller was a stocky old Greek. He was a frequent visitor to this market. With his white beard, thick neck and piercing eyes, and with the forbidding leather whip he held in his hand. He went into the enclosure with a girl he had bought. The girl carried a three-year-old boy. The boy was a healthy and handsome baby. As the slave seller pushed her down and shackled her, she started crying.

'Why do you cry?' He asked the girl. 'Do you want the whip?'

'Why did you seat me here?' The girl sobbed.

'What do you think? Did you not see me pay twenty gold coins for you and your son? Is it not obvious that you are here to be sold?'

'Where? My master told me that my husband is in Vaishali and you would take me to him.'

'If he had not said that, would you not have cried yourself hoarse and disturbed the peace?' The trader smiled without malice. 'Now stop crying, or you will spoil your face, and I will get less money.' He twirled the whip.

The young woman's shoulders heaved, but the threat worked. As her son looked puzzled and wide-eyed at her, she restrained her sobs. She spoke in a low voice. 'So, this is where I will be sold?'

He seemed to debate whether lashing out at her or explaining things to her and opted for the latter. 'Why else would you be here? I buy, I sell. I cannot feed you for too long.'

A prospective buyer had been eyeing the boy. Now he stepped forward and patted his chubby shoulder. 'If you sell this one cheap, I shall buy him now', he said.

'Cheap, indeed.' The trader's face was a mask that was a mix of unconcern and toughness. 'The deal is fair here: good slaves, true prices. See how ready he is.'

'He is too small, though. I cannot get work out of him. I will have to feed him for a few years. I can pay ten karshapanas.'

'And sell him for fifty in six months?'

'And how much do you think I will get if he dies? Be fair, man. All right, I will give you fifteen.'

'Twenty then. You will not regret it. See how fair he is.'

The buyer counted out coins from his pouch. In a thin, quavering voice, the mother said, 'Please, Sir, will you not buy me?'

The trader raised his whip. 'Do not trouble my customer!' He hissed. He took the boy, unshackled him and tossed the wailing boy to the buyer's servant. The mother fainted.

He looked at the customer and rolled his eyes with a thin smile. 'Go now, Sir, you have stared your day well. Go before she recovers and creates more of a scene.'

The buyer and his servant walked away with the sobbing boy. Outside, no one turned to glance at them as they walked towards the clerk who sat at the entrance to get the relevant entries done and receive their certificate.

When the mother awoke, she had a crazed expression. The trader was still soft to her. He said, 'Do not worry. I know that buyer, he is a good man, your boy will live well, and you have one less worry.' The woman looked at him with lifeless eyes. She opened her mouth, but no words came out.

The trader sighed and turned to the next customer, an old Brahman. 'I need a girl', the Brahman said.

'You have come to the right place, as you can see. Do you want a Greek?'

'No, from these parts.'

The trader pointed to a woman. 'I think I would suggest that one. She can speak four languages and can cook and serve you. She is young.' He snapped his fingers and gestured with his hand, and the girl stood.

The Brahman told the slave behind him, 'Go and examine her.'

The slave went to the young woman, inserted his finger into the mouth and ran it along her teeth. He peered into her mouth. Then, without ado, he slid his hand under her thick gown and carefully ran his hand over her body, starting with her breasts, often pausing to squeeze the flesh. The girl looked ahead as if this was not happening to her. He laughed and said, 'She is firm. She will do for you.'

The trader smiled. 'I had told you. She will be forty nishkas. No less', he said.

'That is too much!' the Brahman said. 'Thirty is all right.'

'I see Sir, that you are a Brahman, and a Shrotriya Brahman at that. It is proper that I should sell her to you', the trader said. His smile widened as he bent to open the young woman's shackle. They counted out the coins, and the Brahman left, looking pleased, followed by the two slaves.

Now the trader turned to see Kaumarbhritya studying the slaves. 'What kind of slave do you want, Sir?' He asked. 'Look at this one.' He patted a young boy. 'Good limbs. Let me…' He opened the shackle, and said to the slave, 'Get up and dance.'

The trembling boy stood up and performed a few clumsy steps. Kaumarbhritya smiled, and the trader guffawed.

'He can do better', the trader said. 'Show the Lord how you sing.'

The boy sang in a jarring, wheezing way, struggling to hold his breath. His audience grinned.

Nudged by his friend, Kaumarbhritya pointed to a girl who sat, shrunken, in a corner. 'How much for her?' He asked.

The trader gave him a knowing wink. 'You are a very deep man, Sir, a man of taste. You recognise the best when you see it. That one has come a long way, and I paid a high price to get her and bring her here. She is good at music and dance, cooks, and knows most of the languages spoken in these parts. And look at her.' He took a step to bare the young woman.

Kaumarbhritya gestured. 'That is all right. State your price.'

'Sixty nishkas. Not one less.'

Kaumarbhritya nodded. 'Very well.' He threw a bag of coins, and the trader caught it deftly. There was no talk of counting them. The men had recognised each other.

The trader opened the woman's chains, and said to her, 'Consider yourself lucky. He is a good man.'

The young woman nodded and walked stiffly to join Kaumarbhritya and his friend. She followed them to the clerk's desk, her eyes downcast.

A large line of slaves, men and women, now entered the square. The clerk noted down the slaves' and their traders' details as they marched by his desk. He gave each slave a numbered shackle.

There were men, women, boys and girls of all ages. The oldest seemed to be a woman about seventy years old, stricken with rheumatism, and the youngest a girl of perhaps four. A ten-year-old girl was crying, asking after her mother, who had clearly already been sold. The old woman had suffered the mortification of seeing six of her young children sold over the last three days, while she had no takers. Two women sat hugging each other, one about forty-five years old and the other, about fifteen. They were visibly mother and daughter. They still had on old but fine clothes from their days as free women. Their limbs showed they had lived lives without toil. Someone had gifted them to a Brahman as a tribute after a great yagya. The Brahman had seized their jewellery and sold them.

The centre of the market was now very crowded. There was barely standing room, and the buyers and sellers were shouting to make themselves heard. In a strategic corner, Somprabh stood on a small wooden box, his eyes darting from one slave to the next, making sure he did not miss a single one. His face was wan, and he did not have the aura of the warrior who had defeated Champa. A hand tapped him below the shoulder.

It was Kundani. He helped her up, and she stood next to him. They squeezed each other's hands. Kundani eyes were moist.

Her voice trembled as she spoke. 'It is such a relief to see you. I was so worried, Som!' She stopped to catch her breath. 'I could not do anything for you. Did you come here straight from Sravasti?'

'Yes, I was not too well, and it took longer than I wanted. I have so desperately looked for you.'

'For me, or the princess? Come now.'

Som smiled weakly. 'Where is she?'

Kundani smiled disappeared. 'She has fallen into the hands of this Greek slave trader.'

'You could not save her from that fate?' Somprabh's throat was dry.

'No, Som. At that point, the best I could do was to keep myself free. I fled.'

'So, this man will sell her as a slave?' Somprabh's nostrils had flared, and his hand was on the hilt of his sword.

Kundani gripped his arm. 'Do not do anything foolish, Som', she said. 'He has already sold her.'

'Sold! Where?'

'Into the harem. The harem keeper took her from this market. I saw it happening.'

Somprabh stopped scanning the trading floor and turned to look at Kundani. 'And you stood by and let it happen?' His tone was harsh now.

'What else could I have done? Was I to impede a legal trade? On what basis? I know all about the harem.'

'What do you mean?'

'When King Prasenjit will have married Kalingasena, chief queen Mallika will gift her a young slave woman, according to tradition. Many slave women were brought together, and the harem keeper chose the princess without negotiating. The chief queen has approved of the choice.'

'That is terrible, Kundani! Will you do nothing about it?'

'I only said I could not have stopped the trade. Of course, we must save the princess. But will you have the courage?'

'Will I?' Somprabh said and looked into her eyes.

She waited for him to speak.

'I am still weaker than I was. But be sure of this: if King Prasenjit is proud of his General Bandhul, I alone will smash that pride. I will avenge the defeat of Magadha.'

'Will you be able to do this alone?'

'Not alone. My sword and I will do this.'

'It is well that you have so much faith in your sword. I cannot promise you help here.'

'Why are you so callous about the princess? Why did you bring her here to put her in this miserable state?'

'I saved her from a worse misfortune.'

'Then save her one more time.'

'I can. But not with your plan. With mine.'

Somprabh held back his natural response, keeping in mind all that they had been through together. 'What is your plan?' He asked.

'I will tell you. First, tell me: do you have the courage?'

Somprabh's temple throbbed. 'Do you not see my sword?' Two men turned to look at the two of them. Somprabh glared at them, and they moved on with haste.

'The sword again! Brother, the sword is useless!'

'What is useful?'

'Skill.'

'Do you mean your death kiss?'

'No, no, Som. This is not the Asur's den, this is Sravasti. I am sure I don't need to tell you the executioner's axe awaits us if we are exposed as Magadhans, for they will treat us as spies.'

'Tell me about your plan.'

'We are Magadhans – defeated Magadhans.'

'I do not accept that.'

'There is no point in denying it. But, once again, will you dare to do what I suggest?'

'You test me! Say what you have in mind now. Tell me what to do.'

Kundani laughed. 'That is the plan! I will tell you what to do.'

Som could not help laughing. 'You may as well tell me now.'

Kundani looked around her. The paradox was that discussing a secret in that noisy meat market, now working at a feverish pitch, was safe. No one was paying attention to them, and none could have overheard them.

'You and I will break into the harem.'

Somprabh crossed his arms and looked at her. 'How?'

'Dressed as women.'

'What! How will we do that?'

'Som, trust me. I shall manage the clothes and disguise. But that is where courage lies. Not charging ahead with your sword. Are you up to it?'

Somprabh looked at her earnest face and remembered all they had been through together. 'For you, with you, I may as well do this.' He broke into a broad grin.

It relieved Kundani to see the fire in him still intact, although the events of the dash from Champa had physically weakened him. She looked askance at him. 'Hmm – for me? Or for the princess?'

'Think what you like, dear Kundani', Somprabh said.

'Very well. Now come with me.'

'Where do we go?'

'To the chief minister.'

'What, Arya Varshkar? Are you saying he is here?'

'Yes. First, you must rest, eat and bathe. We shall wait for night to fall before going to him.'

'Let us go.'

They walked out of the slave market, into a maze of crooked streets.

CHAPTER 65

TWO STALWARTS

An old house stood outside the city. Its front yard had a colossal statue of a yaksha, a spirit. Most of the house was underground, and its entrance was through a cave. The statue was made of black stone, and it took on an eerie persona in the darkness. People from the city avoided this area. Sometimes, troubled visitors recited a prayer to the spirit, lit a lamp and stayed for some time in the cave. It was rumoured that the spirit's anger could cause a man's head to roll. At night-time, the residents of Sravasti made themselves scarce.

Kundani brought Somprabh to this house at night. She held Som's hand tight and drew him into the pitch dark cave. Som followed her, groping with his right hand for any obstacles. After what felt an eternity, they saw light at the end of the tunnel. Feeble at first, like the glimmer of a firefly, its intensity increased with each step. As they drew near, Somprabh saw it came from a candle. A man sat erect below the large emitting the light. It was Arya Varshkar. He was the picture of concentration, writing in furious spurts and pausing to think between phrases. When they were within a few steps of him, he looked up, acknowledged their bows and motioned for them to sit. He finished writing, read the scroll through, and closed his eyes to think. Then he sealed the scroll with his clay seal and set aside his quill.

He looked at Somprabh with a stony face. 'Somprabh, young man, the emperor lost the battle before we could be with him.'

Somprabh choked as he said, 'I realised that, Arya.'

'Now, Acharya Vadrayan Vyas has sent me a message. The emperor has reached Rajgrih. I need to get back too as soon as possible. Rajgrih is under attack from Pradyot and Avantivarman. I think I know how to deal with those two. But I have a mission to complete here. What time is it?'

'One watch is over, Sir', Somprabh said.

'Then, Som, keep this letter. Guard it well. I know you will, but I mention the need to do so for a reason. Give it to General Udayi. He is trying his best to reassemble the scattered Magadhan main army. We have a target that he must achieve. It is simple: get the army together, wait for the right occasion and destroy this Rajsuya Yagya that King Prasenjit is conducting.'

Somprabh digested this. 'Arya, do you have any orders about King Prasenjit himself?'

'No specific orders. Do the right thing, at the right time. He is our enemy.'

'Prince Vidudhab?'

'Protect his life. You know why.'

'As you order, Arya!' Somprabh felt a new vigour coursing through his veins.

'Daughter Kundani, you must insert yourself into the harem. And keep in mind, Bandhul Malla is our primary target.'

'As you order, Arya!' Kundani said.

'And one more thing. This is important: Uppali, the potter, is our friend. Keep that in mind. You will find him useful when the time comes.'

'That is all. Bless you both!'

Kundani and Somprabh bowed devoutly and stepped away. The chief minister of Magadha did not rest for long before picking up another scroll and picking up the quill to write again. His concentration on the task did not prevent him from hearing hesitant footsteps coming his way. He threw aside the quill, picked up his sword and stood up in fluid movements.

'Who is there?' A soft voice asked.

'If it is Yogandharayan who asks, the humble Varshkar welcomes him.'

Soon, Yogandharayan stepped into view. 'May you be well, friend, may you be well!' He said.

They embraced with the fervour of two old friends meeting after a long time.

'Be well, my friend', Yogandharayan said, his voice deep with emotion.

'And you, my friend, and you', Arya Varshkar said. He had cast aside his impersonal, stern shell and his fondness showed in his eyes.

They sat down, looking at each other. It was not often that the two great masterminds of the world were in the same room.

Yogandharayan spoke first. He said, 'I am responsible for the defeat of Magadha, my friend!'

'Do I not know that, friend? But I do not blame you.'

'I am happy about that. King Prasenjit had mounted the campaign with a single goal: Kalingasena.'

'I only wonder why Lady Kalingasena set aside King Udayan's love to accept the advances of the old man.'

'I am afraid it was my doing, friend.'

'I see. Does she know about King Prasenjit's age and condition?'

'Why not?'

'Then, why?'

'I came in the way.'

'Why so?'

'For Kaushambhi's sake.'

'Has the wise Yogandharayan perhaps underestimated the value of Gandhar's friendship? It could have extended King Udayan's reach to the northern Kurus.'

'That is so, that is so. Since King Udayan played a positive role in the Dev-Asur wars, King Indra of the Devs has been a close friend of King Udayan.'

'That is well. But – I am still not clear – what came in the way of the love between King Udayan and Princess Kalingasena?'

'I could not allow the king of Avanti to be offended. As you know, after his daughter was abducted, it was an uphill task to please him. And his continued pleasure is essential to my kingdom, Kaushambhi's well-being. We could not afford a marriage between King Udayan and Kalingasena.'

Arya Varshkar absorbed this and nodded. 'That is what I surmised. May I ask why the chief minister of Kaushambhi, the great Yogandharayan, does not set much stock by the friendship of Emperor Bimbisar?' He smiled to show he was not making any threat.

'Why would I not?' Yogandharayan smiled back. 'The chief minister of Magadha knows well that in an earlier era, I went so far as to declare Vasavadatta dead to ease King Prasenjit's marriage to Princess Padmavati of Magadha. That proves the importance I have assigned to relations between Kaushambhi and Magadha. And in my humble opinion, perhaps the dependence in these troubled times is mutual. Perhaps the two – Magadha and Kaushambhi – need each other more than they did in the past.'

'I am relieved to hear these views, friend', Arya Varshkar said. 'You know the king of Avanti has become openly hostile to us. Emperor Bimbisar also opposed King Udayan's marriage to Princess Kalingasena.'

Yogandharayan laughed. 'I understand that. The emperor knows that a union between Kaushambhi and Gandhar only means he must spend much nervous energy worrying about the threat from his north-west. In fact, Magadha taking on and demolishing Kosala serves Kaushambhi's interests. May I also state that King Udayan expected Magadha to be able to deal a body blow to Kosala on its own?'

'Friend Yogandharayan, Magadha's campaign against Kosala is not finished. I, Varshkar, am still alive.'

'The wise old Varshkar's name carries weight for a reason.' Yogandharayan bowed slightly. 'I am pleased the king of Kaushambhi, and I have the friendship of Emperor Bimbisar and you.'

'The emperor has always seen a friend in the king of Kaushambhi.'

'And the king will be pleased to learn this confirmed today.'

'Be well, friend', Arya Varshkar said.

After Yogandharayan had left, Varshkar ordered the items around him neatly and dressed for a journey. Then he strode out into the darkness. At the entrance, he clapped his hands in a pattern. A man appeared in an instant. Varshkar made a gesture with his eyes.

The man bowed. 'I am ready, Arya!'

'Very well. Is my horse ready?'

'Yes, Arya.'

Varshkar pulled his robe tighter around him and walked to the horse.

CHAPTER 66

VIDUDHAB'S DIPLOMACY

King Prasenjit and Bandhul Malla were engaged in a hushed conversation. Prasenjit's lips pursed when he was not talking, his forehead creased, and his eyebrows knit together. He gesticulated with his closed fist to reinforce his points.

A shadow fell over them. Prince Vidudhab had entered the hall.

The king said, 'Come, Prince, sit down. You left suddenly for Sravasti, without a word to me.'

'I had to leave, Your Majesty.'

'Why?'

'An important message.'

'I see. What was it?'

'May I speak freely?'

'Yes, Prince.'

'I received news.'

'Yes, what news?'

'Unwelcome news.'

'From where?'

'The border.'

'Speak now. What was the news?'

'The king of Kaushambhi will attack us at the peak of the Rajsuya Yagya.'

'Is that so? General Karayan knows nothing of any such plans, and he has been at the border for weeks. I hold his letter in my hand.'

'I too have a letter, Your Majesty.'

'Whose letter is it?'

'General Karayan's.'

'And to whom is it addressed?'

'To a friend of his.' Vidudhab handed over a scroll to the king who gave it to Bandhul Malla and ordered him to read it.

Bandhul Malla's eyes traced the letter's contents before reading it aloud. He gulped, shook his head in disbelief, and turned it over to the blank side, flipping it a few times.

'What is the matter, Bandhul? Read the letter!'

Bandhul sighed and read the words out halting as if struggling to make sense of them. 'Right on...the day the army of Kaushambhi will attack Sravasti. I shall pretend to oppose the attack, but please understand that on the ground, I am aligned to support it. Keep a force of city guards ready. What you want to achieve many elude you if you do not.'

King Prasenjit stood up. 'Does it have Karayan's signature?'

'Yes, Your Majesty!' Bandhul Malla was fuming now.

'To whom was the letter written?' King Prasenjit asked.

'To the Mayor.'

Prasenjit turned to Vidudhab. 'How did you come to know if this?' He was shouting now.

'A spy told me. I cannot disclose the source to anyone.'

'And why did you go to Sravasti?'

'To check the city's defences and speak face-to-face with my spy, whom I summoned back to the city.'

The three of them were silent for a few moments. Prasenjit asked Vidudhab, 'What do you recommend now, young man?'

'I would leave it to General Bandhul Malla. He has our trust, and we know he is steadfast.'

'Yes, but I would like to hear your advice.'

'But Your Majesty, you know that you and I do not see things in the same way.'

'But, son, the matter is Kosala's honour!'

'And that led me to Sravasti. I seek to protect the honour of Kosala.'

Prasenjit nodded. He turned to Bandhul Malla. 'Bandhul, go to the border yourself. Take charge there, imprison Karayan and send him here.'

'I object, Your Majesty!' Vidudhab said before Bandhul Malla could respond.

'Why is that, Son?' Prasenjit frowned.

'We need the general here.'

'True enough, but we need him even more at the border.'

'I propose to station the general's twelve men there. The seriousness of the situation demands that all of them control it. They have experience and our trust.'

'All of them stationed at the border? Each of them has official duties here', Prasenjit said.

'I know. But we had a working administration before them, even if it was not as good as it now is. I shall take on their responsibilities, and take help from my aides', Vidudhab said.

The three men pondered for a while in silence. Bandhul Malla did not speak.

King Prasenjit said, 'Bandhul, I made up my mind. Your men will go to the border with a force of twenty thousand soldiers.'

Vidudhab interjected. 'Your Majesty, I have a better plan. We cannot organise such mobilisation in secret. General Bandhul's twelve men should travel as special ambassadors to Kaushambhi. They should invite King Udayan to the Rajsuya Yagya and watch his reactions. Depending on his response, they should start arranging an official welcome for him as a State's guest at the border. That will give them a ceremonial reason to be on the ground. Another person should then organise the army movement in small groups. It should seem to be part of the general mobilisation and should not set off any warnings from Kaushambhi's spies.'

King Prasenjit and Bandhul nodded their assent. King Prasenjit asked, 'Who will organise the additional force? It is no small task.'

'That is a task for General Bandhul', Vidudhab said.

Bandhul spoke for the first time. 'That shall be done. The prince has thought this through well. But what of Karayan?'

Vidudhab said, 'we should summon him to the capital right away. Once he is here, the king can decide the course of action.'

Prasenjit trembled with excitement. He said, 'General Bandhul, issue the orders today. Right away! Prince, go to Sravasti and be ready to assume your new duties as soon as the general has issued the orders.'

When Vidudhab left for Sravasti, his friend Kaumarbhritya travelled with him.

CHAPTER 67

THE BEGINNING OF THE RAJSUYA YAGYA

Spring was in full bloom. The fragrance of the breeze, the colours of flowers and the lush greenery of the surrounding forests seemed to welcome the great King Prasenjit's Rajsuya Yagya. All of Sravasti was being decorated and renovated, with men working round the clock for this once-in-a-lifetime ceremony. Buntings, flags and swastikas adorned every street. Water had been sprinkled on the roads for days to make them less dusty. Massive-scale incense burning made the city smell of sandalwood. These preparations had induced citizens and visitors to spend more time outdoors, and the town had a festive mood.

King Prasenjit had left Saket for Sravasti and entered the city at the head of a triumphant procession. Dressed in all his finery, he sat on the royal elephant, with the twelve Mallas – as Bandhul's men were known – guarding him on horseback. The procession that wound its way to the palace included ambassadors, nobles, village chiefs, Brahmans, monks, merchants and forest-dwelling sages with matted hair.

In the palace, the king entered first to greet his wives. Chief Queen Mallika led a ceremony in which he was worshipped and welcomed back. Then he returned to the general assembly and formally received the invited dignitaries. He took care to also acknowledge each of the notables of Sravasti. A large, open area had been designated for the gifts presented by the guests. The Head of the Republican Council of Kamboj had sent unique objects from the northern path. These included clothing from Nandinagar made from the fur of sheep, cats and mice, and inlaid with gold work. Some dignitaries gifted horses, mules and camels of exceptional quality. From Kuru and Panchala came horses that could gallop like the wind and from Assak, Kalinga, Kampila, Videha and Kashi, valuable carriages, furniture, dresses, ivory armour pieces, decorative arms and ceremonial chariots complete with trained horses to draw them. The king of Sakal sent gifts of gold coins and hundreds of slave women. Madra gifted his kingdom's special sandalwood in golden pitchers, and fine cloth made of golden thread. The gifts' inventory ran into many scrolls and was still being compiled. The largest single present was from Emperor Bimbisar – he sent a hundred elephants caparisoned in gold, and a hundred of the best horses in the land.

Merchants and commoners had brought gifts which, according to their capabilities, ranged from a merchant's priceless ivory cabinets to a forest dweller's honey pots.

The crowd outside the palace courtyard swelled every instant. Ambassadors rubbed shoulders with forest-dwelling ascetics. The guards had formed multiple rings at the main gate. With folded hands, they begged the people to wait for the appointed time to enter the palace, and for the king to accept each gift personally, however small it might be.

Kosala had made elaborate arrangements to receive and pamper the visitors. A temporary force of thousands of workers fulfilled their needs. Accountants documented the presents and issued material from the stores to offer the guests food and comfortable housing. A large kitchen complex was working at full capacity, with material entering at one end, and cooked food leaving at the other, both in enormous quantities.

Among the luminary scholars taking part in the Rajsuya Yagya were Ajit Keskambali, Hiranyakeshi, Bodhayan, Bhardwaj, Shaunak, Jaimini, Gautam, Shambhavya, Kanaad, Aulook, Sankhyayan, Vaishampayan, Sayan and Skand Katyayan. Those scholars represented every earthly knowledge, including calligraphy, mathematics, educational science, art, grammar, etymology, astrology and ethics. To lead the Rajsuya Yagya, eighty-eight senior Brahmans were appointed. The king granted them each sixteen beautiful slave women. Wild cows, bulls and other animals tied at selected points awaited their sacrifice.

Sravasti seemed to be the centre of the world's attention.

CHAPTER 68

LIGHTNING STRIKE

The city was festive. Visiting dignitaries filled the palaces, streets and mansions. The clerks were still scrambling to enter the gifts for the Rajsuya Yagya into the books. Guards, animal trainers, harem keepers and storekeepers struggled to make sure Kosala absorbed them into its resources in an orderly way.

King Prasenjit, the centre of the grand event, was in his bedroom, muttering gibberish in a half-mad state. The entire Malla Brigade had been wiped out – each one of them killed by robbers on the way. The famed Bandhul Malla himself could not bear the shock of the tragedy. He lay, senseless like a log of wood, on the floor where he had collapsed. Prince Vidudhab stood quietly, keeping his thoughts to himself, surveying the effect of the news on the two seniors.

'Has – has Karayan come?' Prasenjit asked in a trembling voice.

'Yes, Majesty', Vidudhab said.

'Then, Son, present him.'

'Majesty, that will not be right. A stunning blow has hit us, a blow of unimaginable proportions. We should not stoke disunity. What if Karayan revolts?'

'Should we not punish him?'

'Why not, Majesty! But perhaps we can just imprison him first. Once the Rajsuya Yagya is over, we shall conduct a proper investigation and punish him according to his crime. We have to protect your reputation for justice, Majesty.'

'Yes, yes, I understand', King Prasenjit said. 'We shall do as you suggest. Arrange for his imprisonment.'

'But he is no ordinary man, Majesty. He is a former general, even if he is not serving any more. I suggest General Bandhul take charge of this matter.'

'Very well', Prasenjit said and nodded to Bandhul Malla.

'Majesty, one task is even more important', Vidudhab said.

'And what is that, Son?'

'Managing the situation at the border. The army lacks a capable and trust-worthy head. There are gaping holes in our defences, and troop morale is low. If Kaushambhi attacks us today, they will slice through our forces. I know that General Bandhul has gone through a heartbreaking bereavement. All the more reason for him to avenge the loss of the Malla brothers. If General Bandhul makes his presence known at the border, our soldiers will take heart, and the enemy will think twice before assuming any weakness on our part.'

'I also have grave doubts', Vidudhab said.

'What doubts, son?' Prasenjit said.

'I suspect the murder of the Malla brothers was not a chance attack by bandits. I see a strategy behind this.'

Bandhul had kept a dignified silence. Now, for the first time, he spoke. 'If that is true, I swear on the ashes of my sons and their cousins that I shall reduce Kaushambhi to ashes.'

'Indeed, General', Prasenjit said. 'You have a cause, and by being on the spot, you will also get a better sense of what led to the great tragedy.'

'Then I shall leave in haste, Majesty', Bandhul said.

'Go, friend', Prasenjit said. 'But I shall feel lonely without you.'

'Majesty, you shall be the cynosure of all eyes during the Rajsuya Yagya. And you have the royal bodyguards to protect you. Have no fear.'

Bandhul rode straight to the border after seeing to Karayan's imprisonment.

CHAPTER 69

THE SLAVE WOMAN

The graceful night was like a swan bathed in moonlight. One and a half watches of the night had passed. The moon had appeared late but held the amber glow from the time of its rising. The cool night air and the clear, starry sky made Som pine with memories of the dash from Champa, with the princess next to him. He was dressed as a woman and trailed Kundani as they walked towards the palace. The beauty of the night had a touch of melancholy.

'Kundani, what if we fail?' He said.

'Quiet!' Kundani hissed. 'I do not think about failing.'

Somprabh marvelled at her composure. They reached the palace. The arches and towers of the beautiful building shimmered in the moonlight. Lines of earthen lamps added to its lustre, and the surrounding air was heady with incense. Strains of music wafted out from the inner rooms.

The harem section was throbbing with people of all walks of life: queens, noblewomen, slaves, courtesans, servants and ordinary city women come to participate in the celebrations. An outer ring of guards maintained a tight security screen while trusted elderly clerks with special tokens went about their routine tasks.

Kundani walked up with confidence to a guard, pointed to him, and said, 'This is the one. She saw the thief take away the slave!'

Unnerved by her confidence and her appearance of a woman of means, the guard stammered, 'Which slave, Lady?'

Somprabh had practised for this moment for hours. In a sugary-sweet voice, he said, 'Be quiet. Take the lady to the chief queen. She will do as she sees fit.'

The guard looked from Kundani to Somprabh. The throng separated him from his nearest companions, and they showed no inclination of coming to his help. In any case, it would be unreasonable to feel threatened by two women, even if one of them was a little on the heavy side.

'We don't have all night!' Kundani raised her voice again. 'Come with us to chief queen Mallika!'

'But Lady …', the guard still hesitated.

'Oh, God! Don't you understand, it is her order! We cannot wait… Are you stupid?'

Now the guard drew himself up to his full height. 'Lady, watch your words.' But he thought better of prolonging the argument. He signalled to the next guard and led the two insistent women inside. They reached the inner door of the harem.

After the guard refused to step in, they agreed, with some wrangling, that Somprabh would go inside to tell the chief queen Mallika of the stolen slave, while Kundani stayed with the guard.

The guards signalled to the others, who let Somprabh enter. Two guards came over to talk to Kundani, drawn by her glamorous looks. With her delicate ivory earrings, her golden blouse with her breasts straining against it, her oiled and styled hair, she could have been one of the harem queens.

The guards were all old men. The oldest of them asked, 'Lady, what happened?'

'We know of a guard who has stolen a slave woman from the harem. My friend has gone to tell the chief queen about him. He will hang for sure!'

The guards looked at each other. 'That doesn't… Do you know his name?'

'Of course, he used a different name outside. But we know where he is!'

'Do you have proof?'

'Proof! Will you be the one to judge my proof? The chief queen Mallika knows me from her visit to Rajgrih! She will decide! Or are you a friend of his?' Kundani frowned at him.

'No, no, Lady! Why would I risk my life at this age for a few nishkas?'

The other guards laughed. This beautiful, outspoken visitor seduced them.

'Lady, where did you find the man?'

'Now, that is a story in itself –'

'Lady!' A reedy voice called out. It was Somprabh, accompanied by a harem guard. 'You are wanted inside!'

Kundani pretended the guards surrounding her did not exist, and they stepped back to let her enter. They followed the harem guard through a series of brilliantly lit corridors that led to open space.

As they approached a shadow area between two pillars, Kundani and Somprabh nodded to each other. Somprabh moved in a flash, and the guard went down in a heap before he sensed the blow to his head. Somprabh made sure that he did not permanently injure the guard. He dragged the guard out of sight. It would take long before the man had possession of his senses.

'Som!' Kundani hissed as they advanced. 'You are not walking like I taught you! Remember the hips!'

Somprabh said, 'I cannot turn into a woman in one day. We shall have to live with this. Where do you think she will be?'

'In the new harem. I found that out. We shall have to cross the crowd, though, and I am afraid that you look too hesitant now – my girlfriend.' Kundani smiled.

'I am trying to look shy, girlfriend!' Somprabh said.

Kundani rolled her eyes. 'It is not working. Stop trying and relax. The test is here now. Follow me.'

They stepped into a brightly lit, open courtyard full of thick, old trees. Here, a group of harem women enjoyed themselves with wine and food an army of servants brought them. Some were in various stages of undress. In a hollow between the trees, a woman sang in a melodious voice, accompanied by musicians. A few women danced without restraint – to please themselves, and not others.

As they cleared the courtyard and came to a door in a wall, they saw another guard by it. He looked formidable, but not at his most alert. Kundani stepped up to him, took out two gold coins and put them in his mouth with a musical laugh.

'Isn't the night wonderful?' She said.

'It is, it is, Lady!' The guard said, also laughing, as he took the coins out and looked, wide-eyed, at them.

'Enjoy the night! We shall not see its par in our lifetime!' Kundani smiled, and they went past him.

They were now on a wide garden path. This part of the complex was less well-lit. The wall in between and the dense trees around filtered the courtyard merrymaking light and sounds. At the end of the path now glowing in the moonlight stood the imposing door to the harem. Greek amazons paced before it, arrows in their hands and bows slung loosely. Somprabh calmed his thudding heart with an effort. The amazons were fair and had long limbs. Jackets and trousers covered their bodies, and they had daggers tied at their waists. Gold that glinted in the soft light studded their shoulder bands. They wore knee-length sandals that seemed to make no noise. There were five of them.

From closer, Somprabh saw they were drunk. Their eyes were blurred, and one of them seemed incapable of taking steady steps. He whispered this observation to Kundani, and she gave him a barely perceptible nod.

They looked at Kundani with curiosity. Kundani was too feminine to arouse their danger instincts. She was obviously not one of the city's ladies, but she looked like a noblewoman, one of the thousands of guests who had flocked to Sravasti.

Kundani took the initiative again, looking so confident no one would have dared to question her. She smiled and said, 'It's boring in the courtyard!' Her words were slurred, to suggest she was half-drunk. She traced the looped earring of an Amazon. 'This is so beautiful!' Next, she pulled out a flask of wine that she had tied at her waist. 'Here, drink this. Let us drink to the great Kalingasena!'

'To Kalingasena!' The Amazon shouted, and the others swarmed in to get their share of the wine.

'I shall meet chief queen Mallika – she does not drink, but she must join the celebration! Come, girl, don't stand there.' She beckoned to Somprabh. The amazons had forgotten all about this demure woman and her fat servant.

They were in another garden. 'Shall we ever get to the centre of this harem?' Somprabh asked. He shook his head in wonder. Kundani put a finger to her lips. They walked past more trees, grown in a rectangular grid. They passed through a patch where the flowers produced an intoxicating mix of scents. He saw Kundani close her eyes and take deep breaths as if she was energising herself with the air.

Patches of red, yellow and blue light played on the ground, giving the garden an unearthly aura. Somprabh looked up over his shoulder and saw that light passing through tinted glass windows in a hall ahead of them produced the colours. As they drew closer, they could hear the symphony of percussion, strings and wind. A large group of musicians entertained the crowd inside, and some women were singing couplets to the applause of others.

The door swung open, and a group of young women came out singing and dancing. Somprabh saw they were sweaty, flushed and totally out of control. In this all-woman enclave, they had let their hair loose, and some had removed their upper garments. Their garlands of many sizes and various flowers had become haphazard. As they approached, Somprabh thought it better to hide behind Kundani, for fear they might ask him to undress with them.

Kundani cheered lustily and sang a few lines Somprabh had never known were in her repertoire. She joined the wild dancing, easily outdoing the most energetic of the other women. But when she saw them reaching for Somprabh, she intervened at once, saying, 'This one is a clumsy oaf! She's a kind soul, but that's all!' She gave a shrill laugh, and the others laughed and danced onwards. Somprabh clutched Kundani's hand and squeezed it in fervent gratitude. Once again, he thought, all his military and political science training were of no importance, while Kundani handled herself with such aplomb. He followed her with his heart thudding.

Two watches of the night had passed. The south-wind carried a subtle fragrance of sandalwood. The trees and vines swayed as if they were drunk too.

Kundani walked briskly towards a door and entered the central tower of the harem without pausing. On any other night, entering this building would have meant inviting death. This was no ordinary night. They passed unchallenged through many halls, staircases, landings and passages, sometimes retracing their steps, but mostly navigating towards the centre of the tower. It was as if the riotous commotion of the gathering outside had sucked out all the life from inside.

As they entered a dimly lit room in the central area, they saw a small jewelled stool with perfumes and make-up, and next to, a gold pot and the ingredients for betel making. Their hearts leapt at what they saw next.

Princess Chandrabhadra lay with eyes wide open, expressionless and listless, on a small cot. Her wet hair made it plain that she had just bathed. There were garlands and silver pots next to the cot, presumably for the princess to serve guests.

The sight transfixed Somprabh. To him, her freshly bathed body looked like the autumn moon covered by clouds. She looked fit to inspire the greatest of sculptors to make a statue of a goddess.

When she raised her eyes at the footfalls, they fell on her companions in sorrow. It took her a moment to realise she was not dreaming. Her eyes shed tears, and her lips quivered. She opened her mouth, but only the slightest of confused sounds issued. Kundani placed her finger on her lips in a gentle movement and smiled to reassure Chandrabhadra.

Chandrabhadra got up unsteadily and looked at a slave sleeping on the ground next to her. Tears ran down her cheeks.

Kundani walked up to the slave and shook her. When her eyes opened wide in fear, Kundani demanded of her, 'Is this how you stay alert, girl?'

The young woman was on her feet but obviously felt unbalanced and groggy. She gulped and lowered her gaze in the face of Kundani piercing look.

'How long have you lazed here?' Kundani asked.

'I think…three watches, Lady. I – everyone is busy', the slave mumbled.

'And you have been sleeping while others ate, drank, got gifts and made merry. Foolish Girl, don't you realise there will be no other occasion like this one? Go now, look for your gifts in the main courtyard.'

The woman gave a blank look at Kundani.

'Have you already got your gift?' Kundani asked.

The woman shook her head.

Kundani rolled her head. 'Foolish Girl! Go now and get it. Run!'

The woman did not stop to think.

The commotion outside reached a crescendo. Drums beats, bass notes and shouts were filtering through to the room. The three of them stayed where they were for a few moments, overcome with emotion.

Then Kundani sat next to Chandrabhadra. She had lost all her poise.

'Princess…I could not…' Kundani sighed and tried to control herself. 'You must run now, Princess.'

Chandrabhadra looked at Kundani through her tears. Her lips parted, but they did not form words. She turned her gaze to Somprabh, who had lost his voice. He could only hang his head in shame. Kundani smiled and said, 'It is Som, friend!' Chandrabhadra's jaw dropped, and a hint of a smile played on her lips. Somprabh felt his heart warm at the sight.

The Princess said, 'What now?'

'Flee!' Kundani said.

'Is that even possible?' Chandrabhadra mumbled.

'Not without danger, that is true', Kundani said.

Somprabh found his voice. 'Do not worry. My sword will protect you.'

Kundani said, 'And what other possibility do we have but to hope, and to show courage?'

'There is one', Chandrabhadra said.

'What is that?' Kundani asked.

'Lord Mahavir.'

'Is he in Sravasti?'

'Yes, he is.'

'If you take my message to him, I am resigned to my fate after that.'

'What shall we say to him, Princess?'

'If you can just tell him the former princess of Champa, the unfortunate Chandrabhadra seeks his shelter with folded hands, and begs his acceptance.'

'But, Princess, that will take time', Somprabh said. 'What if you are harmed before he can shelter you?'

'It shall not. I have asked for three days to fast and pray. No one will touch me until tomorrow evening.'

Somprabh nodded. 'Then, Kundani, I think this is a way out. The princess is better off staying here than fleeing. But I wonder if the sage will help.'

'He will help', Chandrabhadra said, crying again.

'And what if we don't succeed?' Somprabh asked.

'Then do what is right!' Chandrabhadra sobbed.

Kundani said, 'Let us do this. I will stay back here, in the harem. Som, you make a dash to Lord Mahavir.'

'But…' Somprabh frowned.

'Go, Som. But do not use the main gate. Go to the pleasure garden, and there, on your right, you will find a pool bordering the palace wall. Use your skill to fashion a rope from the creepers and scale the wall. I know you can do it. Remember, if I do not see a sign of relief three watches into the day, I shall use what stratagem I can to get the princess out of here. Wait for us at the same point by the wall and help us when it is dark.'

Somprabh thought this through and decided it was for the best. He bowed and left.

CHAPTER 70

THE SAGE WHO WORE NO KNOTS

At the door of the building, a kneeling disciple was learning a sutra by rote, swaying with concentration. His eyes were closed, and his face serene. Somprabh stood in front of him, and the shadow interrupted the boy's trance-like focus. His eyes opened wide in alarm at the sight of the muscular stranger hovering over him.

Somprabh greeted the boy with a namaste and a smile. 'Young Master, I want to see Lord Mahavir. It is crucial', he said.

'Lord Mahavir denies no one, Sir. I shall go to inform him. Who shall I say is waiting?'

'I am a needy man, and my problem is urgent.'

'Please wait a moment, Sir, and I shall rush back.'

He was as good as his word. Somprabh saw him sprinting back almost as soon as he left. 'Yes, the Sage will see you right away', he said. Somprabh followed him through the gateway into a broad field. In one corner was a large banyan tree, and Mahavir sat under it in a meditative posture, his head bowed. He had thinning white hair and a sparse moustache. His limbs showed signs of ageing, but he exuded radiant energy Somprabh felt, even at a distance. As they neared, Somprabh noticed the penetrating and compassionate look of the great Sage's eyes. Even in a still posture and with no king's adornments, his aura was regal and his persona, one of calmness and mastery over the senses. Somprabh prostrated himself before the Sage and sat to one side.

'How may I help you, young man?' Mahavir asked.

'I have a prayer to you for help, Sir', Somprabh said.

'Wait a moment, Gentleman', Mahavir said and nodded to a few disciples sitting around him. They all stood up and left. One student remained. To him, Mahavir said with a smile, 'Go now, and come back later.' The boy who had accompanied Somprabh now hovered with an uncertain air. To him, he said, 'Go back to the door and study there. I will be free when this gentleman has left.'

Mahavir waited until his disciples were out of earshot. Then he told Somprabh, 'Speak now, Gentleman. What vexes you?'

'Sir, Princess Chandrabhadra of Champa seeks shelter with you.'

Mahavir did not lose his composure but stiffened and drew a deep breath. He said, 'So she is alive? Where is she? Tell me quickly.'

'In Sravasti, Sir.'

'Where? I want to see her. She is a pious girl, as good as she is lovely. So, the Magadhans spared her?'

Somprabh lowered his gaze. 'Sir, after the fall of Champa, she headed towards Sravasti and to you. On the way here, slave traders trapped her. They brought her here and sold her in the slave market.'

'Sold her!' Mahavir's eyes closed in anguish for a moment.

'Yes, Lord. The tradition demands that chief queen Mallika offer a slave woman for the king's marriage. The harem keeper bought her for this gift.'

'May the forces of sin be quelled. So, Chief Queen Mallika has bought her intending to gift her to the king?'

'Yes, Lord.'

Mahavir closed his eyes and stayed silent for a few moments. Then he asked, 'Who are you, young man?'

'A Magadhan, Sir', Somprabh said.

'Oh!' Mahavir said. 'And does Chandrabhadra know that her saviour is also an enemy of her people?'

'Yes, Lord.'

'You are the one who helped her thus far, is that correct?'

'Yes, Lord. And another person, a woman.'

'Who is she?'

'She is a Magadhan woman. After the fall of Champa, we tried to protect the princess.' Somprabh gave the Sage a precis of the events that had followed the flight from Champa.

Mahavir listened with concentration. Then he asked, 'What is your name, young man?'

'Somprabh, Sir. I am usually called Som.'

'Very well. Som, wait for an hour in that corner.' He pointed to a small shelter. 'But first, send the boy who brought you here to me. And do not worry, I shall call for you soon.'

Somprabh bowed and went to the shelter.

When the boy came to Mahavir, the Sage said, 'Please tell Prince Vidudhab that I wish to see him now.'

'As you command, Lord!' The boy said, and he left, a cloud of dust trailing him.

Mahavir closed his eyes, but the lines on his forehead betrayed he was not his usual masterful and calm self.

CHAPTER 71

CONFLICT

rince Vidudhab waits for you!' The boy said, panting.

'The prince?' Somprabh asked, surprised.

'Yes, indeed. He has orders from Lord Mahavir!'

Somprabh stood up, and despite the creak in his knees, followed the boy who moved at his usual lightning speed into a small courtyard where Vidudhab sat on the grass. He looked serious. He wore the simplest white clothes and did not carry arms. For someone often said to be a callow youth, he had an air of gravity. He was the picture of humility as he stood up and greeted Somprabh with a namaste.

'Welcome, friend', he said. 'I am Vidudhab. Lord Mahavir has ordered me to protect the princess of Champa, and his slightest wish is my command. I shall take care of her. Please be free of any worry.'

The matter-of-fact way in which he said this pricked Somprabh. 'That is not enough!' he said.

Vidudhab was obviously on his best behaviour, and Somprabh realised he had perhaps been too brash. Vidudhab spoke softly. 'Friend, you speak to the prince of Kosala. Your tone is harsh. Perhaps you may wish to follow the proper decorum?'

'Sir, I am not indebted to the Kosala royal family. Given how she was treated, I do not think the princess will accept the State of Kosala's protection.'

Vidudhab raised an eyebrow. 'I came to know from Lord Mahavir that you are a Magadhan. So, Magadhan Friend, you might believe that we will not treat her worse than the Magadhans treated her family.'

Somprabh felt an uncontrollable rage. He kept his voice low as he said, 'Prince, we Magadhans do not expect to learn etiquette from those of Kosala. Sir, I only wish to state this – you cannot be her protector against her wishes.'

Vidudhab laughed. 'Well, my friend, that is all right. You do not wish to learn etiquette from us, and we have no keen desire to civilise you. Coming to the point, we will arrange for the princess in keeping with her wishes, and Lord Mahavir's advice. You can be free of all worries.'

'I have been her guardian till this moment, Sir. Until I am assured –'

'Please be assured, Sir. I take over her guardianship now.'

'The princess will not accept this. She will not want to be in Kosala's shelter.'

Now Vidudhab smiled, and he did not mask his sarcasm. 'Kosala is not the kingdom that harmed her. Neither have we usurped her father's kingdom, nor have we made her a pauper.'

'But you have made a slave out of her, Sir!'

The prince's hands trembled as if he was controlling his rage. He spoke in a harsher tone now. 'You cross the limits of misdemeanour! Surely you are aware that your being a Magadhan spy is enough to have your head rolling? I do not even need to bring up your entry into the harem in disguise!'

'Prince, this head is not given to rolling. And Magadha's revenge is still incomplete!' Somprabh reached for his sword.

'What on earth are you doing, Sir?' A gentle but firm voice came from behind Somprabh. Mahavir had come in, alarmed by the raised voices. 'The prince has agreed to protect young Chandrabhadra on my request.'

Somprabh gulped as he searched for the right words. 'But –'

'There will not be any buts', Mahavir said. 'The prince is a responsible member of the state. You have to trust him.'

'I – I wish to meet the princess once', Somprabh said.

'That is not possible', Vidudhab said flatly.

'I cannot leave her without hearing her opinion', Somprabh said.

Mahavir laughed. He walked to Somprabh and placed his hand on Somprabh's head. 'I know what is on your mind, young man', he said. 'Set it aside. I shall make sure the princess' welfare is paramount.'

Somprabh stood silent for a long time, aware of the laboured breathing of Vidudhab behind him, and of his own inability to stare down the Sage standing in front of him. With his head lowered, he asked, 'Will the prince keep her here, at Sravasti?'

The Sage looked at the prince. The prince said, 'No, that has its risks. Sending her to Saket under my trusted aides' protection will be better. But we will do this with Lady Kalingasena's advice.'

Somprabh swallowed. 'Do I take it then that she is still a purchased slave, bought by the chief queen for Lady Kalingasena and bound by the conditions of the sale?'

'No, young man', Lord Mahavir said. 'She is under my protection. I shall ensure her welfare. Your work is done, and you are free to leave.'

Again, Somprabh stood undecided for a long time. Then he brought himself to salute the Sage and took a step.

'What? Are you leaving without bidding Vidudhab farewell?' It was Vidudhab, walking to him with his arms outstretched. He embraced Somprabh.

'Prince, I spoke out of turn. I am ashamed that I was so rude', Somprabh said.

'Think nothing of it, friend', Vidudhab said. 'Lord Mahavir saw the dilemma in your mind. And it was not hidden from me either.' Vidudhab looked gravely at Somprabh. 'Friend, hear me, I say this in front of the Lord. I have no other role in matters concerning Princess Chandrabhadra than following Lord Mahavir's orders. Let me be even clearer. If she turned out to harbour a love for you, she would stay under my protection for a suitable time, and I would think of her as your future partner, protecting her as my sister.'

'I am reassured, Prince. I salute your courtesy. And I stay indebted to you.'

'I am relieved too, friend, to part on this note', Vidudhab said.

They embraced once more.

CHAPTER 72

THE RESCUE

Queen Nandini, chief queen Mallika's bosom companion, was busy welcoming the lady guests and carrying out the chief queen's orders. She was a force of orderliness in the chaos that had taken over the harem. Vidudhab made his way through the scurrying and frantic women to reach his mother, Nandini.

He said, 'Mother, I need to consult you this instant. It is critical.'

Queen Nandini frowned, and said, 'Is it that important, son?'

'Indeed, it is, Mother', Vidudhab said.

'Where will we find a safe place to talk, Son, in this crowd?'

'In Lady Kalingasena's house.'

'There?' Nandini seemed uncertain.

'Yes, it will be quiet, and her presence is also essential, as it happens.'

'You say it is essential?' Nandini said, holding out her hand to two worried women who wanted to say something to her.

Vidudhab nodded with gravity, and they left the hall.

When they reached Kalingasena's house, they saw that she sat at a desk, studying a manuscript with calm concentration. She had been left alone, except for one slave woman standing at the door. She noticed their entry and rose in a lithe movement to greet them with an effusive namaste. They returned her greeting.

'Welcome, Sister and welcome, Son!' She said. 'How did you find time in the middle of this frenzy?'

'We had to make time, Mother. It is urgent', Vidudhab said.

Kalingasena saw the matter was serious. 'What is it?' She asked.

'We need to stop an evil deed, Lady.'

'Stop an evil deed?' Kalingasena said. Nandini frowned.

'Yes, chief queen Mallika has bought a slave woman to give to the king on the occasion of your marriage.'

Kalingasena frowned. 'I believe that is your custom. Is it considered evil?'

'Mother, that slave is the princess of Champa, the pious Chandrabhadra.'

Nandini pressed her temples with her fingers, while Kalingasena folded her hands tightly and thought about this.

'Is there a way to stop this?' Kalingasena asked.

'We were ordered to stop it', Vidudhab said.

'Ordered?' Nandini spoke.

'Yes, by Lord Mahavir.' Vidudhab told them the story.

'Where is she now?' Nandini asked.

'In the southern wing', Vidudhab said.

'Let us go now', Nandini said, 'and free her.'

'But how do we do that, Sister?' Kalingasena asked.

'We shall apologise to her on behalf of the Kosala royal family', Nandini said. 'She has been through a horrible ordeal – she must have seen the sack of Champa. And to end up in the clutches of slave traders...'

'Will she be safe?' Kalingasena asked.

'Will chief queen Mallika free her once she knows the story?' Nandini murmured.

'She will', Vidudhab said. 'But I do not have high hopes from Father, and that is why I approached you. I promised to protect her. I would like to send her in secret out of harm's way, to Saket.'

'Go ahead, Son', Nandini said. 'Prepare everything. Meanwhile, we will go to assure the princess she is safe.'

'I have already ordered my small ship to be ready and to have fifty of my best men stationed on it. The ship is the best way to get her to Saket, I think. She will be safe and happy there, and I shall write to my guru, Brahmanya, to take her under his ward and continue her education.'

'That is good. Very well, Son', Nandini said.

'But, Mother, you must still do two things in the next hour. On the left side of the palace's main gate is a palanquin guarded by my men. The princess should get into it with no one recognising her as the slave woman purchased for the ceremony.'

'That will be done', Nandini said. 'What is the second task?'

'Send ten trusted servants to escort the princess. They should go to the dock and climb aboard my ship.'

Kalingasena said, 'I shall help her. Leave these to her. Sister, let us go console Chandrabhadra.'

The princess was speaking in whispers to Kundani when the two queens reached her. When they greeted her with warmth, Chandrabhadra stood up, doubt writ large on her face.

Kalingasena stepped forward and hugged her. 'Blessed Princess, I am the unfortunate Kalingasena because of whom you suffered your most recent ordeal. And here is Queen Nandini, mother of the heir-apparent Prince Vidudhab. We apologise to you on behalf of the Kosala royal family for what has transpired. Our hearts bleed when we think of what you have been through since the savage attack on Champa. But please rest assured your sorrows are now over. By order of Lord Mahavir, Prince Vidudhab has assumed the role of your protector.'

Chandrabhadra eyes were moist, and she cupped her face in her hands.

'We shall send you to Saket, where you will be safe', Nandini said. 'You will go there with ten maids. Remember, take heart from Lord Mahavir's blessings and forget what has recently transpired. Have faith in us. Now come with us. Bring nothing with you. To make sure you no one recognises you on the way, you will go in a veil.'

Chandrabhadra hugged Nandini and Kalingasena many times, sobbing with relief and happiness. 'How shall I thank you? I cannot believe this', she said, again and again.

'Do not thank us. Come now, we must rush', Nandini said.

Chandrabhadra clutched Kundani's hand. Until now, Kundani had remained silent, and the queens had ignored her.

'Who are you, Lady?' Nandini asked.

'I am her servant', Kundani said.

'She lies', Chandrabhadra said. 'She saved my life many times. There is one more person…' She blushed.

Kundani came forward and bowed with humility. 'My Ladies, I committed a crime. I entered the harem in disguise to save the princess. I sent my companion and brother to Lord Mahavir for your mercy to shower the princess.'

'That is well, Young Lady. You saved her. But what now? Do you wish to go with her?'

Kundani spoke without a moment's hesitation. 'No, Your Majesty. My work is done. I shall take leave. Farewell, Princess!'

Chandrabhadra choked as she tried to utter a response. Kundani smiled, forced her hands free from Chandrabhadra's childlike clutches and walked away rapidly, leaving Chandrabhadra in the safe charge of the two queens.

CHAPTER 73

KING PRASENJIT'S CURIOSITY

The grand wedding of King Prasenjit and Kalingasena passed without interruption. As expected, there was chaos and tumult, but the fears of a military crisis proved unfounded. The halls and courtyards choked with gifts that poured in from near and far. Kalingasena's father, the king of Gandhar, had outdone himself with his lavish gifts. Those included a hundred horse-drawn chariots, with horses and charioteers, a hundred Greek slave women well-trained in the arts and in entertaining, and a thousand of the best-bred cows from Mathura. King Prasenjit sent off Gandhar delegation with the choicest gifts of gold and precious stones and ensured he was not found wanting in the spirit of hospitality. King Prasenjit only regretted the time and energy spent on the ceremonies and the Rajsuya Yagya, which had prevented him from spending time alone with Kalingasena, much as he desired.

Prasenjit heard about the disappearance of a slave woman meant to be his rightful gift from the chief queen. His enquiries from his men on the subject drew a blank. It was inexplicable that she could have slipped through the security net of the palace, and yet she had. Several rounds of questioning produced no results. One night, as he lay tossing and turning in his bed, he found sleep had deserted him. He got up, and though the Rajsuya Yagya was still in progress, he went to Kalingasena's palace.

Kalingasena, awaken from her sleep by a panicked servant, dressed in haste and rushed to welcome the king with the protocol due on his first visit. The king sat on the highest seat, and Kalingasena washed his feet.

'Lady Kalingasena, first, I must apologise for not welcoming you myself to the land of Kosala until now. My lapse has borne heavily on my mind, but I could not do as I wished.'

'The king's ministers, the royal family, the servants and the citizens have all welcomed me with open hearts, Your Majesty. I am also indebted to you for agreeing to open the gates of commerce for my homeland, Gandhar, in return for this humble being, Kalingasena. You know well, Majesty, that Gandhar could not have survived without its trade with the Far-East.'

King Prasenjit smiled. 'What kind of talk is this, Good Lady? Why do you measure yourself in these tangled diplomatic terms?'

'Perhaps, Majesty…Perhaps this is not worth discussing.'

'No, no, Kalingasena. It is not indeed. I, I want you…'

'I understand Majesty. You want me very much. I am honoured.'

'And the slave who disappeared? Do you know about her?'

'The one who ran away? Forget her, Your Majesty. You have so many women at your beck and call. One less from a countless number is not material.'

'But I hear she was an extraordinary beauty.'

'That is true, King. There is no one in your harem like her.'

'Excluding you, of course', Prasenjit said with a fawning smile.

'No, Majesty, including me.'

'But you have not seen her.'

'Oh, I did, Majesty. I also apologised to her, when she fled, on behalf of the royal family of Kosala.'

'What! What is that? You say you saw her? When she escaped?'

'Yes, Majesty, I am the one who spirited her away.'

'No! You must be…Why?'

'To free us from sin, from a great burden.'

'What sin?'

'That we made her a slave.'

'But that is very normal, Kalingasena.'

'Unfortunately, in this case, it was not.'

'Why is that?'

'That slave girl was king Dadhivahan's daughter, the princess of Champa.'

'Oh, God! How did she end in that state?'

'It was her fate to fall into this abyss, and our duty to restore her to safety.'

'I see. And is she as beautiful as they say?'

'Indeed, she is, Majesty.'

'But King Dadhivahan has passed away, and by rights, she belonged to me. Have you sent her to Gandhar?'

'I cannot say where I have sent her, Majesty', Kalingasena said with a smile.

'You cannot? I order you to tell me!'

'I shall not, Lord.'

'You have broken the law!'

'I will take the punishment, Majesty.'

'I will dwell on this, Kalingasena!' King Prasenjit stood erect and glared at his new wife, who lowered her eyes but stayed mute.

The King strode off, taking long strides.

CHAPTER 74

THE RAJSUYA YAGYA

The grand sacrifice consecrating King Prasenjit as emperor started with the Samayaag ritual, in which a thousand young men were initiated into their studies. A holy pyre was lit and was to keep burning through the entire ceremony. The whole galaxy of Brahman priests and scholars, led by Ajit Keskambali, conducted the rituals step by elaborate step. The Rajsuya Yagya became a magnet for the sages, forest-dwelling ascetics, scholars and Brahmans from all walks of life. Emperors, kings and ambassadors arrived and left each day, for the ceremony forced each of them to recognise King Prasenjit's supremacy or to prepare for war and defeat.

The best efforts at management could not prevent – as is usual – mismanagement. When such a gathering of rich and powerful men took place, prostitutes naturally flocked, sprinkled perfume on the dignitaries and often solicited openly. They entertained the city folks with ribald jokes and songs.

In the main altar, the sacred fire burnt bright, stoked by an everlasting river of the best ghee flowing from pitchers that formed hillocks next to it. Princes, servants and slaves kept feeding an unending stream of herbs, greens, rice cakes, camphor and sacrificial beasts to the altar. Garlands and coloured garments covered the animals, and the best grass fed the calves, bulls and sheep as they awaited the sacrifice. Their flesh, once offered to the gods, was mixed with deer and boar meat, herbs, fruits, sesame and other seeds and cooked in ghee to make a delicacy called the Khandava raag. That was the most popular dish at the yagya. Abstemious scholars received ample quantities of simpler but tastier dishes such as kheer, rice pudding, bread and lentils.

In the inner circles, the best wines – including the Gaudiya, Madhvik and Draksha – flowed without limit. The rich and the powerful sat with padded bolsters under them, as an army of servants brought wine and crunchy meat snacks. A large complex had been set up to feed the vast congregation.

While an ocean of humanity basked in the joy of the lavish ceremonies, discontent brewed in the city. The ritual's extravagance and the sacrifice of animals offended certain thinkers. The sages Mahavir and Gautam Buddha were then in Sravasti. They had both, in different ways, evangelised simplicity, avoidance of ritual, non-violence and kindness to all beings. The preening and waste of the Rajsuya Yagya and the debauchery outside the altar and the sacred grounds deeply troubled a fraction of the people, cutting across the boundaries of wealth, gender and caste. Secretly, and unknown to the sages, Prince Vidudhab and Ajit Keskambali were fanning these rebellious feelings. Bandhul Malla, the rock of Kosala's defence, was at the border, and the famed Malla Brothers were no more. His own ostensible vulnerability perturbed King Prasenjit. News of the simmering discontentment had reached him.

His first meeting with Kalingasena left him bitter, and since, had not seen her. Deep in his heart, he resented the break between him and the bride he had so deeply desired, and the escape from his harem of the slave girl bought for him. The rituals, the fasts and the conventions the Rajsuya Yagya demanded of him also burdened him. Despite a large contingent of aides, servants and slaves, he still had to worry about the arrangements for the guests and the Brahmans conducting the massive ceremony. All these problems unbalanced his state of mind.

Prince Vidudhab used the opportunity well. He reached out to the visiting kings and ambassadors and befriended them. To those complaining about the excesses and vulgarity accompanying the grand ritual, Vidudhab expressed his secret sympathies and helplessness in front of King Prasenjit's rigidity, lust and obscurantism. He won in this manner supporters among influential merchants, tradespeople and city officials. In a brief time span, he had engineered a groundswell of goodwill inside and outside the palace. He became the centre of a network of ardent followers.

One day, he sought Acharya Ajit Keskambali out between two tasks, when the acharya had rare few moments of freedom. He whispered to the acharya, 'Sir, how long will this fraud ceremony continue?'

'Do not say that, young man. Such a virtuous celebration can last a hundred years, twelve years or eighteen months.'

'And the kingdom? Will it run like during the entire Rajsuya Yagya?'

'Well, the two mutually exclusive possibilities are as follows. Either the king ascends to heaven once he gains even more virtue, or he remains enmeshed in the spider's web of earthly life.'

'He has earned enough virtue! There is no crying need for more.'

The acharya grinned. 'Son, I am not one to forget your interests.'

'But, Acharya, this is our chance. We do not know when Bandhul Malla will come back.'

'Not soon, Son. Not soon. Intrigue and conflict bog him down at the border. The redoubtable Yogandharayan has spun his web around General Bandhul.'

'That is fine, Acharya, but what if I revolt now? Shall I succeed? You know I have many well-wishers.'

'Not now. Today is…the second day of the lunar cycle. The Ratna Yagya finishes on the thirteenth day. Then, there will be fifteen days gap during which they will perform no major rite, and the king will not need to appear in public. This is when you will strike. By then, Payasi will have returned from the border.'

'And do you have a detailed plan in mind, Acharya?'

'I have, Son. And I shall share it with you when the time comes.'

'Very well, Acharya. Then I shall bide my time. I place my destiny in your hands, but I have done much groundwork. Many kings and prominent city men have united behind me. The town people are sick of large-scale animals' slaughter and of the crassness of some visitors, and of our own nobles even.'

'I know. I tolerate the Sage Mahavir and the Shakya Sage because they fan discontent with their speeches preaching simplicity and non-violence and with their own ridiculously simple lives. Let them do their work.'

'What about Karayan? How do we handle him?'

'I shall inform you when the time comes. Not now. For now, stay with the king to give him peace of mind. We do not want him to panic. I am sure you noticed he looks sad.'

'I have been watching, Sir.'

'Good. Keep calm and be sure the time will come when I pour sacred water on your head to anoint you the king of Kosala.'

'And I shall stay eternally grateful to you, Acharya.'

CHAPTER 75

THE PRINCESS

Princess Chandrabhadra settled into a life of ease in the Saket Palace. Prince Vidudhab did his best to make her stay pleasant. He had just glimpsed her as she boarded the ship, and that was enough to set his young heart on fire. However, he prided himself on his character and felt bound by his promise to his Magadhan friend. He kept himself away from the beautiful princess, suppressing an intense longing to meet her. His own ambitions and plans to take the throne of Kosala also burdened him.

After what Chandrabhadra had been through, the tortures she had suffered lingered in her dreams, and she often woke up with a start. The ten Greek slave women Kalingasena had sent were very well-trained. They took every opportunity to entertain the princess with song and dance, sometimes even getting her to join them. For a few moments, the princess would forget the travails of her recent past.

As the days passed, her longing for Somprabh grew stronger instead of fading away. Her separation from him became unbearable, but she found solace thinking he must be nearby, and the obstacles to reaching him no longer existed. The thought energised and pleased her.

Som and Kundani travelled to Saket secretly. Kundani visited Chandrabhadra, who rejoiced to see her. The princess hugged her in so many ways that finally, Kundani, eyes moist, planted a kiss on her forehead and told her to stop.

Kundani held Chandrabhadra at arm's length and gazed at her. 'It is wonderful to see you like this', Kundani said. 'I am so glad for you.'

Chandrabhadra burst at once into a slew of questions. She looked overjoyed and bursting with curiosity about Somprabh. Kundani played with her for a moment, pretending she knew nothing, and then she hugged the princess. She mockingly whispered to her the man of her dreams was in town, and his love for her was not less than hers for him. Although she could have, Chandrabhadra did not wish to invite him to the palace in secrecy. She thought for a while before asking Kundani to tell him he must meet Lord Mahavir and speak his mind to the Sage. He would know what to do.

Kundani and her brother travelled to Sravasti in haste, and Somprabh again presented himself before Mahavir. The young man opened his heart out to the Sage, who has already sensed Somprabh's passionate love for the princess. Mahavir listened calmly and pronounced his view. 'Young man, in your own interest, stay clear of the princess for the time being. I understand what you aspire to, but you must wait. The proper time will come later, and then I shall show you the right path.'

Somprabh was unhappy with this guidance, though he had to accept the great sage's advice. Obstinate, he sent Kundani to Chandrabhadra another time. When Chandrabhadra heard Mahavir's answer, she said, 'Friend Kundani, we must follow Lord Mahavir's advice. It is a pity, but Somprabh must refrain from coming here until we have Lord Mahavir's blessing.'

The message shattered Somprabh, but he kept himself busy fulfilling orders given by General Udayi. He plunged himself into his secret work to keep his mind from straying to thoughts of the princess. A lull in his activity saw his heart get the better of his brain. He landed up in Saket and knocked on Princess Chandrabhadra's door.

The princess had just bathed, and dressed in a chaste white robe, white flowers in her hair. Her eyes danced with joy at the sight of Somprabh standing there, longing in his eyes.

Somprabh lowered his gaze after drinking in at length the pleasure of the sight. He said, 'Forgive me. I could not follow the great sage's orders, I had to come here. I could not control myself, I had to make this transgression.'

'This is not right, my love', Chandrabhadra said.

'But what can I do, My Princess? I am overwhelmed by my feelings for you. I am like a puppet.'

Chandrabhadra blushed and felt a keen pleasure. 'But why the impatience, love? What if Lord Mahavir learns of this visit?'

'My love, I want to hear you say you are mine. Just give me that, and I shall find the right penance for my violation of his order.'

'And what if I do not?' Chandrabhadra said, teasing him.

Somprabh advanced two steps, and before Chandrabhadra could feel alarmed, he went down on his knees, took a fold of her flowing robe in his hand, and kissed it demurely. 'You already said it. I saw it in your eyes. I am content.'

'Then, Sir, make me content, too.'

'Tell me what I must do.'

'Do not come here without Lord Mahavir's consent.'

'Now that – that is unbearable!'

'Do you think it bearable for me?'

'If that is so, I shall bear it.'

'Yes, I am afraid we must bear it because it is right, conforming to moral conduct and sanctioned by the only elder left that I can admire. Now, Som, you must go. I shall be unhappy if someone sees us together breaking the sage's orders.'

'As the princess commands!'

Somprabh retreated, but every few steps, turned to contemplate the lovely woman standing there until she was out of sight. Her eyes expressed her yearning to be united with him.

CHAPTER 76

GENERAL KARAYAN

Prince Vidudhab entered the dark and damp prison cell and said, 'General, you are free. Step out, please.'

Blinded by the light behind the man, the prisoner only discerned a blurred shape. 'Who put me in his debt?' He asked.

'It is I, Vidudhab.'

'How shall I thank you?' General Karayan croaked.

'Let us walk out of this cursed place first, General. We shall talk more at leisure.'

The general staggered to his feet. 'I think…I cannot walk with these chains around my feet.'

'Yes, I see. I have a blacksmith waiting outside.' He went out and returned, followed by a hulk of a man carrying two heavy instruments. The blacksmith's grunts and the clanging of metal echoed in the cell for a few moments only before he broke the chains. The craftsman removed them, taking care not to worsen the cuts in Karayan's ankles. Without a word, Vidudhab bent down, lifted him gingerly off the ground and placed him on a slab outside the cell. He rubbed Karayan's feet and calves and helped him stand. The general closed his eyes, and his shoulders heaved as he winced with pain.

'I am obliged, Prince. Consider me your servant', Karayan said.

'Is it a debt prompted by distress?'

'No, Prince, my indebtedness goes back a long way.'

'I free you from any perceived debt, General.'

'I do not ask you to free me, Prince. I am ready to serve you.'

Vidudhab nodded. 'Here, friend, take this.' He handed Karayan a sheathed sword. 'I appoint you Chief of Staff of Kosala Army.'

'And shall I address you as king of Kosala?'

'If that is your wish.'

'Very well, Sir. What is your order?'

'Take charge of the city, General. Place your men in command.'

'That shall be done. What else?'

'Be present yourself with two hundred horsemen at the main gate at sunset. King Prasenjit plans to go to Jetavan to see the Buddha in the evening. Position yourself and your men after he has left for Jetavan. We shall let him leave, but prevent him from coming back. On his return, imprison and escort him to the eastern border. Leave him alone there. If his bodyguards take their task too much at heart, kill them. Keep your men close by. But do all this with minimum fuss.'

'Very well, Majesty.'

'Will you be fit for action?'

'Not as fit as I used to be, Majesty, but I do not think my abilities will be tested to the limits. And my spirit will make up for my flesh.'

'One more thing. Chief Queen Mallika will be with the king. Ask her to come to the palace and escort her inside. And give. Give the king food and money when you leave him at the border.'

'It shall be done. Anything else, Majesty?'

'Chief, my spies have told me Bandhul Malla is returning to the capital. He must be stopped, even if it means killing him.'

'Bandhul is a friend, but he is also the root of all my problems. I will cut him off, Majesty.'

'Go, then. Bandhul's house is ready for you, and your family is there. Rest and feed yourself before the hour. My men will come to you later. Keep me informed at each step.'

CHAPTER 77

KING PRASENJIT'S EXIT

King Prasenjit was at peace with himself as he made his way back to his palace from Jetavan. The time spent with the Buddha had been a balm to his troubled soul. He saw with surprise that the entrance to the walled area was fortified with obstacles. He had not ordered any such preparations. As he drew closer, a horseman rode out with his sword unsheathed.

It was General Karayan, expressionless and erect in his saddle. He stopped his horse in the middle of the road.

'Karayan!' Prasenjit said. 'Who freed you?'

'The king of Kosala.'

'I am the king! What do you mean?' Prasenjit's breath quickened, and he reached for the hilt of his sword.

'As you please. But I am here to take you prisoner.'

'By whose order?' Prasenjit shouted.

'King Vidudhab's.'

'You dare to… You scoundrel!' Prasenjit unsheathed his sword.

'King Prasenjit, if you wish to meet your death, please come this way.' Karayan spoke without raising his voice. He pointed his glinting sword to the plain on his left. 'We can dismount and fight to the death. I assure you it will be your death and not mine.'

Prasenjit shouted hoarsely. 'Soldiers, arrest this man.'

The soldiers, both those behind him and the ones in front who outnumbered his bodyguards, averted their gazes. Prasenjit's shoulders slumped, and he lowered his sword.

Karayan's eyes were cold even as he smiled. 'It is no use, King Prasenjit. I suggest you follow King Vidudhab's orders.'

'Can I not enter my own city?' Prasenjit said. His voice quivered.

'No,' Karayan said.

'What has your king, that slave woman's son, ordered?' Prasenjit asked.

'That your life be spared if you give yourself up quietly.'

'And if I do not?'

'Then you are to be cut into four pieces, each to be thrown to the four directions, like pieces of sacrificial meat.'

Two tears streaked down the king's cheeks. His sword fell onto the ground. He tore his necklace and its pearls scattered to the ground as well. Next, he took off his crown and flung it to the ground with what vigour he had left. It made a clanging sound and rolled away, coated with dust, as the onlookers gasped. 'Traitor! Do as you like with this old, helpless man!' He shouted.

He got off his horse and patted it. He wiped the tears from his cheeks and took a few deep breaths to regain control of himself. He then strode into the centre of the group of soldiers who stood behind Karayan. A shoulder brushed against his. It was Chief Queen Mallika, who had come and stood beside him. Her servant girls trailed behind her, but she turned to them, and said, 'Women, this is what fate has in store for me. I shall not need you where I am headed. Go back and serve the new king.' She gracefully removed her jewellery and handed it over to the woman who remained stunned next to her. Clasping the jewels into the woman's hands, she asked her to share them equally with the others.

'Chief Queen!' Karayan said. 'I bow before you, as does King Vidudhab. He requests you to proceed to the palace and bless your son.'

'My son Vidudhab's request is proper, General!' Chief Queen Mallika said. 'But I must do my duty. I shall stay by the king. I do bless my son, Vidudhab. Tell him he must protect the dynasty and its traditions. I bless him. May he find fame, live a long life, and bring ever more prosperity to Kosala!'

Meanwhile, the king had gathered all his precious adornments and picked up the ones he had thrown to the ground. He handed the bundle over to a guard, following his queen's precedent. He said, 'When Prasenjit is no longer a king, how can he deserve servants and guards? Bless you all. Take these and go serve the new king.' Then he turned to Karayan. 'Now, traitor, what is holding us? Let us follow the king's orders.'

Karayan ignored the insult. He ordered his men to help the royal couple on horseback. A small core of soldiers formed an escort around the royal couple and Karayan. The slaves stood a few feet away, some of them wailing.

Prasenjit turned around to look at the gates of the city that had been his. Its walls were bathed in a soft orange light. He looked at the far horizon where the sun was a ball of red. The surrounding sky was vermillion, the colour he had seen in the parting of his new bride's hair.

A small group of soldiers would now shepherd the descendant of the sun, as the Brahmans had pronounced him, the destroyer of the once-invincible

Magadha, the ruler of five kingdoms, the king who had sat on his throne for half a century, the one who had been the master of fabulous wealth when he strode out of this gate a few hours earlier, and the man before whom the masters of the universe had grovelled at the start of the Rajsuya Yagya. All he now owned was on his body. And he did not know where they were taking him.

CHAPTER 78

GENERAL BANDHUL'S TACTICS

A web of intrigue caught Bandhul Malla as soon as he reached the border zone. The Vatsa army had established camps very close to their side of the border and planted grown trees to turn the plain into a forest. They seemed to follow a policy of wearing down the Kosala army by attrition. They launched lightning raids with small, fast-moving contingents and robbed cows, animals and crops before racing back to their side of the border with their loot. When the Kosala troops followed them in hot pursuit, the Vatsas ambushed them in the forested areas. Most often, the raids were carried out at night. The overall effect was that the Kosala army was continuously harried and had lost the initiative, though its soldiers were brave and committed. Recently, there had been a few episodes of the Vatsas letting loose war elephants with their soles tied up with leather in the camps of the Kosalas. Many Kosala soldiers were trampled, maimed or killed in the chaos that followed.

Bandhul faced an enemy that had mastered guerrilla tactics, but he also had to face problems on his own side. He received no information from the capital. There was no news of reinforcements, and food was scarce. The army's coffers were almost empty, and the announcement of Malla Brothers' death had damaged the morale. Bandhul's letters to the capital did not elicit any responses. It took Bandhul days to get to know, through some of his most trusted spies, of Prince Vidudhab's machinations.

When he heard the troubling news, Bandhul placed a capable deputy in charge and travelled incognito to Sravasti. He was too late to save the king and observed his exile with his own eyes. He was saddened but also helpless. He had come on his own, and he had no men under his command. Within a few hours of reaching Sravasti, he had met his spies and formed a picture of what had transpired.

He examined his alternatives. He was virtually alone, in a city teeming with Vidudhab's and Karayan's men. The armed forces were in a state of high alert. But for his disguise, one patrol doing the rounds of the city's walls would have arrested him. Bandhul was a better fighter than a politician. But thinking the matter through, he decided his best option was to kidnap Vidudhab. He needed to strike soon, while Karayan was out with Prasenjit, and when Vidudhab least expected such a bold action.

For Vidudhab, the last day's events had been a heady success. He let his guard slip. He was returning from consultations with Ajit Keskambali, accompanied by a single servant. The night was dark, and the royal avenue almost empty. Bandhul and a small group of men shadowed Vidudhab. When he reached a deserted crossing, Bandhul signalled his men to attack. It was over in a few moments. Vidudhab's servant lay unconscious on the street, while three men covered Vidudhab's head with a black hood and carried him away.

So efficient was the abduction that it was a full eight watches before Ajit Keskambali got wind of Vidudhab's disappearance. When they did not see him, the other members of the establishment had assumed he treated of urgent matters related to seizing power. It did not come to anybody's mind that Vidudhab could have been abducted in his own lair.

Kaumarbhritya informed the Acharya that he suspected a sinister cause for Vidudhab's disappearance, the Acharya was alarmed. His mind registered the possibility that Vidudhab had been kidnapped. He sent a message to Karayan and waited for the return of the General. He also issued an alert to the minister for interior matters and the head of counterintelligence. Surveillance was heightened in the inner city and the palace complex.

Bandhul knew of Ajit Keskambali's role in the upheaval. He went to Ajit Keskambali's residence at the end of the next day. He greeted the Acharya politely and took his seat in a corner. Ajit Keskambali was busy issuing instructions to his aides. As he and Bandhul exchanged a glance, a light dawned in Ajit Keskambali eyes. Bandhul knew that the Acharya had surmised the nature and cause of Vidudhab's disappearance. He continued to direct the men around him on the tasks required for the next phase of the Rajsuya Yagya.

The exile of Prasenjit had been seen by only a few men and servants. They had been sworn and threatened into silence. The Rajsuya Yagya continued, and the news of Vidudhab's usurpation of the throne had also not been made public, though rumours flew fast and furious within the city and outside it.

Ajit Keskambali calmly studied two scrolls that were placed before him. He affected complete absorption in this. Bandhul mentally saluted the acharya for the impressive control of his senses.

Ajit Keskambali walked over to Bandhul and greeted him with a smile.

'General! It is such a pleasure to see you', he said with a wide smile. 'Even if it is a surprise. Are you hale and hearty? Is the border…safe?'

'Yes, Acharya, I am well, and the border is safe. And the yagya? Does it proceed well?'

'Indeed, it does, Bandhul!'

'I thought I should not miss the opportunity to see it. After all, it will not happen again in my lifetime. That realisation brought me here.'

'I see, I see. A good idea. But we have completed the Ratna Yagya, and we have a lull of activity in this lunar cycle. The next ceremony will be the Havi Yagya and the sacred bath, on the first day of the full moon.'

'Is the king happy?'

'Yes, he is. He is tired but pleased.'

The two men eyed each other, neither giving anything away.

'That is good, that is good. And is Prince Vidudhab well and happy?' Bandhul asked.

'It is strange – I have not seen him since yesterday. That is most unusual, in fact.'

'Perhaps he is also busy with a new bride? It is his age, of course.'

Ajit Keskambali guffawed. 'Yes, you could say that. Perhaps that is all there is to it.' His eyes remained cold. 'As you see, I am overwhelmed with all that is going on.'

Bandhul rose to his feet and bowed low. 'I shall not disturb the acharya anymore', he said. 'I just came to pay my respects.' He noticed the flaring of anger in Ajit Keskambali's eyes with some satisfaction. 'I shall take your leave, Sir.'

CHAPTER 79

THE WILY BRAHMAN

Acharya Ajit Keskambali's cleverly spun web of deceit came undone with Vidudhab's kidnapping. Ajit Keskambali had no doubt that Bandhul Malla had abducted Vidudhab. As soon as Bandhul left, the acharya pretended to feel unwell and retired to his bed. He summoned Kaumarbhritya.

On Kaumarbhritya's arrival, the two engaged in a hushed discussion. They quickly agreed that the audacity of the act indicated that Bandhul was behind it. They also agreed to keep the turn of events secret. They deduced that Bandhul would not take Vidudhab's life and that his main concern would be the welfare of his patron, King Prasenjit. They focused on the two matters they needed to think about. Where was Vidudhab likely to have been kept? And even if they knew the hideout, how could they free Vidudhab from the formidable Bandhul Malla? They had no answers to these questions.

Ajit Keskambali said, 'Kaumarbhritya, we will have to wait for General Karayan.'

'Yes. But on the other hand, the prince has one friend.'

'Who is that?'

'A young Magadhan.'

'Where is he?'

'You need to find him, but he is in the city all right.'

'Then look for him, Kaumarbhritya! Meanwhile, I will get a sense of attitudes in the harem.'

When Kaumarbhritya had left, Ajit Keskambali got up and paced up and down, deep in thought. After a while, the lines on his forehead cleared. He had a plan. He called out to a disciple and ordered him to take a message to the harem keeper in Kalingasena's palace. The message was that Ajit Keskambali would arrive there at sunrise to carry out a ceremony of great importance. Queen

Kalingasena was to be requested to bathe and ready for the ceremony, and also to fast in preparation for it.

A worried look descended again on Ajit Keskambali's face. He examined the lines of his right palm thoughtfully. A shadow loomed over him, and he looked up. It was General Karayan, fuming, his muscles clenched in anger. Ajit Keskambali chose not to ask him about his mission to the border.

'Acharya, what is this that I hear?' He said.

'General, be calm', Ajit Keskambali said. 'Think, think through what we must do. And only then act.'

'I must first imprison that Bandhul Malla!'

'No. That will not lead us to Prince Vidudhab.'

'Then, what will?'

'Two things. First, launch a tight vigil on the city. Not a stone should move without your knowing it. Second, make sure your most experienced men shadow Bandhul. He will expect it and should not be able to throw them off.'

'I will do so. Right away. But is that all? We will not do more to save the prince?'

'We will, we will. But first, we must know where he is. The rest will follow. Bandhul is sure to go to Vidudhab to extract information on King Prasenjit's whereabouts from him. As I said, the men following him must be your best experts.'

'They will be. I know the team I will use.'

'And there is another thing. The Vatsa army's senior command should not be able to establish contact with Bandhul. Not at any cost.'

'Yes, I will ensure that.'

'Very well, General. You have your work cut out. Oh, and still another thing.'

'What is that?'

'That young Magadhan? Take Kaumarbhritya's help to find him.'

'Yes, Acharya.'

CHAPTER 80

THE SAD END

Earlier, General Karayan and the captive royal couple had marched for many miles. The inky-black sky lightened in tone, and then a faint light crept out of the eastern horizon. The horses had not stopped for a single moment. Karayan's still-chafing ankles prevented him from sparing a thought for a king who had cast him in irons after extracting a lifetime of service from him. In the soft light, Karayan could see a tower at the end of a long slope. This was the border point that he had been aiming for.

He ordered the troops accompanying them to one side, out of earshot. Then he walked to the royal couple. He said, 'You are free now, King Prasenjit! I have fulfilled my orders. You are free to go where you like. Here is some money for your needs.' He handed over a small bag to the deposed king. It was heavy with gold coins. He turned around and walked briskly to his horse without waiting for a reply.

The royal couple stood there for a long time, lost for words. They were exhausted, and a feeling of helplessness had descended on them. The bag of gold coins slipped from Prasenjit's hand and fell on the dust below. Prasenjit did not notice this cruel act of fate in his numbed state.

They rode for a while, without speaking. Prasenjit said, 'What now, Mallika?'

'Let our fate guide us, Majesty.'

'Then let us go to Magadha, dear.'

'Is it wise to ask Bimbisar, whom you defeated, for mercy? He is not an Aryan.'

'He is an emperor and knows what is right and what is not. He may bear rancour towards Kosala, but he should not equate this Prasenjit with Kosala anymore. I am a helpless man, not even an ordinary citizen. I have lost my kingdom; I have lost the patronage of Lakshmi, the Goddess of Wealth. My friends, relatives, servants – where are they? I only have you, Mallika. When I stand before him, I who gave him my daughter in marriage, he must give me shelter.'

'You have lost the bag that Karayan gave you', Mallika said with a heavy heart. 'We have nothing. How will we get there?'

Prasenjit looked for the bag, realised he had lost it and sighed. 'Why should we live on alms from a man I had imprisoned for treason?'

'What will we eat on the way?'

'Will we not get anything by begging?'

'And will you accept those alms, Majesty?'

Prasenjit lowered his head. Then he smiled as a thought struck him. 'Lady Mallika, we will earn some money.'

'How, Majesty?'

'My teeth have diamond nails. They will stand us in good stead.'

'What sacrilege! Surely you do not mean to uproot your teeth?'

'What use will these teeth be to me now, Mallika? When we have abandoned so much, why not my teeth? My gums have decayed, and it will not be too painful.'

Chief Queen Mallika had been stoic and dignified until that moment. Now, when she did not reply, the king turned to her and saw that her shoulders were heaving. It was as if a cloud had burst. Violent sobs wracked her erect frame, and she sank her head into a silk scarf to smother her cries.

The king went to her side and drew her head to his shoulder. He felt the warmth of her tears, and his eyes became moist. He patted her head.

'Come, let us dismount, and walk onwards. These last signs of our earlier life, these horses, are tired and hungry, and we do not have the means to take care of them. Tell me you are a gardener's daughter. Do you not remember how to make flower garlands?'

Mallika said, smiling through her tears, 'I am not sure. But I have made many in my childhood. I shall remember.'

'Then let us settle on that to make our ends meet. Let us go.'

She smiled at the unlikely idea. He held her hand, and the infirm couple started on their long walk on the uneven, lonely path. Neither mentioned it, but their feet were already hurting from the contact with the hard ground.

They walked for a whole day. The sun rose high in the sky, and gave way to a moonlit night, to wrest the sky again the next morning. The two unfortunates kept walking. Many well-meaning people on the road sensed that this was a couple that needed some help. They stopped to talk and offer help, but Prasenjit and Mallika did not answer their queries about their names, and their origins. They met all kinds of people, those who showed them tenderness and respect, and those who insulted and mocked them. They persevered with their journey, ignoring the soreness of their feet and the crying aches of their calves and knees.

Mud caked their clothes, and they bore marks of bushes. Their mouths were dry, and their stomachs cramped from a sensation that they had never dreamt they would encounter – hunger.

At the very end of their tether, having stopped thrice on that seemingly endless march to feed on leftovers and to rest, they reached the gates of Rajgrih. Mallika sank to the ground in utter exhaustion. She was too tired to even make out what Prasenjit said, and he deeply worried for her. Two watches of the night had passed. Prasenjit could see flames from torches moving as guard patrolled the walls. He went to the door and tugged the bell for visitors.

A guard called out to ask who was there.

'Friend, open the door', Prasenjit said.

'Is that an order?' The guard was taken aback at Prasenjit's unusual reply. When he peered down at the unusual sight of a sick-looking beggar couple, he was puzzled more than angry.

'It is not an order, friend. We come from very far.'

'There is a monastery that way', the guard said as he gestured with his torch to a building. 'Stay there for the night. The gate only opens in the morning.'

Prasenjit himself was on the brink of collapsing. He looked at his wife. She whispered, 'Do as he says.'

Prasenjit said, 'We shall do so.' He made an effort to take a ring – the only one of his possessions he still had – off his finger. 'Friend', he said, 'can you kindly come down, take this ring and give it to Emperor Bimbisar later?'

The guard peered one more time, then dashed down the steps. He came out from a small door. He took the ring and scrutinised it. It was clearly a mark of royalty.

'Sir, do you have a message as well?' He asked in a deferential tone.

'No, friend, the ring will be enough', Prasenjit said.

The guard frowned, undecided, but let the couple stagger towards the monastery. He brought up his arm once as if to call out to them, but he had nothing to offer them. He went back to his post.

Prasenjit and Mallika entered the monastery. Its door was not locked. They found a rocky slab in the courtyard and lay on it. Prasenjit saw that Mallika had fallen asleep in an instant, without a word. He reached out to brush her face with his fingers. She was lifeless. He nestled his head on her shoulder and let his life fade away.

At the crack of dawn, the sun bathed the old monastery in a mellow light. A group of horse riders charged towards the sanctuary, their horses at full gallop. It was Bimbisar and two of his ministers, followed by their aides.

Bimbisar ran inside to find the elderly couple dead in each other's arms, their clothes in tatters, and their bodies bruised. The emperor and his entourage stood in solemn silence and prayed for the souls of their former enemy King Prasenjit and his revered chief queen.

Bimbisar cremated the couple with full State honours and declared a state of mourning.

CHAPTER 81

THE MASSEUSE

A Masseuse lived alone in an impressive house in an outer part of the city. The house was a mud structure, but it was clean, large, and imposing. The Masseuse's youth had withered, but not her beauty. She was an attractive and voluptuous woman. Dark lines around her brown eyes set off their brilliance that hinted at sorrow and gave her a certain mystique. When she laughed, her peals had a musical quality. She was an acclaimed expert at applying red paint to the feet of her lady clients, at massage and at social intercourse. She was a talented dancer and musician, and she had a limitless stock of the choicest betel leaves. The doors to the harems of the palace were open to her, as were those to lesser establishments in the houses of merchants and nobles.

Somprabh and Kundani had camped at her home. Som had become rather listless and lovelorn on his separation from Chandrabhadra. He went through the motions of organising the Magadha army. Udayi met him very often, in complete secrecy. Somprabh had met many guests during the Rajsuya Yagya and used well these interactions to get a sense of the popular sentiment among the society decision makers. Lately, he had lost his vigour and keenness, and he often spent entire days lazing in the Masseuse's house. Kundani regularly used her skills at disguise and espionage to infiltrate the harem and collect the latest news and rumours. A regular in the harem, the Masseuse, was more than happy to supplement her handsome earnings with the income from her spying activities.

One afternoon, Kundani rushed into the house and shook Somprabh hard to wake him up. 'Som, there is terrible news!' She said.

Som raised himself on one elbow. 'What is it? Have they discovered us?'

'No, no. Both King Prasenjit and Prince Vidudhab have disappeared from the city.'

'Disappeared? Where?'

'No one knows. There are many rumours.'

'Where did you hear this?'

'In the palace, today. Chief Queen Mallika is also missing!'

'But all is quiet in the city. How can that be?'

'They suppressed the news. Can you imagine what would have happened if it had spread?'

'Who did you hear this from?'

'From Acharya Ajit Keskambali himself. He went to Queen Kalingasena's palace today on the pretext of performing a ceremony. They discussed the matter there. Prince Vidudhab has imprisoned King Prasenjit and sent him to an unknown place. He conducted the overthrow swiftly and silenced the witnesses.'

'I see. I was aware of the plan. But Vidudhab?'

'That is most probably Bandhul Malla's doing.'

'Is Bandhul here?'

'He just got here. And as usual, he acted swiftly.'

Somprabh got out of bed and paced the room. He shook his head, deep in thought. 'Kundani, what should we do?'

'Queen Kalingasena wants to see you.'

'Did she say why?'

'Yes. She wants you to help find the prince.'

'And why does she expect me to oblige her?'

'She has a right to. She helped us to free Chandrabhadra.'

'That she did.' Somprabh closed his eyes and sighed, clearly pushing aside thoughts of the princess. He stretched his limbs. After pondering matters for a while, he said, 'The first thing I must do is find General Udayi.'

'And why is that?' Kundani's gaze was stony.

'Is it not obvious?' Somprabh said. 'This is our golden chance. Magadha will get revenge its defeat.'

'Get revenge from whom?'

'From Kosala.'

'And where is that Kosala, Som? Think about it! Are you becoming a traitor?'

'A traitor to my enemy? Where is the betrayal in that? I have a thousand Magadhan men at my command. In two hours, I can take over this city and become king. And then I can deliver freedom to the princess.'

'What kind of freedom?'

'Freedom to become Chief queen of Kosala.'

'I see. So, the wise men are correct when they say that low-born people can only have lowly thoughts.'

'What!'

'I see now that you are a true illegitimate. Until now, I saw your courage, your righteousness, and I mistook you for a great man.'

Somprabh's hand reached for his sword, hanging from a peg in the wall next to him. But he willed it to stop. He sensed he had spent the last few days in a stupor that had deprived him of moral bearing.

'Go ahead, Som! Kill Kundani. Then stab your friend in the back and take the throne of Kosala. And then drag Chandrabhadra into your fold.'

'Which friend!' Somprabh shouted. His head was spinning.

'Did you not declare the prince your friend? Did he not take charge of the princess as an honourable man? Did he and the Queen Mother not help us protect Chandrabhadra?'

Somprabh collapsed on the floor. Trembling, he lowered his head between his knees. His breath became shallow, and his shoulder heaved as he took great breaths to steady himself. He stood without using his hands for support.

'I have not been myself', he said. He was sweating. 'Tell me what to do, Kundani.'

'Can you do it?'

'Is there a choice? Yes, I shall do it. With you by my side, I shall.'

'True, there is no alternative. And I am by your side.'

'Tomorrow, enter the palace.'

'In disguise?'

'Yes, as one of the acharya's monks.'

'Has the acharya said so?'

'Yes. He has a plan. And there is something else.'

'What?'

'If you do not want to, I will save the prince. Even if it means giving my life.'

'I am still alive. Show me the way. After me, you can be the one to act.'

'Then we are ready for tomorrow. But we have one thing to do today. We have to go to Dhihadant's den.'

'That is a rotten place.'

'That is where Ajit Keskambali said we shall get news of the prince.'

'I will go.'

'No, the three of us should go. The Masseuse knows that scum.'

'When do we go?'

'Just after sunset. You will be disguised as a lout and a drunkard. Perhaps you will not have to pretend much.' She gave him an ironic smile.

Somprabh laughed.

CHAPTER 82

DHIHADANT'S DEN

Kundani donned a cotton jacket and bright make-up. She had heavy kohl in her eyes. A crimson silk blouse covered her breasts, and she wore bangles of a matching colour. Red paint lined her feet, and the bells around her anklets tinkled. She adjusted a headband studded with cheap jewels. 'Is this all right?' She asked the Masseuse.

'Not yet', was the reply. The Masseuse stood to smear even more make-up on her face. She marked black beauty spots on Kundani's chin and cheek and then put ivory colour bangles on Kundani's wrists. Next, she tied a garish waistband around Kundani and then stepped back, hands on her hips, to examine her. She nodded with satisfaction. 'Now it is all right!' She said. 'Your turn to dress me up.' Kundani followed the Masseuse's steps, and soon they had identical dresses.

'Now, Kundani, you must act like an acrobat. Will you be able to do it?'

Kundani said, 'Why not? But I am a fresh country bumpkin girl, an untrained calf.' She pinched the Masseuse hard, making her scream. 'Come, let's find out what our friend, the other acrobat, is doing.'

Somprabh had worked hard to transform himself into a gaudily dressed acrobat. His clothes were white and red, and he wore a bell around his neck. A bright saffron turban and a matching wide belt added to the riot of colour.

Dhihadant's den stood in one of the notorious, densely populated areas of Sravasti. Earthen lamps shed a pale flickering light on dirty, mean streets. The fumes of cheap wine were overpowering. When they reached the place, they saw an open compound crowded with drunkards, gamblers and rogues. Every line uttered contained a curse. A few of the conversations audibly involved men negotiating with pimps the prices of the services they wished to buy. Near the main door, a gambler loudly staked his wife. In the next instant, he threatened to break the head of the one sitting opposite him. Between each phrase, he took a swig from a small pitcher. His eyes were only half-open, and his body swayed as if a puppet master controlled it. A plain, thin girl was doing the rounds, keeping the pitchers full and collecting coins in advance as she did so. She bore the lewd behaviour of the customers with a disinterested look.

Kundani, Somprabh and the Masseuse conferred in a dark corner as they surveyed the scene. They agreed on what to do. When the Masseuse stepped forward towards Dhihadant, his wizened face lit up in a broad grin.

'Welcome, My Queen! It has been a long time! Too long!'

The Masseuse put a finger to her lips and beckoned him with her curled finger, smiling at him. He ran to her like a pet.

'I have a bird with me here. She is special. She can do an act every night and serve wine. You will surely find a buyer for her. When the excitement has settled down, sell her, and you will get no fewer than twenty dammas.'

'Well, well! Dhihadant never turns away from the Goddess of Wealth! Is she…a prostitute?'

'No, an acrobat.'

'That is no problem. Is she pretty?'

'See for yourself, pretty is an understatement.'

'Get her to the back door first. Let me look at the goods.' He leered.

'The goods are good', the Masseuse replied. 'I shall take ten dammas. No less.'

'Let me see her', Dhihadant winked.

They walked around to the back door where Dhihadant waited for them. His jaw dropped when he saw Kundani, and his face lit up. He rubbed his hands and said, 'Hmm, good. Very good. Girl, are you really an acrobat?'

Kundani kept her revulsion at the man and his den to herself. She nodded shyly.

'Very good! I will pay five dammas since I must train and feed her.'

The Masseuse glared at him. 'No, you don't have to teach her. Look.' She snapped her fingers, and Kundani performed a few dance steps. Her anklets drew the attention of a couple of rogue guests, and soon, they were all crowding around, wide-eyed.

The man who had staked his wife was drooling. 'Hey, Dhihadant! How much for her?' He shouted.

He got a shove from the man beside him, and in the next instant, sprawled on the ground accompanied by raucous laughter. The man who had shoved him hissed, his eyes boring into Dhihadant's, 'I shall take her. A hundred dammas.'

At this point, Somprabh staggered into the gathering and sat with a loud thump on one table. The maidservant scurried to place a pitcher on his table and collect his money. The other men looked over their shoulders at the well-built but otherwise typical new arrival and turned back quickly to the beauty before them.

Now Somprabh threw three gold coins one by one so that they landed on Dhihadant's table with loud thuds. The men turned back to look at him.

'A round of drinks for all!' The men cheered loudly at this unforeseen bonanza. They crowded around Somprabh to thank him. Dhihadant bowed obsequiously and showed him to a large couch with bolsters.

The Masseuse whispered in his ears, 'Dhihadant, this is the one. Do you know what he has done? He let it slip he kidnapped the prince.'

Dhihadant laughed. 'That I know to be a lie. The ones who did it are there!' He pointed to the two gamblers still fighting with each other.

The Masseuse adjusted her right earring and designated the two men. Somprabh, who had been waiting for this signal, sauntered over to them.

'Well, friend, how do you like the girl?'

One gambler bared his dirty teeth in a satisfied grin. 'Not bad, not bad at all. And she is mine.'

'But Dhihadant has decided to give her to the prince. Prince Vidudhab.'

'Vidudhab!' The other gambler said. 'Then let him! The fool.'

'Why do you say that?' Somprabh asked. 'Is it not a good idea to ingratiate him with the prince?'

'He is a fool.' the gambler said, his voice slurring. The general din drowned out their conversation. They could barely hear one another. 'Vidudhab is a prisoner. In the underwater room, in the fort.'

'Prisoner?' Somprabh widened his eyes. 'Here, have a drink. Both of you.' He motioned to the servant and got them a pitcher each, which they guzzled down. 'So, you were saying…How can the prince be a prisoner, pray?'

The gambler leant forward and whispered. 'Bandhul.'

'General Bandhul?'

'Who else is Bandhul?'

'Yes, yes. I see.'

'Bandhul is our friend. We don't call him General Bandhul. We…he…tonight is our night off, anyway. It's a long story.'

'Friend, I am a good friend of Dhihadant's, but I have to say this – I don't believe you.'

'What? You don't believe me?' The gambler looked askance at his friend, who chuckled drunkenly. 'A bet?'

'A hundred dammas.'

The gambler's eyes widened. 'To what? Show you the place?'

'No – to show me the prince. If I see him a prisoner, then you are not making a fool of me, and I pay. If you can't show him to me tonight, you pay. Here.' He pulled out a bag and displayed the coins.

The gambler pulled out his own small pouch. 'We ask Dhihadant to be our guarantor?'

Somprabh smiled. 'No need. You are an honest man, I can make that out. And so am I. You can see.'

The gambler nodded sagely. 'Yes. Honest.' Then he looked outside as if having an afterthought. 'Hmm, it is night.'

'We won't do this in daylight, shall we?' Somprabh said.

The two gamblers guffawed. Then the one who had placed the bet said, 'But the way is through a forest…'

'Ah, that's all right. I have my sword.' Somprabh twirled his moustache and put his hand on the hilt. 'And I have two horses outside. The time is now. Remember, there is no time like now.'

The other gambler echoed, 'No time like now.'

Somprabh looked for the Masseuse. In the din, Kundani was showing off the last of her dance and acrobatic moves to great applause. Somprabh led the punter to the rear door and stopped to whisper in the Masseuse's ear. She nodded. At the end of the show, she would tell Dhihadant the deal was final, and they would return the next night, after which the girl would not leave. On the way back, Kundani and the Masseuse would share a horse.

Somprabh had not taken a single drop of wine. He had pretended to drink, and the pretence had been easy to keep in the den's chaos. He helped the gambler to a horse, mounted his own, and they rode off into the darkness.

CHAPTER 83

KOSALA FORT

Kosala fort was a forbidding structure on the river Sarayu, about half a mile from Sravasti's outer edge. The river fringed the fortress on one side, and a deep moat on the other three. An exact square in design, each of its sides a thousand feet long, it had two main gates and eight smaller entrances. The wall foundations were about a hundred feet wide, and the mud walls rose to a height of thirty feet. Those walls had inner and outer layers of brick and plaster. The main gates had octagonal towers rising on each side to a height of sixty feet from the top of the wall. At sunset, they were shut, and their massive wooden drawbridges pulled up. The inhabitants then commuted through the smaller doors. A council room built on sixteen pillars stood in the centre of the square fort.

A thick forest lay between Sravasti and the fort, with no well-marked paths through it. Trained soldiers who knew each step of the way escorted the royal family and the nobles quickly through the wood when needed. It was unheard-of for ordinary citizens to cross the forest at night. Wild animals and even wilder men took refuge in the wood.

The commandant of the fort was a venerable sixty-year-old satrap who lived there with his young daughter. He was a silver-haired, mighty-limbed, tall, and gruff man who was admired for his courage. A dark slave woman had looked after his daughter since her infancy. At a point in his life, the commandant's heart had been broken, and he had asked King Prasenjit for a transfer to an isolated posting. He had lived in the fort for seventeen years. In those years, the bright lights and broad streets of Sravasti had never once drawn him. Besides the slave, he had a deaf-mute servant with the build of a bull.

The two servants followed their masters' example, and cut themselves off from all intercourse with the outside world, except for occasional visits to the neighbouring village.

Apart from these four, only eight chosen soldiers stationed inside the fort at night. The rest of the army lived in a cantonment area outside the fort.

A strongroom with thick walls stood near the main western gate, surrounded by a thicket of trees. It was a prison, and the oddity was it had no door. There was a tiny opening in its roof, just large enough to supply air, food and water and take away waste.

Beyond the rampart, across the moat, was a small two-storey building, deserted most of the time. Rare visitors, mostly royals and nobles, occasionally lived there for a few days. A narrow footpath led to the nearby village and the cantonment. The hamlet had just one grocery and one betel shop. In contrast to the gloomy fort, it was lively, and the betel shop had developed into a local centre for gossip.

The latest news was that the prison had an occupant. It was understood that he must be someone important. A squad of eight guards was stationed, according to tradition, around the lockup, changing shift twice a day. The house opposite the prison also had residents. It would take some time for the locals to know who was visiting.

People could see the commandant climbing up the tower more often than was the norm and surveying the land he commanded. Each time he looked, the surroundings appeared quiet on all fronts.

CHAPTER 84

THE CONFERENCE

omprabh was caked in slush by the time he entered the house. Dawn had not broken yet. He patted his exhausted horse and gave it a few lumps of sugar before taking it to the stable. Kundani and the Masseuse had not slept.

Kundani stared at Somprabh when she saw the state he was in. He smiled at her and said, 'I have completed the reconnaissance. The plan worked well, even if it cost a hundred dammas. Freeing the prince will be difficult. Let us meet Queen Kalingasena and seek her advice. I shall be ready in an hour. I need a good scrubbing, as you can see.'

They talked no more. Somprabh took a long bath and dressed up in white from head to toe. 'I am a monk now', he said to Kundani. 'I cannot take my sword.'

'You don't need it', Kundani said.

'We have to infiltrate a fort in broad daylight.'

'Yes. But we will not attack the enemy.'

The three of them walked to Kalingasena's palace. The Masseuse had given Somprabh a flower basket and a pitcher of holy water to complete his garb. The doorkeeper was the Masseuse's friend, and he gave way to them without asking questions. They crossed a labyrinth of corridors to enter Kalingasena's private rooms.

Ajit Keskambali was waiting for them in the common room. Queen Nandini entered shortly after them.

Somprabh said at once, 'Acharya, Prince Vidudhab is held in Kosala fort. It will not be easy to free him.'

'But, friend, you must fulfil this difficult task. You will do a great favour to this dynasty.'

Queen Nandini's eyes were moist. She had lowered her head at the news. Now she raised it and spoke with a tremor in her voice. 'I know that fort. My father was a prisoner there, and he gave me to the king in return for his freedom. Now my son…'

Kalingasena had entered the room. She said, 'Sir, if you hesitate to do what is needed, I shall ride in there with my sword drawn.' Her tone was decisive.

'I am not one to flinch from my duty. I stated that this mission will be difficult. I shall rescue the prince at the cost of my life', Somprabh said slowly.

'Very well!' The acharya said. He looked relieved. 'And you shall have support. I shall ask General Karayan to help you.'

'Acharya, planning will be critical. The gate of the prison is submerged in water. A heavy mechanism is used to lock it. I will need to key to this lock. Outside, Bandhul himself leads fifty of his elite troops who guard the complex. An open clash of arms will not help us in achieving our aim. This is a matter in which diplomacy must aid our force. We must keep in mind that if General Bandhul surmises that we will launch a frontal attack to free the prince Vidudhab, he may even kill the prince. So far, he has not exercised that option perhaps because he wants to know King Prasenjit's whereabouts.'

'I see why you have a certain reputation, young man', Ajit Keskambali said.

'You are kind, Acharya', Somprabh said. 'There is more. The fort commandant is a renowned warrior. He keeps the key to the prison gate and extracting it from him will be challenging. Remember, the total force there is a hundred chosen men, of which fifty are directly under Bandhul Malla's command. The rest of the army is at the cantonment. Eight sentinels guard the prison at all times. The rest is ready to rush in at the slightest sign of trouble.'

The acharya got up and paced the room, frowning. 'What is your plan, Som?'

'I am afraid it is not complete yet, Acharya. I am waiting.'

'For someone? Who?' Ajit Keskambali asked.

'A total lout.'

The acharya raised his eyebrows.

'He was one of the prince's abductors', Somprabh explained. 'He has accepted my gold and promised me an impression of the key. I expect him to deliver it in two watches, though with men like that, one never knows. I have checked he is busy at work.'

'If he is unreliable, can he not deceive us?' Queen Nandini asked.

'I hope not, Lady. He is open to a bribe, and he will receive on delivery more than he could ever imagine putting together in his entire life. He is a gambler. I guess he is not the most reliable man by any means, but he is the right one for us.'

Kalingasena said, 'What do you want to do, Som? I can get to the fort on my own. But I don't see what else I can do. It's not enough.'

'No, Lady, it's not enough, and not proper', Somprabh said.

'What if you do not obtain the key?' Ajit Keskambali asked.

'I cannot say. But I shall find another way. I need to meet General Karayan today. When do you want the prince here, Acharya?'

'Three watches into the day tomorrow is the hour fixed for the anointment. There is still no official announcement of the king and the prince disappearing. I made sure no one denied the rumours because they only add to the speculation. I have asked impostors to show glimpses of both from a distance. My line is that the king is in Queen Kalingasena's palace, and chief queen Mallika observes a period of seclusion. I am doing what I can to keep up the pretence.'

Somprabh nodded. 'Well, Acharya, I shall get the prince here on time. If I don't, it will mean I kept my oath of friendship but did not survive.'

CHAPTER 85

THE IMPOSSIBLE MISSION

The plan was as complete as could be, and they had a copy of the key. Kundani and the Masseuse had left for the fort disguised as acrobats early in the day. Kundani carried her poisoned dagger.

On that day, Somprabh rested. At sunset, he rose, bathed and meditated. He rubbed oil all over his body, tied a loincloth tightly around himself and hid a small sword under his jacket. He had called up Shambh, taking the view that his old faithful had recuperated enough. To be with his master delighted Shambh. He carried a thick, long rope, a bow and quiver full of arrows, and a strong staff. Like his master, he was rested, bathed and oiled. They rode into the forest after sundown, unseen by anyone. Meanwhile, General Karayan took a longer route, riding ahead of a unit of his best troops.

Somprabh had memorised every detail of the path leading to the fort. Even in the dark, it took him and Shambh only two hours to reach a clearing from which they could see the fort's southern gate. They tied their horses and walked towards the looming fort. They wore soft shoes that helped them to move without noise.

The house at the edge of the moat was well-lit, and music was playing inside. At times, raucous noises burst from it. Somprabh deduced that Kundani and the Masseuse had cast their spells and started a bout of revelry inside. The fort wall was not lit, but Somprabh could see shadows of men patrolling. Somprabh selected a stout Ficus tree, knotted one end of the rope around it, and secured the other end to his waist.

He whispered to Shambh, 'You can see two soldiers patrolling at a time. There are eight soldiers, that's all. I shall enter the water now. Keep sensing the rope. When it becomes loose, climb on the tree and keep ready to shoot your arrows. You have sixteen arrows for eight soldiers. Be careful not to waste a single arrow. Do not leave any of them alive. But first – the rope.'

Shambh nodded vigorously, laid down his staff and took a grip on the rope. As he entered the icy cold and bracing water, Somprabh took a long breath and dived in without a splash. In the clear water, the tunnel was easy to find. He had prepared for multiple dives before reaching the underpass, so this was a good start. The tunnel sloped upwards. Somprabh plunged into it, fighting the claustrophobia that enveloped him at once by focusing on swimming faster. His head broke free of water after an agonising time. He gratefully took in great breaths of air, and his heaving lungs made his chest and head throb. He stood on a wet slab, and this part of the tunnel had chinks allowing fresh air and light to enter. He moved carefully now, mindful of a trap or a tripwire. Five large steps on a rough staircase brought him to the famed underground door. He had spent time tracing out the profile of the key. He groped around until his hands touched the lock. It took what felt like an eternity before the key turned, and he felt a surge of elation. He removed the padlock and the chain and gently pushed the door. A flurry of movement made him pull out his sword in a panic. Then he chided himself. A rat could have caused that small noise.

He stepped into the space beyond the door. It was a small, closed room without air or light. He started feeling his way around in that suffocating place. If this is the cell, he thought, where is the prince? And if not, how do I find the prison cell? He touched every part of the walls and then stepped back outside the door to get some air. He sank to his knees in despair.

·

As soon as the rope loosened, Shambh threw a few blades of grass upwards to see how the wind blew. Then he clambered up the tree with his equipment. He found a branch that gave him a firm sitting position, with a clearing in the foliage through which he could observe the fort walls and the building in front. The shadowy soldiers on the ramparts became more precise as he focused on them. The task ahead of him did not daunt him. He had shot at targets from greater distances before.

He regulated his breath, closed his eyes and prayed for success. Then he reopened his eyes, and in a fluid movement, set the arrow, pulled the bowstring and aimed at one of the dark figures. He followed the moving silhouette with his arrow for a few moments and then let it fly. The man on the wall froze as if someone had ordered him to stop and jerked, looking towards the dark forest. The next instant, he toppled from the rampart into the moat with an enormous splash. The second soldier dashed forward and peered over the edge. An arrow took him straight in the centre of his chest, and he fell back. Shambh was sure he would not rise again.

Shambh relaxed his muscles and waited. After what felt like a long time, two more shapes appeared. They darted forward, and Shambh supposed it must be because they had seen their dead comrade. Shambh shot his third arrow, and his aim was unerring again. However, this time the second man stood behind the first. Before Shambh could shoot him, he had taken out and blown his trumpet with all his might. The shrill ringing beat the sounds of festivity in the house and the forest noises. Shambh's arrow cut it off, and the man collapsed, but the trumpet call already echoed over the stones.

In the house, the music came to an abrupt halt. Metallic clangs and agitation filled the night as the men armed themselves and scrambled to action.

General Karayan and his men had moved into position around the house. The general had told his men to ensure the fort guards could not see them and to wait until he sent orders. Now, the trumpet sounds and the noises from the house showed that enemy were readying themselves to rush out, and Karayan told his men on either side of him to attack. The message rippled through to all his men.

Karayan himself unsheathed his sword since he no longer had to worry about the glint of metal giving away their presence to the fort guards. The soldiers in the house could still not see his force. At the moment he expected men to burst out, the light in the house went off, and the sounds inside stopped completely. In the deathly silence, the cicadas' night song grew even louder. The house suddenly showed no signs of life.

This turn of events astounded General Karayan. As he crouched nonplussed, the loud tolling of a bell shattered the quiet. Within moments, the thuds of the cantonment soldiers rushing to defend the fort made the ground shake, some of them on horseback.

A loud creaking sound filled the air, and the wooden bridge started moving downwards. Karayan made a quick decision. He stood up and called out to four aides. The first unit of fifty soldiers was to charge the gate and gain control of the bridge. Some soldiers in that unit had received training to scale high walls. The second unit was to ambush and stop the troops charging in from the cantonment. Karayan ordered the third unit to surround the house and hold the line while he led the charge into the house with the fourth unit.

General Karayan's unit broke down the door with ease and moved in with caution. The house had turned into a ghost mansion. It was as if the earth had swallowed the revellers preparing to charge. Karayan ordered his men to light their torches, and they saw signs of drinking. A heavy scent of wine floated in the air. But of men or women, there was no trace. Karayan stood perplexed for a while. Then he goaded himself and his men into action, with an order for a room-to-room search. The first few rooms yielded nothing. As the men were about to leave the fourth room, a soldier overheard a scratching sound and alerted the others. They opened a cupboard to find Kundani, and the Masseuse trussed up and gagged. Karayan himself cut their ropes and loosed and pulled the rags out of their mouths. He let them recover their breath before asking who they were. He had not met Somprabh before the attack and did not know about the two women.

'Are you General Karayan?' Kundani asked.

'Yes, I am Karayan.'

'General, you must hurry', Kundani said. 'That door' – she pointed to a small door in the corner – ''leads to the tunnel. Sixteen armed men have left that way. They may run into Somprabh, who is alone inside.' Kundani asked him to inform his men that she, the Masseuse and the Asur belonged in the same force of attackers.

Karayan called for sixteen volunteers who were excellent swimmers. He deputed a runner to alert the men waiting outside about Kundani, the Masseuse and Shambh. Then he led the sixteen men into the passage. After a few hundred steps, the light of their torch caught some enemies. There were only four men, and the battle that ensued was one-sided and quick. As Karayan charged on, he saw a closed iron gate blocking the passage. He cursed his luck. He ordered his men to find out whether they could use some of the large stones lying outside the house to break it down.

·

Kundani said to the Masseuse, 'Sister, let us begin the second phase of our work. We need to find Shambh first. I am sure the trumpets and the bell resulted from what he did. He must be outside, in the stretch of forest right opposite us.' They walked out into the night and discerned a blur of movement in the forest. As Kundani had expected, Shambh slithered down to the ground and then ran towards them.

'Shambh, where is Som?' Kundani asked.

'He headed for the prison.'

'How long ago?'

'A long time. A little less than one watch.'

'Then he may be in trouble. You need to be brave.'

Shambh nodded.

'Do you see that point in the moat? That is where your master must have found the entrance to the prison. He may have to fight with sixteen enemies somewhere in that maze. Some soldiers are trying another route to get to him.'

Shambh nodded again, not showing any sign of apprehension. He gave her the bow and arrows, and said, 'Use this if you need to. Anyway, there are many soldiers around here.' I shall use my staff. He smiled and thought for a moment, and then said, 'I shall follow this rope. You must hold on to it. I shall tug it and keep it tight. If I need to come back, I shall use it. But if it turns loose, know that I have reached the goal.'

Kundani took the bow and arrows and fastened them on her shoulders. As Shambh entered the water and then expanded his chest and dived in, she gripped the rope. It stayed tight for what seemed to be an eternity, and Kundani wondered how Shambh had held his breath that long. When she had almost given up hope, it slackened. She slumped in relief, and said to the Masseuse, 'Sister, it looks like Somprabh is not alone anymore. Let us take cover and wait.'

·

Somprabh turned around the room, feeling its surfaces and corners with his hand. Tapping the bricks with his sword did not allow him to discover any hollows. He sank to the ground to recover his strength and to think through his next steps. To go back was to fail, and he had no way forward.

A faint light appeared in a far corner towards the roof. He immediately focused his attention on it. The light flickered as shadows covered it, and four men jumped into the room while Somprabh retreated into the darkness. One man said, 'I will check the prisoner. The three of you guard this room. Open the door now.'

Somprabh heard some grunting and swearing, and the sound of stone rubbing against stone. To his amazement, a thick stone slab came out of the roof. A pillar of light streamed out of it. The man who gave the orders hoisted himself up a rope ladder that had descended from the hole. Somprabh deduced the man was Bandhul Malla.

Somprabh let Bandhul disappear before attacking the three men. One went down, but then, the other two were on their guard and immediately spread out and took their stances. Somprabh realised right then they were highly trained and would not be pushovers. The men circled the room warily. Then, two of them attacked simultaneously. Somprabh was not at the height of his power. He warded off both thrusts, but when he struck one man, the other inflicted a slight wound on his left arm.

Somprabh wondered if his fate was to die in this inglorious hole in the earth. At that very moment, the taller of his opponents crumbled and fell to the ground with his head bleeding. Behind him stood a smiling Shambh wielding his enormous staff.

'What a relief, My Friend! And not a minute too soon – but thankfully not too late!' Somprabh panted, and Shambh grinned. 'Hold this man. I must save the prisoner.'

Shambh nodded and twirled his staff with his right hand while taking out a dagger with his left. The enemy soldier gulped and stepped back at this display of virtuosity. The sight of his two comrades' corpses next to him could not have been very motivating for him.

.

Somprabh raced up the rope ladder, cursing his clumsiness. When he got close to the top, he used all his strength to pull himself up, look in front and roll forward in a single liquid motion, so as not to be ambushed. There was no one in the small, well-lit room, but there was a voice coming from the next one. Somprabh ran ahead.

Vidudhab was in chains but stood erect and stoic before a sword-wielding and ranting Bandhul. 'You have a few more moments to make your choice, Son of a slave', Bandhul said. 'Remember I have spared you once – I shall not do it now. Tell me where the king is. Or die!'

Vidudhab closed his eyes in response, preparing himself for death. He winced as he drew himself upright but stayed silent.

'General Bandhul!' Somprabh's cry echoed in the room. Bandhul turned jerkily to face Somprabh, and Prince Vidudhab opened his eyes and looked upwards, exulting. 'Killing a bound man will tarnish your name. I stand here before you. I have not faced a Malla sword yet.'

Bandhul had recovered from his surprise. He said, 'You will see it. Are you the Magadhan who went into the harem like a thief?'

'You could say that', Somprabh smiled, to infuriate Bandhul.

Bandhul feinted and attacked without warning. Somprabh parried his thrust and backed away to give himself more space. The next instant, the room was full of the clanging of swords as Bandhul and Somprabh each put all their strength into their thrusts and blows. Sweat trickled into Somprabh's eyes. Bandhul came very close to him and Somprabh had to fight him with his arm. They were locked in an embrace, their sword arms and left arms shuddering as each tried to overpower the other.

Suddenly, Bandhul Malla's strength deserted him. Somprabh saw that Vidudhab had stepped up and summoned all his strength to give him a crushing blow with the end of his heavy chain. Bandhul turned and slashed at Vidudhab, who fell to the floor with a grunt. The opening was all Somprabh needed. With all his remaining force, he hit the Bandhul's left shoulder, making him sway and collapse in a heap.

.

General Karayan gnashed his teeth as his men made no progress against the thick iron gate. The men were about to launch a fourth attempt at battering it open when one of them raised an arm to stop the others. They heard sounds coming from the other side. Shuffling feet stopped, and metal creaked. The door swung open, and a group of defenders stood in front of Karayan's men. The sight of the unexpected invaders shocked them. Realising the attackers outnumbered them, they turned back, Karayan's force running after them. As the men fled, they led Karayan's men deeper into the labyrinth. The general could hear sounds of conflict coming from not far away.

As the prince and Bandhul fell to the ground, Somprabh heard the drumming of feet. He turned to see four enemies storming towards him and prepared to say his prayers. But to his relief, Karayan and his men were right behind them, and so was Shambh. His legs gave way, and he sank to the floor in exhaustion, drenched in sweat and splattered with blood. Karayan's men made quick work of the enemy.

Karayan sent one man to call in the remaining forces. They streamed through the hole at the top of the cell into the fort's heart and overwhelmed the defending army. The commandant could not distinguish between his men and the enemies, as Karayan had made sure only a thick armband set his own men apart. The fort capitulated in less than an hour. Karayan took the commandant and his household prisoners.

Kundani and the Masseuse tended to Somprabh and Vidudhab, who were both wounded. They cleaned the wounds, applied turmeric and tied bandages. Somprabh let the prince rest for some time. Kundani requested a glass of milk for him, but the prince turned it down, saying that he could not stomach it.

Somprabh left General Karayan in command of the fort and the prisoners. He wished he could give Prince Vidudhab more time to rest, but the fear of missing the hour of anointment bore heavily on his mind, and he knew that the prince's wound would not allow them to gallop back fast. The sun was scorching by the time a group of seven – Somprabh, Kundani, Prince Vidudhab, the Masseuse, Shambh and two bodyguards – rode out of the fort towards the palace.

CHAPTER 86

THE ANOINTMENT

The ceremonial canopy was overflowing with guests. The high priest Acharya Ajit Keskambali and sixteen scholars were ready with the holy water for the anointment bath. The high and mighty of the land – kings, satraps, councillors, mayors, merchants, courtiers – had settled as well as possible in the limited area. King Prasenjit's absence was talked about in whispers.

An aide murmured something in Acharya Ajit Keskambali's ear. It was as if a pall had risen from his face. He closed his eyes in what seemed to be a gesture of gratitude to the gods. He rose and raised his hands theatrically. The crowded became silent.

'The hour has arrived! The host must present himself and sit at the altar to receive the anointment!'

The whispers of the crowd grew into a commotion at what happened next. A screen parted, and a wounded, visibly exhausted Prince Vidudhab strode in. By his side was Somprabh, carrying a bloodied sword. Two other bodyguards, stalwarts of Karayan's army, followed behind.

Many of the officials rose to their feet at this dramatic entry. Some of the military drew their swords but were unsure of what action to take in the absence of General Bandhul.

Somprabh steered Prince Vidudhab to the altar and helped him sit down. He looked over his shoulder to check that an elite unit of Karayan's men, fresh and rested, lined up at the edge of the canopy. He raised his sword arm and mustered all his lung power to proclaim in loud words. 'Gentlemen, members of the assembly, Brahmans and citizens! Here is king Vidudhab. The hour of anointment has come, and he must receive it. The ceremony may start now. I, Somprabh of Magadha, declare that the king of Kosala is king Vidudhab. He who wishes to oppose this coronation may step forward now and face my sword!'

A stunned silence greeted the announcement. Then, Vidudhab's supporters in the army, the public and the visiting royals, started chanting in unison. 'Welcome to the new king of Kosala! Long live King Vidudhab!'

One official, a faithful loyalist of King Prasenjit, drew his sword and moved towards Somprabh. It was as if a riverbank had burst. At least a dozen others also drew their swords. Prince Vidudhab made to get up, but Somprabh pressed down on his shoulder and advanced. He parried the first two men to reach the altar, his tired shoulder screaming in protest at the jarring shocks. Fortunately, the soldiers behind jumped into the fray. They were slightly outnumbered, but better warriors. Soon, a pile of corpses lay on the floor. Most of the guests stampeded out, and in the commotion, some sacrificial animals also fled. As pools of blood formed near the altar, Vidudhab supporters chanted, 'Victory to King Vidudhab!'

Now Ajit Keskambali stood up and shouted, 'Listen, All! Whoever still opposes this coronation may step forward now!' No one came forward. 'I repeat, whosoever wishes to oppose the new king may step up now and challenge him!' The deserted canopy remained silent. He repeated the announcement a third time.

Ajit Keskambali spoke in a softer voice now. 'Gentlemen! The former king is not present here to be anointed, and no one has stepped forward to stake a claim on his behalf. The kingdom cannot stay without a king for even an instant. The new king is his heir, born from his seed. I declare him to be the host of this yagya! Now, King Vidudhab, say three times that you choose me as the head of this Rajsuya Yagya.'

Vidudhab spoke the statement thrice.

Then Ajit Keskambali announced, 'Oh, Gods of the World! Oh, Brahmans! All men! Listen! We, the sixteen Vedic scholars and I, according to the prescribed law, in this great ceremony, the Rajsuya Yagya, now anoint Vidudhab, the king of Kosala.'

The sounds of many conches joined in a harmony that spread across and beyond the city, signalling a new era.

The formal ritual began. The kings were guided back to their seats, and each received plates full of symbolic offerings. They lined themselves in order of rank and presented the plates and their gifts. The first in line was the king of Videha, and he offered a white steed from Kamboj. A snaking line of kings and other luminaries stood behind him to pay obeisance and present their gifts.

When the submission of the kings was complete, Ajit Keskambali and the sixteen scholars started the anointment proper. They recited the Vedas, two selected kings standing behind Vidudhab with spotless white umbrellas.

Six other kings then fanned King Vidudhab with feather brushes. Once again, eighteen conches were blown together, and their fanfare echoed far and wide. Then, holy water from eighteen sources was poured into those conches, and from the conches, over the anointed king. Throughout, the priests chanted sacred verses.

Next came the drinking of nectar and the sacrifice of animals. After these rituals, a cloth soaked in ghee was wrapped around the king, over which the acharya placed a coloured wool blanket and a long flowing robe. The sages chanted, 'This is the navel of the land!'

One sage gave Vidudhab a bow that had been purified by placing it near the fire. 'This is the arm of Indra, the slayer of Vrata!' The sages chanted. Next, the king received three sanctified arrows. A piece of copper was placed in the mouth of a Brahman seated next to the altar.

The priests recited more scriptures and asked the king to hold the arm of the head priest and walk in a circle around him. Then the king walked a few steps in each direction.

Now, Ajit Keskambali and the priests chanted, 'When you march to the east, may the gods protect you! When you march to the south, may the gods protect you! When you march to the west, may the gods protect you! When you march to the north, may the gods protect you! And when you march upwards, may the gods protect you!' For each direction, the priests recited metres of poetry suitable to chant, parts of the Sam Veda that must be recited, other appropriate scriptures, and the seasons that would be suitable for campaigns.

They asked the king to stand and installed a lead sheet below the tiger-skin cushion he sat on. When he returned to his throne, a golden saucer was placed below his feet. 'May death spare you!' Ajit Keskambali chanted.

A golden crown with one hundred holes was fixed on Vidudhab's head. Ajit Keskambali chanted, 'You are energy, you are immortal, you are victory!'

Then, as instructed, King Vidudhab stood and raised his hands. 'Gods, grant me your blessings!' He said.

The acharya and the other priests again bathed the king in holy water. This time, the water was stored in cups of Flame of the forest flowers. The acharya said, 'Oh Gods, inspire this king such that he has no rival, his kingdom expands, as does his heart and magnanimity. People of Kosala, King Vidudhab in your king now.'

The eighteen conches were sounded again.

The priests then started the ceremony to sanctify the king's chariot, after which the king sat again on his throne. He was declared to be the one upholding the principle of good conduct.

As per tradition, the game of dice began. Within no time, Ajit Keskambali had defeated the king.

The king said, 'Brahman!'

Ajit Keskambali said, 'You are Brahma, the creator, the morning sun that inspires the truth.'

The king said, 'Brahman!'

Ajit Keskambali said, 'You are Brahma, and Indra – the power behind your people.'

'Brahman!'

'You are Brahma and the merciful form of Rudra.'

'Brahman!'

'You are Brahma.'

This brought the anointment to an end.

Ten days later, another ritual was performed. Bowls full of sacred nectar were placed before Vidudhab and nine Brahmans. Others had to bend on to the floor and wriggle to the bowls while naming their grandfathers and the ten ancestors before them that had performed the same ritual. A verse was chanted: 'With the incandescent morning sun, with the voice of the Goddess of Learning Sarasvati, with the forms made by the Sun God Savitreya, with the animals sustained by the sun, with the blessings of Indra, king of Gods, with the creator Brahma, with the radiance of the moon, with the energy of fire, I am inspired!'

Ten men drank from each of the ten bowls. At the end of the ritual, the new king gifted gold garlands to each of the guests who had drunk from the bowls.

Now, a thousand conches were blown, and the anointed king gifted each of the priests a hundred cows with gold-plated horns and eleven beauties adorned with gold jewellery. Other Brahmans received gold, jewels, clothes, slaves and calves in keeping with their stature.

Thus rewarded, the Brahmans left the site, all praise for the generosity, welcome and respect they had received. King Vidudhab also bade farewell to the many kings and other luminaries, giving each of them grand gifts. To those friends of Kosala who could not attend the Rajsuya Yagya, he sent gifts on chariots. He remembered those who had fought for King Prasenjit at the altar by granting positions and honour to their heirs. King Vidudhab's reign began on a firm foundation.

The unfortunate Prasenjit, he who had sought never-ending pleasure in the realm of the senses was forgotten.

CHAPTER 87

SELF-SACRIFICE

Somprabh lay on a bed in a lavish room in the palace. His wounds had healed, but he still felt weak. Kundani sat by his side. Shambh squatted in a corner, head between his knees, looking at his master. All three of them were silent. The creases on his forehead showed that Somprabh was not at ease.

He worried about Princess Chandrabhadra. Was he, with his unknown lineage, fit to marry her? And what of his role in her father's death, the sacking of her beloved Champa, and her resulting misfortunes? Should he not desist from this foolish love? Was he perhaps taking advantage of her in her hour of distress? If she had not been in straitened circumstances, would she have considered marrying him? And where should she live as his wife? These thoughts pummelled him.

He saw Kundani and Shambh scrambling to their feet. His tired mind needed a few moments to realise there was a fourth presence in the room. It was the sage Mahavir.

Mahavir took a seat that was offered to him and spoke to Somprabh without preamble. 'Dear Som, I have come for you. I was told something troubles you. Look inside yourself and see the virtue you have and the happiness. Free yourself from base emotions. Son, this body gives shelter to many ills. Lust, desire, anger and envy are just some of them. It is like an ocean.

'The ocean has many virtues. It ebbs, it rises, and the cycle repeats. It is limitless but also contained within itself. It ingests the dead bodies we humans throw into it. The greatest of rivers flowing into it surrenders its form into the immensity of the ocean. The skies may open up and pour rain for days on end, but the ocean is never incomplete, not congested. It may heave and roar and still keep its equanimity. It has pearls, shells, jewels of all hues, and creatures ranging from tiny shrimps to monster whales.

'Perhaps you wonder what I am trying to say. Son, a life spiritually rich is like the ocean – it has ebbs and spates and repeats its cycles. It has a synthesis of action, direction and command. Some reject this life's demands to gain salvation, while others must exercise their minds and bodies and purify themselves through virtuous deeds. Young man, if you are not a committed ascetic, you must be a part of this grand phenomenon that is life. Live it with zeal, with courage, with virtue.'

Somprabh listened, hanging on to every word the sage spoke, not wanting to interrupt the flow of the great man's words. Now he said, 'Lord, I shall do as you say.'

Mahavir said, 'Son, you helped to make Vidudhab king. You did your duty by your friend. Now, you must consider what to do about Princess Chandrabhadra. And I know it weighs on your mind. It is a load you cannot carry too long without harming yourself.'

'It does weigh on my mind', Somprabh said, 'and I shall do as you say.'

'In short, give her the choice to become the queen of Kosala.'

The blood drained from Somprabh's face. His eyes betrayed the deep, searing pain arising from hearing confirmed the truth he had suspected but not dared confront.

Somprabh gulped as if swallowing this bitter truth. He said, 'Lord, you are right. I cannot carry this weight anymore. It oppresses me, but I dared not free myself of it until this moment.'

'Bless you. I shall speak to the princess and the king. The rest is up to them. But the path I have just suggested is the best for the princess.'

Somprabh sat up in his bed, bowed his head and joined his hands in greeting. His lips trembled as he said, huskily, 'I am eternally grateful, Lord.'

A teardrop streaked down Kundani's cheek.

CHAPTER 88

THIS KINGDOM MUST NURTURE ALL

The Royal Council was convened in the late afternoon when the sun had mellowed, and the shadows lengthened. King Vidudhab of Kosala walked the few hundred feet to the court under an ornate umbrella, with servants carrying feather fans trailing behind him. Somprabh led the way, his sword drawn, and General Karayan followed the king. At the instant the king sat on his throne, one organiser signalled to the palace to blow the conches. A group of priests chanted mantras, and the women of the royal family showered rice on the king.

Two servants brought a sheathed sword on a brass platter. King Vidudhab stood and addressed Ajit Keskambali. 'Acharya, I appoint you chief minister of Kosala. Please accept this sword.' He handed the sword to Ajit Keskambali, who bowed deeply and took it with both hands. The hall waited for him to speak. He cleared his throat, moved to the side of the throne, and turned to face the audience. He closed his eyes and bowed his head for a moment before looking straight ahead and speaking.

'This kingdom must nurture all. It is not for the benefit of one or of the few. I declare the ministers and officials wishing to remain in their posts may do so. King Vidudhab plans to double the salaries of government officials over a time period. Those who supported the erstwhile King Prasenjit have nothing to fear. We shall treat their opposition to King Vidudhab as a sign of loyalty to the then ruler. They only need to prove their efficiency. Those wishing to leave the kingdom are free to declare their intent and take with them their assets and families. The king guarantees he shall not trouble them in any manner. Equally, he shall crush without mercy those working against the fledgling administration from within our borders.'

The crowd's cheers and cries of 'Victory to the king! Victory to the chief minister!' echoed in the hall. 'By the king's orders, and in my capacity as just-appointed chief minister', he continued, 'I salute our esteemed State's guest, Somprabh Dev on behalf of Kosala. His courage and friendship made this auspicious moment possible. King Vidudhab declares Kosala shall be Magadha's eternal friend. Magadha's friend shall be Kosala's friend, and Magadha's enemy our enemy.

'Further, on Arya Somprabh's request, we shall strive for peaceful relations with the Vatsa kingdom. Our ambassador will soon leave to seek an audience with King Udayan and build bridges with him. As a token of our friendship, we gift the great city of Kashi to Magadha and declare it is now a part of Magadha.'

Ajit Keskambali paused, and a ringing round of applause greeted these announcements. Then he said. 'We appoint Courtier Payasi foreign minister and Mahashal Lauhitya, finance minister. Further, I request the group of eight ministers to rise.' Eight men stood off from the front ranks and saluted the king and the audience. 'These eight men will be responsible for the daily administration of the kingdom. We have already appointed General Karayan Chief of the Army and Navy. Our High Priest will be Basubhatta. Besides being of impeccable lineage, he has an unparalleled mastery of the scriptures, and his sense of justice and his knowledge of mathematics and astrology are famous.'

Ajit Keskambali saluted, nodded to an associate and took his seat. The guests stepped forward one by one, as they were called, to present their gifts to King Vidudhab. Somprabh led the procession with his present, a jewelled sword from Magadha. The queue of ambassadors ran the length of the hall. Thus began King Vidudhab's official reign.

CHAPTER 89

AN EMOTIONAL MEETING

The amber morning light was pushing aside the dark night. Somprabh had slept like a log, but when he woke, he still felt a heaviness in his heart. Worry lined his forehead. The last few days' events weighed on him. He looked at the patterned rays of bright light playing on his bed and imagined the bracing cool air outside. He looked at the clear blue sky framed by the window. The sight did not lighten his face.

Shambh sat wide awake at the foot of the bed, looking unhappy at his master's state of weariness. There was a time when Somprabh would have leapt out of bed and scolded him for not being awake and active. Now the master lay in bed, gazing at the sky, smiling wistfully and without joy.

Footsteps sounded in the corridor, breaking their trains of thought, and someone knocked at the door. Before Somprabh could answer, Kaumarbhritya walked in. He bowed low and saluted Somprabh, saying, 'The king wishes to see you immediately, General, Sir!'

Somprabh did not say a word. He nodded and signalled to the visitor he would obey the summon right away.

.

King Vidudhab lay on a small cot, eyes closed. He gave Somprabh a fond look and struggled to sit up. Somprabh felt a pang of sorrow at his friend's enervated state. Vidudhab raised both hands towards Somprabh and said, 'Brother, I wish I had done more for you. I did not even express my gratitude properly. It's all been too much for me. But you know I owe my rule to you.' He spoke slowly, and with effort.

'I am at peace, Majesty. And my services are at Kosala's disposal', Somprabh said.

Vidudhab's eyes were only half-open, as he gazed through a window at the azure sky straddled by a single dazzling cloud. He sighed and said, 'I wished to have you by my side. But Lord Mahavir and Kalingasena recommend that we should part. Politics dictates my life's choices even more since my coronation. Politics drives a wedge between you and me.'

'It does, Majesty. It does much more than that. But politics is the prime force of our lives. We must bow before it', Somprabh said.

'So, I must sacrifice my friendship? And I should turn away from he who saved my life at the risk of his.' King Vidudhab choked. He strained with his hands to lift himself to his feet and held his arms open.

Somprabh embraced him and felt the flutter of the king's heart. It told him here was a man who deeply felt for him and grieved at their forced separation. He patted Vidudhab's shoulder and stepped back. 'I wish you all success, King Vidudhab', he said. 'The people and the nobles support you. I have done my work here, and I must leave.'

'You leave after giving everything to Kosala!' Vidudhab said. The king seemed about to totter. Kaumarbhritya moved swiftly to hold him steady.

'You must rest, Majesty!' Kaumarbhritya said. 'General Somprabh will leave now, but he will surely return to Kosala.'

Somprabh did not comment on this. He turned and left without a word. Vidudhab closed his eyes, as if unable to bear the sight of his friend's retreating.

CHAPTER 90

THE FINAL FAREWELL

She wore a light silk dress, with a red slant border. Her long, black hair was combed and braided to perfection. A pearl necklace adorned her neck and breasts. Her cheeks had a hint of pollen make-up, and red paste outlined her exquisitely shaped feet. Her slender arms resembled Lotus stems in their grace. When she smiled, her brilliant teeth were like jewels. The swell of her breasts was vastly more intoxicating than the choicest wine. Her forehead, adorned by a diamond, glistened with a few beads of sweat. The light of her eyes, and the flush of her dimples, showed she had recovered her vitality.

An orchard of giant Ashoka trees stretched across a vast expanse of the palace gardens. Their red flowers added a vibrant touch to the lush greenery. In the middle of the orchard was a grove of creepers with white-pink scented flowers.

She sat on a stool in the middle of the flowering creepers, absorbed in her painting. Her jacket had come loose, and a strand of hair fell across her cheek. She ignored these distractions. She had eyes only for the dabs of paint she applied to the canvas before her with long brushes. Her breath was ardent as she concentrated all her energy on her work. Sometimes she stepped closer to the canvas and then got up, examining it with a critical eye from a few feet away. Then she scurried back to her stool and dabbed the brush into a pot and applied it again with measured strokes. At times, her forehead crinkled, and her lips formed a pout before her features eased again.

She did not notice Somprabh walking up behind her, and Somprabh used all his skill to prevent a single twig from snapping. She was lost in her work and seeing her first behind the canvas, he had walked around to approach from behind and see what she was painting.

He knew as he stepped closer that these moments would imprint themselves on his mind forever, much as a dream from which he wished he would never wake up. He took a deep breath. The presence of this divine creature, the love of his life, brought a tremor to his heart.

The painting was a portrait – his portrait.

Somprabh held his face in his hands and angrily brushed aside his tears. Did he imagine it, or was that a teardrop falling from the corner of Chandrabhadra's eye as she surveyed her work?

Somprabh called out to her, but no sound issued from his parched throat. He called again. 'Lady!'

She swivelled like a gazelle, the next instant, and her deep brown eyes hooked on his. She lowered the arm holding a brush, uncertain of what to do next. Somprabh rushed to her and stopped himself from embracing her. With his heart thudding, he went down on his knees and took her arms in his. A smear of paint appeared on their hands.

He said, 'Princess!'

Her eyes widened. 'How many cuts and wounds you have, Som!' She bent down to guide him to stand up. 'Come, sit down here.' She pointed to her seat.

Somprabh did not stand on ceremony. He sat, not letting go of her hands. 'So, you forgave me, Princess?' He asked. 'I hoped, I knew, you would. But I shall never forgive myself…'

'You must, Som!'

'You do not know everything, Chandrabhadra! I gave my heart to you when I first saw you in that helpless state. And how much I hated myself for not bringing you to safety. Do you know how low I stooped in my thinking? I was planning to let Vidudhab die, to usurp the throne of Kosala with the men loyal to me, and to make you my queen. All that, just to become worthy of you. I had the opportunity…'

'Yes, I know. But you did what was right. You are that kind of person!'

'And now I must leave', Somprabh said.

'I shall leave with you!'

'No, Princess. That cannot be. I must go, and you must stay. I did not become king, but you shall become Queen. This is what the stars willed.'

'Som, I shall be proud to be your wife.'

'No. The princess of Champa cannot marry a man of unknown lineage, a petty deceiver.'

'I can. I will serve you in every way possible, Som. I will be faithful to you, and I know that you will make me complete and whole.'

'Every drop of my blood, every fibre of my muscles, every breath of mine is yours. My life is yours. But you must become queen of Kosala.'

'But I love you! Only you!'

'And I love you. Do you not know that? But what has love to do with it? If love alone mattered, why would I have rescued Vidudhab? And stood in his defence with my bloody sword, swaying from exhaustion, while he was coronated? Would I bow before him? What is more powerful than the love a man and a woman feel for each other? It is trust and duty. I did my duty. And now, it is your turn to support me.'

Somprabh slid to the ground, took Chandrabhadra's hands in his, and pressed them over his moist eyes. He had exhausted all his words. There was nothing more he wanted to say. The princess felt the warmth of the warrior's tears. Her eyes were dry but red, and her head and shoulders slumped.

She shuddered as she wiped his tears. She resisted the urge to pull him close to her, to clasp him tight. She staggered to her feet with her eyes closed. 'Dear Som, I knew you would do this. Every part of my being is yours forever. It will remain so after I die.'

Somprabh stood up and drew himself erect. He spoke in a calm, measured tone now. 'Queen Chandrabhadra of Kosala, may you be blessed. May fortune smile on you, sweetest of beings! I salute you, Your Majesty!' Somprabh bowed and touched his sword to his head, in the traditional manner.

The princess said, 'Somprabh, I have run out of words. When you go, you must take my horse Dhumraketu. Give it your care.'

'I shall do so, Majesty', Somprabh said. He turned and walked away without a word. Kundani and Shambh were waiting for him outside the palace when he rode Dhumraketu out of the main gate. A contingent of the king's bodyguards lined the road on both sides, touching their heads with their swords.

Somprabh, Kundani and Shambh galloped towards Vaishali without glancing back.

GLOSSARY

Acharya – A highly learned person

Arya – Used in this text as an honourable prefix for a male. Pronounced aar-yuh.

Aryaa – Feminine equivalent of Arya (see above). Pronounced aar-yaa.

Ajivika – An ascetic sect that emerged in India about the same time as Buddhism and Jainism.

Akshauhini – A battle formation of 218,700 warriors.

Asur – Traditionally, demons who fought against the Devs or gods. In this work, the term should be interpreted as a tribe of aboriginal people.

Ashwamedha Yagya – Sacred ceremony demonstrating sovereign power. It ended with the sacrifice of a horse.

Bhoj – Feast.

Brahma – The creator, in the Hindu Trinity.

Brahman – The caste of priests.

Bhagwat Gita – Hindu religious and philosophical text.

Chakra – In traditional Indian medicine, one of seven centres of energy along the spinal column.

Chandal – A 'lower' caste, responsible for disposing of corpses.

Charvaka – Ancient philosophical school emphasising materialism and rejecting ritualism.

Dasyu – Aboriginal people, hostile to the main characters of the novel.

Dharma – The rightful path

Gandharv – Heavenly being. Also used for skilled singers.

Havi Yagya – A type of yagya. Yagya is a ritual done in front of a sacred fire, often with mantras.

Jiva – A living being

Kshatriya – The warrior caste.

Madhvik – A type of wine.

Maharaja – Great king.

Maireya – A type of wine.

Manav – Literally, human. Used in this work as a term for the Asur Aboriginals to refer to non-Aboriginals.

Mantra – Sacred verse.

Moksha – Salvation.

Namaste – Greeting in which the two palms are joined in front of the chest.

Nirukta – The science of etymology.

Raja – King.

Rajsuya Yagya – A grand and sacred ceremony that established the consecration of a king.

Havi Yagya – A ritual, part of the Rajsuya Yagya.

Ratna Yagna – A ritual, part of the Rajsuya Yagya.

Samadhi – A state of meditative consciousness.

Samrat – Emperor.

Sangha – Literally an association or community; the organisation led by the Buddha.

Shudra – The lowest caste

Siddha – The perfect one.

Sutra – Literally a thread, but generally used to mean a related collection of tales or texts.

Vaishya – Caste of traders, merchants and professionals.

Vihara – Monastery.

Vratya – Wandering ascetic.

Veena – Ancient Indian plucked-string musical instrument.

Yagya – Sacred ceremony.

Bodhi tree – The tree under which the Buddha attained enlightenment.

www.ingramcontent.com/pod-product-compliance
Lightning Source LLC
Chambersburg PA
CBHW021336150726
47989CB00005B/2011